TM & Copyright © 2012–2019, Warren Murphy Media
All rights reserved, including but not limited to, the right to reproduce this book, or any portion thereof, in any form or by any manner.

Official website: www.Facebook.com/LegacyBookSeries/

Art by Gerald Welch: http://www.jerrywelch.com

Published by Destroyer Books http://www.DestroyerBooks.com

First printing: February 2019

SPOILER ALERT: Some of the information in this omnibus is contemporary with the end of Legacy #8, which means that certain areas will contain spoilers.

NOTE: If you purchased this book without a cover, you should be aware that you're missing some really cool artwork as well as valuable stain-resistant features!

This is a work of fiction. All the characters and events portrayed in this novel are products of the authors' overactive imaginations or are used fictitiously.

LEGACY

OMNIBUS, VOL. I

TM & Copyright © 2012–2019, Warren Murphy Media

All rights reserved, including but not limited to, the right to reproduce this book, or any portion thereof, in any form or by any manner.

Official website: *www.Facebook.com/LegacyBookSeries/*

Written by Gerald Welch: *http://www.jerrywelch.com*

Art by Gerald Welch

Published by Destroyer Books *http://www.DestroyerBooks.com*

First printing: February 2019

Printed in the United States of America

PROCEED WITH CAUTION

SPOILER ALERT: Some of the information in this omnibus is contemporary with the end of Legacy #8, which means that certain areas will contain spoilers.

THIS VOLUME IS DEDICATED

TO THE HONORARY MASTERS OF

CAMERON BAILEY

MASTER OF CANADA

RICK DREW

MASTER OF CHICAGO

GERALD WELCH

MASTER OF CREATIVITY

IN 2004, WARREN MURPHY RECOGNIZED THE ACHIEVEMENTS OF THOSE WITHIN THE DESTROYER COMMUNITY WHO HAD GONE ABOVE AND BEYOND AS HONORARY MASTERS OF SINANJU. EACH WAS GIVEN A CERTIFICATE AND NAMED HONORARY MASTER IN A SPECIFIC AREA SO AS TO NOT OFFEND CHIUN. WARREN SPECIFIED THAT EACH WAS A MASTER OF SOMETHING THAT BEGAN WITH THE LETTER "C."

INDEX

FOREWORD

Sometimes the smallest decisions change the course of your life, and on a gray October weekend in 1985, choosing which movie to see did just that.

I looked at the four posters displayed outside the theater; having already seen *Commando,* I chose the one with the guy hanging from the Statue of Liberty. I had heard that *Remo Williams: the Adventure Begins* was a James Bond-type movie. It was fun, but apart from the character of Chiun, it didn't really make a huge impression on me. I only found out weeks later that it was based on a book series called the *Destroyer,* and I began devouring them.

It drove my Army recruiter crazy when I told him that I wanted to be stationed in Korea. He said that I should get a posh job at the Pentagon. But after serving three years in The Land of the Morning Calm, I returned stateside as a dedicated Destroyer fan.

I connected with Warren Murphy — one of the original creators and authors of the *Destroyer* — in the late nineties, when I found his email address and volunteered to contribute graphics for his website.

It had always been my dream to be an author, but I didn't think I was good enough. Then, on my 38th birthday, I had an epiphany: *no one starts out good enough*. I gave myself ten years to succeed, and began work on my first book series, *The Last Witness.*

In 2004, Warren said that he'd be glad to look my work over. A week after I sent my manuscript, he called and the first thing he said about my book was: "You suck."

Ouch.

"But," he continued, "it's fixable."

I took detailed notes as he went through his notes, and I began making changes, writing and rewriting and editing until it was better. Finally, in 2005, I released *Resurrected Destiny* and *The Arterran Chronicles.*

In 2009, when Warren announced that he was taking submissions for a compilation of fan-written *Destroyer* stories in an anthology named *New Blood,* I submitted two stories: *Monuments* and *Intermission* (*under the pseudonym Richard Ellington Logan*). I was elated when Warren accepted them.

After *New Blood* was published in 2010, I began thinking of making *Monuments* into a spin-off series called "Masters of Sinanju." I knew that I was going to get one shot at pitching to Warren, so I came up with a Plan B: a series featuring Remo Williams' children, Stone and Freya, called "*Young Destroyers.*"

Warren liked Plan B better, and asked for me to come up with a fleshed-out synopsis for that series, with characters strong enough to sustain it.

Technically, that's when I started work on the omnibus. Because of my love of comic books, I have always fused story with art. In fact, it's difficult for me to see one without the other. So when I first started thinking about Legacy, I started making sketches, layouts, diagrams, and drawings, to help me visualize who — and what — I was writing and thinking about.

That's much of what the encyclopedia part of this omnibus comprises: my collection of sketches, layouts and profiles, rendered as professionally as possible.

Since *Legacy* exists in the Sinanju universe, I deferred to *The Destroyer* and my frequent conversations with Warren to ensure that, *as much as possible*, everything fit in 'Sinanju canon.'

Though *Legacy* stands on its own as a series, it simply could not have come into being without the *Destroyer*. This omnibus is my tribute to the world of the *Destroyer* that Warren Murphy and Dick Sapir created. I designed it to be the ultimate Sinanju sourcebook, and included as much detail as I could without spoilers, minus an Easter Egg or two (*or the 54 that I will publicly acknowledge…good luck finding them!*)

I love the world of Sinanju, and want to share it — but I also know that this book will help me, too: it's going to serve as a Sinanju Bible whenever *I* have a question.

Work has already begun on the second omnibus. It will include updated versions of books four through six and have its own unique entries — but hopefully, this should keep you busy until then.

Warren and Dick created a universe that tens of millions of people have enjoyed for almost five decades. This omnibus, then, is part homage and part compass, for anyone who wants to explore the wild, hilarious, exciting world of Sinanju. Warren and Dick may be gone, but their characters and ideas remain.

I'm proud to help keep that tradition alive…and really glad I went to the movies all those years ago.

All my best,

Gerald Welch

신안주 모두가 마스터에게 활을 다

FORGOTTEN SON

SINANJU, KOREA: 1612 A.D.

Master Nonga's chest rose defiantly against the deep rattle that had already claimed his lungs. His once powerful body lay still on a small slab of stone in the center of the cave of his ancestors. As was the tradition in the House of Sinanju, candles circled the dying Master's body to light his way into the Void.

As his heir — and reigning Master of Sinanju — Kojing stood solemnly at his father's side. The old man's ragged breathing told him that Master Nonga did not have long to live, because proper breathing was a Master of Sinanju's fuel, allowing him to exercise almost superhuman power.

Throughout history, it would be recorded how lesser men could sometimes access a tiny portion of that power and use it to lift an automobile from their loved ones or walk over hot coals without being burnt. But the full power had first manifested in the tiny Korean village of Sinanju, and only the Masters of Sinanju had unlimited access to the full strength, speed and reflexes of the human body that they would often be described as gods in ancient texts.

These masters hired themselves out to pharaohs and kings, emperors, and chieftains to feed their poor fishing village in Korea. They conquered armies and overthrew entire empires, shaping history beneath the shadow of their symbol — the slashed trapezoid that appeared in the records of all civilizations.

For the history of Sinanju is the history of man.

"My son," Nonga whispered, fighting for one last breath.

"Yes, father?" Kojing asked humbly. Despite his blindness, Nonga had been a great Master, and over the course of his life had brought enough tribute to feed their village for many years to come.

"Shiva," Nonga wheezed. "...the House."

* * * *

Nonga held his breath one last time and looked around. Though blind, his eyes seemed to focus on something in the distance and then, he slowly released his breath.

Kojing extinguished the candles surrounding his father and pulled the sheet over his body. His father's last cryptic words were puzzling. Kojing had taken over the writing of the scrolls a decade earlier, recording the history of the House of Sinanju as past Masters had for nearly five thousand years. Yet while the last words of all Masters were preserved for posterity, Kojing had never read of a Master calling on the aid of a god.

The answer would have to wait for another day and another age. Tomorrow, the villagers of Sinanju would publicly grieve the passing of their master, and Kojing wanted time to privately grieve the passing of his father.

The next twelve days were filled with ceremonies and rituals filling the village with mourning and feasts and lauded speeches boasting the skill and bravery of Master Nonga, who would forever be known as the Blind Master.

In the years that followed, Kojing would go on to become a great Master of Sinanju in his own right, but he would never discover the meaning of his father's cryptic last words. Nor would his son, Master Sambria, or his son's son, Master Go.

That secret was reserved for Kojing's twin brother Kojong, who had exiled himself to whatever the fates held for him on the other side of the Great Eastern Sea.

CHAPTER ONE: THE PRESENT

Freya Williams sat silently on the hillside, wondering what the fates held for her.

The setting sun slanted across the vast expanse of the Sonoran Desert, bringing out the deep reds and oranges in the low hills and flat Arizona mesa. The hot desert wind stirred the few blond wisps of hair that had escaped her braids. She would have to find another way to hold her hair in place. It did not matter how invisible her Sinanju training allowed her to be if her hair gave her position away.

Freya watched her half-brother Stone as he slinked into the growing darkness beneath her, unseen by the men pulling a cart through the scrubland to the south, past a signpost that warned them they were leaving Mexico and entering the United States.

No, Freya thought, correcting herself. While the territory was technically within the boundaries of the United States, this land belonged to the Sinanju tribe. *Her* tribe. Freya looked down at her bare arms. Unlike the bronze skin of her Sinanju tribesmen, they were an almost porcelain white. She never tanned, nor did she burn. But white or not, this was her land. It was the first stable home she could truly claim in her short fifteen years of life.

Freya had spent the first eleven years leading a nomadic existence with her mother, the warrior princess known as Jilda of Lakluun. They were wanderers, banned from returning to their native Scandinavian village. Jilda would never speak of Freya's father, but she had promised the girl that she would explain what happened when Freya was old enough to understand.

But Jilda was killed before that day had come.

Freya finally met her father and was brought to the Sinanju reservation. That was when she found out his name was Remo Williams and that the curious and deadly art he mastered was called Sinanju. Unlike her mother's wizardry with the blades, Sinanju used no weapons, favoring only their hands. She only saw her father, Remo, a few times after that, when he had come to the reservation. Each time she meant to ask him about his life with her mother but she never did. Perhaps she was afraid to question anything because she had finally found a place to truly put down roots.

And now she was worried that she would be uprooted again.

Her grandfather, Bill Roam, known better as Sunny Joe, the tribe's chief and protector, had put down his cup that morning at breakfast, clearing his throat.

"You have a birthday soon, little one."

Freya shrugged. Birthdays meant nothing to her. She smiled each year when they brought out a cake, and enjoyed opening presents, but she did that more because she knew her family enjoyed making her smile. She didn't need presents to be happy.

"You turn sixteen next week, an adult by Sinanju standards. Have you thought what you would like to do?"

"No, grandfather," she replied, looking down at her breakfast. *I'd like to stay here,* she thought, *and continue helping you and Stone.* But she knew that was not what her grandfather wanted to hear.

"You've already graduated the home school programs. Maybe you should think about college."

She had promised him she would think it over and let him know before her birthday next week. But as she sat cross-legged, watching her brother track the smugglers below her, she could not bring herself to think about college or even her future. All she could think of was the roots she had found in her long-lost family, her brother Stone, her grandfather Sunny Joe.

They needed her and she needed them.

* * * *

Stone Smith did not need anyone.

He winced as he shifted his weight. A few pebbles slid down the side of the small hill. He would have to be more silent. At just over six feet tall, it was not easy hiding his large frame, even with the Sinanju techniques he had been learning.

Stone turned to scan his surroundings. Nobody was around but the illegals heading his way. At least he had managed to ditch his pain in the ass half-sister. He had been a loner all his life, so it surprised him just how protective he had become of her. He had been raised as an orphan, living in boarding schools and military academies, until he joined the Navy SEALs, and he did not have much use for anyone except his grandfather and Freya. But he did not need her here. She had no business patrolling the border with him. It was just too dangerous. Despite her advanced training in Sinanju, Freya was still a kid.

Stone quietly snorted. His SEAL training allowed him to thrive in conditions that would kill an ordinary man. He could fieldstrip and reassemble any firearm under combat conditions in total darkness. He could sneak up and disarm a man before that enemy knew what happened.

As a SEAL, he was the best of the best, the toughest of the toughest, and none of that would even remotely impress a Master of Sinanju like his grandfather Sunny Joe.

Stone had begun training with his grandfather after arriving at the reservation three years ago, but he still had trouble trusting it. He was raised to believe in physics and punching and grunting when using your muscles; Sinanju reached deadliness through silence.

The Mexicans advanced to the outcropping Stone was crouched behind. He quietly grabbed a breath and centered himself as he waited for the men to pass him.

Carlos Martinez was tired of walking. The skinny *soldado* wiped his forehead with a sweat-stained piece of cloth.

"Ay! Armando, the wagon. When's it my turn to ride?"

"*Silencio, ojete,*" snapped Armando Ortiz. The leader of the cartel's expedition, Armando stood above the others, six foot five, with a shaved bullet of a head. "Keep your eyes open and your big mouth shut. This is the valley of *muerte.*"

"That's just talk," one of the other men spoke up. Two missing front teeth gave his words a sibilant hiss. "Border crossing is always dangerous. This section's not any worse than anywhere else."

"Wrong about that, *muchachos!*"

The voice had come from behind them. The men turned as one, hands reaching for guns and rifles. They had not heard anyone approach. A shot rang out. One of the men spent his last breath on a curse and dropped his rifle to the ground moments before he joined it.

"Nobody move! Keep your hands where I can see them. Slowly now — you first, tall and ugly — no, the one with the tattoo on his neck. No, the one with the scorpion tattoo. Take your machine gun by the stock. Throw it over there; as far as you can throw it."

Stone waited until each man had thrown his weapon out of reach.

"Okay, Uncle Sam says kneel, hands on your head. Slowly, very slowly. I don't want to start shooting again."

When the four men were still, Stone risked gliding over to the wagon they had been pulling. Not taking his eyes off his prisoners, Stone held his gun in one hand while the other reached over to the tarp. Then the tarp moved by itself and a large man launched from his hiding place, knocking Stone over. The man grabbed Stone's arm, pushing it up. Both men fought for the weapon. The other men didn't waste time looking back.

They lurched to their feet, running for their weapons. Stone head-butted his attacker and felt the satisfying crunch as his nose broke. The man cried out in pain. Stone brought the butt of his gun down, cracking the man over the head. He collapsed to the ground. Stone rolled toward the wagon for cover. His heart was racing as he struggled to maintain his breathing.

Then time seemed to slow down.

His body jerked hard to the left and then to the right as two bullets passed him. It was as if he was on a violent roller coaster, unable to adjust to the sharp turns of the track. His body had reacted on its own as his Sinanju training kicked in to dodge the bullets.

"Blast it!" he shouted.

Stone hated the loss of control that went against all his military training. Now behind one of the wheels, he squeezed off four rounds. Two of the men fell. The remaining two men, knowing they were vulnerable in the open, froze in awkward positions.

Stone rose to his feet, panting.

"Smart move." He began to walk over to them. Next time he would bring rope and tie them up first.

Armando Ortiz felt the first stirrings of real fear. This *idioto* wasn't behaving like any Homeland Security agent he had ever heard of. He knew civilians patrolled the border, but they were always organized. They never worked alone and they only warned border crossers away or reported armed men to government officials.

Armando saw the tarp move again. His last man was only armed with a blade. Needing a distraction, Armando grabbed Carlos from behind and began using him as a shield.

"Hey, I'll just shoot through your friend," Stone said.

"Armando?" Carlos shouted.

Armando ignored the pleading voice and snapped Carlos' neck.

The distraction worked. A small man had slithered out of the tarp quietly and grabbed a knife from the sheath on his calf. He straightened up, raising the knife. Stone's back was a large target, mere yards away. But then the knife seemed to develop a life of its own.

It left his hand.

He turned.

A slim white hand was holding it. He had only an instant to see the tall blond woman who appeared out of nowhere, before he didn't see anything at all. He slid to the ground, dead before his body could feel the pain from the blow to the chest that stopped his heart.

Stone noticed Armando looking beyond him in fear.

"Don't think you can try that old trick, making me turn around," Stone sneered.

Then he heard a familiar voice behind him.

"There was another man in the wagon, Stone."

Annoyed, Stone's head turned of its own accord. How had she found him? He had been so careful.

Armando didn't waste a second. He made a break to the left, arms reaching for his dropped machine gun. He never saw the knife that sliced through his neck, severing his jugular vein. He bled out into the desert sands.

Stone's head snapped from Freya to the fallen cartel *soldado* and back again. Freya had bent down, grabbed the dead man's knife and swung back up, throwing without seeming to aim.

"How many times have I told you not to follow me?" Stone yelled.

"You're welcome." Freya said, folding her arms.

"You have to stop this, Freya. You're going to get me killed one day."

"You're kidding, right?"

"I had it under control! I was just about to turn and take care of him when you butted in!"

"You didn't even know anyone was behind you!" She knew Stone was embarrassed. "You're good, Stone. But everyone needs help sometimes."

"Knock it off," Stone said. He hated the hurt look that came over Freya's face. But he had to be a little cruel, if that was the only thing that could get her to stop mothering him. "Go back to the village. Everyone's dead here. Nobody left to question. If there's something big brewing, we won't know it now."

Stone looked inside the cart. Except for a few empty snack wrappers, it was empty.

"The cartels know a lot of their men disappear on this stretch of the border," Freya said. "They were probably trying to catch you. I can help you clean this up."

Stone shook his head. "I'll take care of it. We're going to have a talk with Sunny Joe when I get back. Serious, sis, you can't keep tagging along behind me."

"You haven't told Sunny Joe, have you?" she asked.

Stone looked at her as if he didn't know what she was talking about.

"You got a job offer to be a field agent for some organization, remember?" she reminded him.

"How did you know about that?"

"I'm your *'crazy stalker sister'* remember? Besides, you're not very quiet on the phone."

"Yeah, I told him yesterday. I've been going stir crazy."

"Let me help you."

"Don't even think about it," Stone said, glaring. "Grandpa would tear me a new one if he thought I let you come."

Freya realized she wouldn't get anywhere with her brother, not in the mood he was in, though he was right about one thing. They *were* going to settle this, but she would wait until he had calmed down. Leaving Stone a disdainful glance, Freya turned and set off for the village, breaking into an easy lope that ate up the ground beneath her at a pace more suited to a cheetah than a human.

CHAPTER TWO

Benjamin Cole stared at the unmarked package, wondering when it would explode. It had been sitting on a desk in the middle of a darkened room and though it raised every red flag he had developed over his twenty-seven years of being an agent, the truth was that he just did not care.

He tilted back the bottle of vodka he had nearly emptied and tried to squeeze the spent lime slice back in, but merely crushed it. Ben abandoned the slice to the floor and sat down behind the box. Then the box began vibrating.

"Sara," he whispered, fighting back tears. If he was going to die, her name would be the last word coming from his lips.

In the mid-eighties, his name had been Benjamin Maugaine. He and his wife were stationed in Egypt as part of an Israeli sleeper cell, assigned to monitor activities of local militant Islamists and report back to Mossad, Israel's famed intelligence agency. They had seen the ascent of a radical wing of Islam taking over larger and larger regions. But after living a peaceful life as the owner of a small electronics repair shop for three years, Sara fell under the lustful gaze of a provincial governor. She was invited to his mansion and survived multiple rapes over the next three days.

When she returned, Ben reported the matter to the police. They went to trial within days, but Ben was prepared. He built an ironclad case that proved that the governor had raped his wife.

Which only made it worse when the judge used that evidence to convict Sara of adultery. He threw out the charges against the governor and sentenced Sara to be stoned.

After the sentence was read, Ben had to be forcefully removed from the courtroom as Sara was led out a backdoor. Facing her own death, but knowing the pain Ben was in, she managed a smile and blew him a kiss.

Her body was returned to him that evening with a court order to have her buried within twenty-four hours. He sat with her body the entire night, cradling her head in his lap.

As he thought back to that day, Ben hurled his empty bottle toward the wall, smashing it into a thousand shards. They both knew what they had signed up for. They knew they were risking their lives for the promise of a better future. And they both knew that if they were caught that they would be executed, but this?

This was not part of the plan.

The next day, Ben buried his wife and his humanity. He sent one last detailed message to his handler and then Benjamin Maugaine went to work. He studied the travel patterns of both the provincial governor and the local judge.

He killed them both the next week. Ben found himself wounded and on the run. His local intelligence contacts were of no use. The governor had been too high a target.

In desperation, Ben tracked down a CIA agent he had often worked with. The man stitched him up and smuggled Ben into the United States. Ben changed his last name to Cole in honor of the agent and over the next decade, became one of the CIA's top covert operatives. When terrorists attacked on 9/11, every report Ben had filed became a national security must read. Ben was the first choice to head up the foreign studies division of the newly-formed Department of Homeland Security. His department was responsible for the killing or capture of over eighty terrorists and he excelled at his job.

So, when he was removed as head of his department and received an odd order to report to an empty building soon after September 11, finding only an unmarked package on a desk in a darkened room, he had figured someone had set him up. He did not really care. He had lived a productive life. Getting rid of bad guys was more than most people could say.

It was enough.

Ben leaned back and took a deep breath as he opened the vibrating package, only to find what appeared to be a computer tablet inside. It was unlike any tablet he had seen before. It was oblong and the screen was covered with some kind of thin, plated flap. As he opened it, the screen instantly turned on. It performed a quick scan and identified Ben as the only person in the room.

The silhouette of a man appeared on the tablet.

"Agent Cole," the lemony voice greeted.

"Yeah, who are you?" Ben asked, releasing the breath he had been unconsciously holding.

"You may call me Smith," the voice said.

"Nice toy, Smith," Ben said, twisting the tablet in his hands. Even when he applied full force, the tablet twisted and returned, but continued to operate. It was made of some kind of compound metallic material, but was deceptively light.

"Hmm...bulletproof?"

"Possibly, but it is inadvisable to test in that manner," Smith replied. "The unit is called a FORtab and there is nothing else like it in the world. I have remotely activated the synchronization routine, which will bind this FORtab for your use only."

The screen immediately turned into a rapidly blinking target. The target moved to where Ben's eyes looked on the screen. It was disturbing and felt confining.

"It can only be unlocked by a combination of vocal and retina scan. Follow the target with your eyes and when you think of a good password, just speak it."

Ben looked down at the small blinking target and scratched his beard as he took a second to think of a password.

"Gimlet," he said and the password took. Ben had seen a lot of advanced technology in his years with the agency, but had never seen anything like this. Sleek lines covered the face of the tablet, appearing to be a leather cover, but when he logged in, they disappeared into a very sharp screen. The texture of the screen had actually changed.

"I will make this short," Smith said. "You have been chosen to head a new department that detects and disposes of terrorist cells."

"And who chose me?"

"That is not important," Smith said.

"Okay, try this question. How big is this department?"

"Two, counting yourself."

"Look I'm drunk, not stupid. You can't do this with two men."

"You will not be going into the field. However, you will be allowed one field agent."

"That won't be enough."

"This man has...special training that makes him specifically suited to this job."

"I'm gonna need at *least* twenty men. If — no, *when* your 'specifically suited' guy gets shot, and he will — I'm going to need another. Look, if you've read my stuff, then you know what's coming. And we can't stop it with just two men."

"That's the offer."

Ben lowered his face only long enough to break eye contact with the FORtab. There was something that he was not being told, but he would not find anything from the outside.

"Okay, count me in. Forgive me for being drunk the first day on the job. I thought this was a setup to kill me."

"And you still showed up?"

"There are more important things in this world than my life," Ben answered soberly. "So, who's my field agent?"

"His name is Stone Smith. He was a member of Navy SEAL Team Six and..."

"A single SEAL isn't going to be able to..."

"He is also a student of the martial art known as Sinanju."

"So, what, he can break bricks with his head?"

"He can dodge bullets."

"So, let me see if I understand you," Ben said, trying to use his serious voice. "You just put a drunk guy in charge of an organization that has authority to use lethal force and is armed with alien technology and a guy who can dodge bullets?"

"I would not have worded it that way, but you are basically correct."

"Okay, I'm in. What now?"

"You will set up your office and then travel to Arizona to meet your field agent. It is important that you brief yourself on all files referring to 'Sinanju' on the flight over."

The file appeared even as Smith spoke. As Ben began scanning the information, the tablet reacted to his eye's movements, automatically moving text and pictures as soon as he was finished viewing them. It was awkward, but only for a few seconds. Then his eyes adjusted and he sped across the information.

"Agent Cole, your forecasts are incredibly sobering, but your limited knowledge of the forces operating in this world cause them to be short-sighted."

"I don't know what I'm supposed to say."

"At the end of a conversation, the traditional thing to say is 'goodbye.'" And the man on the other side disappeared.

Ben leaned back in the chair. As he let go of his FORtab computer tablet, the screen returned to its original pattern.

"Ben, Ben, Ben…" he moaned. "What have you gotten yourself into?"

CHAPTER THREE

Kylie Holcomb bit her lip. As Liz Worn's campaign manager, Kylie had been told that if she helped Liz get elected to the Senate, she would be placed on a fast track in Washington politics. How hard could it be? The last election had produced a Republican win but that was a fluke not seen in the previous fifty years. Returning a Democrat to this Senate seat would be about as hard as getting a baby to poop.

She had no idea.

The first thing she found out after taking the job was that she was Liz Worn's sixth campaign manager in three months. The second thing was that the self-styled "People's Senator" had a nasty habit of taking bad news out on the messenger and today the papers in her hand made Kylie the messenger. She quietly entered the luxurious office and left the papers on Liz's handmade oak desk.

But before she could turn to leave, Liz looked up at Kylie and flashed her famous 'everyman' smile.

"What's that, hon?" she asked in the sweet tone that had become familiar over the past few weeks of the campaign.

The short straw, Kylie wanted to say. "All the local papers are running this story tomorrow, page one."

The smile disappeared from Liz's face and the age lines, carefully masked by four-hundred-dollar-a-bottle makeup and multiple Botox treatments teased their way back to her face. Liz slowly read the story and her scowl quickly disappeared into her jowls.

"I don't see the problem," she said, tossing the paper into the recycle bin.

Being green was a convenient way to justify multiple shredders in every room.

"The story says that you claimed to be Native American to get jobs at Ivy League schools," Kylie said, puzzled. *Had she even read the story?*

"Dang right I did! The idiots wouldn't just hire me because I was a woman. They said they already had their quota on women, so I had to do something."

"But you took jobs that should have gone to real Native Americans."

"Aw, crap-a-poo! I used some obscure tribe that no one's ever heard of. I don't even remember their name. Besides, it was just to get into Harvard."

"They are called the Sinanju tribe and you actually did it eight times! The Sinanju were contacted for the story and they have no record of any of your ancestors being a member of their tribe."

"Pssh. It'll all blow over."

"Ms. Worn, it is not going to blow over. Two newspapers are already calling it 'potentially racist.'"

Liz tilted her head in condescension.

"Young lady, do you realize who I am? I am the founder of "Integrate Diversity In Overtly Troubled Societies!" They're not legally allowed to call me racist!"

"Ms. Worn, our research shows that unless you get the tribe to acknowledge your heritage, this could get ugly."

"Forget it. We have more important issues in this campaign, like finding out if my opponent cheated on his high school science project. How's that coming along?"

"We're talking with one of his old girlfriends, but she's having trouble remembering the exact details and we can't afford to go public until she's consistent."

"Get on it," Liz said, no longer with any pretense at a smile on her face. "Now!"

Kylie rushed out of the room, relieved that she still had her job.

Liz watched Kylie leave the office and her temper broiled over. How dare she imply that Liz Worn, supergenius professor and champion of the underdog, was a racist? Liz buzzed the receptionist.

"Yes, Ms. Worn?" the receptionist asked.

"Make sure that girl never works in politics again."

CHAPTER FOUR

"You can't just keep tagging along!" Stone said, slamming the door behind him. "This isn't kid camp!"

Freya swiftly entered before the door had a chance to fully close. "Everyone's saying that I'm turning sixteen, so it's time to start acting like an adult. Then, in the next breath, they tell me that I'm too young to do anything!"

"Look, I'm sorry," Stone said, putting his hand on her shoulder. "I know you're good at Sinanju and I know you want to help, but there's a whole world out there that you're just not ready for yet."

"Really? I spent the first eleven years of my life traveling across Europe, watching my mother fight off rapists, murderers and drug dealers and I've saved your sorry butt at least twice! And you think I'm naïve?"

"You can't work with me and that's that."

Freya stood directly in front of Stone.

"If you can stop me from reaching your back door, I'll stay."

Stone locked eyes with Freya and took in a deep breath. The first Sinanju lesson that his grandfather Sunny Joe taught him was proper breathing. Ninjitsu, Kung-Fu, Karate. Each was based on a small splinter of Sinanju and as such, each was a pale comparison.

The air flooded his body with strength and his awareness expanded as the world around him slowed to a crawl. The dust that had been lazily dancing in the air froze in place. The steady click-clack of the clock on the wall turned into a slow, almost imperceptible tap.

And then Freya smiled and disappeared.

One moment she was standing in front of him and, during the time it took him to blink, she was gone. Freya was suddenly behind him, holding her finger to his throat as if it were a knife.

"You're not naïve, Stone. You're just dumb. And stubborn," she said, walking out the door.

"That's cheating!" Stone yelled without turning around.

Stone cursed. She was trained well enough to kill just about any man on Earth — but that wasn't the point. He couldn't get by this blasted feeling of protecting her. When she first arrived at the reservation, she was the outsider. It took a couple of years for her to fit in. There were arguments over who got to date her.

Then, at fourteen, when she was trying to break up a fight, one of the guys actually tried to hit her. While the guy eventually recovered from his broken bones, Sunny Joe had to make a rule preventing any Sinanju boy from dating her. But that only further isolated her, preventing her from bonding with the tribe. She was always 'the outside girl,' 'the princess,' the unobtainable girl that caused all sorts of teenage angst in local dating patterns as other Sinanju girls were inevitably compared to Freya.

It was not like that for Stone. He had arrived earlier and was quickly able to connect with someone at a family level for the first time in his life. There had never been an emotional attachment to the uncle who raised him, but now Stone's grandfather, Sunny Joe, was always there and he was able to recognize the Sinanju tribe as home.

Stone knew it was different with Freya. Despite her outside toughness, Stone could see the walls she had erected to hide behind — to protect her from the social environment where she was truly vulnerable. He knew her well enough to see the fake smiles and could tell when she was being polite.

He could almost hear her silent screams…for the mother she had lost, and for the father that she had met only fleetingly.

Stone shared the same father, this Remo Williams, but whatever affection he might have had for the man had been transferred to his grandfather Sunny Joe. And all Stone knew of his mother was that she gave birth to him and then left town. It really didn't bother him.

A knock at the door. Sunny Joe had just finished speaking with Freya. Stone opened the door and motioned for him to enter.

"Grandpa," Stone greeted. "Freya's been bugging me to tag along with the patrols. I tried to tell her…"

"She's right, you know," Sunny Joe said, interrupting. "This is her home, too."

"But she's only fifteen," Stone protested. "I was a punk at fifteen."

"You're still a punk," Sunny Joe said, laughing. "But you're family and yeah, she may be fifteen, but your sister is tougher'n you think."

"I just don't want to see her getting hurt."

"Remember that boy that tried to punch her a few years ago? He's good enough to walk with a cane now."

"I get it; I know she's a natural when it comes to Sinanju, but grandpa, she needs…I don't know. She needs some down time. Learn how to be normal."

"Neither one of you is ever gonna be normal. You got Sinanju blood. This is her tribe, too. Let her help defend it."

Sunny Joe turned to leave.

"But…" Stone started to protest.

"Next patrol, she's going with you. No buts. Don't make me kick yours," Sunny Joe said as he left.

CHAPTER FIVE

Manuel "Manny" Gonzalez could almost feel the wrinkles that had taken hold at the edges of his eyes. Age had begun to claim the fifty-eight-year-old Mexican drug lord. Involuntarily, he turned to glance at the reflection in his large glass window and flexed his arms.

A strapping barrel chest stretched his shirt, but something wasn't right. Manny rolled up his sleeves, revealing his thick, hairy arms. There was something about bare arms that made a man a man. Kids these days did not understand things like that.

He looked around. His newest mansion had been the kind of palace that he once would never have even dreamed of visiting, much less owning. It was a four-story citadel built in the Old-World style of stone and mortar, sitting on the plushest eighty acres this side of Mexico City, complete with a double basement and a twelve-car garage. He boasted twenty servants, a real marble floor and a heated Olympic-sized pool that he had not used in years.

From an empire built on drugs and blood, Manny Gonzalez had it all.

That was when he realized the truth in the saying that life is a journey, not a destination. After thirty years, Manny Gonzalez had arrived and found there was nothing left to do at the end of the path he had taken. He had saved more money than he could spend in a dozen lifetimes. But for every professional and family goal that he had ever achieved, Manny Gonzalez was merely another man on a leash and the only way to get off the leash was by retirement or death.

The holder of his leash was only known as Helmut, a European man perhaps a few years older than Manny and educated in fine Western schools. Manny never even graduated from high school, but he knew that schooling did not create intelligence, just as being clever was not a substitute for wisdom. But such maxims did not apply to this man who was learned and intelligent as well as clever and wise. After Helmut's first devastating show of power that took the lives of both of Manny's more powerful rivals, Manny learned not to question the leash.

It was not all bad. Helmut had given Manny the kind of protection that allowed him to grow his empire to the size of a small country, but the fact remained that the leash was still there. As his laptop beeped signaling an incoming video call from Helmut, Manny felt it tighten around his neck just a bit more.

As Manny answered the video chat on his laptop, Helmut appeared, giving Manny a perfunctory smile.

"You will receive a package by personal carrier that will be delivered to a location I will later detail," he said without greeting in a way that was neither rude nor rushed. "This package is more important than your entire empire."

The tone of his voice was serious, but Manny knew that he was not making a threat. He was merely spelling out expectations. Helmut never threatened, but Manny knew from personal experience that bad things happened whenever Helmut did not get his way.

"When will it arrive?" Manny asked, knowing not to ask what was in the package.

"It is at your doorstep right now. It will only be released to you and you will keep it in your presence until it is ready for delivery."

"I shall do as you say," Manny said humbly. Hearing the voice of a servant come from his mouth only made his decision to retire easier. "My friend, I am old and this is a world for the young."

"You are thinking of retiring?"

"Yes, for many months now."

"All is well as long as our arrangement is followed by your successor. I assume your nephew Tomás is next in line? I know how much your own sons have disappointed you."

Manny never questioned how Helmut knew things. At first, he tried to deny what Helmut said, but Helmut would just grin that knowing grin and smoke one of those large cigars of his and remain silent until Manny realized that it didn't matter how he knew.

He just knew.

"Sí, he is a smart boy with a strong heart."

"A piece of unsolicited advice about Tomás. Your nephew is a crass brute who hides his murderous impulses behind a computer screen. I would exercise great caution."

And that was that. The conversation ended and Manny thought about what Helmut had said. He was right. Manny could not trust his fat, lazy sons and his daughter was certainly not a leader of anyone other than her boyfriend of the week.

But despite Helmut's warning, he would hand over reins of his empire — and more importantly, he realized with a sigh of relief, hand over his leash — to his nephew. Tomás was ruthless, yes, Manny knew this, but he also had a business sense about him. Born of the internet generation, Tomás knew computers and over the past two years had brought the Gonzalez Empire into the twenty-first century. No longer would they use phones and hand-delivered letters. Tomás had created extensive networks of electronic messaging. Video conferencing allowed him immediate access to remote parts of the empire. Manny never tried to understand the workings of this new electronic age. He preferred working directly with people, so in Tomás, he saw a future for himself, away from the business. Time to spend with his family.

He had always wanted to take his wife Maria to Thailand. It was beautiful there.

Manny received the package from the courier. It was neither larger nor smaller than a breadbox. For all he knew, it was a breadbox — some kind of perverse last test from Helmut to validate Manny's loyalty.

It didn't matter what was inside. He could not risk the box falling into the wrong hands, so he had probed until he found an unguarded spot on the southeastern Arizona border.

The first two groups of men he sent to survey the area never returned. At first, Manny thought they were taking advantage of the occasion to remain in the United States for the good paying jobs that didn't exist in their home country.

That was before their heads started showing up.

The heads were found on the Mexican side of Agua Prieta, mounted on the top of a billboard that urged caution when crossing the border. Manny had not seen anyone stand up to him like that in years and a small spark of the man he once was actually looked forward to the challenge. Then the moment passed and Manny reminded himself that this was no longer his challenge, no longer his empire. This challenge was Tomás' and it would truly show whether or not he was ready to lead the Gonzalez drug empire.

If Tomás survived, Manny would give him the keys of his kingdom. Manny sat back and took a long swig from a bottle of tequila, hoping Tomás was every bit the brute Helmut claimed he was.

CHAPTER SIX

Liz looked at her watch. She had eight minutes to make her decision. To her left she had made a stack of newspapers that had begun to investigate her claims of Native American lineage. On the right was the sole paper that had not covered the story: a local high school paper that wasn't allowed to cover politics. Seven other local high school newspapers were in the pile to the left.

"Crap-a-poo!" she said.

This was getting serious.

Not only had two of the papers actually used the term 'potentially racist' which was a clear violation of their agreement with Liz's organization, three of them had gone so far as to actually pull their endorsements. She would appeal the use of the "R" word, but it was too late. The damage had already been done. Some of her most ardent supporters were privately asking questions. Her largest financial supporter, sensing blood in the water, pulled back any further support "until this blows over."

She was going to have to do something fast, but what? Liz buzzed the receptionist.

"Yes, Ms. Worn?" the woman asked.

"Send in my campaign manager."

"You fired your campaign manager, ma'am."

"Well, how am I supposed to run a campaign without a manager? Find me another one!"

Nikki Jarrell quickly left the office. She had been Liz Worn's original campaign manager, appointed by the Vice President himself, but was fired after Liz was videotaped sleeping in the middle of a policy briefing. She said that Nikki should have had a 3D likeness of her ready for situations like this to allow her to nap. When Nikki tried to explain that such technology didn't exist, Liz called her a Luddite and fired her.

Nikki took over the position as receptionist when Liz threw a stapler at the original receptionist, who promptly quit. Going through campaign managers had almost become a sport. Nikki had been secretly running the campaign from the receptionist desk since then, hiring a bench of campaign managers as phone staff. She had privately promised each one an opportunity at running the campaign, but she was already down to four people. But if Liz kept firing campaign managers at her current rate, they wouldn't make it to the election.

Nikki walked to the front desk of the phone staff office where a very serious-looking man was seated.

"I've been waiting," the man said, adjusting his tie. Unlike others in the campaign manager reserve, Christopher Scott was a child of privilege. Though he was handed the finest things in life, Christopher worked hard to amplify his already impressive beginnings. He graduated at the top of the best private schools, and at the top of his class at Harvard.

"Mr. Scott, are you sure you want this job?"

"Ma'am, I have never failed at a job," Christopher said, gathering his folders.

"Good luck," Nikki said, returning to her desk.

"Unnecessary," Christopher said, entering Liz's office.

Liz smiled as he entered. Christopher smiled back and offered his hand.

And then the door shut.

"Hi, I'm…"

"Get your ass over here!" she barked, dropping her friendly demeanor and pointing at her laptop. "I have four minutes to make a decision. Do I issue a press release that details my opponent's high school cheating scandal or the one about the Indians?"

Christopher handed Liz a folder detailing the Sinanju tribe controversy.

"Our research has shown that the Native American story is not going to go away," Christopher said. "You've either lost or dulled the support of most of your key constituents. I've already prepared a press release that will adequately deal with the issue as well as garner more support."

Liz opened the folder. It was all neatly printed out with graph charts of polling results, categorized by constituency. The press release said that the recent stories about her not being a Native American were the result of a misunderstanding with the tribe and that Liz planned to personally travel to Arizona to straighten things out.

"Where is Arizona?" she asked. "I don't have a passport!"

"Arizona is an American state west of Texas," Christopher replied, unfazed.

"Do they have cows there? I don't like cows."

Christopher wouldn't allow her to sidetrack him with one of her well-known tangential statements. "We will make an anonymous donation of five thousand dollars to create a Sinanju college fund. I can arrange it with the chief now, so all you will have to do when you get there is to complete the rite of passage ceremony."

"Is it hot there?" Liz asked.

"Yes, ma'am. The reservation is located on a desert. Temperatures typically pass one hundred degrees."

"What? My hair can't take heat like that!"

"I'll arrange for research to get us accurate costume and hair styles for Sinanju women. We don't want to insult them and risk them not giving you a new name."

"What do you mean, a new name? I'm Liz Worn!"

"To claim kinship to the Sinanju tribe, you will have to assume a tribal name, at least until the election is over."

Liz gritted her teeth and jutted her chin out to show the world that she had come to a decision.

"Book me in a five-star Saint Joe hotel! If the press wants a real Indian, they're going to get one! We're going on the warpath!" she screamed, placing the palm of her hand against her mouth and whooping.

Christopher glanced at the thick folder at the top of his stack of folders, which contained a psychological profile of Liz Worn.

It was obviously outdated.

CHAPTER SEVEN

"Are you ready?" Smith asked Ben through his earplug.

"Yes. And before you ask, I'm sober."

"Your condition was never in question," Smith replied.

"I just assumed since you called me to a bar that you would want to know."

Not that this was the type of bar Ben frequented. If a building could have a hangover, then Mike's had been hammered since the sixties. The bricks had grimed together into a solid mass of texture and the sign had been painted over so many times that the original logo was nowhere to be seen.

"Your profile didn't display a tendency toward alcoholism," Smith said

"Let's get on with your big tour, because if you've read any of my reports, you know that 9/11 is just the start. We've got a lot of work to do."

Ben opened the door to Mike's and a cool breeze flowed from the inside.

The bar was smaller than it looked from the outside. Eight tables and four booths surrounded a twelve-foot bar. No one was inside except for the burly man behind the bar who matched the picture of Mike on the wall behind him. Mike looked up and nodded to Ben, then went back to wiping the bar.

"Mike is CIA," Smith's voice said over the earpiece. "He is your gatekeeper."

Ben walked to the bar and sat down.

"What'll you have?" Mike asked with a modest smile.

"Tell him that you're his new boss," Smith's voice said.

"I'm your new boss," Ben said.

Mike's smile disappeared. He pulled a shotgun from beneath the counter so fast that Ben didn't have time to duck.

"I own this joint," Mike said. "I ain't got no boss."

"Tell him that the pond is cool in summer," Smith said.

"The pond is cool in summer," Ben dutifully replied.

Mike paused for a second, as if he were memorizing Ben's face. He lowered the rifle and placed it back in its guard.

"I'm Mike. Just remember, boss or not, drinks ain't free."

"I'll remember that," Ben said.

"Walk toward the restrooms," Smith instructed. "Past the men's and the ladies' room is a door marked 'Employees Only.'"

Ben walked to the back corner of the bar. It was dark, but he could have sworn he saw the glint from a camera lens.

"Cameras?" Ben asked.

"There are forty cameras located from the parking lot outside to the elevator."

Ben found the employee entrance. A worn touchpad was on the right side of the door.

"A high-resolution facial recognition camera is mounted inside the peephole. It has already scanned your face and enabled the keypad. The code is 9 – 1 – 0 – 6 – 4," Smith said.

Ben entered the numbers and the door smoothly opened.

Behind the door was a small corridor that led to a room with an elevator on either side. A solitary down button rested on the wall between them.

"Never take the elevator to the left," Smith warned. "Once an elevator alarm is triggered, an incapacitating agent is released into the air-tight confines of the elevator, rendering the subject inert."

"Knockout gas?" Ben asked.

"It is much more complex than that, but we can discuss it at a later time."

Ben pressed the elevator button and only the left elevator door opened. Ben looked at it and was about to say something when the right door finally opened.

"There is a ten-second delay to lure intruders into the left elevator," Smith explained.

Buttons one through four began blinking as Ben entered.

"Choose three," Smith said.

Ben pushed it and the elevator began descending.

"Sensors are located in the elevator walls to scan for weaponry, identity and heat signatures. The floor tiles hide sensor plates that measure weight and temperature."

The elevator doors opened to a single large room.

"This room was originally designed to be one of the President's bunker control rooms. It was constructed here because of its close proximity to the nation's fiber-optic hub. Every bit of processed information in the United States passes through here."

And the President won't be missing this office if there's an emergency?" Ben asked.

"This is only one of his twenty-two bunkers. The safety of the President is not in question."

Ben was almost embarrassed at the opulent fixtures that adorned the walls. An exact replica of the President's desk sat toward the back center of the room. A fake window was behind it, making the room look like the Oval Office.

"Where do the other doors lead?"

"Besides the elevator, there are six individual apartments for the President and his security team."

"I'll be living here?"

"For the most part, yes."

Ben sat in the desk and the leather creaked comfortably to accommodate his weight.

"Is Stone ready? I hope you're right about Sinanju."

"You'll see soon enough. You and Stone will fly from Tucson. Then he…"

"I would rather drive."

"Why is that?"

"No distractions, just two people in a car riding hundreds of miles. There's nothing like a road trip to really get to know someone."

CHAPTER EIGHT

"Tomás, what do your computers tell you?" Manny asked anxiously.

His nephew sat in Manny's chair, the only other person in the entire cartel allowed to do so. Tomás was engrossed by the laptop in front of him. His fingers moved nimbly over the keyboard, inputting commands with confidence. He tapped a key in response to his uncle's question and turned the laptop so that Manny could see it.

"There is a reservation in the area we are attempting to bypass. I think the Indians are beheading our men as a show of force."

Manny huffed. "It is a game of escalation, my nephew. If someone punches you, you just have to punch back harder. Every man has a point where escalation is no longer worth the cost. Find that level and then continue hitting. The package must go through this week. We don't have time for another test run."

"Yes, uncle, I have been preparing," Tomás said, tapping another key. A map of Arizona appeared on his laptop and it zoomed into the southeast corner, focusing on a city on the American side of the border called Douglas. A small group of arrows appeared to the east of Douglas, pointing north through the Sinanju reservation.

"Our next move will involve a small army that I shall personally supervise. I shall not fail you, uncle," Tomás said with the cold smile of a killer.

"I am so proud of you, Tomás. If only my sons were men like you," Manny said, cupping the back of Tomás' head. "Your mother is very proud of you."

Tomás looked sadly up at his uncle. "The doctor does not give her any hope."

"Doctors are not God!" Manny said and spat on the marbled floor. "They told me to lose weight twenty years ago and look at me! I am a strapping bull of a man!"

"I just worry about her," Tomás said. "She's all I have."

"Your mother will be fine," Manny said, laughing. "You just need to find a good woman, that's all."

"When I have my own house and steady income, then I will look for a girl, uncle. Until then, I am your soldier."

"Good boy, Tomás," Manny said, messing his hair up. "Good boy."

Tomás ignored the sentimental gesture and pointed to an area on the map. It was the only route they had not tried.

"This is where we have to hit them uncle, and hit them hard. I will personally carry the package, surrounded by a small army. If we move quickly, there will not be time for them to react."

"Is that area even passable?" Manny asked, squinting. The satellite map showed large landmarks stretching horizontally. "Those fortifications look to be as large as the river."

"Those are only trenches and unmanned ruins left over from the last century. We will move our army through this pass," he said, pointing with his finger. "Three waves. The first wave of men will overwhelm any resistance, allowing me to pass through with the second wave to our contact in Tucson. The third wave will follow, protecting our flank. After delivery of the package, our men will disperse throughout the country and return separately within the month."

"You think like a general!" Manny said, impressed. "How many men will you need?"

"Three hundred," Tomás said, remembering a movie he had once seen about three hundred men who had fought against a million. He forgot about the part where they died. "I need three hundred of your best men. We can no longer be seen as soft."

"I don't have three hundred men to spare on this short notice. I shall give you ninety of my best men."

"I can work with ninety, but we will need an advantage. Some of our soldiers now fear the border."

"My soldiers are a superstitious, cowardly lot," Manny admitted. "They fear what they don't know. We need a disguise to strike terror into the hearts of our enemies. We must become something terrible, dark…a creature of the night!"

Tomás looked to the ceiling for just a moment as his uncle's words triggered a memory from the earliest part of Tomás' childhood.

"I have it!" Tomás said and began furiously typing on his keyboard.

Manny looked at the odd words his nephew was typing into the search bar. Tomás triumphantly clicked on IMAGES and the screen was filled with people dressed in dark masks and suits carrying all manner of weaponry.

"We will dress each of our soldiers thusly, striking fear into the heart of our foes!"

"Who are these people?" Manny asked, impressed with their dark, savage look. Many of them carried three-pronged knives and slim blades.

"They are the most feared people on the face of the Earth, uncle. They are silent, deadly, and no known force on Earth is their equal," Tomás said gleefully.

"I have never heard of these…niñas," he said, reading the screen.

"No, uncle, not niñas, these are *Ninjas*! They conquered Asia through their martial arts, invisible assassins who cannot be stopped!"

"My men know nothing of these neen-ja or how to fight like that," Manny said. "They only know the gun and the knife."

"But in the United States, everyone knows of the ninja. They are the most feared assassins in the world! Many movies have been made of them. Just by placing our men in these fierce dark uniforms, we take back the advantage. I shall build a great Mexican Ninja Army and our enemies will crouch in fear at their coming!"

Manny smiled. He did not know what Tomás was speaking of, but this was his test and he would be allowed to pass or fail on his own.

CHAPTER NINE

It was just past noon, in the hottest part of the day. Ben drove up the sandy trail that had at one time been a paved road. The cracks would have sprouted weeds, had vegetation actually been able to thrive in the area. But, like the rest of the Sinanju tribal grounds, sand had long ago taken over any plants that had tried to grow there. It had become the de facto yard for each of the small houses that peppered the southeastern part of an otherwise uninhabitable desert.

Looking for any sign of life in the small shantytown, Ben shook his head. The town consisted of a bunch of small houses scattered around a row of buildings attached to each other by a small wooden sidewalk. It was almost like traveling back in time. Ben imagined that Tombstone might have looked like this after it had been abandoned. None of the buildings was clearly marked, so he pulled in front of the largest one, a storefront that had once been red decades ago. The remaining chips of faded maroon paint defiantly tried to maintain a semblance of their former color.

Only after he placed the car in park did Ben notice the girl standing at the front of his car. She had not been standing there when he pulled in. Her blonde hair and piercing blue eyes most certainly did not look Native American. Cautiously, Ben placed his index finger on the pistol in his jacket pocket and slowly exited the car.

"Didn't see you there," Ben said, remaining behind his open car door. "I'm looking for Stone Smith."

Something is very wrong, Ben thought as he looked around. It was too quiet. There were no signs of any vehicles. And the girl...she was not there when he pulled in. She just appeared out of nowhere. The way she stared at him, dissecting him with her eyes, Ben felt like he had just pulled onto the set of a horror movie. The girl looked to be no more than sixteen, but he clearly felt an air of danger around her. For all he knew, this was a ghost town populated by a lone teenage girl.

"Stone's my brother. How do you know him?" she finally asked.

"Only from his resume," Ben said, keeping his hand in his pocket.

"Unless you're looking for trouble, you need to ditch the gun."

Surprised that someone her age had noticed that he was packing, Ben slowly placed his pistol under the driver's seat and locked the door. "My apologies. Do you know where Stone is?"

"Everyone's at lunch. It's our weekly communal meal."

"Then why aren't you there?"

"You ask too many questions," Freya said and turned. "Follow me."

Ben walked the length of the wooden sidewalk behind Freya until they reached the last building on the strip, a green-painted monstrosity that acted as the village's assembly hall. The building had seen better days and those days had obviously been in the middle of the previous century. Inside, a group of twenty men sat eating at various tables. They were talking and laughing until the door opened.

Everyone stared at the visitor standing beside Freya. After a moment, they resumed eating, but remained quiet except for whispers and quick glances at the foreigner.

As Ben looked around, he saw mostly older men in western cut shirts, but Stone was nowhere to be found. His research on the Sinanju put their number around eight hundred. This must be some kind of council leadership meeting.

At one time, the Sinanju tribe numbered in the thousands, but that was before construction jobs in the nineties and the siren song of bright American cities began luring their young from the old ways.

The Sinanju were a dying tribe.

"You must be Ben," a firm voice said from behind him.

Ben's training kept him from showing that he had been startled for the second time in five minutes. That was twice someone had sneaked up on him. Maybe this was a ghost town.

"Sunny Joe Roam," the tall man said, extending his hand. "But you can call me Bill."

While studying about Stone, Ben learned that he was being trained by the man standing before him. Sunny Joe stood tall for a man in his seventies and though his thin frame still looked powerful, Ben couldn't imagine a guy who looked like a beardless Abraham Lincoln teaching any kind of martial art.

Ben smiled and shook Sunny Joe's hand.

"Afternoon, Bill. I didn't know I was expected. I'm looking for Stone."

"I know," Sunny Joe said. "He'll be here momentarily."

"I have a few questions while we're waiting, if you don't mind."

Sunny Joe led him off to the side so they could talk privately.

"The court records show that your tribe is called Sunonjo, but everyone else is calling it Sinanju."

"It's always been Sinanju. Some stupid government surveyor misspelled our name in the 1800's and we've been fighting to get it changed ever since. Just imagine if they had been spelling your country 'Murika' for almost two centuries. It literally took an act of Congress to fix it last year."

"And the martial art? To be honest, what I've read seems unbelievable. You're their teacher?"

Sunny Joe leaned toward close to Ben's face. "You know what they say about Fight Club?" he asked.

"The first rule of Fight Club is that you do not talk about Fight Club," Ben replied.

"That's because they're afraid we'll find them and kick their asses," Sunny Joe said with a confident wink.

Before Ben could pry further, the back door slammed open and a young man with dark hair stormed toward the front of the room. Stone was carrying a small duffel bag and wearing an old button-up shirt.

"You're my ride?" he asked Ben.

"Something like that."

Stone nodded and then said to Sunny Joe, "She's not supposed to be here." He still had not looked at Freya.

"Freya, don't embarrass him," Sunny Joe replied in Korean.

Ben wasn't sure, but it sounded more like an Asian language than a traditional Native American tongue.

Freya stepped behind Sunny Joe, but kept her eyes on Stone.

Stone's eyebrows knotted in frustration.

"Are you ready?" Ben asked Stone.

"Yeah," Stone replied, glaring at Freya. "I am now."

CHAPTER TEN

Sunny Joe watched Ben and Stone leave. It took several minutes before the dust cloud from the car became too small for him to see. He entered the small building the tribe used as City Hall and entered his office. He sat behind the wooden desk built by his father as a ceremonial gift for taking over as Sunny Joe.

But Bill Roam had never wanted to lead the Sinanju tribe.

His father was a serious man dedicated to the old ways, but like others his age in the early sixties, Bill had been more worried about finding out who he was than maintaining the status quo. He couldn't do that under the constant thumb of tradition on the reservation. After mastering all the basics of Sinanju at twenty-seven, he left to seek fame and fortune in Hollywood. Bill quickly became a famous stuntman, able to perform amazing feats of strength and endurance that audiences attributed to trick edits or special effects. But Sinanju didn't help his acting ability, so he was pigeonholed as Hollywood's go-to stuntman, eventually becoming the man behind the suit in the famous *Muckman* movies. It took two decades for Bill to discover that he could not find what he had been looking for in Hollywood, so he returned home, to his father, to his people and to the old ways.

Perhaps it was because he was wiser, or perhaps the call to be the next leader of the Sinanju tribe was subconsciously trapped in his mind, but at forty years of age, Bill Roam knew what he was meant to do.

His father ignored the time Bill had been gone, and over the next two decades, finalized his training in Sinanju. Unlike their Korean counterparts, who were the greatest assassins of all time, Sunny Joes concentrated mostly on the defensive aspects of the art. The Tribe of Sinanju was not to directly compete with the House of Sinanju. There would be no killing by contract.

That was forbidden.

And his father continued teaching Bill about the history and legends of the Masters of Sinanju. The most important one, the legend that was repeated every year on the anniversary of the tribe's establishment in Arizona, was the story of the twins Kojing and Kojong.

As Bill remembered the story, he heard it spoken with the voice of his father.

There was once a Master of Sinanju by the name of Nonga. He was fearsome in battle and, more importantly, brought much tribute to the small fishing village on the Korean bay.

But something happened on one of his missions — something that cost him most of his eyesight. Because their training placed their bodies at the pinnacle of human development, Masters of Sinanju could see farther, more clearly and even in the dark. One of Nonga's scrolls mentioned that he had an accident, but provided no details of the incident.

Masters of Sinanju never had accidents.

The scrolls of Sinanju detailed every Master even before the Great Wang, who first discovered the Sun Source. The scrolls were the living history of the House of Sinanju, handed down from one Master to the next. Nonga didn't explain how it happened, but his grandson, Master Sambria, blamed the god Kali.

When he returned, Nonga could barely see, so when his wife bore twins, she was able to hide one of them from Nonga, for there can only ever be one Master and one pupil. Kojong, as the second twin, would have normally been cast into the sea. But his mother had him trade places with his brother Kojing every other day, teaching each other the lessons they had learned from their father.

Nonga had completely lost his eyesight before the boys began training in earnest. And when he died, for the first time in history, there were two Masters of Sinanju. Kojong, sensing the unrest the pair had inadvertently caused, volunteered to exile himself. He assembled a small raft and took with him the barest of rations and set sail over the Great Eastern Sea.

The greatest story in the Tribe of Sinanju was the story of the journeys of Kojong Shiva. When Bill first heard the story, he scoffed. Despite all the superhuman achievements of the Masters of Sinanju, Bill still questioned old world gods.

When Kojong reached the American coast, he was greeted by attack from various tribes, until he reached what is now known as Arizona. A small tribe of people welcomed him into their homes. They housed and fed him. The people were poor, like the Korean fishing village he grew up in, and Kojong grew to feel a kinship to these beleaguered people.

When they were attacked by a rival tribe and the chief was killed, Kojong defended them and the invaders fled. The tribe then crowned him with the feathers from the dead chief and Kojong assumed command of the tribe.

He was given the chief's daughter as a wife and she bore him a son and named him Gerah. Soon after his birth, survivors of the rival tribe assembled an alliance of other local tribes to attack them. They used poisoned arrows, flaming arrows, and even a few newly-acquired Spanish rifles in an attempt to overwhelm the tribe.

In Bill's mind, his father's voice always lowered for the next part.

Then came a mighty earthquake, which shook until the men were thrown off their horses. Lightning struck from the sky. Kojong's eyes darkened and his voice filled the plains.

"I am created Shiva, the Destroyer!" Kojong Shiva cried. "Death, the shatterer of worlds! The night tiger made whole by the Master of Sinanju! Who is this dog meat that dares challenge me?"

The armies, unfazed by what they considered to be a trick to scare them, descended as one. Hundreds of men from surrounding tribes moved to assault Kojong with their knives and their bows and their guns, threatening to overpower them with sheer numbers. And then they died.

They all died.

After their enemies lay dead, Kojong's eyes returned to normal. His fellow tribesmen, fearing him, whispered the name they had heard him utter as best they could in their own tongue.

"Sunny Joe! Sunny Joe!" they chanted.

The tribe was renamed Sinanju and the heirs of Kojong were called Sunny Joe. Each taught his eldest son the secrets of Sinanju, only for tribal defense, careful not to interfere in the outside world lest they compete against the House of Sinanju in Korea.

The goal was always to eventually return to Korea and somehow reunite the two factions of Sinanju, both the House and the Tribe. And now Bill Roam — Sunny Joe — found himself violating two of his ancestors' most sacred rules in order to accomplish that goal.

It was forbidden to train more than one pupil. Their very existence in Arizona was due to a violation of that principle. More importantly, tradition strictly prohibited a woman from ever being trained in Sinanju.

Even though he was not as fervent a believer as his father, Sunny Joe felt a little guilt. But he had a reason. His own son, Remo, had returned as the reigning Master of the Korean House of Sinanju, and left Sunny Joe to care for his children, Stone and Freya. Sinanju tradition demanded that Sunny Joe only teach Stone. But Stone was stubborn, favoring his military training while Freya was a natural in everything he showed her. He could tell that she had been breathing correctly most of her life, while Stone had only started after moving to the reservation.

Stone could only maintain a Sinanju center for short peaks before his body had to recover. Until he stopped smoking, he would not be able to retain his center indefinitely like Freya.

She was the key to the future.

As daughter of both factions of Sinanju, she could reunite the House and the Tribe. But it was too large a burden to share with her until she was older.

The door opened, but Sunny Joe knew who was on the other side before it opened. He would recognize the frantic heartbeat of his tribal caretaker Mick Walker anywhere.

"What are they telling you now, Mick?" Sunny Joe asked.

"Sunny Joe," he greeted, removing his ever-present cowboy hat as he entered. Mick was shorter than Sunny Joe, and he had begun packing some extra weight in the last few years. The harsh tan line running across his forehead revealed that he had spent more time outside than in.

"They said they'd give the tribe ten thousand dollars to set up a college fund. All we have to do is say this woman is a member of our tribe."

"You told them no," Sunny Joe assumed out loud.

"Well...ten thousand dollars would help some kids who want to go to college."

"Sinanju ain't for sale, Mick. You're the tribal historian. You know that better'n I do."

"It's not like we're competing with the House, Sunny Joe. You know I'd never do that. I'm just thinking of the kids it could help."

"Answer's no."

"I told her you'd say that, but she insisted that I ask," Mick said sheepishly. "Said she wants to visit to see if she can change your mind."

"Politicians coming to visit?" Sunny Joe shook his head. "God help us all."

CHAPTER ELEVEN

Freya centered her breathing while lying in the trunk of Ben's rental car. Her weight was perfectly distributed. She could easily hear Stone's breathing from where she lay. Sunny Joe would be embarrassed. It was unseemly to breathe like that in front of an outsider.

Ben said that they had a twenty-one-hour drive to a place called Roxana, Illinois. Freya adjusted her body to a more comfortable position, careful to remain silent. The temperature in the trunk quickly rose past one hundred and thirty degrees, but Freya altered her body temperature to accommodate the stifling heat, sipping small wisps of cool air that leaked through the back seats. In the stillness of the trunk, Freya's mind wandered as it did just before she went to sleep.

And in the stillness, her senses expanded.

She was able to filter out the subtle knock of the engine caused by cheap gas and the slight vibration in the rear axle, which caused an unnecessary bump every time it struck a line in the pavement.

Had she made the right decision, stowing away like this? Stone was right about one thing. This wasn't some kind of kid's camp, but Freya wasn't a kid. She never had been, not really.

Freya unconsciously frowned as she thought of her childhood. Would her mother Jilda be proud of her? Jilda was killed when Freya was only eleven, leaving her with so many unanswered questions.

Her father and mother had only known each other for a short time during the Masters' Trials. Opponents sworn to fight to the death, both were masters in their respective arts. They only survived because Jilda declined to continue the Trials, upsetting centuries of order.

Though he was the current master of the Korean House, Freya's father carried the decidedly non-Korean name of Remo. As daughter of the reigning Master of the House of Sinanju, this made Freya mistress of both the House of Sinanju and the Tribe of Sinanju. She would make Sunny Joe proud of her. She could tell that he had big things in mind for her. Even his Sinanju training couldn't keep the prideful smile from breaking his stern face when she learned a new movement perfectly.

Freya never had to ask if she had performed her moves properly. Her body *knew*. She didn't remember when she first started breathing correctly, for she had always remembered breathing this way. She remembered running through the forests of Eastern Europe, escaping one mob after another, connecting with nature, living off the land, being an integral part of the universe in a way that even her mother never understood.

Then her mother was killed.

And the one man on the face of the Earth who did understand how she felt, who should be with her to help answer the questions she had — her father — had just dropped her off at Sunny Joe's as if she were a piece of luggage. He visited every year for her birthday, and she assumed he would be here for her birthday this year as well. But it always felt more obligatory than familial.

And that was something that proper breathing could never replace. Sunny Joe told her that her father, Remo, was a good man doing good things and he missed his daughter terribly, but that work for his country always had to come first. She hoped that was true.

Then the car stopped. They were still in the desert; perhaps she had inadvertently made a noise.

Had she been discovered?

CHAPTER TWELVE

"So, who do we work for?" Stone asked.

"People who don't like to be named," Ben replied. "Have you read over your mission brief?"

"It's why I signed up. Cartels have been sending more and more smugglers through our border in the past couple of weeks. They're up to something big."

"This is bigger than you know," Ben said. "Our intel says they're getting ready to move something really important. I don't know if it's nuclear or biological, but we need to stop them."

"Why is it coming from Mexico?" Stone asked.

"If you want to do something criminal, go to a country that has no tradition of enforcing any laws. That's Mexico. You know, if they're coming across the border, your people may want to consider allowing our government access just long enough to place security fences on your southern border."

"Sunny Joe isn't gonna let a single soldier on tribal land. Don't get him worked up. He's a nice guy, but you don't want to be on his bad side."

"But doesn't he realize that your people are in the most danger from this package?"

"They have to get through me first and that's not going to happen."

"Because of your Sinanju training? Look, kid, I know you're a pro. You don't become a SEAL without being one of the best, but right now, you're sounding awfully naïve."

"There are about forty guys who tried to come through our border who would disagree with you if they were still alive. Sinanju isn't a martial art. At least, not like you understand the term."

"Yeah, about that. I'm not sure I believe in the whole bullet dodging thing," Ben mused.

"Dodging bullets is simple compared to some of the stuff I've seen Sunny Joe do," Stone sighed. "You know how good a karate master is?"

"I hold a fourth-degree black belt in Isshin-ryū," Ben said. "We're not overly impressed with Karate."

"Sinanju's even less impressed with Isshin-ryū," Stone said, allowing a prideful grin. "Pull over."

Ben pulled the car to the side of the road. They exited and almost immediately started sweating in the Arizona heat.

"Grandpa...Sunny Joe...says sweating is a sign of weakness," Stone said. "I haven't gotten that far in my training yet. My sister Freya would be making fun of me right now. She's a natural."

Freya allowed herself a smile as she lay still in the trunk. Stone would never compliment her to her face. She huffed just once to continue regulating her body temperature, but did so against the back of the seat to muffle the sound. Stone would be able to regulate his body temperature if he would just stop smoking and put more effort into Sunny Joe's training.

"Your sister, she's trained in Sinanju?"

"Yeah, but she's been breathing properly since she was a baby," Stone said with a bit of pride. "If she were older, you would probably want her for the job, not me."

"Okay, now what?" Ben asked.

Stone walked until he was twenty feet from Ben and then held his hands out to his side. "Try to shoot me."

"Bullet dodging," Ben mused, pulling the custom Glock from his jacket pocket and aiming it at Stone. "You realize that if this is some kind of magic trick, you're dead. You can't fool me with jerky movements. I was trained as a sniper when I was a child."

"Unless you can somehow bend the trajectory of a bullet, I'm more than..."

Ben pulled the trigger in the middle of the sentence, to catch Stone off-guard. He aimed for the shoulder. No need for a mortal wound.

Stone had time to smile before the bullet reached him.

Though he was not in control of his body when Sinanju took over, when the shot was expected, the roller coaster turned into a ride. As he started to say the word "ready" the bullet came at him and he felt the sudden surge of power to his frame as it moved him to the side, allowing the bullet to pass harmlessly by.

Ben blinked, but Stone was no longer standing where he was before. He was standing slightly to the right of where he had been. The move was timed so perfectly that it seemed to Ben that the act of pulling the trigger had caused Stone to appear elsewhere.

The moment was so surreal that Ben looked at his gun. If he had not felt the kick of his custom hand-loaded bullets, he would have thought he was firing blanks.

Stone moved two steps closer and bowed.

Clutching his pistol with both hands and spreading his stance, Ben steadied his aim. There was no way he could miss at fifteen feet, no matter how fast Stone was. There simply was not enough time for the neurons in his brain to react to a bullet being fired this closely.

So he fired again.

And again.

And again.

And again, and again, and again, the bullets missed their target.

"Impossible!" Ben cried out, unable to accept what his own eyes were showing him.

He reached into his pocket for his backup pistol, but in the second it took to reach his weapon, Stone was standing directly in front of him. Ben brought the gun up, firing as he did, but Stone had already moved to his side. When Ben turned to look where he stood, Stone was holding both of his pistols.

A sly smile stretched across Stone's face.

"I'm not fully trained yet or I would have done something fancy," Stone said, handing back the pistols. "Sunny Joe does this thing where he grabs a pistol, unloading it at the same time. The bullets fly out like popcorn."

"That's not...I don't..." Ben stammered. "What kind of trick is this?"

"I've been trying to tell you, it's not a trick," Stone explained, shrugging his shoulders. "It's Sinanju."

CHAPTER THIRTEEN

The media had all but destroyed Liz Worn's claims to a Native American heritage. Everywhere she looked, another newspaper or television station was attacking her. Late night comedians were starting to call her 'Liz Worn Out.' Local television anchors, who had all but endorsed her before the controversy, were all but calling her a liar for claiming to be Native American.

"Okay, maybe it was eight jobs," Liz thought out loud. "But they're still blowing it out of proportion!"

It was worse than her pre-Harvard days when one of the local New York papers — *The Times* — criticized her 1981 study that conclusively proved that all men were homosexual. The only consistent difference between heterosexuals and homosexuals that the $4.2 million study could find after a painstaking three days of research was that the heterosexual men were attracted to women.

That was the only difference!

Liz grimaced. The establishment. They were always trying to find some way to keep the minority down and she was a double minority, both female *and* 1/64th Sinjanan… Sunjanoa… whoever they were!

Liz was going to settle this issue once and for all. She accepted a live interview from one of the local television morning show hosts. Liz booked the interview in front of a food bank to show the little people that she cared about them.

The interview would take the heat off of Liz's Native American claims. Liz would use the interview to break the story about her rival's high school cheating scandal. The television crew arrived and was setting up their equipment when a middle-aged lady walked up to Liz unbidden.

"Good morning, Ms. Worn. I'm Megan. I manage the food bank," she said, offering a handshake. Liz looked around, but the cameras were not set up yet, so she wouldn't get credit for shaking one of the little people's hands. Liz put on her professional smile and ignored the extended hand.

"We're so glad you could make it," Megan said, ignoring the snub. "Donations have been down lately and we have more people to feed than ever. Would you and the camera crew care to share breakfast with us this morning?"

"This isn't about you," Liz said, shooing away Megan as if she was diseased. "Go away, you fat little turd!"

Megan tensed and then frowned. She turned and sadly walked away.

"Hi, I'm Trish Hill," a voice said behind Liz. "Who was that?"

Liz turned and flashed her professional smile. "Who? Oh, that's just a nobody."

Trish watched Megan walk away, shoulders down. Trish had seen and interviewed cocky politicians her entire career, but this took the cake. Trish narrowed her eyes for just a second before returning to her own professional smile.

"Ms. Worn, please, have a seat over here. We will be live in a few seconds. You received our advance questions?"

Liz winked at Trish. "I'm ready!" she said as the microphone was being pinned to the front of her blouse.

A cameraman held his hand out, all five fingers splayed. Liz had been doing this long enough to know that meant a five second countdown. The fingers counted down to one, and then he pointed to Trish.

"Good morning Boston! We are live at the Mercy Pantry food bank with Senatorial candidate Liz Worn. Good morning, Liz."

"Good morning! Doesn't that food smell great?"

"I hear that's partially thanks to you?" Trish asked.

"I've been a huge supporter of food ever since I was a small girl," Liz admitted, smiling. "People have got to eat and what better way to eat than at a bank? My opponent only thinks about money when he hears the word bank!"

Liz laughed at her little joke.

A small crowd had gathered behind the two women. Trish was used to it. People naturally gathered whenever they saw a camera. Normally, her peripheral vision was cut off and reserved for her guest, but Trish could not help but see Megan sheepishly walk to the front of the group. Trish's eyes narrowed.

"What do you have to say about the controversy surrounding your claim of being a Native American?" Trish asked.

Liz's eyes darted back and forth. That was not one of the approved questions.

"To get back to the issue at hand," Liz said, ignoring the question. "There are some very serious questions in this campaign that need to be addressed!"

"That is what your opponent is saying about your claim. Are you or are you not a Native American?"

Liz swallowed.

The camera was live. There was no way out. She could see herself in the monitor, fidgeting. Liz blinked once and then regained control. She forced her professional smile back on and leaned forward, taking charge of the interview.

"That's because he wants to run from the issues that really matter in this election," she said with a granite confidence chiseled in Harvard debate class.

What's this bimbo trying to pull? Liz wondered. *After this interview's over, you can kiss your career goodbye, sister!*

"You haven't answered my question," Trish continued, leaning in to match Liz's move.

Liz leaned in even closer. "I don't understand the question," she said, trying to keep the vein in her forehead from destroying years of plastic surgery.

Trish leaned in until the two were almost nose-to-nose. "Several papers are reporting that you claimed to be 1/64th Sinanju to get a job at eight different Ivy League schools. What is your response?"

"Look Trudy…"

"It's Trish."

Liz shuddered. She wanted nothing more than to smack the smile off her happy face.

"Trish, I'm here to connect with the people and talk about real issues. Serious issues. This distraction was engineered by my racist opponent. I'm extremely proud of my Saint Joe heritage, but the people of Massachusetts want to hear about serious issues, like what my opponent says about cheating on his high school chemistry project!"

And just like that, it was out.

Liz leaned back and smiled victoriously. Live television was her friend. If the reporter wanted to go off-topic, Liz would give her something to scorch the headlines. Now she would *have* to address the true controversy in this election. Liz's research team had verified that her opponent had been caught cheating on his junior year chemistry project and as a result was sent to summer school.

"Ms. Worn," the reporter continued, ignoring Liz's triumphant smile. "You still have not answered my question. Do you still claim to be Native American?"

Liz froze.

For the first time in her life, she did not know what to do. As one BBC reporter would later describe the scene, "You could almost hear the crickets chirping as her mind unsuccessfully tried to find a dignified way out."

So Liz slipped back into her friendly smile and panicked.

"I gotta go pee."

And she unplugged her microphone and bolted for the women's room.

The video went viral within minutes. Several websites had already turned Liz Worn's video statement into a meme. Her voice was superimposed over any scene where a character turned to run away.

An action hero, walking away from a bomb blast in a movie, was overdubbed with Liz's voice.

"I gotta go pee!" he said as he ignored the blast behind him.

One bright user even matched it to Rhett's exit speech in *Gone With The Wind* so when he stood at the door, he said, "Frankly my dear, I gotta go pee!"

CHAPTER FOURTEEN

It was late when Ben pulled into Mike's parking lot. He had told Stone about the bar during their trip, but it was obvious from the look on Stone's face that he had not believed how rundown it looked. The men walked into the bar and Ben nodded to Mike, who only grunted. Stone looked at Mike and felt his probing eyes. He could tell by his posture that Mike was armed.

Ben walked Stone to the employee entrance and showed him the code.

"There are cameras everywhere, including here," Ben said, pointing to what appeared to be a peephole. "If you're not in the database, the keypad won't work."

"This is supposed to impress me?" Stone asked as the door swooshed open.

"It should. No one can access this part of the building without triggering a dozen alarms."

"Who's the guy at the bar? He's armed to the teeth."

"Mike's the gatekeeper. No one gets in or out without his permission," Ben said, leading Stone to the elevators. "Never take the left elevator."

Stone looked around. Something was not right.

"There's no one else here?" Stone asked.

"Just you and me," Ben replied. "Well, and Mike out front."

Ben waited for the right elevator to open and the men walked inside.

"Only choose the third floor," Ben said. "Any other button will ruin your day."

The elevator slowly descended the three floors, but, as the elevator bell dinged and just before the doors opened, Stone felt it again, but much stronger; the slight wince in his bones that something was not right. It was the same feeling he got right before being shot. Adrenalin flooded his body with energy and his nerves automatically forced Stone to center his breathing.

Had he been led into a trap?

No, he could tell by Ben's stance that he wasn't expecting anything. As the doors opened, Stone shoved Ben toward the cover of the side of the elevator and prepared to take on whatever was on the other side of the doors.

"Hi, Stone," a distinctly familiar voice said as the doors opened.

Ben's FORtab began the dull pulsating vibration that signaled an intruder.

Freya stood on the other side of the door with a weak smile on her face. Recognizing her from the reservation, Ben pulled out his FORtab and stopped the alarm.

"I thought Stone might need some help," she said. "We met at the reservation, remember?"

"How...what's she doing here?" Ben yelled to Stone.

"Your security won't stop her," Stone said to Ben as they exited the elevator and then turned to Freya. "You ride in the trunk again?"

"For a secret headquarters, you don't have any alarms on top of the elevator itself," Freya pointed out.

Ben stared at his FORtab. It signaled that security had been breached and the location of the intruder. But she still did not register on the screen. His FORtab lit up and Ben stepped back into the elevator to answer it. There was only one person on the other end of the FORtab and he knew that an intruder alarm would be dealt with in a serious manner.

Stone pulled Freya back away from the elevator.

"You're gonna blow this for me. I'm here to help the tribe and you're getting in my way again."

"I can help you, Stone."

"No, sis, you can't," Stone said softly. He looked at Freya and then lowered his head. "Sis, I know you mean well, I really do. But..."

"Give me a chance," Freya said, nodding to Ben. "If I can't get him to say yes, I'll go home."

Stone paused. "Deal. But after this, you gotta go home, okay?"

"Cole," Ben said, answering his FORtab. How could he have let a girl waltz into his office? "Boss, I screwed up."

"There actually is an intruder?" the voice on the other end of Ben's FORtab asked. "I had assumed you were demonstrating security protocols with Stone."

"No, it's Stone's sister. I have no idea how she got in. I guess she has Sinanju training. How many of these guys are there?"

"Tradition calls for only one Master and one pupil. The girl must be an exception. If so, her abilities are beyond your scope to deal with. This organization will not incur the wrath of a Master of Sinanju by attempting to harm her. Why is she there?" Ben noted that even the FORtab couldn't filter out the annoyance of Smith's voice.

"Says that she wants to help Stone. So, what's the call? Protocol states that I'm supposed to kill all intruders, but another protocol says I'm prohibited from harming any member of the Sinanju tribe for any reason."

The voice was silent on the other end for a moment and then Ben thought he heard the creak of a chair as if its owner leaned back in thought.

"You now have two field agents," Smith said. "Make it work."

Ben wondered how that was going to work.

"One more thing; the package we are trying to intercept is in a small wooden box."

And the FORtab signed off.

"Mr. Ben?" Freya asked shyly as she approached the elevator door.

"You're in," Ben said. "But you follow my orders or you're gone."

"What?" Stone asked in disbelief. "No way!"

"I won't let you down, Mr. Ben," Freya smiled.

"She's your responsibility, Stone," Ben said. "Bring her up to speed on operations and teach her whatever you can. I'll set up security to clear her here."

"It's really no problem, I can just bypass…" Freya started.

"No!" both men shouted.

CHAPTER FIFTEEN

Kylie sat her things down on the desk and turned on the computer. She had lost her job as campaign manager and no matter where she went, no one was willing to hire her, so she quietly returned to the Liz Worn campaign as a researcher. That's how she started in politics and she was good at it.

It was a major step down, but at least it was work. She would just keep to herself and hope no one recognized her.

A man came and sat down across from Kylie and looked at her oddly.

"What are you doing down here?" he asked.

"I'm just doing research for the campaign," she said.

"Jonah…Jonah Miller," the man said, offering a handshake. "Don't worry about it. I was her fourth campaign manager. You know Lou, the guy who drives her, right? He was the campaign manager before me. You're lucky that you only got demoted. She drove me so crazy that my wife divorced me and took the kids."

"I've never seen anything like it," Kylie confided. "She is Jekyll and Hyde."

"What did you do to get fired?" Jonah asked. "I forgot to pick up her dry cleaning."

"I was the one who broke the news to her about her Native American heritage."

"Ouch. I'm surprised she didn't throw something at you."

"Well, she threw my career out the window," Kylie said.

"Hey, wanna have some fun and maybe get payback at the same time?"

Kylie smiled. "I like the way you think. Nothing illegal, right?"

"Nah. Our current mission is to research this 'Sinanju' tribe."

"I'd never heard of them before this," Kylie said.

"That's probably why she chose them," Jonah said. "They pretty much stay on their reservation, so she figured no one would ever be able to challenge her claim."

"So, what can we do?"

"She wants to know everything about them, what they wear, what they eat, things like that. Guess what I found?"

Kylie moved her chair to his desk and sat down so she could see his monitor. It displayed several images of a tall man dressed in what could only be described as a very campy 1950's Tonto uniform.

"That's so much of a stereotype it's almost racist," Kylie said, wincing.

"It's an actual picture of their chief. Well, they don't have a chief. The official title of the tribal leader is 'Sunny Joe,' but that's him."

"Well, except for the campy costume, he's hot."

"Don't get too worked up. These pictures were all taken in the seventies. Get this; he left the tribe for about ten years to become a Hollywood stuntman. These are various set shots of him playing bit parts in sixties westerns, but they're definitely him."

Kylie smiled. "Oh, my God. I know what you're thinking."

"Yeah, we tell her these are pictures of him and find some cheap costume shop to get her dressed up in a Pocahontas suit. Let her make a fool of herself."

"Oh, you're bad," Kylie said. "I like you."

"There's just one problem," Jonah pointed out. "Her new campaign manager."

"Yeah, he's so serious, he's scary."

"We won't have to worry about him for a few days. I booked him on a three-day junket with the Vice President. They're traveling to Ghana. Just him and the VP."

"That's just wrong," Kylie said.

"It's about to get wronger," Jonah said, opening a folder full of sketches and handwritten notes, spreading them across his desk. "Here's what we're going to do."

That afternoon, Kylie and Jonah met with Liz for their weekly briefing.

Liz looked curiously around the room as if she were missing something.

"Did I fire another campaign manager?" she asked.

"No, ma'am," Jonah said. "He will be with the Vice President for the next three days."

"That guy's a retard," Liz said, rolling her eyes. "So, what did you two find out about these Sinjuns?"

Kylie stood to give her presentation. She was both upset and relieved that Liz did not seem to recognize her.

"The Sinanju tribe is not what you would consider a traditional Native American tribe," Kylie began. "They are of Korean descent. They travelled to America sometime in the late 16th or early 17th century."

"That's racist, isn't it?" Liz asked. "Why are Koreans pretending to be Indians?"

"They aren't pretending. This is how they live their lives. We've taken extra time to study the customs of the tribe and have found out all the basics."

Kylie nodded to Jonah. He turned on the projector.

The first slide showed a man's face with the title SUNNY JOE ROAM below it.

"This is their chief, Sunny Joe Roam."

The next slide showed a younger picture of him in one of his bit parts in a 1960's western. He was dressed in a campy brown Indian suit, complete with tassels and a feather in his hair.

"I thought chiefs have a full feather headdress," Liz pondered.

"Oh, this was back when he was just a young Indian," Jonah said, pushing the button. The next slide showed Sunny Joe in a full headdress. He was holding a cavalryman's head in his armpit, pulling on his hair. It was a set photo from "*That Darn Injun*," the only comedy credited to Sunny Joe.

"Now, that's more like it!" Liz said, smiling and clapping.

Kylie rolled her eyes. "We've arranged for a tribal uniform to be custom-made for you. But understand, we have to use the same materials they use for it to be an authentic tribal uniform."

"Is it itchy?" Liz asked, already scratching her arms. "I hope it's not wool."

"I'm sorry, but you'll only have to wear it for as long as it takes to complete their rites of passage," Kylie said, making a mental note to construct the entire costume from wool. "If you don't show up in an authentic uniform, some clown on the internet will say that you're wearing a rival tribe costume and that will just stir the controversy even more."

"Whatever I have to do, let's just get this over with. What does Slim Joe say?"

"We contacted him again today. He still wants no part of it, but the reservation has no known security, so you're going to just show up Tuesday dressed like this, offering a peace pipe."

Liz's eyes widened.

"Do they smoke pot?" she asked, smiling hopefully.

"No, that was a figure of speech," Kylie said.

"Are you sure this is going to work?"

"We have no other choice."

"Ms. Worn!" a man yelled, entering the room, holding papers as if he were strangling them. "Bad news!"

Jonah and Kylie smiled. They had given the intern twenty dollars to bring the article to Liz's attention.

"Now what?" Liz asked.

"A paper has found another one of your college applications. They're releasing a story tomorrow that says when you applied to MIT you claimed to be 1/32nd Jamaican."

"So what? I never attended MIT, you idiot! Those jerks wouldn't let me in."

The intern became nervous, not knowing what to do. Liz leaned into his face.

"Are you waiting for a cookie? Run away, you little turd!"

The intern ran out more quickly than he had come in.

"You claimed you were part Jamaican?" Kylie asked innocently.

"Yeah. I overheard one of the department heads saying that they needed more black people. I hired this black guy once and he came from Jamaica, so I thought if I could just imitate his accent that it would help me get in. But do you know what those idiots said? They dared to say that I wasn't smart enough! Sexist…racist…woman-phobes! Everyone knows that they rig those tests so they're hard on purpose!"

"This isn't good," Kylie said, faking the concerned look already showing on Jonah's face.

"What are we going to do?" Liz asked, copying their worried expressions.

"We can't do anything that would take away from your claim to be a Native American, but you're going to have to do something to address your alleged Jamaican roots."

"I *am* Jamaican!" Liz protested.

"I thought you just claimed that to get in."

"I did!" she screamed. Then when they continued staring at her, she asked, "What?"

"I know what she needs," Jonah said, snapping his fingers.

"I know what you mean," Kylie said, smiling.

"Dreadlocks," they said in unison.

"You've got to be kidding me," Liz said.

CHAPTER SIXTEEN

"Tomás!" Manny barked as he burst into his office, displeased with his nephew for the first time in his life. "Please, make me understand what you have done!"

"Uncle, I cannot have untested men enter the battlefield," Tomás said, his eyes remaining on his laptop. "They need the experience of battle."

Tomás watched the live video feed as his Mexican Ninja Army advanced on the battlefield. While none of them had been trained in any martial art, the sudden appearance of ninety black-clad soldiers had startled the guards stationed at the house of José Moreno, head of a competing cartel.

"You are attacking my friend," Manny said. "We have a pact. We have been at peace since childhood. I am the godfather of his children and now he is on the phone asking me why I am attacking his home."

"That was his mistake, uncle," Tomás said coldly. "We need a trained army and José had let down his defenses."

"How many of my men have died?" Manny asked, seeing a few ninjas lying on the ground.

"Thirty-two," Tomás said.

"I gave you ninety men! No, Tomás, this is something that you cannot do!" Manny said, closing the lid of the laptop.

Tomás simply continued to stare forward as if nothing had happened. Manny thought he saw a slight smile crack Tomás' otherwise harsh face.

"Uncle, you have given me a very difficult mission; one that you have not been able to accomplish yourself, even though you have tried twice. If I am to complete this mission, then I will need to think outside the box."

"But José is my friend!" Manny said, standing back. "You cannot attack my friend!"

"This is why I attacked your friend," Tomás said, opening his laptop. The screen turned back on. After a click of the mouse, the screen began showing a video of José and Tomás' mother in an unflattering situation. Tomás made sure the audio was turned all the way up.

"How can he do this to me?" Manny shouted, inflamed.

Tomás changed the screen back to the video feed from one of the ninjas. The walls to Fortress *Jefe Duro* had already been breached and the fortress had been set ablaze. The ninjas waited for the people to run out of the burning building, only to gun them down as they did.

"Shoot them harder!" Manny yelled.

Tomás turned the laptop away and looked his uncle directly in the eye.

"This is only the beginning, uncle. No more family cartels. We rule them. All of them."

Manny's cell phone began ringing. No doubt that *capullo* José was begging for mercy. Manny answered the phone without looking.

"We need to talk," the cool voice of Helmut said as he answered. "Alone."

Tomás noticed the change in his uncle's demeanor and saw a look he had never seen before on the face of his uncle: fear. Manny waved Tomás on with the war and exited the room.

Tomás made a mental note to follow up on this weakness his uncle was showing.

"This call has nothing to do with José or the small war your nephew has just launched." Helmut's voice over the cellphone was brisk and sharp.

Manny looked back at the closed door of his office and in his mind's eye recalled Tomás gleefully watching the death and destruction from his computer as if it were just a video game. There had been no sign of human empathy, just the cold eyes of one machine killing another. It was the curse of this generation. They thought people were just like games or machines.

"You are in danger," Helmut continued. "An American agency has sent two agents to kill you and your nephew; a man and a woman. I will send pictures of the two to your computer and inform Tomás of the orders. I would prefer they be kept alive for interrogation," Helmut said. "This is very important to me, Manuel. You cannot allow your nephew to interfere. Do you understand?"

Manny lowered his head. Though he could not see the smug look of Helmut's face, he could still feel the leash.

"It will be done as you say," Manny replied.

"Good. I want to find out who sent them. After that, you can do whatever you want with them. It is imperative that the package be transported this week. Then you can retire, Manny, and live out the rest of your life just as you wish."

Manny did not hear the phone disconnect, but knew Helmut had hung up. He placed the cell phone to his pocket and returned to his office. Tomás was still at the computer, speaking commands into a microphone.

"We have trouble," Manny said.

"Is it this email that keeps popping up?"

"Click it," Manny said. "These two have been sent to kill us."

Tomás clicked on the email and as he did, the screen flashed a couple of times before displaying the attached pictures. A voice began talking through the laptop speakers.

"Hello, Tomás," the voice of Helmut said through the computer.

"Who is this?" Tomás asked, bewildered. "How are you talking to me? I have this thing firewalled and encrypted! This *perra* is locked down like gravity!"

"These are two American agents who will arrive at Mexico City tomorrow," Helmut said. Manny and Tomás studied the image of a dark haired American in combat fatigues and a thin teenage girl with long blonde hair.

"That girl is an agent?" Tomás asked. "She can't be sixteen, man!"

"They have been sent to kill both you and your uncle. I want them captured alive to find out what they know first. Be careful. Your lives depend on this, gentlemen."

The screen returned to fighting. They saw a pair of ninjas crash through the front door of José's drug cartel headquarters. One of the maids had obviously been forced to carry a gun and fight, but the woman dropped the rifle and screamed when she saw the masked men. They shot her and continued inside.

"Who was that?" Tomás asked his uncle.

"The man who helped set up my empire," Manny replied, deflated.

"Your empire?" Tomás mocked. "The one you 'built with your own hands'?"

"Everyone has help, Tomás, even you."

"I don't need your help, uncle. You gave me a situation and I handled it and now I find out that you aren't even in charge?"

"Don't fool yourself, Tomás. I run this cartel. Helmut merely assists from time to time."

"Europeans don't assist, uncle. They take over your society and change it to theirs."

"We will do as he says," Manny said, trying to regain the upper hand. "Or you will not live to see another sunrise."

A group of screaming ninjas took their attention back to the laptop. A large man in striped, bloody pajamas was dragged into the hallway. His face was lifted to the camera for identification.

"*Te odio,*" Manny whispered.

"Take him outside!" Tomás yelled.

Manny wasn't used to seeing someone sitting in his desk shouting out orders. Did he look this foolish when he barked commands? José was dragged through the yard and forced to his knees in front of a statue of the Virgin Mary.

"*Madre!* Have mercy, Manuel!" José pleaded.

"Can they hear me?" Manny asked. Tomás nodded. "*Chinga tu madre y muerte, puto! Disparale!*"

The ninja holding a gun to José's head just stood there.

"I thought you said they could hear me?" Manny asked.

Tomás whispered an order into his microphone and the ninja kicked José to the ground and emptied his AK-47 into the drug lord's body.

"Why didn't he do what I said?" Manny asked.

"This is my army now, uncle," Tomás said.

Manny felt a chill race down his spine.

For the first time, he looked around and noticed that his office did not look like it used to. The painting of his childhood horse was no longer displayed over the large stone fireplace. The small medallions that once proudly hung over the bar had been replaced with a gaudy picture of a cartoon figure with the words "All Your Base" at the bottom.

Suddenly Manny felt another leash had just been slipped around his neck and the other end was tied to the pistol now brandished in his nephew's hand.

"You can leave," Tomás said.

Manny stormed down the stairs, but as he looked at the guards, he realized that he didn't recognize any of them. As he reached the front door, he saw the butler. A trusted member of his family for decades, Manny finally found someone he knew. Somebody who could help.

He raced toward the butler, eyes frantic with questions, but the butler merely opened the door, glaring at him as he would a panhandler. Manny looked down in shame. As he walked by, the butler placed his finger against the back of Manny's head like a gun.

Manny froze in place.

"Do not come back," the butler said and then motioned as if he had pulled the trigger.

Manny ran to his car. Screw this. He was going to retire early.

CHAPTER SEVENTEEN

Liz Worn cursed her Native American heritage.

"This is horse crap!" she screamed. "If I had known I was gonna have to go through all this trouble, I would have claimed to be Asian. They talk funny, but at least they have air conditioning!"

"Ms. Worn, after you complete the Sinanju rite of passage, you will never have to talk about this again," Kylie said. "Just follow my lead. I've prepared a speech written phonetically in the native Sinanju tongue. It's just a couple of lines, but you'll need to memorize them."

Liz snatched the papers from Kylie, but began fanning herself with them instead.

"I will do no such thing! I went to my prom in a helicopter. I'm a Harvard graduate. Heck, I dated a guy from Juilliard! I'm not spending one more brain cell on this than I have to for these goomy goomps."

Kylie had no idea what a 'goomy goomp' was, but she hid a smile. She knew that Liz would never memorize anything.

The small motorcade drove into the main road of the Sinanju reservation and pulled up to the building marked 'City Hall.' Liz remained in the car, placing her lips on the air conditioning vents to suck the cold air out of them while Kylie went inside.

"Uh, hello?" Kylie asked the empty room.

She tapped the bell on the counter, but before her hand could return to her side, a man appeared next to her. He had not been standing there a second earlier.

Startled, she jumped back.

"Whoa! Where did you come from? We're here to see Sunny Joe Roam."

"That's me. You from the papers?"

The man was tall, thin and old, but there was something hard about his face. As she looked closer, Kylie recognized his eyes and smiled.

"Hi, I'm Kylie Holcomb from Senator Worn's campaign," she said, extending her hand. Sunny Joe shook her hand and returned to his statue-like stance. "Uh, we called you a few days ago about the future Senator completing a rite of passage?"

"I've already told your people no. She has no ancestors here and I'm not gonna let her turn our tribe into a political punch line."

The door slammed open and Liz Worn, fully decked out in a wool version of a 1950's television Indian costume spilled into the room. Sunny Joe looked at her as if she was diseased.

"What are you supposed to be?" he asked.

"Shut up!" Liz barked. "Someone tell me where the goddam air conditioning is in this place!"

Kylie winced, but motioned her forward.

"This is Sunny Joe Roam," Kylie said formally. "He is the leader of the Sinanju tribe."

Liz panicked.

Not knowing what to say, she pulled out the script Kylie had prepared for her and started reading.

"Oh, great chief of the Sun…Sinjana…onjono, ah, whatever. We have traveled many moon for rite of passage. Make a sweeping arm movement," Liz said.

Then she realized that she wasn't supposed to read the last part and made a sweeping arm movement. "We give much moolah to make great wigwam for chief."

"Your press lady already came here and checked on this a few months ago," Sunny Joe said, annoyed. "You don't have any ancestors here."

"You speak English?" Liz asked, glaring at Kylie. "Why didn't anyone tell me?"

Liz tossed the papers to the floor. "Look, Tonto, before the cameras get here, let me make this worth your while. Do you know you guys don't have a casino? I thought all Indians had casinos! After I get into the Senate, my number one priority will be to get you the casino you deserve. The white man has held you captive long enough!"

"We can have a casino anytime we want, lady. We choose not to."

"What kind of Indians don't have a casino?"

"Sinanju," Sunny Joe said proudly.

He had almost had enough of this idiot when the camera crew came in the door. Liz fell to her knees in desperation. It would only be a moment before they started rolling.

"I need a Suntajano name," she pleaded. "Just give me your blessing!"

Sunny Joe looked down at the Senatorial candidate. Her faux Indian makeup was already streaking down her flushed red face. Sunny Joe kept his anger inside. Everything about this woman offended him, but if she wanted a show, Sunny Joe would give her a show.

He waited until the cameras blinked on and then raised his hands over her head.

"You, who are not of my tribe, light of skin and small of brain — if you can but pass the Sinanju rites of passage, you shall receive a tribal name."

Liz looked back at the cameras and smiled, giving them a thumbs-up. Her Indian makeup dripped over her cheeks as she smiled.

Sunny Joe looked outside the building and then reached behind the counter to grab an old broom.

"Wow," she asked as Sunny Joe handed her the broom, handling it like an heirloom. "Is this a magic broom?"

"It is the first task in the Sinanju rite of passage. It is said that only a Sinanju warrior can sweep the street clean," Sunny Joe said, pointing out the window.

"But…that's a dirt road," Liz protested.

Sunny Joe continued pointing outside, unmoving as a statue.

The cameras focused on Liz as she looked out the door for a moment of protest and then, magic broom in hand, went outside and began sweeping the dirt street.

CHAPTER EIGHTEEN

Helmut Belisis leaned back in his chair, breaking the seal from his box of Gurkha Black Dragons. Though he had long ago accepted such benefits as a normal part of the life of a VIGIL Director, he was still able to enjoy them. He clipped the end from one of the cigars and lit it, officially beginning his daily ritual. The smoke lingered just long enough in the air to take a second hit from his mouth.

Helmut, like the director before him, had been genetically selected to lead VIGIL. Occasionally, others were allowed to join the organization to bring in new wealth and energy, but the real power remained tied to the same bloodline; a bloodline with purple eyes.

It indicated the key gene that identified a member of the distinct VIGIL bloodline. Most people would never have known the eye color existed, except for one VIGIL board member's daughter who insisted on becoming an actress.

VIGIL had been formed in the first millennium A.D. by an Iberian monk who had looked to the skies, not for God, but for knowledge. This unnamed man was well-read in history and seeing all the war and disease that man had survived, knew that it would only be a matter of time before man became as extinct as the unicorn. He gathered political and religious figures to form a community to ensure mankind's survival for the next thousand years.

VIGIL began gathering wealth and power at the turn of the first millennium, hiding behind such public organizations as the Knights Templar and Freemasons in the Middle Ages. Its membership fostered thinkers like Botticelli, Raphael, Vasari, and Salieri, and with their increase in knowledge, VIGIL's mission was extended to ensure mankind's survival for the next million years.

It all boiled down to population control. The greater the population, the larger number would survive a cataclysm. VIGIL's mission until the mid-twentieth century was twofold: increase the population and keep them occupied by entertainment or by supplying artificial enemies through racial or class warfare. Prevent all wars that could wipe out civilization.

Then the day they had feared arrived on July 16, 1945.

That was the day mankind proved that it could destroy itself when the power of the atom was unleashed in a remote corner of New Mexico.

Lars Papadakis, director of VIGIL at the time, was said to have locked himself into his office upon hearing the news. When he called an emergency meeting of the VIGIL board two days later, he provided new and more powerful directives. He said that mankind didn't have a million years.

It might not even have a million minutes.

The full resources of VIGIL were allocated to bringing World War II to a close and then, for the first time, VIGIL began actively manipulating world governments. Their advocates infiltrated the governments of every major nation on Earth. But as they had done with all of their operations, they needed a boogieman to distract the people from what was really happening. Taking advantage of cultural biases, VIGIL allocated money and power to fringe groups all over the globe. From organizations dedicated to protecting wildlife and animals to abstract groups protesting humanity itself, VIGIL kept attention away from their manipulation of the political systems of nations all across the globe.

Lars realized that even silly arguments had to be addressed once they had been placed on the table of serious political debate. It would take time and money to defeat such arguments and VIGIL had an abundance of both.

International organizations, setup for contingencies such as this, were flooded with money. Ambassadors were replaced with VIGIL-friendly operatives. Radical organizations and religions were given serious precedence over well-established ones. For the first time in history, VIGIL played one of its four doomsday cards. It was time to occupy mankind.

Once the international community was firmly established as a serious political organization, it became easier to target and eliminate nationalistic goals that ran counter to VIGIL's worldwide mandate. And Lars' plan worked. Within a decade of World War II, nation after nation had fallen under VIGIL's financial onslaught and political machinery. Lars saw the ultimate dream of VIGIL at his grasp: a world government with VIGIL behind the curtain, controlling the world's leaders.

But one nation stubbornly defied him: The United States of America.

Despite being flooded with campaign donations, favorable media coverage and outright bribery, the people of America refused to believe the stories they were being fed. They clung to their guns and their religion, ignoring the loud voices trying to overwhelm them. They elected an actor who had his own ideas. And then they elected somebody who acted like a cowboy and he knew where he was going, too.

The foundation of America was built on the belief that every man had an opportunity to improve his lot in life. This foundation was taught to every child, in every school, and in every church. They were boldly featured in movies and literature.

Lars realized that he had been looking at a twenty-year plan and, for most of the world, that was long enough for the plan to take root. He had to look for longer-term solutions and plan into the next century. He had already begun grooming Helmut Belisis as his replacement. Helmut would see the fruit of his labor long after Lars' body was placed at rest in the Tomb of the Keepers.

Lars began to turn over day-to-day operations to Helmut while Lars turned his full attention to America. Through court appointees made in the forties and fifties, he struck the foundational structures of American schools and churches so hard that it would take decades to repair. He simultaneously followed with attacks on the core unit of American society, the family. It started out small as comedy bits questioning the structure of the family and then sparked into documentaries that highlighted perceived injustices in the family structure and enflamed as scientific study, quickly entrenching itself as a part of American cultural history.

VIGIL worked its way through the American government over the next three decades, attempting to choke out the spark that made it unique. But each time they ran into interference from a small organization that they would later identify as CURE.

Lars would die only days before a man who had never served in the military took the oath of office. Helmut's first act as director of VIGIL was to meet with the new President in a room supposedly reserved for the First Family. The meeting lasted fifteen minutes, only long enough for Helmut to spell out his expectations.

Helmut met with each succeeding President in the same room, immediately after their inauguration. Some meetings were successful, like his most recent visit, some less successful, like his stubborn predecessor. But Helmut Belisis had learned Lars' lesson and thought in terms of centuries and millennia, not decades. Any setbacks by one President could be easily overcome with the next.

Helmut leaned forward and picked up his FORtab. Even with the most advanced technology known to man, he was still somehow unable to access the computers of this organization called CURE which had foiled their plans for almost a half-century now. Helmut did not like things that he could not access. Without access, there was no control. But that would all change soon, he thought. Very soon.

CHAPTER NINETEEN

Two men carried Liz back into Sunny Joe's air-conditioned office. The cameras followed her in and Kylie allowed them to videotape her snoring. Kylie was surprised that Liz had actually been able to sweep for two whole minutes before collapsing. The small pile of dirt she had swept up had already blown back onto the road. As Liz was laid on a bench, she stopped snoring and unconsciously flashed her professional smile.

Oh brother, Kylie thought. *She's even campaigning in her sleep.*

Sunny Joe brought in an old pail and dumped water over her head.

"Oh, my God!" Liz sputtered, instantly awake. Her wool costume was now a sticky, clingy mess. "Why did you do that?"

"This is the Sinanju cleansing ceremony," Sunny Joe said. "It rids a person of evil spirits and stupidity…most of the time."

Noting the ever-present cameras, Liz forced a smile back on her face, but was clearly gritting her teeth.

"I gladly receive your cleansing as a part of acceptance into the Sinjonanan tribe and I thank…"

"This does not make you a member of the Sinanju tribe," Sunny Joe interrupted, standing over her with a look of disappointment. "For you have failed the first test of a Sinanju warrior."

"There are…more?" Liz asked, wide eyed.

"There are forty tests to become a Sinanju warrior."

"Forty? How many to make me a Sanjo princess?"

Sunny Joe's caretaker Mick ceremoniously marched into the room, holding a butterfly net in front of him like a flag. Sunny Joe raised an eyebrow. Mick just shrugged his shoulders and grinned. When Sunny Joe had asked him to bring something in, he had told Mick to be creative.

Mick ceremoniously held the butterfly net out in his hands and bowed. Sunny Joe moved his hands over the net, blessing it.

"Sheesa notta too-uh smarta Mick!" Sunny Joe intoned over the net in a fake Indian voice. "Stoooooo Pidwuh muuuun! Stoooo Pidwuh mun!"

Mick grunted to stop from laughing.

"What's that?" Liz asked as Sunny Joe handed the net to her.

"It is a...Sinanju spirit net," Sunny Joe said after a moment of thought. "Only a true member of our tribe can harness its power. You will have fifteen minutes to try and capture a Sinanju spirit."

"But how do I..."

"Fourteen minutes and fifty-five seconds," Sunny Joe said, looking at his watch.

Liz grabbed the butterfly net and raced out the door. The cameras scrambled after her, leaving Sunny Joe and Mick alone.

"Five bucks says she comes back and claims to have caught one," Sunny Joe said.

Mick put ten dollars on the counter.

"You're on," he said, shaking his head. "Ain't nobody that dumb."

Liz walked back into the heat, keeping to the shaded walkways. While that took her out of the direct sunlight, it also took her out of the slight breeze that had kept her cool. She sipped air while trying to figure out what to do, facing away from the cameras to hide her anger. What kind of idiot did they think she was? Everyone knew you had to have one of those dream catcher things to catch a spirit. She would trick them at their own game. Liz stopped walking and began looking around. The cameras zoomed in on the suddenly serious look on her face.

"It's her, my ancestor!" she squealed, pointing to an empty spot in the air.

The cameras began focusing on the area she was pointing toward, but saw nothing.

"She's come back to tell me something!" Liz shouted. "What is it, oh great-grandmother? I'm what? It can't be!"

"What did it say?" one of the cameramen asked.

"She says that I am full blooded Suntonjonian!"

Liz made a slow, swooping motion with the net and, spirit of her great-grandmother in tow, triumphantly returned to the storefront. As she approached the door, it opened suddenly, banging her in the head.

"Oops," Sunny Joe said, pulling the door back as Liz collapsed to the wooden plank sidewalk. "Did she catch one?"

Liz awoke ten minutes later, her butterfly net nowhere to be seen. The camera crew was packing up and Sunny Joe and Mick stood grinning by the counter.

"What happened? What's going on?" she asked, panicked at seeing the camera crew leaving. "What's the next test?"

"I don't think you would survive another," Sunny Joe said, shaking his head.

"Bull! You're just afraid that a woman can be a better Suntan Indian than you! Get those cameras back here! I'm not finished yet!"

The cameraman looked sheepishly at his producer, who reluctantly nodded. If nothing else, they would record the candidate's meltdown for later play.

"Okay, Sunjo, I played your game," she said. "It's time you recognize me as Sunjanian."

Sunny Joe's top lip curled in disgust.

"I will not declare you a member of the Sinanju, but you show spirit. I will honor you with a Sinanju name."

Liz waited until the cameras were rolling to take her place in front of Sunny Joe.

"That's better. Now get to it! I don't have all day."

"Slow-witted one, not of our tribe, you have failed every test given to you, but you show great spirit. Though I do not make you a member of the Sinanju tribe, I will grant you a name. Everywhere you go, members of the Sinanju tribe shall recognize you as such."

Liz smiled. Finally! Now the papers could work on her opponent's high school scandal.

Sunny Joe looked at Mick and held out his hands for something. Not knowing what to give him, Mick opened the refrigerator behind the counter and handed Sunny Joe an old fish. Sunny Joe slapped it over Liz's shoulders until her woolen smock smelled of dead fish.

"Hear ye, citizens of Sinanju, now and forever more! This woman shall be known as …"

Here it comes! Liz thought. *The end of my long nightmare. Freedom from this fake scandal. The Senate Seat that once belonged to the Lion of the Senate handed to me on a silver platter!*

"…'Crazy As a One-Eyed Mule.'"

Sunny Joe turned to leave and Liz came unglued. Her anger ignited to the point that she forgot the cameras were on. She tried to attack Sunny Joe from behind, but ended up sprawled on the floor, her damp brown skirt above her head.

"Well," Sunny Joe said as he exited the room. "Maybe not as smart as one, though."

Liz stood, suddenly remembering the cameras. She ignored Sunny Joe and smiled her professional smile before turning around.

"You heard him!" she yelled. "He named me. I'm in."

CHAPTER TWENTY

In Mexico City, Stone exited the terminal first. He knew without looking that Freya was behind him. Not from a sound she made; she was always too quiet, nor from a scent; she was pheromonally invisible.

It was because her name was Freya and she was told to follow him.

"Why won't you talk?" Freya asked. "We're on a mission. Shouldn't you be telling me how we're going to do this?"

Stone stopped and turned around.

"See, that's the problem. You have all of this training and no experience. I shouldn't have to tell you how we're going to do something. You should just know what to do."

"Here's what I'm going to do," Freya said, leaning toward Stone. "I'm going to slap you silly if you don't stop talking down to me. You said you're a professional, so you ought to start acting like one. Keep the personal attacks for when we're not on a job."

Stone grunted. She was right. Besides, she was already here and there was nothing he could do about it.

"Deal," Stone said. "Here's what we're going to do."

Stone spent eight minutes detailing the plan to Freya, who asked surprisingly informed questions.

"Stone, I can do this," Freya said, pulling the large sunglasses down to cover her eyes.

"I sure hope so," Stone said, following behind at a safe distance.

Juan "Beef" Torres sat outside the Mexico City airport, staring at the main entrance. He took a quick glance at the photos of the two people he was looking for: a guy and some chick. Beef took an extra-long look at the girl. She was pretty young, with the emphasis on pretty. Hiding the pictures under his seat, he pulled up in front of the taxi gate and waited.

It did not take long for the girl to appear. Beef stepped out of the taxi and looked around for the guy, but he was nowhere to be found. The other cab drivers got out of his way as he approached the girl.

Good thing for her that the boss told him not to touch her.

Freya walked out the door and instantly felt eyes crawling all over her body. One set of eyes though, was looking at her for a different reason. A large man with meaty paws lumbered out of his cab, walking her way. He was six feet tall, about eye level to Freya, but at least four times as heavy and ten times as hairy. His low cap and sunglasses made him look like a seventies cartoon character. He even had a toothpick in his mouth.

Freya walked directly to him, smiling.

"I surrender. Take me to your leader," she said.

Beef stared at her and then looked around. Was this a joke? He was supposed to intimidate her into the taxi, not the other way around.

"What?" he asked, momentarily confused.

"You're here to take me somewhere," Freya repeated, smiling. "I'm ready. My bags are over there."

Beef didn't know why, but he picked up her bags and carried them to the cab. The other cabbies, even the ones who feared him, were smiling.

"*¡Cállate!*" he yelled and the other cabbies gathered together to talk about the situation. He would take care of them later. Beef loaded both small suitcases into the trunk and sat in the driver's seat. He looked in the back seat.

Freya was already sitting there.

Stone rushed out the door, only to see Freya grinning at him as she drove off in a taxi. She should have delayed the cab driver so Stone could follow in another cab. And while a dozen cabbies stood near the airport entrance, they were too busy laughing about something. Frustrated and unable to speak much Spanish, Stone grabbed a deep breath.

Sinanju training or not, he hated running.

The oxygen flooded power to his thighs and he followed the cab. The traffic kept the taxi from going over thirty miles per hour. Though Stone could normally run faster than that, the smog was so thick that he would not be able to maintain the speed for long.

Air slowly seeping through his lips as he ran, he leapt across a busy intersection, ignoring the stares and pointing fingers. Mexico City was just too crowded. Keeping one eye on Freya's cab, Stone looked around. There had to be another ride.

"Sis, when I catch up..." he whispered, careful to keep his breath tightly inside.

Stone leapt silently inside the back of a passing truck bed and, sensing the driver's curiosity at the small bump, leaned closer to the front, out of sight.

Stone waited until he could no longer sense the driver's attention and then released his breath. Spots appeared around the edge of his eyes. He had been at peak too many times in the past week. Sunny Joe told him that his body was still processing poisons that had built up in the first two decades of his life. Once the time of the purification came and his body acclimated to its Sinanju bearings, he would be like Freya.

But with his smoking, that was still years away.

Until then, he had to manage peak cycles and when he stayed at peak too long, his body began to decay. Sinanju was too powerful for an impure body to process. Once, his fingers and toes had turned black as if they were frostbitten.

Sunny Joe saved them from being amputated by applying a poultice that smelled like goat cheese and waffles. Stone had to repeat novice breathing lessons for the next week to make sure his body was once again balanced.

CHAPTER TWENTY-ONE

Tomás' fingers flew across the keyboard. Over the past few months, he had wormed his way into his uncle's life and slowly began to loot each of his uncle's bank accounts under the pretense of improving security at the fortress. From there, it was a simple matter to bleed enough money to hire new guards. It only took two weeks to replace the entire staff, except the butler. He could not risk firing the man his uncle saw on a daily basis. Tomás was surprised that it only took five thousand dollars to pay off the butler. He had been with Manny for two decades, but from the way the butler shooed him out of the house, it was obvious he had not been a happy employee.

Manny never saw it coming.

After Manny left, Tomás took his money back and spent twenty dollars to bury the butler behind the water fountain he loved to sit at during break.

Tomás accessed each bank account, leaving a single dollar as he transferred the funds to a single new offshore account. He had almost forgotten how many separate accounts his uncle had accumulated over the years. Anytime he received a large sum of money, he opened a new account. Tomás found over a dozen accounts that his uncle had forgotten about. He had always lived the life of luxury, flaunting his cars and girls, leaving small trinkets as the only support to his large family. Tomás resisted the urge to have one of his men — and they were now his men — hunt Manny down and shoot him.

Tomás had bigger plans for his uncle.

He began typing on a search page when his screen darkened, only to be replaced with the face of Helmut.

"Good afternoon, Tomás. I see that your uncle failed to heed my warning."

"I was wondering when you were gonna show your face," Tomás said, leaning back in his chair, propping his feet in the direct line of the webcam.

"It doesn't matter to me who is on the other side of the camera, Tomás. Only that my instructions are followed without question."

"Hey man, you're not gonna push me around like my uncle! I'm not weak like he was."

"Correct," Helmut replied. "Your arrogance makes you far weaker."

"Eurotrash! You think you're better than us! You come down here, flash your money and your fancy technology and expect us to hop. Well, I ain't nobody's hopper!"

"This is purely a business relationship, Tomás. If we are to do business together, you will need to set aside your personal…"

"My uncle's first mistake was allowing a man to talk to him like that. You're done here, *puto!*" Tomás interrupted, powering off his monitor.

Instantly, the music on his stereo stopped. The steel doors to the office slammed shut. The window bars slid into place and the lights turned off. His monitor turned back on and the face of the smiling European returned.

"Your uncle was a wise man, Tomás," Helmut said, taking a moment to puff on his cigar. "But like you, he had to learn a lesson about power. I made Manuel a king. In my world, he was just a lieutenant, but he knew his place. Tomás, you are a barbarian, but you will do what I say or you will be replaced."

Tomás was about to unleash a string of curse words harsh enough to sting his ancestors when he heard a hissing sound. Gas.

Sealed inside the room, there was nowhere to go, nowhere to hide.

"Don't worry, it's not lethal," Helmut replied. "But you will soon wish that it was."

Tomás allowed an angry glare at the monitor while he held his breath. If it was not lethal, he was going to show this *puto* just who he was dealing with. Then the first wisps of gas began to brush across his face.

It crawled across the cellular membrane of his skin with the sensitivity of battery acid. Tomás' expression instantly betrayed his fear. As the gas became stronger, he instinctively covered his eyes, but the gas made him nauseous and as he opened his mouth to regurgitate chef's sliced beef tips, the gas invaded his throat. Scalding nerves all the way down, Tomás could barely hear himself surrender before passing out on the floor.

Helmut hit a switch and the gas nozzles shut off. The vapors receded. On the screen, he left a list of what Tomás was expected to do when he recovered and appended a note: "Never be rude to me again, you ignorant peon."

CHAPTER TWENTY-TWO

Kylie tried to straighten the rounded collars of Liz's Indian costume. The wool had gotten wet during the trip back to New England and was a wrinkled mess. It had taken nearly an hour for Kylie to dress Liz in a way that honored both her Indian and Jamaican heritage. Kylie carefully took over twenty minutes to apply the war paint to Liz's face.

"There, finished," Kylie said, smiling.

Liz sat straight up and looked around as if she had just woken up.

"Do I look like I'm on the warpath?" she asked.

Kylie looked at her and smiled even more broadly. "You look absolutely savage!"

Liz stood and looked at herself in the full-length mirror…

…and giggled like a schoolgirl.

"Here, let me take that," Kylie said, removing the peace pipe from Liz's hands. Liz poked out her bottom lip as Kylie stashed it behind the dressing room door.

"It's time to go," Kylie said. "The debate starts in a few minutes. You need to get onstage."

Liz looked at the clock, but she could not read it. Numbers were blocking the face. She laughed as she saw the number ten.

Who ever heard of ten o'clock?

She had originally declined the peace pipe, telling Kylie that smoking would hurt the ozone. But Kylie said it would put her in touch with her true animal self.

Liz reached for her head as the world expanded around her. She tried to hold her breath to slow down her carbon monoxide assault on the ozone, but that only made her laugh all the harder. Her stomach growled.

"I hope they have snacks afterwards," Liz grumbled.

Kylie looked around. The hotel staff had provided wine, cheese and small sandwiches, but Liz had drunk the entire bottle of *Grand Cru* and used the platter of cheese to finger-paint a peace sign on the wall. She hoped that Liz wasn't too drunk and high to reach the stage.

"I'll get you something to eat after the debate," Kylie promised.

"Debate?" Liz asked groggily. "Oh yeah, the debate thing with the guy."

The guy.

"It's time to go," Kylie said, leading Liz to the door.

Liz played with the door handle only for a few seconds before exiting the dressing room. Kylie led her to an area just behind the curtain.

"Wait right here until they call your name," Kylie said slowly.

Liz looked like she didn't understand. Kylie leaned in and spoke slowly. "Stay here until you hear your name," she repeated. "Then go to the podium," she said, pointing to her side of the stage.

Liz tried to find the spot Kylie pointed at on the floor, but gave up. All the wood looked alike. She cringed. That sounded like something a wood-racist would say.

"They won't let me stay here, but I'll be sitting in the front row with the staff," Kylie said, leaving Liz alone.

Then it became very quiet, Liz noticed. She looked up and…

…all the way across the stage

Behind the curtains on the other side…

There was the guy.

…the racist guy who wanted to take over the world.

He was standing behind the curtain on the other side.

Son of a bitch!

He didn't own that curtain!

Liz tried to ignore his friendly smile and polite nod.

But as she thought about his nod, it reminded her of a bobble head.

His head was bobbing.

Up and down and up and down and up and down.

Liz had a bobble head dog in her car.

It always agreed with her.

The man is agreeing with me.

Liz got angry and kicked the curtain. She was his fierce warrior Indian opponent!

Liz smiled back, waving at him and then flipped him the bird.

Hi, Mr. Evil!

Liz snickered at her joke.

Hey, it's cold in here, she thought and then scolded herself. *It's always cold here, stupid!*

Liz wiped the corners of her mouth, careful to stay away from her tribal war paint. She was ready to kick some white boy ass!

OOOH, look at the confused look on his face.

That's right, stupid man! You can't understand what you never understood! Did you drive your little truck tonight? You're gonna kill the ozone in that thing, you idiot!

Did he just give me a look? *Did he just give me a look?*

I have something to give you, Mr. Judgmental! Bet you never expected this!

Liz turned around and hiked her skirt, mooning him.

Assface! I bet it's like looking into a mirror, isn't it? She thought.

Liz laughed and laughed and laughed.

What's wrong with him?

Why is he puking?

You are one sick moon unit! she thought.

CHAPTER TWENTY-THREE

Kathy Courage took a deep breath. She had not wanted to be here, but corporate said that moderating this debate was her last chance at keeping a network position. The woman who once owned morning television took her entire network into a personal kamikaze-like ratings dive when she became anchor of the evening news. She grabbed a donut from a tray and took a big bite.

A local high school gymnasium had been redecorated in red, white and blue. Two serious-looking lecterns stood almost facing each other, and in front was Kathy's moderator desk. She shooed away the makeup artist who was trying to follow Kathy's instructions of "you better take twenty pounds off my looks or you're fired" because she saw a small streak of makeup that had rubbed off on her expensive suit jacket when she grabbed the donut.

"Fum un ceen me up!" she yelled in an explosion of powder donut.

A stagehand rushed over to Kathy with a handful of baby wipes, trying to remove the mixture of donut powder and makeup. It only caused the mixture to smear even more on the dark jacket. Kathy grabbed a wipe for her mouth and pushed the woman away.

"Where's my backup jacket?"

Another stagehand rushed the jacket to Kathy who quickly ditched the grimy jacket. That makeup artist would get the cleaning bill, Kathy swore. She pulled the jacket on, only to realize that she had indeed gained twenty pounds since she last wore it, but it was too late. She unbuttoned the jacket so she could breathe and hoped no one would notice.

The debate logo swirled around the screen of one of the monitors as the broadcast went live. Blasts of trumpets matched the tempo of the graphics as if war had just been declared. An animated elephant and donkey rushed toward each other and when they collided, burst into a million tiny red and blue smiley faces, revealing the I-can-be-serious look of Kathy Courage.

"Good evening. I'm Kathy Courage. Tonight, the fate of the seat once held by the Lion of the Senate will once again be determined. Will it return to its safe home or stay in the hands of their racist opposition? Let's welcome the candidates!"

A spotlight turned on at the right side of the stage and a middle-aged man dressed in a smart business suit walked to the podium. The man was smiling and waving to the crowd. A few audience members started to clap.

"May I remind our audience to remain silent until the end of the debate," Kathy Courage scolded and the applause died down. "Ladies, gentlemen and those of an undeclared gender, Scotty Black."

Trying to keep a look of irritation from his face, Scotty walked to his podium, waving at various people in the audience.

Then, all the lights in the auditorium went out as a slow drumroll started playing. The stage lit up with disco lights and laser beams. A fog cannon filled the stage with mist and Kathy Courage stood to her feet in applause. The producer turned on the echo effect for her voice and it sounded as if they were at a wrestling match.

"And now! The next Senator for not just her state, but all of America! Everyone please give a warm welcome to your candidate and mine, Liz Worn!"

Liz stepped out into the lights and explosions of confetti announced her arrival. A rock band track punched in the background. She looked around and smiled. It was like walking into the middle of a Pink Floyd song…

Kathy squinted. In the middle of the fog and staccato laser beams, it was hard to make out what Liz was wearing, but it looked like…

Liz walked out in her 1950's all-wool Indian costume. Dark makeup chevrons streaked across her cheeks and large red dots adorned the tips of her nose and her chin. With the addition of her new blonde Jamaican dreadlocks, she looked like a zombie version of Raggedy Ann.

Liz walked over to Scotty Black, who had his hand extended. She was trying her best not to giggle. Liz ignored his hand and, her chin jutting forth, walked back to her podium.

The producer said something to Kathy, but Liz's appearance had caused her to zone out.

"What did you say?" Kathy asked.

"She only wants to be referred to by her Indian name," the producer said. "Crazy As a One-Eyed Mule."

"Crazy Ass what? No way! We can't do that!" Kathy said in an angry whisper.

"No, it's just the opposite. We have to do it. It is illegal to censor a federal campaign. If she wanted to streak onstage while singing the theme song from the *Brady Bunch*, we couldn't stop her."

"I'm not conducting a debate calling someone Crazy Ass… Mule or whatever!"

"Too late, we already changed the crawl. You're back in three…two…"

Kathy forced a smile and then remembered where she was. She glanced down for a second and put on her serious face.

"Both candidates have agreed on the terms of the debate. Since we're in America, the

Democrat gets to speak first," Kathy said, victorious in her refusal to call Liz by her Native American name.

Liz looked sadly into the camera, a victim of the establishment. The black part of her Indian makeup was already starting to run under the heat of the studio lighting. Her mind had wandered among all of the lights, but it looked to those in the audience as if she were demonstrating her victimhood. The floor director snapped his fingers to make Liz turn back to the teleprompter.

"Good evening to the oppressed peoples of America," she said with her fake Jamaican accent, staring straight into the camera. "I am 'Crazy As a One-Eyed Mule.'"

As if to confirm, a crawl appeared directly beneath her in a formal font reading "CRAZY AS A ONE-EYED MULE."

"I come as a representative of the Sinon…Sanj…the St. Jonono tribe and the persecuted peoples of the Philippines."

"Don't you mean Jamaica?" Kathy asked, trying to help.

"That is what I said, white woman," Liz said, scowling at Kathy. She then returned her innocent gaze to the television cameras. "I seek your vote in the coming election to save this planet from one man. That man, right there," she said, pointing to Scotty Black.

"This man, like all white men, tried to fool all of us, even me and it is my job to set the record straight. During his junior year in high school, Scotty Black was charged and convicted of cheating on his chemistry lab report, as has been detailed by bloggers at *liberalsrule.com* and the *Hermitpost.* He was sentenced to four weeks of extra schooling. Hold up four fingers."

Liz grunted and smiled as she looked at her hand. She finally held up four fingers.

"I am sad to bring this to your attention," she said, tearing up. "For the warrior within me yearns…it desires, no…it demands a worthy opponent, not one who cheats on his chemistry lab report in his junior year in high school. That is all."

Liz stepped back and lowered her head. The streaking makeup freely dripped down on her costume like black tears.

"Mister Black!" Kathy yelled, judgment dripping from her microphone. "What do you have to say about Crazy Ass One Eye…"

"Excuse me?" Liz yelled, returning to the microphone. Any pretense at a Jamaican accent was long forgotten. "Did you just call me Crazy Ass?"

"Ms. Worn, I…"

"Don't call me by my slave name! Don't you *dare* call me by my slave name! You will address me by my rightfully-earned Santa Joe Anna Native American name!"

"Yes, Ms. Mule."

"That's better! That's better! Now, what's my first name?"

Kathy paused and looked hopelessly at the camera before looking back at Liz.

"Crazy Ass?"

Liz's eyes opened like saucers. She jumped off the platform and dove over the desk at Kathy. The two disappeared behind the debate table. Scotty Black came down in an attempt to break it up.

Unfortunately, security didn't see it that way.

Off-duty police officers, they had been extensively trained in hate crime legislation and merely saw two liberals — in fact, two liberal women — merely engaged in a heated discussion. But as Scotty Black descended toward the pair, it instantly alerted them to a plethora of potential hate crimes. Male-on-female, white-on-minority (multiple minorities in the case of Liz Worn) and worst: Conservative-on-Liberal.

Security tackled him from behind, mad glee in their eyes.

"Taze him!" one guard yelled at the top of his lungs. "I said, taze him, bro!"

The scene collapsed into chaos, as audience members began throwing water bottles and chairs.

The producer smiled.

The debate was a wreck, but she could already see Jerry Springer-sized dollar signs as she ordered the cameras to pull out and record the entire scene.

CHAPTER TWENTY-FOUR

Stone leapt silently from the passing truck and snuck behind the antique cannon mounted at the front of Manny's fortress. The car carrying Freya entered the compound, disappearing behind a large gate. Stone took inventory of the situation. Nineteenth-century fortress. Reinforced stone and brick. Four guards at the entrance, with dozens more inside.

All dressed like ninjas.

Blast it, Sis! Stone thought. *This wasn't part of the plan.*

It was almost dusk. The sun would not set for another hour, but he didn't have time to wait. Stone would have to try to meld into the landscape and sneak past the guards. Grabbing a deep breath, Stone centered himself once more and moved toward the fortress.

Freya was carefully studying the entryway. A relatively modern system, electronics had been crudely strewn across the base rock that formed the foundation of the fortress walls. Freya could feel the cameras as they captured her and, with a little effort, she managed to filter them out. With proper training, the body's natural electric field was able to interfere with electronic signals, including video signals. So, once she felt the cameras' invisible touch, Freya simply adjusted her field. If they saw anything, it would be a blur at best.

The taxi stopped in front of a blocked moat entrance and waited for an escort. The entrance had been boarded over sometime in the last twenty years. It looked like the only thing holding up the side posts were multiple layers of brown paint. Why anyone would paint wood brown was beyond Freya's comprehension.

An armed group of soldiers opened the door and motioned for her to follow them. Two more armed soldiers followed behind, their pistols out of the holster but at their sides. Though the dialect was different, she could understand what they were saying from her time in Spain.

"He gonna kill her?" the tall one asked.

"I don't know. Shut up, Felipe," the other said.

"She's hot," Felipe said, looking back at her sternly as if he were just trying to make sure she wasn't attempting to escape. "I want her so bad!"

"Shut up, Felipe!" the other said. "Tomás wants her alive."

"You ask him for a raise yet?" Felipe said. "I hate this costume! It's too hot. I can barely see through the little slit in the mask! How am I supposed to kill someone if I can't see them?"

"You better just worry about getting that package through. Tomás isn't as nice as

Manny."

"My kids make fun of me and call me 'Ninja Turtle,'" Felipe said. "I don't like it."

Freya saw the door they were approaching at the end of the long hall. As they walked down the hall, she felt a system similar to the cameras she had sensed earlier. But while she had easily managed to block the electronics from the field cameras, whatever this was simply passed through her. She didn't feel any different and the guards weren't showing any abnormal effects, so she continued down the hall with them. But as she approached the steel reinforced lead door, she could tell that there was a large electronic device or devices behind it. The small hairs on her arm began to rise the closer she got.

The guard at the door listened to something on his earpiece before looking at Freya. He opened the door and Freya entered by herself.

"Have a seat," Tomás said in English.

"You left your guards outside," Freya said.

"I don't need them against an unarmed girl," Tomás said boldly. "That hallway you walked through is full of sensors. I was able to count the number of bobby pins in your hair."

"I don't have any bobby pins," Freya said.

"Exactly!" Tomás bragged and then frowned. "The point is that I could have counted them if you had any."

Freya just stared at him. "Brilliant," she said. "What do you want?"

Tomás walked behind her and allowed himself a glance below her waist.

"I want to know what a teenage American girl is doing in the company of a known American spy," Tomás said, reading from the questions Helmut left with him.

"I'm his partner," Freya answered honestly.

"Like a secretary?" Tomás asked, puzzled. Perhaps he had not understood the word the way she meant it. English was tricky like that.

"No, we are equal partners," Freya said. "We are trained to kill."

Tomás began laughing. "Little girl, you are in my castle. I am the only killer here."

"Then you know what they're trying to smuggle through the border," Freya said.

"Of course, I do! The king knows everything that happens in his castle, but..." he said, glancing back at the paper of questions, "I would like to know your name."

"My what?"

"Your name. Is it Valerie or Jaime or maybe April? I have always liked the name April."

"That's none of your business. Where is the box you are supposed to deliver?" Freya looked around the room but saw no sign of any package or box. *Had it already been shipped?*

Tomás looked down. He would find her name later. "What is your partner's name?"

"You haven't been doing this very long, have you? You're barely older than I am."

Tomás dropped the page in anger. He didn't need any of the Eurotrash's silly questions. He would beat the answers out of this American girl. But before he could raise his hand, the fortress alarm rang. Tomás walked back to his laptop and motioned at Freya.

"Stay put!" he ordered, pointing to a spot on the Persian rug. He opened his laptop as eight guards rushed into the room, bolting the massive door shut behind them.

"Secure her," Tomás ordered, pointing to Freya. "It's an intruder. Ah, it's your 'partner.'"

The guards moved toward Freya. One of the men reached for her arm and then found himself reaching for the Pearly Gates. The other guards stared, transfixed at the scene. Felipe had simply reached for the girl's arm and then fell over like a robot with its switch turned off.

Had he suffered a heart attack?

While they were confused, Freya moved into their midst. Before they could react, she slid her fingernails beneath their collarbones, disabling the part of their central nervous system that controlled breathing. The men fell to the floor, gasping for air as they tried to manually keep their lungs inflated. They dropped their weapons, flopping on the floor like a basket of fish spilled onto a table at a farmer's market.

"What did you do?" Tomás demanded. He pulled out his pistol and aimed it at her.

But Freya had already crossed the room and slapped the gun out of his hand. His arm instantly became numb below the elbow. Freya held him at arm's length while looking at his laptop. The screen was setup to see all four cameras at once. In the first three, men dressed as ninjas, armed with high-powered rifles standing at the top of the circular courtyard in the middle.

In the fourth, she saw Stone, about to enter the courtyard.

"Stay put," Freya said, slapping Tomás hard enough to crack several teeth. When he regained his senses, he scrambled for his gun and looked around. He had not heard the massive door open or close. But the devil girl was gone.

CHAPTER TWENTY-FIVE

Stone walked cautiously along the shaded part of the entryway, careful not to make a sound. He brought out his pistol and it became a silent extension of his hand. Sinanju frowned on the use of weapons, but Stone trusted them more than his own hands. With his enhanced Sinanju senses, he was a deadlier shot than he had ever been with SEAL Team Six.

Centering his breathing, Stone glimpsed the small part of Sinanju that he had access to: a world of vibration and motion, senses and nerves.

As he walked toward the center courtyard, he noticed something odd. It was not something that had triggered his senses, but the exact opposite. Unless there were no more guards, he should have felt the pressure from their attention, but he felt nothing.

Something was wrong.

Twelve men lined the roof over the exposed courtyard. Following Helmut's specific orders, Tomás had told the men to remain looking up at the sky, thinking random thoughts. When the command was given, they were to aim their rifles at a specific door and immediately open fire. The orders confused the men, but being soldiers, they obeyed.

The thick dark robes of the Mexican Ninja Army burned hot in the early fall sun and a few of the men had to wipe their brows to keep the sweat from streaming into their eyes.

One ninja glanced at the ninja to his right. The man had been looking at the sky and as the first ninja blinked, the man disappeared. It was as if he were sitting there one instant and after he blinked, he was gone. He turned around to look at another ninja. Again, when he blinked, the man disappeared.

And then another.

And another.

When only he and another ninja remained, he saw a plume of long, golden hair.

Freya was thrown off-balance as a large section of her hair came loose from the stretch band she used to keep her hair in place. The small amount of unaccounted for personal weight was just enough to shift her center, reducing the power of her attack, leaving her intended target with the rifle still in his hand.

The man turned, swinging the butt of his rifle at Freya's head, but she grabbed her hair with one hand while ducking the wooden stock. She recovered and struck the man's throat with enough force to dislocate his head from his shoulders. Attached only by skin and arteries, his head lolled to one side and he collapsed lifelessly to the rooftop.

Sloppy! she cursed herself.

If Sunny Joe had seen that stroke, he would have been embarrassed. She needed to find a way to keep her hair more secure in the future, or else she would end up dead.

The bullets suddenly heading her way peppered the air with individual pressure waves, reaching her skin a millisecond before the bullets did. Freya twisted away from each round, slapping away the ones too close to dodge, returning them to their point of origin.

The ninja's body wiggled in pain as his own bullets found their mark in his abdomen. The man fell backwards, into the courtyard four stories below.

Glancing around to make sure that all of the roof ninjas were vanquished, Freya leapt into the courtyard below.

* * * *

Stone approached the courtyard, mindful of the doors surrounding him, when he heard gunfire from the roof. He glanced up just in time to avoid the body falling towards him. Then he detected motion to his left. Bringing up his pistol, he placed a bead on the target, only for the target to disappear.

Freya came from behind and Stone lowered his pistol.

"I'm not even gonna ask," Stone said, looking at the dead man in the ninja suit. He tapped his earpiece and was instantly connected to Ben.

"What's going on?" Ben asked. "You should have already left."

"The guy upstairs knows about the package," Freya said. "We're just about to have a talk with him."

"We got this, boss," Stone said, but heard nothing but static.

"What happened?" Freya asked.

"Dunno. Sounds like our connection was cut."

A small buzz entered his fingernails as Stone centered himself again. He made a quick promise to stop smoking and ran toward the doorway.

As they approached the staircase, both felt the telltale pressure waves of incoming bullets. There were so many that Stone almost lost his bearing. They hid behind a small wall at the bottom of the staircase.

"Yeah, even you can't dodge that many bullets," Stone said. "Here's your chance to shine. You got a plan, sis?"

"Let them come to us," she said.

Freya moved to the center of the wall. She felt the vibrations of an electric generator behind the stucco. She tore through the plaster, pulling the six-hundred-pound unit from the wall, revealing the electrical grid for the entire fortress.

Instantly, the lights went out and several ninjas could be heard screaming above. They had been leaning on the metal rail that lined the old staircase and their bodies had made a perfect conduit.

As their weapons clattered to the ground, Stone grabbed a quick peek and returned behind the wall. A barrage of bullets struck the wall just as he pulled his head back in.

"At least forty guys still up there. This isn't gonna be easy."

"I have an idea," Freya said. She yanked on the cable, dragging the generator all the way through. She pushed it toward the staircase.

"What are you doing?"

"Providing cover," she said.

They both heard the sound at the same time, but only Stone knew what it was. The stairwell's foundation creaked menacingly and Stone realized in horror that it supported the entire fortress wing. He threw his body toward Freya as the foundation above them ruptured, knocking her to the floor behind the generator. Tons of stone and brick collapsed, filling the chamber with debris. Stone shook his head to regain his senses. Freya lay quietly in the dust as the ninjas started down the stairs.

CHAPTER TWENTY-SIX

Ben's fingers raced across his FORtab, trying to re-establish a connection with Stone and Freya. Twice he almost had the system bypassed, but then it reinstated a new firewall to stop him. The edges of the screen slowly blinked as a dull buzz emitted from the computer. He was receiving a call.

Not now, Ben thought and then sighed.

Maybe his mysterious boss would have a suggestion for this situation? Ben answered the call and a man appeared on his screen. Unlike Smith's usual hidden shadowy image, this man sat boldly in front of a camera. He wore an immaculate business suit, and behind him was a well-stocked library shelf. He was barely older than Ben, perhaps in his fifties, with finely coiffed gray hair and a trimmed beard that stubbornly retained a few brown hairs. Ben quickly tapped the 'record' function of his FORtab for later investigation and sat it on his desk. He blindly reached for his coffee. Something was wrong. Why would Smith establish secrecy so totally, only to abandon it now?

"Good afternoon, Ben," the man said with a slight nod. It was not Smith's usual sour-sounding voice.

"Why are you showing your face now?" Ben asked, taking a drink from his coffee.

"I am not the man you have been speaking with. My name is Helmut. You need know nothing else."

Ben swished the coffee around his mouth for a second before swallowing it.

"Well, 'Helmut', I'll tell you what I already know. Your name and mannerisms are German — East German to be exact — but your accent is Greek. You speak slowly and methodically, so you're probably well-educated, and the way you're talking to me suggests that you are or were in charge of something you consider important. But while you know who I am and most likely what I do, you're arrogant, or at the least feel that I pose no threat."

"Impressive, but I already knew that about you. Right now, you are attempting to save your agents and are being frustrated by the FORtab which I possess," Helmut said, seeking a reaction from Ben. Finding none, he continued. "Yes, Smith told you there were only two prototypes of this amazing computer, but obviously he is incorrect. I have the third and unless I authorize it, the security protecting the fortress will not be released, and both of your agents will die."

"Cut to the chase," Ben said. "You believe this is a bargaining chip, so what do you want?"

"I am going to have to update my file on you," Helmut said, in a voice that almost sounded respectful. "You are correct. I need something. A name. Just the female's."

"This is the part where I ask how I know you will keep your word."

"And this is the part where I tell you that you cannot. But the math is simple. I can just print her after her death or you can give me her name now."

"First, mind telling me why you're interested?" Ben said.

"Actually, I don't mind at all. She's young and female. This is not a usual profile for spies; I would like to know more about her to find out if some new agency has arrived on the playing field."

"Fair enough," Ben said without hesitation. "Her name is Freya. I don't know if she even has a last name."

Helmut looked down at his FORtab. Ben was telling the truth.

"That is very intriguing. You must have been placed in quite an interesting situation to accept an agent you hardly know. Perhaps one day you will share the story with me?"

"Perhaps you better shut down those defenses," Ben said.

Helmut looked down, seemingly occupied by something on the screen.

"You take caramel in your coffee?" Helmut asked. "How juvenile."

Ben continued to stare forward, but he knew that Helmut had been delaying him so the FORtab could scan as much information as it could. Helmut was letting Ben know that it even scanned what kind of coffee he was drinking.

Damn, Ben thought. He was going to have to learn more about the FORtab's capabilities.

"I am sorry Ben, but there many ways to bypass our deal without violating the actual wording or even spirit of the deal. The bottom line is that I choose not to disable the security at this time. Thank you for providing me with a name. It will assist me when I search her fingerprints. I do not like being kept in the dark. One last thing," Helmut said. "Our assessment did not indicate that you would develop this level of attachment to your agents, at least, not this early. Perhaps you will learn a lesson with your next agents."

"You traded the only commodity we could possibly share — trust — for a simple name? I've learned something else about you. You don't think too far ahead, because we will definitely meet again," Ben said, closing the connection.

He slammed the palm of his hand on his desk in frustration. He would keep trying to bypass the fortress' security, but his analytical mind kept coming back with the same conclusion: Stone and Freya were on their own.

Ben bit his bottom lip and said a quick prayer.

CHAPTER TWENTY-SEVEN

Stone looked around. The generator Freya had pulled from the wall was large enough to provide temporary cover, but he was out of ammunition, leaving them open to attacks from both sides. Freya was dazed, but at least she was conscious enough to lean against the wall.

Her eyes were open but didn't seem to be focused on anything.

"Sis, you've got to snap out of it," Stone said, gently shaking her. "And I mean right now."

The men above were at the bottom of the stairs, almost in Stone's direct sight. They began firing again and the bullets ricocheted all around them. One of the bullets struck the generator, triggering an electrical spike to the floor.

Unable to dodge, unable to move, unable to escape the biting electricity, Stone could do nothing but stand as the fillings in his back teeth grounded to each other. The short discharge ended in seconds as the machine exploded into sparks. Stone was able to relax his muscles, but Freya collapsed.

She was not breathing.

Then, the air itself began to shudder, with pressure waves seeming to come from every direction at once. Stone tried to block it, but his Sinanju training was partially based on sensing pressure waves. Every nerve in his body seemed to tremble as the sensation increased. Whatever was happening was creating sound waves far below the normal range of human hearing, but to Stone's Sinanju-trained ears, it was a low rumble that was vibrating his internal organs, keeping him off center.

Infrasound.

While in the SEALs, he had heard about it being used to disperse crowds, but until this moment, he had not personally experienced it. Whatever was producing it, there was no protection from its piercing sound waves. And beyond the wave of deadly sound, he sensed the rest of the Mexican Ninja Army as they descended down the stairs.

CHAPTER TWENTY-EIGHT

Ignoring the aural attack and the incoming army, Stone leaned Freya against the generator and was about to administer CPR when he found himself sprawled back against the wall, dazed. Whatever had hit him had shredded his bulletproof vest.

He glanced back toward Freya and sighed in relief. She was standing again.

But as he looked closer, he could tell that something was wrong. Freya's eyes were dark. Alien. She looked around as if she did not know where she was. And she was still not breathing.

One of the Mexican Ninjas rounded the corner and Freya instantly separated the man's head from his body. The movement was so smooth and so fast that the man's momentum was enough to keep his body running for a few steps before realizing it had no head.

Then it collapsed to the floor.

Others came around the corner and Freya turned toward them. That was when Stone realized that the infrasound was originating from Freya. The soldiers did not stand a chance. They were so close to the infrasound and so afraid, that they forgot they held guns in their hands.

Freya opened her mouth and tilted her head back, and though her lips did not move, her voice roared and froze the men in their tracks.

"I am created Shiva, the Destroyer! Death, the shatterer of worlds! The night tiger made whole by the Master of Sinanju! Who is this dog meat that dares challenge me?"

She tore into the men, reducing them to a whirlwind of bones and gore. Stone had to hide behind the generator to shield himself from bone shrapnel. Freya advanced past the guard, moving up the stairs toward Tomás' top floor office. The floor seemed to spin beneath Stone's feet as his sister slowly advanced toward the remaining ninjas. Just before she disappeared up the stairwell, she turned to look Stone in the eye and smiled.

Stone followed quickly behind.

CHAPTER TWENTY-NINE

Tomás cursed his laptop. He had not asked the Eurotrash how to contact him and now, with his empire crashing around him, Helmut was nowhere to be found. The scene below was sheer carnage as his ninja army fell before the two American agents. Tomás grabbed his Uzi and loaded the magazine. He was not going to go down without a fight.

Tomás was not regretting his decision to take over, but in hindsight, maybe he should have waited. No matter. He had two problems and thirty bullets. The math was on his side.

Tomás took a shooting stance behind the steel-lined desk. If the agents somehow found a way to get through the door, he would have a direct line of fire to them while they would only have access to the top of his head.

Then he heard the footfalls.

Like a giant coming down the marbled floor hallway, each step was a slow declaration of power. Tomás glanced at his laptop. The hallway monitors merely showed a barely-visible blob moving toward his door. It was as if the marbled floor itself was warping in the direction of his office. In fact, he could have sworn he heard the marble crack with each step. He switched off the safety and wiped the sweat that had gathered on his brow and waited.

He did not have long to wait.

The steel-reinforced lead door caved in a single, thunderous blow, surrendering its massive weight to the floor before Tomás. Without thinking, he squeezed the trigger as the girl, who now had black eyes, walked toward him. And although he aimed the pistol directly at her, the bullets never hit their target.

Had he been able to see the bullets in slow motion, he would have seen each bullet slowly turning through the air, directly toward Freya. Then he would have seen their trajectory change, as if each bullet bent out of the way so as not to offend her. The bullets went left and right, up and down, everywhere but at Freya.

Tomás advanced at the small girl. He would just have to pistol whip her to death.

Stone entered the room as Tomás advanced toward Freya. Instinctively, he aimed his empty pistol at Stone and pulled the trigger. "Madre!" Tomás shouted.

"Sis!" Stone yelled, trying to get her attention. Freya did not turn around.

Stone had to find some way to get her breathing again. Her fingers were already turning black. Stone tried to kick her in the abdomen to force her to breathe in, but his foot somehow missed. Without a target, the force of the kick almost tore his leg out of its socket.

Stone howled in pain.

Freya grabbed Tomás.

"The box," she said.

"Too late. It has been shipped."

Freya snarled at Tomás and in one ragged motion, tore his body in two. She dropped the pieces and began roaring at them, releasing the last bit of air stored in her lungs.

Then she wobbled for a moment and fell to the floor.

Clutching his hip, Stone limped toward Freya, mindful of the groaning sound of the building around them. Though the infrasound had stopped when Freya collapsed, it had already damaged the foundation. There was not much time left.

As he leaned over, he heard a thin wisp of air as it entered Freya's lungs. She was breathing on her own again, but it was very shallow. Her fingers were still black, so Stone grabbed a deep breath and centered himself. The air flooded his body, but he felt like he was hyperventilating.

He had been at peak for too long.

But he would not fail. Freya was hurt and she needed him…she needed her big brother. That's what he was — the big brother — and anyone trying to get her would have to go through him.

Stone threw Freya over his shoulder and began descending the stairs three at a time. They exited the building directly into the middle of a dozen ninjas. The men had been injured, but survived Freya's initial assault. When they saw Stone, they reached for their weapons, only to remember that their fear upon seeing Freya slice through their fellow ninjas had caused them to drop their weapons inside.

As one, they attacked.

Stone had no choice but to drop Freya to the ground so he could confront the men. Spots began to enter his peripheral vision as he moved into their midst. The first two men surrendered their diaphragms as Stone's fist punched through their spines, but the third man managed to connect with a right cross. Stone reeled back from the punch, but was able to twist his body enough to sweep kick the man to the ground.

A heel to the throat later and there were only nine men left.

Two of them turned toward Freya. Stone ran over to them and dislocated their necks from behind, but the attack left him open to the others. They began pounding and kicking him until his air was gone and he dropped, dazed, to his knees.

He was not going to make it.

The ninjas were screaming in Spanish as they tackled him to the ground, pummeling him. Stone tried his best to block their attacks, but his thoughts were becoming murkier with each blow.

And then the fists didn't matter and the pain didn't matter because Stone Smith lay helplessly on the ground.

CHAPTER THIRTY

Freya Williams' mind was awash with near-forgotten images of what had just happened. She remembered some of it, but it was more like seeing someone else's memories. As she began to take stock of where she was, she heard the sounds of the beating before she opened her eyes. As she looked at the origin of the sound, her eyes opened wide.

Seven men were beating and kicking Stone. Freya could not tell what shape he was in, but he was not defending against their attacks and their kicks were so hard that they shook his body.

One of the ninjas jumped on top of him, pulling out a long ceremonial blade of some kind. But before he could strike, he looked up to the sky, screaming in pain. He dropped the knife and collapsed on Stone.

The others began screaming.

"*Ella ha vuelto!*" one of the men yelled. "*Huye!*"

Freya sliced into the men like a dervish, fury burned into her face. The next man froze in his tracks as she reached him. Still woozy from her experience, she pulled away, smashing his face into putty. She lifted the next man off his feet so quickly that she tore the collarbone from his chest. The rest of the ninjas, remembering what she had done to the men inside, ran.

Freya rolled the dead man off Stone's chest and sat him up, inspecting him.

Stone blinked once, then twice. He tried to laugh to assure Freya that he was okay, but was only able to produce a painful cough. His entire body ached, but he was alive.

Thanks to Freya.

"What happened back there?" he asked as Freya helped him stand. Her eyes had returned to normal, but her fingers were still a deathly black.

Freya only looked at her brother with tears in her eyes and hugged him tightly.

"Let's go home," she said. "We're done here."

Answers would come later.

CHAPTER THIRTY-ONE

The next morning, Ben stared at his FORtab. As he read back over the report Stone filed, he could tell several things were missing. Most of the report was immaculate, but it was far too brief in its description of what happened to the Mexican Ninja Army and how Tomás was killed. It said that the box that was to be shipped into the United States was already gone when Stone and Freya had arrived.

No mention was made of Freya's actions in the mission. That should have been mandatory. Stone was not incompetent but simple competence was not enough. In an operation like this one, trust was everything. It took time to earn an agent's trust, but first Stone had to trust Ben with all available information, or else Ben could give orders that would result in their deaths.

The FORtab screen lit on the edges, indicating an incoming call. Ben noticed that the FORtab had categorized the call and it wasn't the familiar red hue indicating a call from the mysterious Smith.

Helmut was calling.

Ben tapped the screen a few times and then answered. Helmut leaned forward with a smile.

"Thank you for taking my call," Helmut said.

"Knowledge is power," Ben said. "And each call empowers me a little more."

"Then this conversation will make you a very powerful man. Let me inform you of a secret American organization called CURE."

"Sure, I'm all ears, but what's that got to do with me?"

"It's who you work for."

"And of course, you expect me to believe that you know my boss?"

"Not personally. I was but a young man when my predecessor chose Harold W. Smith for the job. He is officially listed as the Director of Operations at Folcroft Sanitarium in Rye, New York, but that is merely cover for his real job as director of CURE."

"So why is he hiding his face if everyone but me seems to know him?"

"Don't be a fool. There are fewer people who are aware of CURE's existence than VIGIL's."

"You're dropping a lot of names for someone who likes to keep secrets," Ben said.

"Think of it as my way of thanking you for your assistance. Your agents caused such widespread destruction that the Mexican nationals were spending all of their attention on the cartel attack, allowing my agents time to quietly and safely escort my package across the border. It is now in safe hands."

"I figured as much," Ben said. "Whatever it is, it's still in play, so it can be stopped."

"That's what I like about you. Smith has no imagination, but you, Benjamin Cole, you are an inquisitive man. You grew up reading comic books, making almost weekly trips to the theater. Smith's persona is based on the thin notion of patriotism. Yours is fed by living out your childhood adventures. Though you would deny it, this is just a game to you. Our very conversation has already been reduced to one of 'good guy versus bad guy' in your mind."

"So why are you telling me this?"

"Because I want you to know that I personally chose you. I made sure that your name was put before Smith. Your very existence in this program is thanks to VIGIL, and whether you want to admit it or not, your agency's mandate is a result of VIGIL's worldwide goal."

"And that goal is?"

"A peaceful world," Helmut said.

Ben laughed. "Run by you, of course."

"Naturally."

"Good luck with that. So now what?"

"You have a very important decision to make, Benjamin Cole. You know the secret of VIGIL's existence, which even the director of CURE is unaware of, but what will you do with it? If you inform Smith, he will no doubt declare CURE impossibly compromised and disband it, resulting in both of your deaths. Or will you attempt to take your rightful place as director of CURE?"

Ben glanced down at his FORtab as the program running in the background signaled completion.

"Neither. See, I'm a pretty clever guy and I've learned a thing or two about my FORtab since our last conversation. For instance, I discovered how you accessed my tab to obtain images of my agents. And that allowed me to connect to your FORtab during this conversation. Those images, along with all information dealing with CURE, have been deleted from your unit."

For the first time, Ben saw a crack in Helmut's confidence. Turning his attention from Ben, Helmut began searching his FORtab. The only files he found were compressed videos of old Three Stooges movies. He switched to the directory where he kept his secured VIGIL files.

It was empty.

"You know what was really cool?" Ben said. "Some of the files were locked, so I had to delete them, but I was still able to copy eight thousand files. And don't bother trying to access either my FORtab or my boss's. You'll find that I set up a firewall. This will be the last time we talk, until I put a bullet between your eyes. Have a good day."

Ben closed the connection.

The small satisfaction that he felt from electronically sucker punching Helmut had already disappeared as he digested the information he had been given. Ben had worked in psychological operations long enough to know data manipulation when he heard it, but he also knew that the best manipulation always contained a large kernel of truth.

The question was, how much was truth?

It was late. Ben pulled the bottle of vodka out of his drawer and headed to his room. Though he was on call 24/7, he was calling it a night. He would file his report in the morning.

No one owned his soul.

CHAPTER THIRTY-TWO

Inside a stone chamber deep under the ruins of an old French castle, the twelve Watchers who made up the inner council of VIGIL took their place at the round marble-topped table. Originally designed during World War II to house various government heads in case of aerial attack, the thick-walled complex of offices and sleeping quarters had gradually been forgotten over the decades. It was one of three nuclear bunkers acquired by VIGIL.

The organization's inner council consisted of thirteen members: one male Watcher and one female Watcher from each of the populated continents. Each wore a tunic representing the continent of their birth. The thirteenth member was the director. The men and women who served as Director varied in race and age, but they all had purple eyes.

Helmut sat at the director's chair at the head of the table and after each Watcher was in place, called the meeting to order.

"The Senior Watcher from Europe has called this meeting," Helmut said, nodding to a middle-aged man with a dark tunic and a tempered glare on his face. "Europe Senior, you may proceed."

The man stood to his feet and locked eyes with his peers before returning his gaze to Helmut.

"Director, VIGIL has been compromised and the council is extremely displeased by your failure. Exactly how much does this Benjamin Cole know?"

Helmut stood to address Europe Senior. "It is likely he only has access to a few of our short-term operations."

"You said that he claimed to have access to eight thousand files."

"That is correct."

"Did the FORtab indicate that he was lying?"

"No, but it did detect some kind of deception on his part. It could be possible he has eight thousand icons with no data attached."

"Or it is possible that he has our home addresses and phone numbers," Europe Senior said. "We cannot underestimate an intelligence failure at this level."

"Security has been increased at each of your stations," Helmut said, annoyed that a council member would show personal concern above that of the organization. A show of weakness like that would normally have been fodder for the other council members, but

Europe Senior's words carried a ring of finality to them.

"America is just too powerful," the Junior Watcher from Asia said. She was known by Helmut to be a close ally of the European Watchers.

Helmut paused before he spoke again.

"Before going any further, perhaps we should all remember that the mission we set out to accomplish has been a success. It was our plan to ship into the United States the antidotes to all the viruses now being developed by the destructive savages in the lunatic nations of the world. If such viruses are ever unleashed, only America will have the capacity to create cures and preventatives for them. This was our goal and we have accomplished it. The anti-viral programs are now safe."

He looked around the room to see if the council had understood that they had accomplished a great deed for humanity, but the Watchers were not listening to him.

Of all Watchers present, the most senior was the short woman from Africa. She rarely spoke at meetings, but she now called for Helmut's attention.

"This is the largest intelligence failure in VIGIL's history," Africa Senior said. "After centuries of working to create a sane and stable world, you say we have succeeded, but because information concerning VIGIL has gotten into the hands of those who will not support our efforts, we may be faced with destruction. And so I ask, is it time that we consider launching the Carnage program? Is it time to strike first against those who would destroy us?"

Helmut paused as he considered the card just played. The woman had been trying to put the Carnage program into play for the past two years. She was nearing the end of her life cycle and was unwilling to have her successor enjoy the fruits of her labor.

Carnage was the most dangerous program that VIGIL had ever launched. It was an armageddon effort, designed to destroy any standing army. It had been limited to a test field of one hundred candidates. Because of the strenuous nature of the program, only twelve had survived. Of those twelve, it was projected that only four would ever maintain enough sanity to be of any real use. In the next phase of the program, they would serve as models for VIGIL's first army, an insurmountable cadre of faceless, fearless, deathless killers. Even with access to advanced biological technology, it was still decades away, but with the sensitivity of the current situation, Africa Senior's appeal held stronger ground than it normally would have.

"This is not the time for panic," Helmut said, trying to reassure the council. "The Carnage Program was not designed to be triggered by anything less than a doomsday card.

And despite this temporary setback, we are not there."

"But we may be soon. This is the perfect opportunity to move the program further ahead," Africa Senior said.

The other council members murmured amongst themselves.

"The Carnage Program is not designed for such a measure," Helmut cautioned. "If Carnage appears too soon, it will open itself up for counter-measures...and we will lose."

"I call for a vote," Africa Senior said, ignoring Helmut.

Helmut nodded and stepped outside the chamber into the formal greeting room. Council votes were reserved for members of the council. As director of VIGIL, he had final say on anything other than a unanimous decision. There had been very few unanimous decisions in VIGIL's history.

He poured a cup of chamomile tea while he waited.

The door buzzed open twenty minutes later and Helmut resumed his seat at the head of the council table.

Africa Senior turned to Helmut.

"Director, VIGIL has come to a unanimous decision. A limited Carnage test has been authorized."

"Its target?" Helmut asked.

"Benjamin Cole and his Sinanju agents."

"I wish the record to note my strongest disapproval," Helmut said. "If you are correct and Cole possesses information concerning VIGIL's whereabouts, we will not withstand a direct assault."

"All the more reason to initiate a first strike," Africa Senior said. "You have ninety days to prepare for the demonstration. And, Director, this council will not tolerate subversion of its decision."

Helmut said nothing as the meeting concluded.

He would do as they directed, but he would ensure that the council would come to regret its decision.

CHAPTER THIRTY-THREE

"You did not intercept the box?" the lemony voice on the phone asked.

"No. It was gone before we arrived," Ben said.

There was a pause on the other end of the line. Ben could almost hear disappointment.

"This is your entire report? Were there any abnormalities that I should be aware of?"

Ben recognized the tone. It was the same one he had when thinking about Stone's lean report. Ben had realized that something was missing and was frustrated that he had not earned Stone's full trust. And now he was doing the same thing to his boss.

"Yes, something big," Ben admitted. "I would like to meet with you to discuss it."

"One of the conditions of your employment was that we could never meet."

Ben paused and looked down at his FORtab. When he first found it, he thought it was a bomb. Now, he knew that it did not need to be a bomb. He smiled grimly to himself at the fact that his entire office was lined with explosives, all of which could be remotely detonated by the man on the other end of the FORtab.

"There is a third FORtab," Ben said.

"That is impossible. Only two units were manufactured, at my direction."

"That's what I understood as well. But the fact is that a man contacted me from a FORtab and he seemed to know a lot about you...Doctor Smith."

There was an awkward pause.

"And you thought to leave this out of your report?" Smith finally asked.

"Only because I wanted to directly speak to you about it."

"Who is this man?"

"I don't know how much I can believe. My FORtab says that he's telling the truth, but there's something odd that I can't put my finger on. I can only say for sure that his name is Helmut," Ben said, uploading a screen capture he had taken of Helmut's face. "Facematch software is unable to find him in any of my databases. He claims to work for something called VIGIL."

"VIGIL disappeared over two hundred years ago."

"You asked and that's what the documents say. I'm sending them over as we speak."

The files transferred in a matter of moments. Ben gave him a few minutes to study the files.

"How did you come by these documents?"

"The first time he contacted me, he took me by surprise. I did a little digging into the network security on my unit and discovered..."

"That it is controlled by my FORtab," Smith said, completing Ben's sentence.

"Yes, and before you wonder, I didn't try to change that. The way you have it set up, I don't even know if it's possible. But I did notice that the device Helmut has doesn't have any sort of security protocol on it, almost like he wasn't expecting me to connect to his device. The second time he contacted me, it was easy to copy most of his files."

"There isn't much data here."

The man on the other side of the screen was silent as he scanned the rest of the files.

"What else did he say?" Smith asked.

"He said that if I repeat what he told me, you would pull the plug on me. I need to know if that's true."

The other side of the connection was silent.

"I'll take that as a yes," Ben said. "And, to be honest, I understand why. But if even part of what Helmut told me is true, then we both know what must be done. I love this country just as much as you do. It gave me a new life when mine was over. America alone holds the promise of a better world. That is, if we can hold it together."

For some reason, Ben began thinking about Sara. "Look, if my life is the price to keep your secret and help hold this country together, so be it, but I think I deserve a chance to tell you why I should live. Why we should both live and fight this enemy together."

There was no reply except the sound of fingers softly tapping a keyboard.

"You will board a 7:15 AM flight to La Guardia," Smith said and the connection was dropped.

Ben's screen filled with an itinerary, which ended at a small building seven miles away from the New York City airport. He opened the drawer next to him and looked at the bottle of vodka. Then he shut the drawer.

He waited ten full minutes before leaving his office, just to make sure that the building wasn't going to blow up around him.

He retired to his room though it was difficult to sleep. He had escaped death. But how would this CURE agency of Smith's go after VIGIL? Would Stone and Freya be his permanent weapons or did Smith already have other resources in CURE?

The answers would be interesting. *One way or another*, Ben Cole thought, *things are going to change tomorrow.*

CHAPTER THIRTY-FOUR

Stone stared out into the cool desert evening. The moon tinted the sands a light blue, giving the horizon an almost alien feel. He took a deep drag from his cigarette and held in the smoke. It processed its way into his lungs, spreading nicotine into his system. He knew he should stop smoking. If he had stopped when he first started training, his body would probably already be functioning at full capacity and he wouldn't have to worry about peaks.

But, like most things in his life, it just was not that easy.

Stone took a glance back toward Sunny Joe's house. Everyone was inside celebrating Freya's sixteenth birthday. He had handed her a present and told her he would be back after a walk, which was his code for getting a smoke. Normally, Freya would ask for a sixty second delay so she could try to talk him out of it, but whatever had happened to her on the Mexico mission had spooked her to the point that she had avoided talking to him.

It was hard for Stone to think about. He had never seen eyes like that. And the way she tore through those guys…it would have been hard for someone to understand unless they actually saw it. She ripped a heavily-reinforced steel door off its frame. Stone didn't know if even Sunny Joe could do something like that.

When they had returned, she made him promise not to tell anyone. He only agreed to the promise if she would talk about it later. She nodded and then put on a smile for her party, but he could see the worry behind her eyes.

He glanced to his side and Sunny Joe was sitting next to him. He had not heard him sit down, but then again, when Sunny Joe wanted to be quiet, no one could hear him.

"You should be inside, celebrating with your sister," Sunny Joe said, keeping upwind of Stone's cigarette.

"She doesn't need me," Stone said, stomping the cigarette into the sand.

"How are your hands?"

Stone looked at his hands. The feeling was back in his fingers, but they were still dark from blood loss.

"Your sister's hands look better," Sunny Joe said with a knowing look. "I never heard of that happening to someone who could center themselves."

"She doesn't want to talk about it," Stone said truthfully.

Sunny Joe looked down at his own hands for a moment.

"I've killed twenty-six men with these hands. I understand the need for secrets, but you have to realize that in our line of work there are very few people to confide in and some secrets can be fatal."

Stone looked down at the sand again. He would not betray Freya's trust. Who would believe him anyway? Stone had never seen anything like it. The way she just tore that guy in two like a ragdoll…it wasn't human.

"Your dad's here," Sunny Joe said, changing the subject. "He's asking about you."

"I saw him and Master Chiun come in. That's another reason not to go inside. You know, when I was growing up, I would have given anything to meet my father. But now? I don't know. We just don't see eye-to-eye."

"That's funny, because that's exactly what he said about me years ago. He always wanted to find me and then he did and he didn't come back because we just didn't see eye-to-eye."

"But he's not…"

"I'm not through," Sunny Joe said. "When you're a kid, you think your father is perfect. A titan. As you grow up, you begin to question his decisions. At one point, you start to realize that he's just the guy who happened to marry your mother. That process normally takes years, but for you and your dad, the process went from superhero to mortal in two seconds flat. No man — and I mean no man — can withstand that kind of scrutiny, not even a Master of Sinanju. But don't ever discount what your father is. His entire being is magic."

"You're a better father than he is," Stone protested.

"Don't put me on that pedestal. I was a selfish bastard when your dad was born, trying to make it big in Hollywood. My pop wanted me to come back to take charge of the tribe and then Dawn had Remo. It felt like everyone was trying to chain me down and drag me back to the reservation. It was just too much. But when I finally met your dad as a grown man, something inside of me changed. I went from being an unattached dad to doting father in two seconds flat. After realizing who he was, I imagined him growing up without me. I could see him learning to ride a bike by himself. See him picked on because I wasn't there to teach him how to defend himself."

Sunny Joe's voice trailed off and he cleared his throat. "When your dad told me about you and Freya, I agreed to keep you both to try and set things right with him. At first, I was just paying off a debt, taking care of you two like I had failed to take care of him. You're part of my family, too. You're my grandson. Freya's my granddaughter."

Stone looked off into the distance, digesting Sunny Joe's words. "I just need to find out where I belong."

"That's just life," Sunny Joe said. "I'm your grandfather and I have some skills. But Remo…your dad is a Master of Sinanju. You may not know it yet, but that is some strong cheese. And Master Chiun…well, he is from a different world. And all of these things are part of you, part of your sister. If you have any questions about who you and your sister are, you could do worse than speak to your father.

"And now since you want to know where you belong, I suggest you belong at your sister's party, celebrating her birthday. So get in there before I kick your ass."

"If he doesn't get in there soon, I'll kick his ass myself," Freya said from behind.

For the first time in a long time, Stone smiled when he heard her voice.

"I'm gonna see what Master Chiun is up to," Sunny Joe said, excusing himself. "He's probably bragging about his dragon soup recipe again."

Stone remained seated and Freya sat beside him. She waited a moment before she spoke.

"Thank you," she said. "For not telling grandfather."

"What was I supposed to tell him? That you turned into some kind of non-breathing killing machine?"

"We'll talk about it later, I promise," Freya said. "It happened to me once, before we came to the reservation. I just need time to think."

"We both do," Stone said. "And…hey, thanks for saving my hide back there."

"Thanks? Aww, that's the best birthday present I've ever received," Freya said, smiling.

"Not as good as that horse!" Stone said. "I thought they were kidding when they said they were getting you a horse. I thought it was gonna be a pony or something. I didn't know they made horses that big!"

"It's a white Andalusian!" Freya said, excited. "Master Chiun said that they are extremely rare! The King of Spain gave it to him for my birthday."

"Just handed it over to him, uh huh," Stone smirked. "I would have loved to seen that conversation."

"I'm going to name him Thor!"

"Where are you gonna keep him?"

"Grandpa said that he'll make a special stall in the stable with the camels."

"Hey, as long as you take care of it. Don't expect me to shovel its crap."

Freya laughed and then turned toward Stone with a serious look on her face.

"You know that I'm not doing this just to get in your way, don't you?"

"I know. That's not what bothered me," Stone admitted. "I felt like I had finally found my calling…my place in this world. I think the real reason I didn't want you to come along is that maybe you were going to prove that I'm not even necessary there."

Freya paused a moment, then spoke quietly to Stone. "Without you, I'd be buried under rubble someplace south of the border with some mariachi band playing over my corpse. Don't you ever forget it. I won't."

Freya grinned, and Stone couldn't help but grin back.

"Yeah, maybe so."

The two stood and Freya placed her arm around Stone's shoulder as they walked back to the house.

"I know a couple of things that you don't know yet…but you can learn," she said. "And you know more than I'll ever know about how the real world works. That makes us a pretty good team."

"Stone and Freya, master assassin team," her brother said whimsically. "We might be the first in the world."

"I think our father, Remo, and Master Chiun might have a different opinion about that," Freya said.

Stone chuckled. "We'll just tell them that they're yesterday. We're tomorrow."

Freya giggled, a happy child sound, and Stone came to the sudden understanding that no matter what her skills were, she was still a sixteen-year-old girl. And the kid sister he would be responsible for.

"You know I love you, big brother, but you've really got to stop smoking." Freya said, waving the air before her. "Your breath smells like someone burning leaves."

"Tomorrow," he said.

신안주 모두가 마스터에게 활을 다
THE KILLING FIELDS

THE SCROLLS OF SINANJU
KOREA, 1612 A.D.

WRITTEN BY SAMBRIA, MASTER OF THE HOUSE OF SINANJU

The contract with Thamma, King of Siam, has been fulfilled. His gold has been placed in the storehouse, and his ivory and teakwood offerings have been added to the Master's House.

The Sleepwalkers who threatened his Highness, the King, have been destroyed. The head of their mistress now adorns the pike before his throne.

This mission started like many others. Underestimating the abilities of the House, the client lied about the true threat they faced...

* * * *

Master Sambria moved through the sweltering forest as silently as fog. The eight Siamese guards walked slowly ahead of him, swords drawn, occasionally looking backwards to ensure that Sambria remained unharmed. Each time they glanced at him, he politely bowed his head.

The guards were an embarrassment to Sambria, but he knew the King had sent them as a gesture of respect. To refuse them would have been an insult to Siamese tradition. As the reigning Master of Sinanju, a house of assassins over five thousand years old, Sambria understood the value of tradition — just as the King understood that the most dangerous assassin alive did not need royal bodyguards.

The soldiers plodded through the dense foliage, sweating and grunting in their leather armor, but Sambria felt no weariness. He was no more troubled by the temperature and humidity of the Siamese forest any more than the biting cold air of Sinanju, his village in Korea.

He was more concerned with observing his surroundings. Unlike his escorts, Master Sambria had noted signs that a large contingent had moved through the area recently.

* * * *

The captain of the Royal Siamese Guard had not wanted to hire the Master of Sinanju.

The captain called the army of dead men 'Sleepwalkers' because they appeared to be sleepwalking, a clear sign of demon possession in their culture. He asked the King how a single unarmed man, regardless of his training, could possibly succeed?

At first, the King had found the captain's story unbelievable. But then the Sleepwalkers attacked an outpost north of Tak, and he ordered the captain to send a legion of his finest soldiers, and armed with the best weapons Siam could provide. Even though the Sleepwalkers were shot with arrows and hacked with swords, they could not be stopped. After they overran the outpost, the Sleepwalkers killed the soldiers and the survivors claimed that they began devouring the flesh of their victims.

The Sleepwalkers began their slow march south until it was apparent that Bangkok was their final destination. Fortunately, King Thamma knew of Sinanju and had enough gold to procure their services. Sambria could tell the captain was lying about something, but could not discern what it was.

* * * *

These thoughts filled Master Sambria's mind as he moved through the jungle. Oddly, he smelled his targets before he heard them. A lingering and heady spice overwhelmed his senses. Soon after, he felt the light vibrations of their footfalls — slow and melodic, like an ancient drum. He estimated their number at no more than twenty. Not knowing which part of the captain's story was a lie, Sambria fell back into the shadows of the jungle to observe the approaching army. To his handlers, he merely appeared to lean backward before disappearing from sight.

The men turned around to search for Master Sambria when they first saw the slowly-marching column of Sleepwalkers. Sambria continued to observe from a perch in a nearby tree. He could not concern himself with their fate. They were, after all, merely soldiers.

The Sleepwalkers wore torn and bloody clothing. A fine white powder covered their faces and vests, and they smelled strongly of the pungent spice Sambria had detected earlier. They moved in silence, a ghost army with blank stares. One of the Siamese bodyguards fired an arrow into their ranks. In silent unison, the Sleepwalkers turned, attacking with terrifying speed. Before the guard could fire a second arrow, he lay dead on the ground, bitten and bloody.

The remaining soldiers drew their swords. Sambria could tell that they had been trained well, but though their swords found their marks, piercing hearts and lungs, the attack by the ghost soldiers was not slowed. They moved like an unstoppable wave, tearing at and biting the soldiers.

A soldier toward the rear spun with his sword, cleanly slicing the head off of one of the Sleepwalkers. Sambria noted that this one fell and did not move again. The remaining Sleepwalkers quickly overcame the bodyguard, and they turned as one to feast on his still-living body.

Sambria dropped from his perch in the tree, but as he attacked the first line of Sleepwalkers, he noticed that his blows were having no more effect than the soldiers' swords. A nerve strike that should have exploded the creature's heart only slowed it for a moment. A stone blow that collapsed a Sleepwalker's sternum into his chest cavity merely caused it to take a step back before continuing his relentless advance.

Then Sambria felt the first of the Sleepwalkers touch his robes.

They were moving too fast for humans not trained in Sinanju, and for the first time in his life, Sambria became concerned for his own safety. While no human was as fast as the Master of Sinanju, their sheer number threatened to overwhelm him. A Sleepwalker raked its bloody fingers across Sambria's back, shredding his cloak. Turning like a dervish and repeating the one effective move he had seen, Sambria sliced through the necks of the first three Sleepwalkers, watching their heads fall to the ground.

They did not move again.

The rest of the Sleepwalkers charged without a glance to their fallen dead. The fear of the living was nowhere to be found in their eyes. One managed to grab Sambria's arm, and he was as strong as he was fast. He tried to bite Sambria's arm, but the Master of Sinanju removed his arm from his shoulder before quickly removing his head from his body. Sambria's hands flashed back and forth, decapitating all of the Sleepwalkers.

* * * *

Returning to the palace, Sambria told the King that the Sleepwalkers would no longer terrorize the land. As he explained that it had been an assassination attempt upon His Majesty using an odd white powder, he noticed that the scent of the spice was faintly present in the throne room. Walking slowly before each of the thrones, Master Sambria stopped at the throne of the princess.

With a downward glance, the princess surrendered her guilt, and with a single stroke from Master Sambria, she surrendered her head.

"The princess!" the captain of the guard shouted, drawing his sword.

Sambria moved toward the captain, and with a single, lightning-fast movement, took his sword from his hands in mid-swing and used it to slice through the princess' pouch. The same white powder Sambria had seen on the faces of the Sleepwalkers fell to the ground, covering the throne room floor.

Though distressed over the death of his favorite daughter, the King paid Master Sambria's fee in gold, and rewarded him with a bonus of ivory carvings and teakwood. Sambria returned home to Sinanju with a small pouch of the spice in order to teach future Masters its scent. His entry in the scrolls would ensure that others would be warned, but he would never reveal that it was the only time in his life he felt fear.

CHAPTER ONE: THE PRESENT

Stone Smith sat down at the front of the training hut, crossing his legs. The morning Arizona sun shimmered through the small gap in the curtain behind him, cutting a swath of light across the room. Stone glared in frustration at the rock placed at the front of the one-room building. The Founder Stone, legend said, was where Kojong stood when he claimed the land for Sinanju.

The cool of the night had not yet been washed away by the morning sun, and Stone shivered for just a second before seeking his center. He had spent the last week healing, performing breathing rituals to cleanse his system. Like every student and Master of Sinanju for the past five thousand years, breath was his fuel. But unlike his sister Freya, who had been breathing properly since she was an infant, Stone could only maintain a Sinanju center for short periods of time. This past week, trying to save his sister, he had centered too often.

His weakness had almost gotten both of them killed.

"Again," Sunny Joe said. In contrast to Stone's look of annoyance, the chief's face showed a perfect calm.

Stone exhaled slowly and deeply, and as the breath filled his lungs, his awareness expanded. He could smell the soft, bitter scent of the few blades of grass peering at the steps of the small hut. He could hear the individual beats of the wings of a fly that weaved lazily around him, and felt the tiny pressure waves from its wings as it moved through the air.

He turned his attention to a small granite ledge on the Founder Stone. He stared at the grain of sand, impossibly and perfectly balanced on the end of an impossibly and perfectly balanced needle, until it filled his vision and was all he could see. Stone was deeply focused, and he could see the grain of sand as clearly as a small boulder sitting atop a metal spike.

All he had to do was knock the grain of sand off without disturbing the needle.

In Sinanju, one did not practice a stroke — one performed a stroke. So, while he would have at one time practiced like a golfer preparing his swing, Stone sliced his right hand at the needle. His fingernail sliced through the air at a perfect angle and connected with the grain of sand. Stone felt victorious until the needle fell to the floor.

His breathing was right, but Stone could feel the small tickle of nicotine as it wormed its way through his lung tissue.

"Sloppy," Sunny Joe said. "I can hear you wheezing from over here."

"I get it. I need to stop smoking," Stone said, rolling his eyes. "But it's something else, I can feel it, Grandpa. What am I doing wrong? The stroke was right."

"I've been telling you. You're gonna have to lose some of that muscle. You're naturally lean like Freya, but you've spent years bulking up."

"I like my muscle," Stone said, subconsciously flexing his arms.

"If you want to be a Master, you have to master your own body first. Right now, your two biggest problems are smoking and your diet. Stone, the way we empower our bodies, it is very easy to bulk up, but Sinanju does not rely on muscular strength for its power. You've got to get that out of your head."

"I know, I know, it's all about breathing."

"It all *starts* with breathing," Sunny Joe said, correcting him. "Do you remember your first lesson?"

"I remember that you tore my favorite jacket," Stone muttered.

"You're missing something important, and I'm not going to keep repeating it. Close your eyes. Think back."

Stone gave Sunny Joe a small glare and then closed his eyes. He knew his grandfather meant well, but that did not make it any less frustrating. He thought back.

* * * *

The first day Stone agreed to attend training with Sunny Joe was a month after he moved onto the Sinanju reservation. He had met Freya, his twelve-year-old half-sister, just before they arrived. She was excited to find out that she had a brother, even though they only shared the same father. Every day, Freya invited him to her training sessions with Sunny Joe, and every day he declined. One day, bored stiff and unable to find anything else to do, he agreed.

Sunny Joe was spry for a man in his seventies, but Stone was a Navy SEAL and a black belt in Tae Kwon Do. So, when he first entered the worn-out shack that served as Sunny Joe's dojo, he could barely keep himself from laughing.

The outside of the shack had been beaten to death by the sun and wind, and the inside had not fared much better. He could see through the wall planks in several places. The room had probably not been painted since Sunny Joe was taking lessons himself, but Stone decided that he would be a good sport. He would humor his grandfather. He might even learn a couple of moves before he showed Sunny Joe how things worked in the modern world.

Sunny Joe led Freya and Stone past the large stone at the front of the dojo to the center of the training hut. It was a bitterly cold December morning, and Stone wore a bomber jacket to keep warm. Sunny Joe and Freya were wearing tribal robes, which Stone assumed was their training *gi*. Staring at the brightly colored and patterned robes, Stone stifled another laugh. The robes looked like they had been designed by someone from the sixties. While they were high.

Freya nudged him, pointing downwards at a pair of worn bamboo mats and promptly knelt. Stone rolled his eyes and sighed deeply before slowly folding his legs to the ground. He coughed, feeling the urge for a cigarette, and lifted his face, waiting for Sunny Joe's first piece of wisdom.

"Breathe," Sunny Joe said, crossing his arms behind his back as if he were waiting for Stone to perform a trick.

"What?" Stone asked. He thought Sunny Joe just told him to breathe.

He glanced over at Freya, who was looking at him with her big eyes, also waiting for him to breathe.

"Is this a joke?" Stone asked. "I'm already breathing."

"Fill your lungs with air, son. Inhale. Exhale. I have to see how bad your breathing rhythms are."

Stone smirked and breathed in. And then out. He tilted his head and the smirk became a smile as he breathed in and out. In and out.

Sunny Joe bent forward slightly. He studied Stone for a moment before shaking his head sadly.

"Don't take it personally, son, but you just don't know how to breathe. You just suck air in and blow it out without thought. We'll have to untrain your body."

"Grandpa, I'm here out of respect, but I think I know how to breathe."

"That's your problem," Sunny Joe said, moving behind Stone. "You think you know."

Sunny Joe placed his left hand over Stone's sternum and pushed, forcing out the dead air at the bottom of his lungs, while his right hand manipulated the nerves at the base of Stone's spine.

Stone's eyes shot open. His skin tingled as if waves of water were cascading over him. He arched his back as a breath, deeper than any he had ever taken, flooded his lungs with fresh air. The moment turned in onto itself and Stone felt awareness for the first time in his life. Sunny Joe, Freya, the room, the breathing — everything was there, and it was right. In that instant, Stone knew that it not only *was*, but that *it was meant to be.*

For one brief moment, Stone Smith was whole. Complete. With purpose and direction and...

The feeling left as he exhaled, leaving him alone and empty.

"What was that?" he gasped.

"That's what it feels like to take a real breath. It begins with the center, filling you with energy, and flows outward. Once you understand that, your body and mind will start to function like they should."

Stone tried to suck the air back into his lungs to reclaim the feeling of wholeness, but no matter how hard he tried, his lungs stayed as flat and useless as they always had been. Except now, he knew they were useless.

"Sinanju is based on this one fundamental truth: everything starts with breathing. Others have never grasped this truth. This is why some of the Masters of Sinanju have been called gods who walked the Earth. You've heard of some of them. Hercules. Thor. Ogoun."

Stone looked into Sunny Joe's eyes with disbelief. "You're telling me that all those guys were real and they were Sinanju?"

"Each myth and legend comes from a splinter of truth that is Sinanju."

Stone sat back, this time considering his grandfather's words.

"It is a simple premise: if you cannot breathe correctly, you cannot move correctly. I will show you. Hold out your arm."

Stone held out his arm. Sunny Joe sliced through the sleeve of his jacket with a fingernail, exposing Stone's bare arm.

"Hey!" Stone yelled.

Sunny Joe ignored him and used one of his fingernails to gently prod Stone's exposed arm. Stone's muscles involuntarily flexed as if he were posing in a bodybuilding contest. Despite the pain, Stone took pride in the curvature of his muscles.

"See those muscles you've been building for years? You've spent so much time on developing the size of your muscles that you've abused the body's most important organ. What's worse is that you think you've accomplished something."

"What are you talking about?" Stone asked, shaking the feeling back into his arm.

"Skin is the body's largest organ. Man has forgotten how to breathe with it. All of those muscles are pressuring your skin, stretching it beyond its normal capacity. In other words, your muscles are suffocating it."

"Look, I don't know what you did with that breathing thing a while ago, but I'm a black belt and these little tricks don't mean squat in the real world!"

"Okay, let's see your attack," Sunny Joe said, taking a standard defensive position.

"Grandpa, I'd cripple you."

Freya snorted, then quickly cupped her hand over her mouth.

"Then by all means, cripple me," Sunny Joe said, cordially bowing.

Stone assumed an offensive stance. He would not seriously hurt his grandfather, but he would make sure that he realized...

Sunny Joe was gone.

He had been standing in front of Stone. Stone had blinked and he had disappeared.

"Start whenever you're ready," Sunny Joe said from behind.

Stone instinctively wheeled around, leading with his fist. He would use the side of his fist so he would not cause any real harm.

But his fist went through where Sunny Joe should have been.

He saw it with his own eyes. His grandfather was standing just behind him. His mind told his fist to recognize the impact on the side of his grandfather's head. But he felt confused when no such sensation followed, and his arm went sailing through the air.

Sunny Joe grabbed Stone's arm in mid-swing and increased his momentum until Stone hit the dirt floor face first.

Stone smiled.

Okay, so his grandfather had a few moves. Good, because so did Stone. He just hoped his grandfather could take a punch. Stone stood to his feet with a dominant stance and this time Sunny Joe did not move when he swung. Stone was going to knock his grandfather to the ground. Though not fatal, a blow to the temple would likely render him unconscious.

Stone's fist hit a stone wall.

He thought he was aiming at the side of his grandfather's head, but he must have accidentally hit the wall behind him, because his fist collapsed into a limp, shaking thing as pain shot up from his hand to his shoulder as if he had struck a tree. Stone howled, grabbing his right hand with his left.

But when he looked up, he saw that he was nowhere near the wall. His grandfather remained standing where he had been before Stone's punch, with the same curious look on his face, as if he were watching a child learn how to dance.

Stone felt rage tear through his body and his eyes narrowed. He leaned forward and charged.

"No, Stone, don't!" Freya yelled, recognizing the madness in her brother's eyes. She moved between them to defend her grandfather.

But it was too late. Bloodlust had overcome Stone, and as he moved in for the attack, he tried to push Freya out of the way.

His hands never touched her.

Stone saw the smile disappear from Freya's face and felt a dozen blows to his body, ranging from his chest to his hip, each blow a sledgehammer to his central nervous system. Stone dropped to his knees in shock as waves of pain overwhelmed him. Then he fell to the ground. In his last moment of consciousness, he saw Freya leaning over him, teary-eyed.

"I'm so sorry!" she said.

* * * *

Stone opened his eyes, returning to the present.

"I forgot that was the first time Freya kicked my ass."

Sunny Joe smiled. "Do you remember what I said about muscles?"

"Yeah, I actually do. But why didn't you just tell me?"

"Once something has been learned, it cannot be unlearned. It can only be forgotten. You have to be able to remember the important things yourself. I won't always be here to tell you. And if you don't like getting your ass kicked by your little sister, you've got a lot of catching up to do."

"I'm not like Freya. She's been trained longer. Even before she came here, Master Chiun taught her how to breathe right. She's been doing this since she was a baby."

"Son, even I didn't learn Sinanju as quickly as her, so you can either make excuses or you can fix the problem," Sunny Joe said, pointing at Stone's head. "Besides, no one is like Freya. The more I see that girl in action, the more I know why they didn't want women to become masters. They're damn near unstoppable. In a dozen years, she's gonna pass me in skill. In twenty, she'll catch up to your dad. Past that? Well, that's just unknown territory."

Stone would not tell his grandfather, but he had already seen what happened once Freya entered 'unknown territory'. Last week, they had been in Mexico, where a small army had been raised. To shield them from bullets, Freya had ripped a large generator from a wall, causing part of the building to collapse on her. She had been injured and stopped breathing, but when she finally awakened, her eyes had blackened and the voice that roared from her mouth sent shudders down Stone's spine. The voice was not Freya's. It was a dead voice that seemed to come from beyond this world. When she found the leader huddled in his office, she ripped through the steel-reinforced door and tore the man in half as if he were a piece of paper.

Sunny Joe noted the worried look on Stone's face, but ignored it. When Stone was ready to talk, he would talk.

"Again," Sunny Joe said, balancing the grain of sand on the needle.

CHAPTER TWO

Her name was a number and that number was 14. She was one of the test subjects in the top-secret 'Carnage' program, though their caretakers called them "Premiums." From the original hundred subjects selected for the program, only a dozen Premiums now remained. The rest had either died or mysteriously disappeared before she was twelve. By the time she was twenty, just three Premiums were battle-ready. The remaining nine were still in training.

At 5 A.M. the lights came on in 14's small concrete cell, beginning her daily routine. She slid smoothly from her padded bunk, stepping into the metallic diagnostic unit in the corner. The size of a small closet, the metal box measured her vital readings four times a day.

14 closed her eyes, trying to hold on to the few remaining fragments of her dream. For the past week, she had been dreaming deeply. Each night, it was the same dream and each morning, it was gone. Shutting her eyes even tighter, 14 remembered a doll with blonde hair…and the sound of screams. She tried to remember a name. *Lauren?* She shook her head from side to side.

No, it was something else.

The machine whirred with a constant, dull hiss. 14 tried to ignore it, but it seemed to grow louder and louder the more she tried to focus. She finally opened her eyes in angry frustration, and, in that moment, the hiss of the diagnostic unit brought the name back to her. *Lisa.* 14 knew that it had been more than a dream. It was a memory, and it roared back to life in her mind.

* * * *

When 14 was six years old, almost half of the Premiums remained of the original hundred. One afternoon, they were taken outside the compound to a small hospital, where they were politely called "guest visitors."

During their visit, a young intern had made the mistake of accosting one of the Keepers, a burly man in a blue lab coat. Stepping away from the anatomical model he was assembling, the intern said it was "utterly heartless" to call the girls numbers instead of names. When his body was found later that day, his heart surgically removed and placed in the chest cavity of the dummy, the whispers stopped. The visits continued.

For their weekly excursions, each Premium had been paired with an 'outsider' girl.

These girls were allowed to grow their hair long, and, in contrast to the Premiums' matching grey jumpsuits, they wore an explosion of brightly-colored dresses, bows, and ribbons. Each week, the outside girls were escorted into a large room filled with toys, dolls, and games.

14 was partnered with a girl named Lisa, a shy girl with long, blonde hair. Lisa wore a pink dress and shiny black shoes. Despite being surrounded with new toys, Lisa always brought a decrepit, filthy doll with her. She held it tightly to her chest, hiding her face in its hair. The doll was threadbare, missing an eye, and starting to tear at the seams, but Lisa never put it down. Every few moments, she would peek out from behind the doll, look at 14, and immediately bury her face back in the doll's dirty, blonde mane.

14 did not understand the purpose of dolls. Lisa's doll did not even look like a real girl: it had an enormous head, and each hand only had three fingers.

As the days passed, Lisa grew less shy. She still clung to her doll like a life preserver, but she no longer stood on the opposite side of the room from 14. One day, she slowly sidled up to 14. After staring at the floor for several minutes, Lisa handed 14 the doll.

"Here," Lisa said quietly. "She needs a new friend."

14 felt something soft stir inside her. A smile crept slowly across her face as she began to cradle the doll.

Then she heard the screams.

Her eyes darted wildly around the room. All of the Premiums who had been playing with toys and dolls were being led out the door by the men in blue lab coats. Even at six years old, the Premiums knew that if the men in blue lab coats took you away, you never came back.

14 looked down in horror at the doll in her hands. She lightly stroked the doll's face, feeling its softness and its warmth. She tightly shut her eyes, turning her head to the side before ripping the ancient doll in half.

Forcing herself not to cry, she hurled the pieces at Lisa, who began to scream. 14 grabbed Lisa's hair and pulled her to the ground. She bared her teeth and leaned close to Lisa's neck. To everyone in the room, it looked as though 14 was trying to bite the screaming girl's jugular.

"I'm sorry," she whispered.

Her handlers — in white lab coats, she noted with relief — pulled her off Lisa and led her to one of the vans outside. Back to the compound. Back to safety.

They never returned to the hospital.

* * * *

The diagnostic unit beeped, showing that 14's blood pressure and body mass were perfect. Her bone implants were carrying a strong signal. 14 slid her fingers over her nearly-bald head. All Premiums had scars from multiple surgeries once they reached puberty. Their bones, including their skulls and torsos, were lined with thin rails of hyper-structured carbon, making them nearly unbreakable. Their knuckles, elbows, and heels were doubly plated to ensure maximum damage when attacking.

The Carnage program chose only females to be Premiums, because the primary chemical used to alter their DNA — an ancient Siamese potion once thought to animate the dead — was absorbed more quickly into the female body. That, along with females' faster development than males, made them optimal subjects.

Each Premium had been given special hormonal injections for the first twelve years of their lives, which greatly increased their strength, speed, and endurance. The injections also caused many to suffer heart failure and strokes. Unlike the weaker Premiums who sought medical care when their chests began to tighten up, 14 remained in her bed and grabbed her pillow until the feeling passed.

The food tray opened, and her bowl of high-protein gruel passed through the slot. 14 sat on her padded bench and dutifully ate the tasteless porridge. There were no artificial colors or flavors. It was merely designed to amplify her energy output and maintain a low body mass.

As 14 ate, her food tray opened a second time. A piece of paper was pushed through and slowly floated to the floor. 14 stared at the paper while she continued eating. She could not see the writing from where she was sitting. When she finished eating, 14 slid her tray through the waste slot and picked up the paper. She could tell by the sloppiness of the handwriting that it had been written hurriedly.

14 — Return to your diagnostic unit immediately.
Do not move from it until you are ordered to do so.

She had never received a personal message before. Having been trained all her life to obey orders without question, she started to walk to the diagnostic unit, but felt uneasy. *Was this some sort of test?*

14 glanced at the camera monitoring her cell, then looked at the steel unit in the corner

of her cell and dutifully entered. The instant she stepped into the metallic chamber, she noticed a rumble. The glass in the machine began to rattle, and her feet could feel vibrations coming through the floor. Looking up, she saw dust begin to flutter lazily from the ceiling. She saw one flake of paint fall, watching it drifting downward, slowly and elliptically. It was less than an inch away from the ground when she heard a sickening groan, and then the terrible roar of the building exploding around her.

* * * *

14 looked around, dazed. The blast had knocked her to the floor. A large wooden beam that had once supported the ceiling now lay inches from her face, split like an enormous toothpick. She touched her face; pulling back her hand, she saw that it was covered with blood and dirt. She didn't know if she had been out for minutes or for hours, but she was being shaken back to consciousness by a man in a chemical suit.

"Let's go!" he shouted, gesturing wildly. His words were easy enough for 14 to understand, even though she could not hear him. All 14 could hear was a single, deafening high-pitched ringing in her ears. The man in the chemical suit urgently motioned for her to follow him, turning from her cell into a long hallway.

Sensing that more of the ceiling would collapse soon, she cautiously walked behind him, maintaining a safe distance, though she noticed that the man was unarmed. As she passed through the piles of smoldering rubble that had once been her home, 14 was shocked to see so many lifeless bodies strewn throughout the facility. This was not a freak explosion; it was a massacre. Those who had not died in the blast had been riddled with bullets, Premiums and Keepers alike.

As sounds began to become audible again, she could hear gunshots and screams. Instinctively, she took a defensive stance. 64, the only Premium that she considered her equal, had survived the blast, and was fighting against a squad of armed guards. Their bodies fell as she tore through them.

The man escorting 14 stopped when he saw 64 and lifted his radio to his face. "We have a runner!" he said.

The radio crackled back a response. "Do not engage! Get your Premium off campus now!"

"Yes, sir!" the man said, and they continued through the rubble to a limousine parked outside the compound.

The back door opened, and 14 was ushered inside. The door slammed behind her. For the first time since the explosion, 14 was able to take a calming breath.

The young man sitting across from her in the back seat wore a dark suit and sunglasses, despite the dim lighting inside the limousine. His musky cologne was so strong that it was almost unbearable. The man turned to glance at 14 as if she was a present.

"You are the sole survivor of the Carnage program," he said. "Congratulations." A small, cruel smile cracked the sides of his mouth.

14 relaxed and allowed a restful sigh.

"We have an assignment for you," the man said as the limousine pulled away.

Looking over her shoulder at the compound again, 14 watched 64, bleeding and injured, dispatch the last of the guards before limping weakly into the forest.

CHAPTER THREE

Mick Walker entered his small office and turned on his computer. As he waited for the monitor to come to life, Mick removed his ever-present cowboy hat and took a sip of coffee. As chief historian for the Sinanju Tribe, his job was to catalog tribal events.

Over four hundred years of scrolls, chronicling everything from wars to tribal dietary habits filled the small storage room next to his office. A few months ago, Mick had started transcribing the scrolls to a digital format so future Sinanju chiefs would have easier access to the histories. There were so many scrolls and fragments that Mick figured it would take a decade to completely convert the older parchments.

Looking at the piles of papers stacked on top of his desk, Mick leaned back in his chair and sighed. Today was not a day for transcribing. The first day of the month was reserved for his monthly entry, logging new events. Next month would be his annual entry, a much more detailed report chronicling the entire year's events.

When Mick took over as historian, he dreaded the job. His father had been a meticulous man who thought everything that happened in the tribe deserved an entry. Temperatures, weather patterns, crop harvests — nothing was too small for his father to record. After a year, Mick found out why his father was so meticulous: until Stone and Freya arrived, nothing worth recording ever seemed to happen in the small Arizona tribe.

The chief of the Tribe of Sinanju, Bill Roam, was Mick's childhood friend. After a squabble with his father Bill left the small Arizona reservation for Hollywood, where his Sinanju training quickly made him a highly sought-after stuntman. But just as Mick got the courage to follow in his friend's footsteps, his father died, leaving him the scribing duties that had been a part of their tribe since Kojong first settled the land they now called home.

Bill eventually returned to finish his father's training. When Bill's father passed away, he took over the role of Sunny Joe, the name given to every Sinanju chief. And when he did, something inside him changed. He started attending council meetings, and looking into ideas like irrigation proposals and land usage, things that he would previously have considered a waste of time.

Another major change in Sunny Joe's life happened a few years ago, when he took in his grandchildren, Stone Smith and Freya Williams. The daughter and son of Sunny Joe's son, Remo Williams, Freya and Stone were perennial outsiders like their father. It took months for them to acclimate to the reservation.

And that's when Sunny Joe started breaking the rules.

When Sunny Joe first started training Freya, everyone on the council was worried. It was a cardinal rule never to train a female in the art of Sinanju. It simply was not done. A few council members began to murmur to Mick. One even asked him about the process of removing a sitting Sunny Joe. Mick smiled, informing the councilman that no such procedure existed, but if he would like to attempt to physically remove Sunny Joe from office, he was more than welcome to try.

That was the last Mick heard about impeachment proceedings.

Mick told Sunny Joe about the council's discussion, but Sunny Joe ignored their concerns. He had the right to train whomever he chose. That was Sinanju law, and Mick had to admit, when there was a conflict, the chief had final say.

But then, as if to poke the council in the eye, Sunny Joe also started training Stone. Training two pupils was not just one of the central taboos of Sinanju, it was a very personal taboo to the Sinanju tribe. In fact, it was the very reason they had been separated from the village of Sinanju in Korea hundreds of years earlier.

A past Master, Nonga, had twin sons, Kojong and Kojing. Because Master Nonga was blind, he could not see when Kojong sometimes took his brother's place during lessons. Thus, although Nonga believed he had trained only Kojing, he had actually trained both his sons.

When it came time for Kojing to become Master, Kojong knew that he needed to leave the village. With sadness in his heart, he journeyed across the Great Sea, settling far away, in what was now Arizona. There, he found a home with a small tribe of Native Americans. After he single-handedly protected them from a tremendous attack, he was made chief. The tribe asked him where he had become such a great warrior. His answer — Sinanju — was a difficult word for non-Koreans to pronounce, so they called him "Sunny Joe," a title given henceforth to every chief.

Though chief of a desert tribe, Kojong never forgot his home. Farming had been impossible in the small Korean village, for the air was cold, and the soil filled with clay. The jagged, sharp rocks of the bay made commercial fishing too dangerous for even the most skillful fishermen. The village's only protection against famine and death was the gold earned by the House of Sinanju, the greatest assassins in the world. For over five thousand years, the Masters of Sinanju were hired by those who could afford them, and fear of their skills ensured that each Master was paid handsomely.

Kojong understood why his ancestors had decreed that there must be only one Master and one pupil: training many in Sinanju would render a Master's services less valuable. If there was only one Master, he could charge any fee he wanted, and someone would willingly pay it. Having more than one Master meant lower earnings for all, and the Korean village would eventually starve. Kojong saw that this was why it had been forbidden to train women: to keep them from passing that training on to their children.

By training both Stone and Freya, Sunny Joe was blatantly violating the tribe's sacred traditions. Mick's charge as tribal historian demanded that he catalog the actions for future Sunny Joes, but he did not want to betray his friend. And even though Sunny Joe had never asked him to cover his actions, Mick had wanted to know why his childhood friend was acting erratically. Earlier that day, Mick finally confronted Sunny Joe.

"But why?" Mick asked. "Why train Freya? Why train two pupils at all?"

"I think the girl might be the key," Sunny Joe said. "If one of these two can unite the Tribe with the House in Korea, even the council won't care that I broke the rules."

Mick smiled widely. He had wondered the same thing at Freya's sixteenth birthday party the week before, but he had kept the idea to himself. Even though Stone was training, he could tell that he was not as serious as his sister. Freya, on the other hand, trained as if that was her purpose. He had not wanted to allow himself to get too hopeful. But now, having heard Sunny Joe say it aloud, Mick started to feel optimistic that it might actually come to pass in his lifetime.

Maybe Mick would even get to see the village before he died.

His ancient computer finally finished booting up, and Mick began typing. Monthly entries took an hour or two, and they were mostly filled with minor tribal news. Mick recorded births, deaths, and any new events, all of which were rare for the tribe. The last portion of the report was always reserved for commentary on the Sunny Joe's activities for the past month. Mick paused for a moment, before leaning over the keyboard once more.

Sunny Joe continues training both Stone and Freya, to the dismay of many. Stone appears to have great potential, but he stubbornly clings to many of his Western ways. Until he learns to fully accept Sinanju – and quits smoking – his training will progress more slowly than either he or Sunny Joe would like.

Freya is another matter. She has adapted to her Sinanju training more quickly than any pupil I can find in the histories. Sunny Joe suspects that this is because she is a female, but the girl is naturally gifted like her father, Remo

Williams. His skills are considered to be equal or above those of Chiun, Master of Sinanju, who calls Remo his son and considers him a fellow Master.

Last week, both Master Remo and Master Chiun attended Freya's sixteenth birthday party. At the celebration, Master Chiun regaled us with many tales of Sinanju that I did not previously know. I asked whether his astonishing deeds had ever been properly chronicled. Perhaps I misunderstood what he said in Korea, but I believe that Master Chiun's response was a forceful tirade of curses directed against "drunken Irish scribblers." Had I known it was a delicate subject, I would not have asked.

Master Chiun treated us all to heaping portions of his "dragon bone soup." The festivities of the day, however, must have lessened our appetites; none of us could finish more than a few bites.

Master Remo hardly spoke to his father, Sunny Joe. Their relationship has always been tense. I know it is a source of sadness to Sunny Joe, but he does not talk about it.

Master Chiun told me that Freya approaches the "Night of Salt" which is the first rite of passage for a future Master of Sinanju and shows that Freya is further advanced than I had guessed.

I had hoped to ask Master Chiun for more details, but Master Remo interrupted us. He said that enduring a hundred Nights of Salt would still be better than eating another bowl of 'duck poo stew.' Master Chiun left to scold Master Remo, who had darted away, and I was unable to ask him any further questions.

After the Night of Salt, Freya will have to obey the strict diet of a Master of Sinanju: rice, fish and, on special occasions, corn and roadrunner. Roadrunner is a favorite of Sunny Joe's. He calls it "Arizona duck."

If Freya is approaching this level of training, this quickly, then this may be a dangerous time for her. No one yet knows what the female cycle will do to a Sinanju-trained body.

Stone and Freya have accepted employment with a government agency. As leery as the tribe is about working with the government, Stone and Freya were successful in stopping a Mexican drug cartel from overrunning the reservation. In doing so, they saved countless lives.

Sunny Joe has said that both Stone and Freya performed admirably, but something is different about Freya since her return. She is more quiet than usual. I suspect something serious happened in Mexico.

Sunny Joe and I will soon take a few men to the Southwestern Tribal Meet in Phoenix. Once a meeting of great tribes discussing our collective future, it is now little more than a sale of tribal arts and crafts. That being said, it has become an important source of Sinanju income. Sales last year grew by twelve percent, and we hope for a good sale this year.

Mick printed his report, putting it in the rusty file cabinet near his desk. He was surprised to see that it was already ten o'clock, much later than he expected. He hoped his wife would still be awake when he got home. Mick wondered if Sunny Joe felt lonely, since he had never looked for another wife after Remo's mother had died. When Mick opened his front door, he saw the smile drawn across his wife's face. He would not trade that for anything in the world.

CHAPTER FOUR

Freya sat on the couch in her small house, staring at the wall. She had just finished her evening training, trying unsuccessfully to focus on the lesson. Spinal manipulation was usually one of her favorite subjects, but her mind kept drifting back to the events in Mexico. When Sunny Joe asked her what was wrong, she lowered her head and said she was fine. It was the first time Freya had ever misled her grandfather, and she hoped it would be the last.

But what could she tell him? She did not remember much after Stone knocked her out of the way of the falling ceiling supports. She found it hard to believe what Stone said, but the look in his eyes told her that he was telling the truth.

On the way back from Mexico, Stone said that she had become some kind of monster.

"A monster?" Freya asked as a worried look spread across her face.

"No, don't take it that way! You asked! Besides, you saved my ass. It was still you, but...your eyes were all black and your voice was...scary."

"You? Scared? How?"

"After you stood back up, your body began radiating an ultra-low sound, like a sub-woofer, but lower. In the military, we called it infra-sound. It's a classified weapon. Normally it's too low for the human ear to hear, but it was so powerful that everyone could hear it. We could feel it, too. The Mexican ninjas standing in front of you were so afraid that they forgot they had rifles in their hands. It was strong enough to freeze me in place."

"What did I say?"

Stone took a second to think. The scene had been so surreal that he had wanted to forget it, but the words came easily.

"I am created Shiva, the Destroyer," Stone said, and as she remembered his words, a memory woke inside Freya.

It was the same feeling she had in Mexico before blacking out. She had felt this way once before, before she moved to the reservation. She was only eleven, and she remembered a man was attacking someone. The man had metal arms, like a robot. With his steely grip, he grabbed the woman who was protecting Freya and began choking her.

Freya's mother had taught her to run in circumstances that she was not prepared for, but before she could turn to run, she felt something flowing beneath her skin like an unstoppable river of power.

It turned her fear into anger.

Instead of running, Freya had walked directly to the man. When she reached him, the man did not even glance down at her. After all, what threat could an eleven-year-old girl possibly be?

Freya breathed in deeply as she grabbed the offending arm nearest to her. Her long fingers reached around one of the polished metal pistons controlling the arm. She squeezed, and the metal bent like warm candle wax. With a futile groan, the artificial bone collapsed. A quick turn of her tiny wrist and the arm snapped off. The hand holding the woman sprang open.

"Meddlesome little bitch!" the man said in disbelief as his arm collapsed to the ground.

"Run, Freya!" the woman screamed as he released her.

"I've got an idea," the man said, striking the woman with his remaining hand and turning to Freya. "Why don't you mind your own damned business?"

But something inside Freya would not let her run from this lesser being, this non-threat. Her eyes remained fixated on the man with one metal arm, and she felt nothing more than the peace of a calm stream as he moved toward her.

In the distance, she remembered hearing chimes…

Then she had said the words.

"I am created Shiva, the Destroyer; Death, the shatterer of worlds," young Freya said to the man standing before her.

And then there was silence.

Freya's memory was interrupted by the taste of salt flooding her mouth. Her mouth opened involuntarily and she began gasping for air. She ran to the kitchen and drank a glass of water, but the overpowering taste remained. Something was seriously wrong.

Stone rushed to her side. "What's wrong? You look like you're about to puke!"

"Get out," she croaked. "Now!"

Grandfather would know what to do.

Freya sprinted the hundred yards to Sunny Joe's house in seconds. It was late, but surely, he could help her. Freya rounded the corner. Sunny Joe was sitting on his porch swing. She looked up at Sunny Joe with tears in her eyes.

"What's wrong, little one?"

"Grandfather, something is wrong with me!" she said hoarsely. "My mouth is dry…"

"And you taste salt," Sunny Joe said, chuckling softly. "Delicious, right?"

"It's awful…wait, how did you know that?" Freya asked between gasps.

"I knew you were close. Sit down. There's nothing you can do about it."

Freya sat beside Sunny Joe. "What is happening to me?" she asked.

"It's called the 'Night of Salt.' It's the first rite of passage that every future Master has to go through. It means that your body has fully accepted Sinanju."

"I can't stand it! When will it stop?"

"It'll stop in a day or so. Until then, you need to stay put. There are other…symptoms."

"Like what?"

"It's the last vestiges of your pre-Sinanju self being expelled from your system. It will make you doubt yourself. I was sixteen when it happened to me, too, and, well, I'm still embarrassed," he said, lowering his head.

"What did you do?" Freya asked.

"Let's just say that the bottom of the Founder Stone used to point to the sky."

"You rolled the Founders Stone?" she asked in disbelief as she thought about the large boulder that sat at the front of their training hut. It weighed several tons.

"I said it was embarrassing."

"Why didn't you just roll it back?"

"Pop wouldn't let me. Said that I needed a lesson in humility."

"Are you're saying that I'm going to do something crazy?"

"Maybe not crazy, but you need to be careful. Just make sure that you don't do anything to hurt someone close to you."

"What can I do to get this taste out of my mouth?"

"Not much you can do. It lasts a day or so, but from this day forward, you'll have to stick to a strict Sinanju diet. Your body will now refuse to process some of the food you've been sneaking when I haven't been looking."

"Sorry, Grandfather," Freya said, blushing. She thought that Sunny Joe had not noticed the occasional bite of chocolate. It was her favorite food since arriving at the reservation.

"Chocolate has all kind of nasty chemicals that dull your senses. I could smell it on your breath, but I knew this day was close, so I didn't say anything. If you eat chocolate after this, it'll put you in a coma, or worse."

"Why?"

"Your body has just become fine-tuned for Sinanju. You'll find that you're stronger now; faster. Everything your body does has just went up to eleven and that includes your stomach. From now on, it's gonna strain every nutrient from anything you eat. Processed stuff is too much for it to handle. Ask your dad what happened to him when he tried to eat a cheeseburger." Sunny Joe chuckled.

Freya continued trying to get the taste out of her mouth, but she laid her head on Sunny Joe's shoulder and tightly closed her eyes. She had gone to Sunny Joe because she knew that she could trust him.

She wondered if that trust extended to monsters.

CHAPTER FIVE

Chicago was the largest city 14 had ever seen, and every bit as barbarous as she expected. Like most American cities she had read about, waste was everywhere. The lights of a hundred empty office buildings reflected on the wet, dirty streets. People walked by, consuming greasy chunks of artificially-colored poison without thinking. 14 grimaced. They gave no thought to self-defense. Their manner of dress placed them at a clear tactical disadvantage.

14 arrived at the destination marked on her map, a condemned building at the end of a dimly-lit street. Following the instructions that she had been given, 14 pried up a loose floorboard in the building's decrepit foyer and found two small boxes. The first contained a dress and heels, a photograph, and further instructions. The second contained a different outfit, a VIP pass to a nightclub, and five crisp hundred-dollar bills. As she picked up the bright, stiff dress, a furtive smile crept across her face. This would be the first time she had ever been allowed to wear a dress. She remembered her weekly visits to the hospital, and how pretty all the outsider girls looked. Holding the dress up in admiration, she closed her eyes and smiled as her thoughts drifted to Lisa and the soft, threadbare doll that she had briefly cradled.

The squeak of a rat snapped 14 from her reverie. Stripping free of her gray jumpsuit, she donned the dress and immediately scowled. Though perfectly sized for her, the garment greatly restricted her range of motion, and the stiletto heels compressed her toes painfully. She sliced the dress to the top of her thighs to allow her legs free movement, and tottered awkwardly around the deserted building.

In frustration, 14 snapped the heels off the shoes and broke the soles with her hands until the shoes were level with the ground. Though she understood the need for disguise, battle-readiness came first. She wondered how women were able to walk, much less fight, in such impractical footwear.

14 picked up the photo of her target from inside the package and studied it closely. The girl had platinum-blonde hair with red streaks. She was a young girl with small eyes and widely-curved eyebrows. An obviously doctored, turned-up nose and a round chin from a lack of dietary discipline. A small dove tattoo wrapped around the right side of her neck.

14 committed all the details to memory and, following instructions, tore the photo and her assignment into tiny shreds. Irritated by her outfit's lack of pockets, 14 tucked the money

and the pass into the front of her dress, put the box back under the floorboards, and began walking to her destination, Club Stray.

As she walked, her stomach growled with hunger. Noting that she still had over an hour before she was due at her destination, 14 looked at the money she had been given. It was a curious, alien thing. She had been taught how currency worked, but felt skeptical that a piece of green paper could be exchanged for something of actual value.

14 looked at all the brightly-colored signs designed to entice people into restaurants. It was rare for any of them to show pictures of their food. Even though her studies had showed her places like this, she had never entered one and was curious to know what their food tasted like.

Not knowing a better way to choose, 14 walked into the restaurant with the most colorful signage. The place smelled like a mixture of sweat and fried fat. A figure of a queen wearing clown makeup greeted her upon entering. 14 stood quietly by the entrance. She wanted to observe the technique used to purchase food.

Two girls, standing on the other side of the counter, were taking orders from customers. Their costumes were similar to the Clown Queen. 14 watched one man approach the counter and stood closely behind him. He looked at the brightly-colored menu above and chose a specific item, asking them to add things to it. He called them 'condiments.'

She had no idea what a condiment was, nor did she know what it would do to her metabolism. But she knew meat. If the sign was correct, the patty was one hundred percent beef. After squeezing out the grease, she would need a pound of meat to handle her daily protein needs.

Timidly, she walked to the counter and waited for the girl behind the counter to notice her. The girl was smiling while talking to someone on her cell phone. 14 raised her hand and waved it in front of the girl's face.

"Rude!" the girl exclaimed. "I'll call you back. I got another one of *those* customers."

The girl took the gum out of her mouth and mindlessly tacked it beneath the counter, adding to the growing clump that blocked the drawer from opening. She looked at 14 with a fake smile. While 14 was not aware of the cultural upbringing, she recognized it as a challenge.

14 returned the same smile.

"Welcome to McBurger Queen," the girl said in a droning manner. "We'll make it how you want, but don't be ridiculous."

"I need four of your full-size meat patties and a large cup of water."

"You want just meat and bun?"

"No, I just need the meat patties and a cup of water."

"But what do you want on it?"

"Nothing. Just four of your one-hundred-percent meat patties," 14 repeated. She had not blinked once during the entire conversation and the girl behind the counter felt uncomfortable.

"I'm gonna have to ask my manager about that."

"But you said that you would make it the way I want," 14 protested.

"Yeah, I also said 'don't be ridiculous.' I told ya not to. But ya did."

14 watched silently as the girl walked toward the back. She approached a large, middle-aged man behind the grill and pointed back to 14. The man looked to the front, smiling and pushing up his thick glasses. He approached 14 with a condescending smile. His glasses had slipped down his nose again.

"You just want meat patties?" he asked. "May I ask why?"

"Everything here is covered in fat and grease," 14 replied honestly. "Hopefully, I will be able to squeeze most of the grease out of the patties."

"Ma'am, I assure you, we use only the finest ingredients," the manager protested.

"Meat patties," 14 repeated sternly. "I want four of them. And a large cup of water."

The manager felt 14's glare, followed by something much sharper pricking the center of his chest. He slowly glanced down and saw a thin blade pointed directly at his heart. 14 was holding his tie with her other hand. He tried to move back, but she pulled on his tie and he felt the tip of the blade on his skin.

"I need four patties!" he yelled to the back. "Right now!"

14 looked at the counter girl and smiled, but there was no hint of friendliness in the gesture. The girl's eyes shot wide open and she ran to the back screaming, leaving her manager to his fate. A few moments later, the cook slowly set the bag of meat patties and a cup of water on the counter and ran back to the grill.

14 handed the manager one of the hundred dollar bills she was given.

"They're on the house," the manager said nervously.

"On the house?" she asked, pushing a bit harder on the knife. She had no time for trickery.

"They're free! No charge…all yours," the manager sputtered.

14 grabbed the bag of patties and water and bolted out the door, passing the policeman standing outside. The Mayor had promised to enforce city ordinances

mandating the maximum size of soft drinks. This particular establishment had been caught trying to sell sixteen-ounce drinks several times in the past month, mandating a full-time officer.

"Stop her!" the cook shouted, pointing at 14.

The policeman stood and looked around.

"What size was her drink?" the policeman asked.

"I don't know! She attacked Ted with a knife!"

The policeman leaned back against the wall.

"Not my jurisdiction."

14 ran several blocks before she stopped to eat. Even after squeezing as much fat out of the patties as she could, the thick taste of grease penetrated the meat. She quickly took a sip of water. If the food had been half as good as the water, she actually could have enjoyed the meal.

CHAPTER SIX

Benjamin Cole sat in the back of the nearly-empty 737, trying to remain inconspicuous. He wore jeans and a sweater emblazoned with a metallic red dragon. When people noticed large or bright objects, they tended to forget surrounding details. Someone might remember Ben's sweater, but they would forget his face. His sunglasses were bland, but very dark, and he had booked the adjacent seats so that no one could sit near him.

Though he leaned his head next to the window, Ben was not remotely tired. He knew that he was traveling to his death. He tried thinking of every possible outcome, but it kept coming back to the same conclusion: Benjamin Maugaine Cole was going to be executed by his boss, Harold W. Smith.

Ben shifted in his seat as the events of the past few weeks ran through his mind. He had been appointed director of a small, clandestine agency whose mission was to protect the United States from terrorists. Ben had been chosen due to his extensive past work with Mossad, Israel's famed intelligence agency. He had also been chosen because he knew the value of not asking too many questions. Though Ben knew he worked for the United States government, he was never given more information than that, nor did he ask.

Ben had expected to command a small squad of highly-trained intelligence operatives and weapons specialists. He had been dismayed to find that his "elite team" would consist of only two people: an ex-Navy SEAL named Stone Smith and himself. At first, he didn't think it would be enough. It was simple math: *one* unarmed man — no matter how well-trained — was likely to die when faced with *many* armed men. But the more he learned about the mystic martial art of Sinanju, the more he began to believe in the young man.

He was extremely impressed when Stone dodged bullets fired at point-blank range, but he was awed and somewhat embarrassed when Stone's sister, Freya, had somehow sneaked into his top-secret base, demanding to work alongside her brother as a field agent. Freya was not even old enough to get a learner's permit, but she had bypassed one of the most advanced security systems in the world, and had avoided setting off any of the base's countless weapon systems designed to neutralize any would-be intruders. Ben began to hope that with Stone and Freya, his small team might actually be able to succeed.

A small Mexican army had been raised in order to transport a small box safely across the border. With the advent of nanotechnology, Ben knew that an atomic bomb far more devastating than the one dropped on Hiroshima could be made smaller than a toaster. A container of weaponized anthrax, smaller than a shoebox, would be enough to eradicate half the population of New York City.

Stone and Freya had defeated the small army, and eliminated its leader, but Ben had still failed: he had been unable to intercept the box. He should have known better. The army had been a diversion. The box had probably left Mexico before Stone and Freya had even arrived. He had risked Stone and Freya's lives for nothing.

But a weapon, no matter how lethal, could still be stopped if it had not yet been deployed. What could not be stopped was the intelligence Ben had accidentally leaked.

When Ben accepted his position, he had been given a small tablet called a FORtab, more powerful than any computer he had ever seen. He was told that only two had been made: the one in his possession, and the one operated by his boss Smith. Ben had used the device to extensively research Tomás, the leader of the small Mexican army. Tomás did not have enough resources, nor was he smart enough, to pose a dire threat. Ben knew that the Mexican jefe was just a small part of a larger plan, and that he must have been following orders from a superior. But who was it?

Ben did not have to wonder for long, because the mastermind, Helmut Belisis, contacted him personally. Not only did he also have a FORtab, he seemed to know more about Ben's job than Ben himself. Helmut said that Ben unknowingly worked for an agency named CURE, and revealed that his boss was Dr. Harold W. Smith.

On paper, Smith was listed as the director of Folcroft Sanitarium in Rye, New York, but he had actually been director of CURE for decades. CURE's mission was simple: eliminate criminals who could not be brought to justice using the conventional legal system. Because CURE was often responsible for assassinating hostile dictators from other nations, the government could not officially acknowledge its existence, or the international community would turn its backs — and soon, its missiles — on the United States.

Ben did not know why Helmut had told him this until after the call ended, when he discovered that Helmut had stolen vast amounts of data from Ben's FORtab during their conversation. Helmut did not know Freya or Stone's names, but he had pictures of them, and knew that they were being trained in Sinanju. Though Ben had eventually managed to erase the information from Helmut's device, taking some of Helmut's confidential files in the process, he knew he could never erase the information from Helmut's mind.

Ben had learned from their conversation that Helmut was the director of a group named VIGIL, equal to CURE in its secrecy. VIGIL had been founded in the sixth century by a monk whose goal was the preservation of mankind. That had been VIGIL's sacred duty for the past fifteen centuries, but Helmut had warped and distorted that goal. He was determined to eradicate Sinanju, and had almost killed Stone and Freya while they were in Mexico.

Helmut's vendetta against Sinanju began when he discovered that the mythical martial art was being used to defend the United States. Ben knew that Helmut's eventual goal was world domination, and as the only nation able to pose a substantial threat to his plan, the United States, would have to be destroyed in the process. Ben did not know how, or when, this would happen, but he knew with an absolute certainty, that he had failed his mission. Not only had he failed to prevent the box from entering the United States, he had inadvertently leaked confidential information. And thanks to Helmut, he knew too much about Smith and CURE, and posed a grave security risk.

And for that, he knew that he would be killed.

Ben had played out in his mind how it would probably happen. The location that Smith had chosen was in a rundown part of town, a block full of vacant warehouses and factories. No one would hear a couple of gunshots. He would meet Smith, would be debriefed on what he knew, and then Smith would do something to distract him. He would probably tell Ben that he would not be killed, in order to get Ben to let down his guard. Then Smith would shoot him. It would be a clean chest shot with a final tap to the head. Messy, but relatively quick and painless.

Ben knew that his organization held great promise, and truly believed in his cause. He just wished he could live to fulfill his mission.

Ben headed out of the airport with his small bag of clothes and the fake identification that identified him as Benjamin Wheat. After he died, he did not want to leave anything that might link him to CURE.

Ben had left the FORtab at his office, and even though he had just obtained the device, felt naked without it. Designed and built by a mysterious organization known as FORTEC, the thin, oblong tablet was the most powerful computer Ben had ever seen.

Moore's Law was the measuring stick used for every computer on Earth. Since the sixties, it had successfully dictated that computers doubled in power every eighteen months. But the FORtab did not just break Moore's Law — it shattered it.

The tablets were so advanced that Ben had actually begun to wonder if they were a product of alien technology. No matter how hard he searched, he could not find any information on their manufacturer. When powered off, the screen's texture actually changed from its normal glassy display into a roughly-grained plating. He did not know its storage capacity, but it had already downloaded every law enforcement database in the country with ease.

Yes, if he were to remain alive, the FORtab would have been invaluable in his job.

Ben allowed himself a moment to think of what he could have accomplished had he been allowed to live. Accepting his fate, he squashed the thought. He was glad that he had recorded a video to be played back after his death, thanking Dr. Smith for a quick death and the opportunity to serve.

Ben arrived at the site a few minutes early. He did not like being late to anything, even his own death. He looked around for any external activity and, seeing none, entered. Triggered by opening the door, Ben's cell phone showed a change of location. Smith sent new directions, directing Ben two blocks away. Smart, Ben thought, realizing that Smith had just dramatically reduced the possibility of a double-cross.

It only took a few minutes for Ben to reach the new destination, an abandoned church. It looked as if it had been boarded up for several years, but it had been kept clean.

Ben felt a faint glimmer of hope. Maybe Smith would not kill him in a Christian church. It was just as likely, however, that Smith was using the building to lull him into a false sense of security. No one expected to be shot in a church, even a deserted one.

Ben opened the door. As he entered the long blackness of the vestibule, he heard the hammer of a pistol being pulled back. He closed his eyes, said a quick prayer, and waited for the shot.

CHAPTER SEVEN

Helmut Belisis looked at his FORtab. Before his access to Ben Cole's FORtab was cut, Helmut was able to access many of his files. He had photos of Ben's two agents, and knew that they were a brother/sister team. The most important fact he had learned had come as a shock to him: both were being trained in the mystical art of Sinanju.

Helmut knew first-hand the powers of Sinanju.

When he was first nominated for the position of VIGIL's director, two Watchers protested: both of the watchers from Africa. The nomination process took several months and Helmut's predecessor, Lars Papadakis, was dying. He confided in Helmut that if he died before the nomination process was completed, the African Watchers would have enough influence over the other members to prevent him from becoming director.

Helmut had asked how he could stop them without causing a revolt among the other members. With a soft smile, Lars patted him on the hand and said "Sinanju."

"I highly doubt an imaginary martial art will help us," Helmut had said with a scoff.

Within a week, Africa Senior and Junior were both dead at the hands of the Master of Sinanju and Helmut was approved as VIGIL director before their replacements could be found. Lars died a few weeks later.

As director, Helmut had access to files that were off-limits even to VIGIL members. He was able to access sealed records of the Masters of Sinanju: where they worked with VIGIL's plans and where they had not. When the First World War spun out of control, VIGIL knew that they had to take Sinanju out of the equation if they were to control the situation. Though they could not kill a Master of Sinanju, they could isolate them by removing the knowledge of their existence.

Over the next decade, VIGIL conducted a worldwide mission to destroy all records relating to Sinanju. The few who passed on the legends of Sinanju were scoffed at. It was the twentieth century: a time of technology, the scoffers would say, time to leave behind stories of magic and wizards and Masters of Sinanju. Fewer people considered Sinanju a part of history and, after one small job near the end of World War II, Sinanju became silent on the world stage.

Helmut saw that the modern record of Sinanju began toward the end of the twentieth century, and that file was extensive. Sinanju had been hired by the organization VIGIL created to stabilize America: CURE. Then he realized what his predecessor had done. Lars had assigned both Africa Senior and Africa Junior to a critical mission involving the transportation of biological weapons, while secretly alerting CURE.

Helmut admired the old man's cunning. He knew that CURE would send the Master of Sinanju, thus disposing of both Watchers from Africa and ensuring that Helmut was voted in as the new director of VIGIL.

But Sinanju once again stood in VIGIL's way. America had grown too strong, too stable. It was harder to seize power from a strong, well-defended nation than a chaotic, crumbling one, so Helmut realized that he had to eliminate Sinanju. If America would fall, so be it.

The Council may have thought they had frustrated Helmut's plans by playing one of VIGIL's Doomsday cards and initiating the Carnage Program, but Helmut would deploy the Premium to his own ends. Her actions in Chicago would force Ben Cole to act. Ben would send his Sinanju agents to terminate the Premium. But their lethal powers would be useless against what he was planning. Their demise would be in a place that had no bullets to dodge, or soldiers to easily defeat in battle.

Helmut's FORtab had made it easy for him to locate the nuclear missile stockpiles located within the United States. Four installations had been abandoned since the Cold War, but still had live nuclear weapons. They were deserted and the men who built and staffed them had long since retired. Despite their nuclear contents, they had been classed as "low risk" by the military.

Their electronic security systems were easily bypassed by Helmut's FORtab. With a few clicks, the St. Louis nuclear arsenal was completely under his control. Though the bombs were not attached to rockets and buried under twenty feet of concrete, they could still be remotely triggered. No one, Sinanju or otherwise, could survive the blast of a nuclear bomb. The Sinanju-trained agents would be incinerated.

No one would know what had happened until it was too late.

Helmut would send 14 there and leak small bits of data to Cole's FORtab. Cole would send his agents there, but they would not return. They would be dust.

The explosion would cause widespread international panic. CURE would be disbanded for its blatant failure to protect the country. The Eastern United States would be contaminated with radiation fallout, and what little was left would be destroyed by its terrified, angry population. With its people sick and its economy in ruins, the United States would collapse, followed quickly by the world economy. Helmut would use the time of crisis to seize power, and the world would be his.

It was a good day to be Helmut Belisis.

CHAPTER EIGHT

Harold W. Smith had only risked making a face-to-face appearance with his new agent to find out what he knew. After his FORtab alerted him that Agent Cole had arrived at the original meeting site, Smith ordered a change of destination.

Smith knew that Cole assumed he was going to be killed, and briefly wondered if Cole would try to attack him. Smith did not believe that he would. Benjamin Cole was in that rare one percent of the population who truly believed in their cause, and Cole's psychological profile suggested he would not attack. Smith contemplated this while checking the bullets in his gun. He knew that being prepared was better than being hopeful.

The question that remained was whether or not Smith should kill him. For decades, anyone who had found out about CURE received an automatic death sentence. Anyone and everyone who had found out about the country's greatest secret forfeited their lives.

Because CURE was an admission of failure.

It was not that the Constitution was not strong enough. Two centuries earlier, the Founding Fathers had crafted a nearly-perfect document when building the foundation for their country's future. But the people defending it were not strong enough. Over time, people had placed their own personal opinions over the original intent of the founders. By doing so, they allowed their feelings to warp centuries of jurisprudence, mutating the Supreme Court into a sick parody of its original lofty purpose.

CURE was the balance. CURE would find those people who had escaped the weakened federal system and bring them to justice. But they were not taken to the plush, air-conditioned legal system of the twenty-first century. Crimes that were important enough to come across CURE's radar were worthy of only one sentence: death. There was no twenty-year string of appeals between the guilty and their fate. There was only Harold W. Smith.

A high school graduate at sixteen, Smith had joined the Army immediately after graduation — not out of obligation, but of a genuine love of country. His company commander had noticed that the young man was extremely bright, so, fresh out of boot camp, he was removed from the other privates who were sent to infantry and tank school. Smith was assigned to work in military intelligence.

Harold W. Smith became part of the first generation of superspies, a secret weapon deployed whenever the government needed results. And Smith always provided results. His analytical mind tore through problems that normal men struggled with, even when they used computers. So, when the President of the United States asked him if he would serve his country in a new capacity, Smith said yes.

But that was a long time ago, when he had been a younger man.

Over the next several decades, CURE had held the United States together, with Smith at the helm. Mark Howard had become his assistant a decade ago. Though Smith had no immediate plans on handing over control of CURE, Mark Howard had always been there as a contingency in case of Smith's incapacitation or death. When he disappeared in Afghanistan, it left the full weight of CURE on Smith's shoulders once again.

Smith tried to start over by trying a remote assistant, but that turned into a different type of mission. When he searched again, he was frustrated to see that only three names matched his criteria. At the top of that short list was a man who had not even been born in the United States. Benjamin Cole had been an ex-Mossad agent who had run into trouble with his government. Highly intelligent and disciplined, he had been one of Israel's top sleeper cell agents. But when his wife was murdered because of a loophole in Egyptian law, Cole wiped out the men who killed his wife, becoming a man without a country.

Not knowing where to go, Cole contacted a local CIA agent he had worked with in the past. He found Ben, injured and close to death. He treated Ben's wounds, and they hid out while Ben slowly recovered. After two weeks, Ben was healthy enough to be smuggled onto a ship heading for the United States. CURE had a long and bloody list of those who believed America was worth a life.

CHAPTER NINE

Ben opened the front door. As he entered the church, he heard Smith cock the hammer. Ben closed his eyes and froze. To his left, Smith held a well-used .45 caliber pistol.

"Agent Cole," Smith said solemnly.

Ben could tell by the voice that the man holding the pistol was old, but the barrel was steady. One pull of the trigger and Ben would become just another statistic. Maybe, if he were lucky, his body would be found in a couple of months and given a proper burial.

"I am Smith," the man in the gray suit said, introducing himself. "Are you armed?"

Ben slowly removed his sweater.

"No, sir," Ben replied.

"This way," Smith said, motioning for Ben to move to the sanctuary.

Ben walked ahead, keenly aware of the pistol trained on him. Smith was smart to keep him a few feet in front. Most people would stick a gun in the center of the back, which placed the gun too close to the target.

"Do you go to church, Smith?" Ben asked.

"Yes. Sit in the front pew," Smith ordered.

Ben moved to the small bench at the front of the sanctuary and sat down. The pew had been heavily worn before the church was closed down. The specific spot he chose had lost any pretense of wood finish long ago. Ben wondered if the person who had last sat there had known it was the last time they would see their church. And if they did, would they have done anything differently?

Smith sat down directly behind him.

"The church is where I first learned about sacrifice," Smith said. "And the concepts of good and evil."

"You're ahead of most of the human race," Ben said. "I don't think they believe that evil exists anymore."

"Why do you think you can make a difference?" Smith asked abruptly.

This is it, Ben thought, bracing himself for the shot. But it did not come.

He took a breath and looked around. Holy images adorned the walls, the ceiling, even the few pieces of stained glass that remained. Though Ben was Jewish, he felt a connection — a single thread that led from his pew, back to the carpenter who inspired the pew, to the man who delivered his people from Egypt, all the way back to the garden that first connected mankind.

"I believe that people should be able to live their lives without fear. I believe that people should be allowed to chase their dreams, no matter how stupid they appear to others. I believe in God. Country. Family. Love. I believe that we must protect them by any means necessary. And I believe that takes men like you and me."

Ben leaned back in the pew and exhaled. He was ready for his fate. Smith did not respond for almost a minute. And when he did, Ben could have sworn that he almost heard a crack in the older man's voice.

"There was a time when men like us were a staple of American society. Yet, out of four thousand potential candidates, only three people match the proper psychological profile. That is as dangerous as any direct threat to America."

"If America has a soul, we're losing it," Ben said.

"That may very well be true," Smith replied, his gun still aimed at Ben. "It is regrettable that you leaked information, even if you did so accidentally. You have endangered national security. Furthermore, you were told to keep America's borders safe. The package was allowed to be delivered across the border despite the guidance you were given. You failed."

Ben slowly turned around and looked Smith in the eye. If Smith was about to fire, Ben wanted to see it coming.

"I know, sir. But I will do better. I will not let America die," Ben said.

Smith looked icily at Ben. Finally, after what felt like ages, he holstered his pistol. "I do not give second chances frequently, Mr. Cole, and I will never give a third. You are alive now because your mission is too important to abandon. You must protect our borders."

"I can't fully guarantee our borders, sir, but I promise to try. It doesn't hurt that we have alien technology and a couple of kids who can dodge bullets."

"I have never found humor to fit in our line of work, but I have learned to accommodate it. This is a life-long mission, Agent Cole. There is no retirement from this agency."

"I signed up for life when I entered United States soil," Ben said. "But what about Stone and Freya? Are they in it for life too?"

"No. This agency will not provoke a Master of Sinanju by treating them as employees," Smith said. "They are independent, at-will contractors and will be treated as such."

"Yeah. Stone said that Sunny Joe had asked when they were going to sign a contract."

Smith groaned. He had many years of experience negotiating contracts with the House of Sinanju, and always came out on the losing side. He expected that dealing with the Tribe would result in a similar outcome. "Be careful whenever you speak with Sinanju about money."

"Stone said they only accept payment in gold?"

"Traditionally, gold is their base salary; it is issued as a payment to the tribe. Anything else is considered a tip to the Master who is working for you. Given the powers of Sinanju, it is, shall we say, customary, to tip."

"But Stone and Freya aren't yet Masters."

"Then perhaps you will not bankrupt us," Smith said. "Send me a copy of the proposed contract and I will help you negotiate terms. When it is time, I will make arrangements to have the gold shipped."

Smith reached for something in his pocket and handed Ben a small pillbox.

"This is for you," Smith said.

Ben opened the lid. Inside was a small coffin-shaped pill. A single glance between both men provided an unspoken understanding of its purpose. Ben started to reach for the pill, but Smith protested.

"Do not touch it. The surface is toxic if held for more than a few seconds," Smith explained.

"Booby-trapped pills," Ben mused.

"Return to your bunker," Smith said, turning to leave. "We have a great deal of work ahead of us."

CHAPTER TEN

His name was Miguel Espinoza III. His family, a long and distinguished line of military officers and statesmen, had been powerful in Spain since the days of the conquistadors, when Alvarado Espinoza had slain an entire village and plundered its gold. Since then, the Espinoza family had been given the nickname 'Los Amantes de la Muerte' — 'The Death Lovers.' They were known as much for their cruelty and ruthlessness as their vast wealth.

But even Miguel's family could not stop his mother from being taken to Germany immediately before his birth. A power far greater than the Espinozas had chosen him for a great honor: he would be VIGIL's next European delegate. When the former Europe Senior suddenly died of a stroke, Europe Junior assumed the rank of Senior, and Miguel became Europe Junior. Though he was two months shy of graduating college, VIGIL seated him on the condition that he would complete his studies.

His first month in VIGIL was hectic and heady. His collegiate courses were effortless compared to the information he was required to learn. Per VIGIL regulations, all records of Miguel Espinoza III were erased as if he had never existed. The only name that mattered any more was what he was called in VIGIL: Europe Junior.

He immediately noticed a powerful sense of tension between some members of the VIGIL council and their director, Helmut Belisis. When he was assigned his first mission, Africa Senior convinced Europe Senior to let her guide the new Watcher. During their many private meetings, she warned him about the danger Helmut posed and said that he was not to be trusted.

Africa Senior was the council's oldest member, and widely respected by her peers in VIGIL. Even though his senior partner technically held sway over him, Europe Junior always listened to Africa Senior's opinions. He knew the value of a powerful ally.

"VIGIL's goal," she said, "has always been to ensure the survival of mankind. For nearly two thousand years, we have done this by keeping countries from becoming too powerful. This has usually been accomplished by wars, which keep any one empire from getting too large. But since the nuclear age, wars have become more and more dangerous. Now, with the push of a button, anyone with access to nuclear weapons can destroy the entire world. This is why the United States must be weakened. It has more nuclear weapons than any other nation, while at the same time, it continues to make shortsighted political decisions that are designed to enrage other countries."

"I understand our directive," Europe Junior said. "But why do you despise the Director? He himself has admitted that the United States is too powerful, and everyone in VIGIL agrees. Even now, you are defending his ideas. Why should I — why should we — not trust him?"

"Helmut is using 'protecting mankind' as an excuse," said Africa Senior. "He claims that he is fearful that the United States has become too powerful. This is true. But his plan is to destroy the United States, and to use the chaos that follows to take power. His goal is not a more balanced world, and certainly not a peaceful world. His goal is world domination. Watch him carefully, young man. His desire for power is dangerous."

CHAPTER ELEVEN

14 arrived at Club Stray in immense pain. Her stomach felt as if she had swallowed a bottle of lye. As she looked at the crowd gathered around the club, she tried not to vomit.

An unmoving line of people waiting to get inside snaked around the side of the building. Girls in skimpy dresses shivered in the night air, huddling next to their friends in a vain effort to stay warm. Although she had been told that her target would already be inside, 14 looked at the people waiting in line. Her lips curled derisively. No one posed a threat to her.

14 walked around the crowd to the guarded VIP entrance, the people in line whispered and stared. With her tightly-cropped blonde hair and large sunglasses, many thought she was a celebrity, even though she had not arrived with an entourage.

14 presented her pass to the heavily-tattooed man standing at the door, peering past his huge form into the blackness of the club. He slowly looked over 14, his eyes pausing on her cracked, heel-less shoes. He did not know that she had already sized him up. He had a small pistol tucked under his arm, 14 noticed, but she had already mapped three ways to kill the man if her credentials were questioned. He would be dead before he could reach his gun.

The man forced a smile as he returned her VIP card and unchained the velvet rope, allowing her in. She could hear the loud thump of the music from outside, and knew that the people inside would never hear her until it was too late. If she thought the music had been loud from the outside, inside the club was deafening. The interior was dark, with the exception of flashing lights on the dance floor, and soft lights above the tables to the sides.

14 slid her hands over the blades hidden discreetly under her dress. They were short, but sharp enough to cut through bone. She sauntered through the club almost invisibly, just another brightly-dressed girl in a sea of people trying to find meaning and purpose in a roaring beat. Ignoring the drunk men who tried to make eye contact, she walked toward one of the side booths that stood slightly above the crowd and spotted her target.

Daphne Steinem giggled as the cork burst out of her fifth bottle of Dom Perignon. As the cork sailed somewhere into the darkness of the club, half of the bottle foamed onto the ground. She continued to giggle as she stumbled around her private table.

Abandoning her brief search for a glass, Daphne put the bottle to her lips and took a long swig. More foam leaked from the corners of her mouth, followed by a long, roaring belch. Though aware — and annoyed — that the blaring music had drowned out her stentorian emission, she nevertheless took a deep bow, unknowingly mooning half of Club Stray in the process. "Excu-u-u-u-se me!" she squealed. Overwhelmed by her own soaring wit and charm, her giggle erupted into maniacal laughter, punctuated by loud snorts and wheezing.

Daphne's father, Senator Jesse Steinem, Jr., was one of Washington's most powerful figures. In Washington, money always followed power. Supporters funneled money, officially and unofficially, through his office. It happened almost overnight. The day after her father was elected, she was given keys to a swanky penthouse apartment in one of Chicago's most upscale and chic neighborhoods. A small attached note told her which of her father's supporters had bought it for her.

She did not bother to read the note.

Daphne did not care about politics. She could not even say which party her father belonged to, though her father tried to tell her several times. It did not matter to her, though, because Daphne Steinem had never voted in her life.

Daphne had once entertained the notion of college. When she was a little girl, she had wanted to be a nurse. Then her father got into politics and became rich. Since then, she had lived the life of a party girl. Tonight was no exception. Earlier in the day, she had dumped her boyfriend of the week and was on the prowl for the next one. Daphne had paid the lighting guy to highlight her every few minutes. This was her night to shine, and the world was hers.

When the blonde woman with the wicked smile showed up in front of her, Daphne ignored her. She would have a talk with security later about who they let approach her table. When the woman came up and gave her a hug, Daphne screamed.

Rather, she tried to scream. The hug concealed the two blades the woman carried, which pounded into Daphne's chest with the subtlety of baseball bats. Seeing her blood pour out onto her dress, Daphne looked angry. The woman stepped back and watched Daphne fall lifelessly to the floor.

"Not my favorite dress!" was Daphne's last thought.

To those around her, it seemed that Daphne had just fallen down. Her friends thought nothing of it. Daphne was known to take drunken spills from time to time. But when they saw the growing pool of blood surrounding her, they began screaming too, drowned out by the thump-thump-thump of the blaring music.

14 went to work.

Moving from one person to the next in the cordoned-off VIP section, she extended her blades squarely through their backs, leaving a bloody mass of falling bodies, as if they were all dominoes and someone had just pushed the first person down.

The music stopped and a panicked roar filled the dance floor. People bolted for the doors. Club security was unable to stop the stampede.

The woman in the flowing, bloody dress paused to write something on the wall. In blood, she drew a symbol: a trapezoid bisected by a slash.

14 paused for a moment, admiring her handiwork, then walked outside into the cold Chicago air.

CHAPTER TWELVE

Europe Junior had been called into Helmut's office to receive his orders. Entering the room, he was motioned to sit in the chair placed before Helmut's large walnut desk. The man behind the desk was in his sixties, but only his graying beard betrayed his age. Otherwise, Helmut Belisis was as healthy a sixty-year-old as he had ever seen. His eyes had a youthful intensity to them and his smile was eminently politic and professional.

"Are you familiar with the pair of agents you will encounter?" Helmut asked.

"I am familiar with the Premium we have developed," Europe Junior said. "Her training and biological augmentations place her outside the threat of 'agents.'"

"For most, that would be a fair assessment. These two, however, are unique. They are students of Sinanju."

Europe Junior tried not to laugh. "Director, are you trying to tell me that you believe in the legends of Sinanju?"

"Every Watcher acolyte learns about the Masters of Sinanju," Helmut said.

"As a part of ancient history, yes, but those accounts are about as historically reliable as Hercules' twelve feats."

"Which were based on the feats of a Master of Sinanju," Helmut noted.

"Director, even if I were to believe this nonsense, we live in the twenty-first century. We have guns and electronic systems."

"None of which posed a threat to a teenage girl who has just begun training in Sinanju," Helmut said, interrupting.

He tapped his finger on the top of his desk, signaling his FORtab. The lights to the room darkened and video of a hallway showed on Helmut's wall.

"What am I supposed to be seeing?" Europe Junior asked after a few seconds. "I can barely see anything."

"Keep watching."

The hallway scene shrunk and moved to the upper right as a picture-in-picture. The main view now showed inside the office at the end of the hall. A young man brandished a pistol from behind his desk, aiming it at the door. Europe Junior noticed how nervous the man seemed to be. Even on the grainy film, he could tell that the man's hands were shaking, and he wiped his forehead with his shirtsleeve every few seconds.

Then the steel door exploded inward, and Europe Junior saw the girl with the black, dead eyes.

She had not been there a second before. She faded into view like a ghost. Thin, with long, blonde hair, her eyes seemed to absorb the light around her. She did not move when the young man fired his pistol at her from point-blank range.

The plaster of the wall behind her exploded in small puffs of smoke, as if the nervous man were trying to outline her with bullets. Not one bullet hit its mark.

Another man came in behind her. He shouted at her, but she ignored him. He swung his leg toward her in a wide, arcing kick, but she was no longer standing next to him. The man's kick did not connect with its target and Europe Junior could see the man howl in pain as he collapsed to the floor. The girl grabbed the man who had the gun with both hands.

Then Europe Junior saw something that would haunt him for the rest of his life. The girl lifted the man above her head, and, with no more effort than she would have used on a piece of paper, ripped him in half. She smashed the bloody halves to the ground, cracking the heavy concrete, and roared heavenward before collapsing into a crumpled heap on the floor in a dead faint.

The young man with the injured leg hobbled over to the unconscious girl. With what must have been monumental effort, he slung her over his shoulder and carried her out. Despite his obvious injury, there was something elegant and beautiful in the way he moved. While the girl had exuded power and terror, the man's movement represented absolute control.

"That was real?" Europe Junior asked, fighting pangs of nausea.

"Yes. These are the two agents 14 will face."

"But…how? If they are as lethal as they appear, how can she defeat them?"

"The Premium is only there to force them from the shadows," Helmut said. "For some time now, we have required a small favor from Senator Steinem of Illinois. Regrettably, he has ignored our attempts to communicate with him. The Premium's actions will remind him that no one ignores VIGIL. She has already completed her mission, and left this mark behind," Helmut said, handing Europe Junior an image of a trapezoid with a slash running through it.

"This is the symbol for Sinanju. Are you trying to goad them?" Europe Junior asked. "Director, after what you just showed me, provoking them seems very risky."

"VIGIL has tolerated the existence of Sinanju long enough. America must be weakened. By defending the United States, Sinanju has made that task almost impossible. This is why the Premium was deployed. Her actions in Chicago will force the Sinanju agents to follow her. You will talk to the Senator, and she will lead the agents to an abandoned warehouse in St. Louis, where they will be eliminated."

Helmut handed Europe Junior two syringes. They smelled strongly of a pungent spice. Europe Junior's nose crinkled.

"What are these for?"

"It is an ancient Siamese formula that VIGIL has modified into a weapons-grade chemical. Handle it very carefully. You will give these shots to the Premium, twenty-four hours apart. They will greatly augment her strength and speed and with luck, will give her an edge over the Sinanju agents."

Europe Junior took the syringes and looked at them. They contained a liquid that was the pasty white of old glue. He placed them in his briefcase.

"If your plan succeeds, Director, what will be done with the Premium?"

"It is expendable. The second dose is a concentrated dose…lethal, but while it is active in her system, she will be the deadliest human alive. Her goal will be to kill both agents, after which, she will die."

"Director, is there no one else you can send? This is a very dangerous mission. What if she kills me first?"

"That is a risk I am more than willing to take," Helmut said slowly, a cruel smile stretching across his face. "You see, Europe, I am well aware of how Africa Senior feels about me, and I know that she is attempting to turn you against me as well. So, I offer you a choice. I plan to send information to Ben Cole's agency. Should you refuse your orders, the information will appear to come from your computer, and you will be executed immediately for committing treason against VIGIL."

"And if I go?" Europe Junior's voice trembled, for he already knew the answer.

"Then they will appear to come from the computer of Madame Africa," Helmut replied. "It is your choice, Europe. Ask yourself which is more important: your friendship, or your life?"

After what felt like an eternity, Europe Junior looked up at Helmut. "I will do my duty."

"You have made a wise choice, Europe. You leave tonight. You will find your bags have already been packed. Welcome to VIGIL.

Europe Junior shuddered as he walked out of Helmut's office, knowing that he had condemned his best friend and closest ally to death.

CHAPTER THIRTEEN

After burning her blood-soaked dress from the nightclub, 14 changed into one of the new outfits she had been provided. It looked more suited to a typical teenager than a trained killer. The T-shirt and jeans were restrictive — though better than the dress, she noticed with relief — but she genuinely liked the shoes. The hot-pink Vans were flexible, and even more comfortable than her training shoes. Though she had lied to everyone at the facility, saying that her favorite color was black, she had secretly loved the color pink ever since she first met Lisa.

The wail of sirens and the distant flash of red and blue lights constantly intruded upon her attempts to rest. She was not afraid of the police; she knew that she could easily eliminate anyone who might try to arrest her. Her mind was restless with confusion.

14 had obeyed her commands, but they had violated every principle of secrecy she had been taught. Every time she closed her eyes, she could imagine the faces of the others who had died at her hands. They were weak and soft people, certainly, but they had done nothing wrong. 14 took pride in executing her mission swiftly and efficiently, but she could not shake the nagging feeling that she had done something bad. Even in this city of waste and squalor, the nameless dead had lived for something more than training and missions and duty. But for her, there was nothing more. The mission was everything.

Shaking the negative thoughts from her head, 14 thought of her next task. She was to travel south, to a city named Alton. There, she would meet a member of the VIGIL council to receive her next assignment.

She traveled quickly, hitching rides with truckers unknowingly as they stopped to fuel up. She waited at gas stations, watching for any vehicle with an open back that was traveling south. When a truck pulled in, she climbed into the back, finding a spot she could safely squeeze into.

Once she reached the city limits of Alton, she struck out on foot. The endless noise of Chicago was gone. The air was still and peaceful. After climbing in the window of an abandoned building, she quickly fell asleep.

CHAPTER FOURTEEN

Freya stood alone in the old shack that doubled as their training hut. Sunny Joe and Mick had already left for the Great Southwestern Tribal Meet, and Stone was packing for their flight to Ben's headquarters. He would not pick her up for another half hour. Freya's bags were already packed. At the front of the hut was the Founder Stone, always standing behind Sunny Joe as a symbol of the masters who had come before him. As she paced, her eyes never left the stone.

She could not sleep the night before. In the few moments when she was not gagging from the taste of salt, she was overwhelmed with feelings of inadequacy. Although she realized that her feelings were the result of the Night of Salt, she had been blinking back tears all day. All the self-doubt she felt since she arrived at the reservation had surfaced.

When she had first begun training with Sunny Joe, rumors and gossip traveled quickly through the reservation. Men and women would stop talking in her presence, and it didn't take Sinanju perception skills to feel their eyes as they judged her.

It was worse in school. Though she would never give them the satisfaction of knowing it, Freya had heard the kids making fun of her, and it stung. The boys avoided her, and the girls teased her. She knew that her classmates called her 'Freddy,' a boy's name, for training with her grandfather. Girls were not meant to be trained, they said. The tribal council even held meetings to protest her presence on the reservation. Sunny Joe defended her and the council relented, but it was clear to everyone that she was not wanted and would never fit in.

Freya was the pale girl.

The odd one.

The outsider.

She wanted to prove to the entire tribe that a female could be a Master of Sinanju. She would do that by proving that she was as good as Sunny Joe had been at sixteen. When saw the Founder Stone, she knew what to do. She would duplicate Sunny Joe's feat, and correct a mistake he had made at the same time. Then they would all know that she *was* worthy!

It felt odd to actually touch the stone. Sunny Joe had always described it in reverent tones; it was the Sinanju tribe's Plymouth Rock.

Freya steadied herself, grasping it from the base and lifting skyward with all her might.

The stone did not budge. It had been embedded into the hardened desert clay for decades, and the ground refused her attempts. Moving around the stone to get a different grip on it, Freya tried again, but again, she failed.

Hesitantly, Freya thought back to Mexico. Whatever had happened to her there had given her superhuman strength, even by Sinanju standards. Perhaps she could learn to harness that strength. Even though she knew no one else was around, Freya glanced out the front door. No other building was within earshot. Feeling slightly embarrassed, Freya tried to remember what she had said when she had transformed in Mexico.

The words flowed easily from her mouth.

"I am created Shiva, the Destroyer! Death, the shatterer of worlds! The night tiger made whole by the Master of Sinanju!" she shouted, fearful but curious to see what would happen. She expected to feel the vast ocean of power rushing through her, like it had in Mexico when her senses were heightened and her body capable of impossible feats...

But nothing happened. She remained the same.

Freya knew with certainty that she had spoken the correct words, but the power she had felt in Mexico was nowhere to be found.

Freya leaned back against the stone, stomping the ground in frustration. The thought kept returning to her that Sunny Joe had accomplished the same feat when he was sixteen. In her mind, he simply rolled the stone around the shack like a hula-hoop. The sixteen-year-old Sunny Joe in her mind's eye looked like the boys at school, mocking her: "Girls can't be taught Sinanju! You're too weak! You're a failure!"

I am a failure, she thought. *Maybe they're right. Maybe I don't belong here or deserve to be trained in Sinanju. I'm such a disappointment to Grandfather. No wonder Stone didn't want me to join Ben's team.*

Negativity and rage filled Freya's mind until nothing else existed. Infuriated at her own weakness, she turned her attention to the Founder Stone. *Stupid rock!* Her mind became a laser of focus and she made a decision: The stone was going to move. *I'm going to move this dirty old rock,* Freya thought. *And if it doesn't move, I will smash it into dust!*

Freya took a deep, slow breath and grabbed the stone.

Screaming with fury, she drove her legs upward. The stone burst out of its clay womb with a thunderous crack. Freya smiled with gleeful vindication. *I told you that you would move, rock. Glad you finally listened to me.*

The stone's boxy shape made moving it awkward and cumbersome, but Freya slowly maneuvered it around the shack, trying not to hit the walls. The hut was almost ready to fall down on its own, and she didn't want to explain to Sunny Joe how she had destroyed their training hut.

After fifteen minutes, Freya had placed the stone back in its hole. The bottom proudly faced the sky once more. She had only damaged a few wall planks, and the front of the dojo was now a mess of upturned dirt.

The Founder Stone is back in its original position, Freya thought. *I've fixed Sunny Joe's mistake. And I'm as strong as he was when he was sixteen!*

As she gazed fondly at the now-inverted Founder Stone, Freya noticed that the taste of salt that had plagued her for the past day had finally left her mouth. A wide smile broke across her face as she savored the taste of the cool, dusty air.

Her enjoyment was interrupted by Stone honking the horn outside. As she left the shack, she suddenly felt overwhelmingly sheepish about what she had done, though she was still deeply glad to be rid of the taste of salt.

Stone drummed his fingers on the side of his old jeep as Freya approached. He glared at the sky in frustration.

"What took you so long?" he asked. "The first part of professionalism is being able to show up on time."

"I...had something to do."

Stone finally looked down at his sister. His eyebrows shot up in surprise. From head to toe, Freya was caked in dirt.

"Something to do? What was it — a last-minute mud wrestling match? You can't go to the airport looking like that. Blast it, sis, now you gotta clean up!"

"I won't take long, I promise," Freya said sheepishly, hopping into the jeep.

"You're cleaning the car when we get back," Stone said, pointing at his now-filthy passenger seat. "What were you doing in there, anyway? Grandpa's going to be ticked if you made a mess."

"Tell me about it," Freya said, biting her bottom lip.

CHAPTER FIFTEEN

Stone and Freya's short flight to St. Louis was uncomfortably silent. Stone could tell something had been disturbing his sister. As he watched her feign sleep, he grew more and more worried. It was one thing to be physically injured during a mission. It was another to be mentally injured. Freya was normally quiet around everyone but her family, but ever since returning from Mexico, when she had made her terrifying transformation, she had been quiet around them as well.

Sunny Joe had asked about her, but Stone would not betray his sister's confidence. Besides, he honestly did not know or understand what had happened.

"So, are you going to pretend you're sleeping the whole trip, or what?" Stone asked.

Freya opened her eyes, but did not move.

"I know something's wrong. Come on, sis. It's me. You've gotta talk to someone."

Freya turned away and looked out the window at the wide expanse of land beneath them.

"Do you think I should leave the reservation?" she asked, finally turning to face Stone.

"No! Of course not. Why would you even say that?"

"The tribe has accepted you. They think of you as one of their own. Not me. I'm still an outsider."

"You think they don't talk about me behind my back? I'm the kid who just came to the reservation who all of a sudden thinks he's good enough to be trained by the chief!"

"But you're not a girl. And I don't remember the council calling for a special session to protest you getting trained."

"They're coming around," Stone said. "Even Councilman Jordan said that you're a pretty good fighter…for a girl." Stone squeezed Freya's shoulder and smiled.

Freya sighed and lowered her face.

"You know, I love Grandfather, but I think you're the only one who understands me," she said. After a long pause, she spoke again. "I think I'm ready to talk about Mexico."

"Are you sure?" Stone asked, as a worried look crept back across his brow. After Freya solemnly nodded, Stone took a deep breath. "Okay. What happened to you down there?"

"I don't really know. I remember there were a lot of men shooting at us. I pulled the generator out of the wall to give us some cover."

"Except that made the wall collapse. Smooth move." Stone grinned broadly. "Maybe you should ask next time."

Freya bowed her head in embarrassment before continuing.

"It was like watching a movie. After the wall fell, I blacked out. When I woke up, I heard the sound of thunder, and felt a rumble in my bones. Then I felt myself moving and heard myself speaking. It was like being a puppet. I was still me, but I wasn't in control of what I was doing."

"Do you remember what happened next?"

Freya lowered her head and frowned. Her eyes seemed to focus on something beyond the seats in front of her.

"I remember feeling that the men around me were not worthy to be in my presence. They had to die. All of them." She gulped. "So, I killed them."

Stone saw tears welling up in Freya's eyes. "I'm sorry, Sis," he whispered. "I know that must have been hard to do. But you saved our lives."

"That's just it, though. It wasn't hard. It was like stepping on bugs. And I think that's what scares me the most."

Stone paused for a few seconds, letting Freya's tears fall on his shoulder. "What happened with the guy upstairs? He shot at you, and you didn't move."

"I was in no danger," she said.

"But I saw him fire his pistol directly at you. How did he not hit you? You didn't even try to dodge the bullets."

Freya pulled away. Holding Stone's hand, she looked directly into his eyes.

"I didn't have to dodge. The bullets…the bullets dodged *me*."

Stone tilted his head. He did not know if he understood what his sister had just said.

"What?" he asked.

Freya leaned in toward him. The momentary pause made the steady roar of the plane engines seem even louder.

"I'm trying to understand this as I'm saying it," she finally said. "It was like being centered, but far beyond that. I could see each of the bullets coming at me, but I wasn't afraid. I knew they wouldn't hit me. I did not permit them to. And yes, I know how weird that sounds. But that's also why you missed when you tried to kick me."

"I was just trying to get you to start breathing again!"

"Thank you."

Freya looked for an emotion in Stone's eyes. But instead of the fear she expected, she saw concern in her brother's eyes.

"How did this happen?" he finally asked. "What triggered it?"

Freya paused and looked to the plane's floor. "I died."

CHAPTER SIXTEEN

Ben sat at his desk, reading through the weekly report of border-related crimes supplied by Smith. Weapons had been smuggled into Detroit through the Canadian border. Drug boats in Florida had begun learning the Coast Guard's patterns, and were now using new routes. Though the news was somber, there was nothing yet that required sending Stone and Freya.

Ben opened the intricately-carved bone chest on his desk and removed a cigar. His FORtab began blinking. Smith was calling.

"I've received a coded message," Smith said. "I've sent it to you. As you can see, it cannot be traced. Curiously, however, the sender has claimed to be Africa Senior, a member of VIGIL."

Ben looked at the incoming message.

"Trace," Ben said, and the FORtab immediately started filtering the hundreds of rerouted addresses the message had passed through. Smith did not take offense at Ben's attempt at verifying the information and, in fact, appreciated it. The trace program finished in moments, unhelpfully stating "Origin Unknown."

"Do you believe she is the real sender?" Ben asked.

"Certainly not," Smith said flatly. "Only another FORtab would be capable of sending an untraceable message, and, so far as we know, Helmut has the only other extant device. Read the message."

It was a detailed report about the brutal killing inside Club Stray. Ben was familiar with the massacre, since it was being covered non-stop by the news. Even though no guns had been used in the nightclub slaying, Senator Jesse Steinem, Daphne's father, had already begun to use his personal tragedy as a platform for gun control legislation.

Having reviewed the security footage, police told the public to watch out for a short-haired woman carrying two blades. Within an hour, members from every college fencing team in Illinois sat in jail, awaiting questioning and wondering what they had done wrong.

But the report Ben read showed that the murders had not been random killings by an "extremely disturbed individual," as the police had said. Daphne Steinem had been assassinated by a highly-trained operative.

One section of the report displayed pictures of the attack. The woman who had assassinated Daphne and killed the others stopped at the door on the way out and scrawled a symbol on the wall in blood.

The symbol of Sinanju.

"Good Lord!" Ben said. "Is she actually trying to call out Sinanju?"

"It appears so. Stone and Freya must handle this immediately. Remo and Master Chiun are currently occupied and we cannot risk exposure."

"They are due for their briefing this afternoon."

"One thing, Agent Cole," Smith said with a grimace. "Using the symbol of Sinanju so blatantly certainly seems to indicate a trap. You will have to be extremely cautious."

The connection closed and Ben sat back.

Ben looked through the gruesome photos for hours, before the light blinking above his door finally interrupted him. Stone and Freya had just entered the bar above him.

CHAPTER SEVENTEEN

The gatekeeper for Ben Cole's secret facility was a burly man who matched the dictionary description of "old-time barkeep." No one would have guessed that Mike Nelson had graduated Summa Cum Laude at Princeton, or that he had majored in Criminal Justice and Psychology.

He had never envisioned himself working for the government, and certainly not the CIA, but after being forced out of the Marines, he paid attention to the thin man with a gray suit asked if he wanted to run a bar.

The official title of the position was "gatekeeper," and its mythic, foreboding quality appealed to Mike. But when he told his wife that he was going to purchase a bar that had no customers, she thought he was crazy. He told her there was a loophole in the new tax system that would allow him to run the bar for free. Hidden inside the President's latest proposal was a provision for businesses with very few customers.

If a business was accepted into the program, the government would finance it for a decade. The results would be researched at the end of the program and studied to see if the businesses were helped or harmed. One hundred failing businesses would be given the full faith and credit of the United States Government.

Of course, ninety percent of the applications came from black book operations that would never have to declare what the funds would be used for. The ten percent of private businesses who were allowed into the program would satisfy the one percent of annual audits, as they were constantly recycled through the auditing system.

Mike's wife had thought they might finally get to travel but instead, he was spending ten or more hours a day standing around unused liquor bottles in a bar with no customers. She sighed, decided that she had married an idiot, and booked a trip to Paris — for one.

What no official CIA document revealed was that Mike's bar was the front for Ben Cole's agency. Mike's job was simple, but crucial: prevent unauthorized people from accessing the headquarters, both during the eighteen months of its construction, and once it was in use by Ben. If he failed and there was a security breach, then the headquarters would be sealed and an armed satellite orbiting 22,300 miles above the Earth would be activated. The resulting blast would level the block surrounding the bar.

When Mike reported that the bar had zero customers to qualify for the government program, he was slightly exaggerating. The bar had actually sold a grand total of five drinks over the past year. Mike knew, however, that those few patrons were a distraction from his more important task, so he was as rude as possible to the unlucky few who wandered in.

But as the months passed, Mike's boredom and loneliness grew. When he was a Marine, he had friends. Now, he was alone in a constantly-empty bar. In an effort to draw in some foot traffic, he placed a small sign in the window: **all drinks free!**

His plan had not been a success. The bar remained desolate. Mike, wondering if the lack of decoration kept people away, placed a gigantic neon sign behind the bar, the colors endlessly shifting between the red, white, and green of the Mexican flag. Yet despite the sign's jaunty invitation for people to "¡Have a Cerveza!", the bar still attracted no patrons.

Looking in the mirror at his reflection, it dawned on Mike: maybe it wasn't the location or the ambiance that kept people away — maybe it was him. He knew he looked tough; he was hulking and strong, with arms like braided steel. While there was no way to look smaller, he decided that he could look less intimidating. So, abandoning his collection of department-issued black polo shirts, Mike donned a brightly-colored Mexican serape and an enormous sombrero, and vigorously shook maracas every time someone entered the bar.

Despite his valiant efforts, Mike still made most people feel ill at ease. While brandishing his maracas at customers who walked in, he never broke eye contact with them, which made entering the bar feel like a wordless interrogation. Of course, that was true: by the time a person ordered their first drink, Mike had made sure they were unarmed, and that the security camera had taken a close-up photograph of their face. Mike's desire to have guests was still infinitely less important to him than following proper security protocol. No matter how tense the atmosphere, however, free drinks eventually brought people in, and within a few months, Mike had his first regulars.

Four Vietnam veterans came in, without fail, every Tuesday and Thursday night. Mike enjoyed talking with them about America and how it had changed. Without its soul, the five agreed, America had become Europe Light.

Though the place was merely a front, Mike found himself liking his cover job more and more. Once he retired and handed the bar off to the next gatekeeper, he planned on opening a real bar.

Mike saw people approaching. Grabbing his maracas from behind the cash register, he waited for them to enter.

CHAPTER EIGHTEEN

Stone and Freya walked into Mike's and headed to the door that hid Ben's secret elevator. Neither had really spoken to Ben's sullen, sombrero-clad gatekeeper, and he had never tried to speak with them. Freya wondered if he was quiet because he wanted to be or because he was ordered to be.

Freya took a chance at friendliness and smiled at Mike, giving him a small wave.

"Just a second, *missy*," Mike said. "I have a question."

Stone stopped and his eyebrows arched. "What did you just call her?"

"Missy. You speak English, don't you?"

Recognizing the irritated look on her brother's face, Freya placed her hand in front of Stone.

"There is no need to be rude, Mr. Mike," she said.

"Not rude — curious. You aren't even old enough to be in here as a customer, much less an employee. Something isn't kosher."

"That is probably because I am not Jewish," Freya explained simply.

"Everyone's a comedian." Mike leaned in until his huge face was all Freya could see. "I just want to know one thing, kid."

"My name is Freya."

"Okay, Freya. Cole told me that you bypassed my security. How'd you do that?"

"Quite easily," she said, shrugging.

Stone and Freya took the elevator down and Ben motioned them to take a seat.

Stone recognized stale cigar smoke lingering in the air, even though Ben tried not to smoke around him. It made Stone cranky.

"What's wrong with Mike?" Stone asked. "That guy's got an attitude problem."

"Pot, it sounds like you've met kettle. He's just concerned about security, and I honestly can't tell him how a fifteen…sixteen-year-old girl bypassed his sensors."

"It's hard to explain," Stone said. "Just think of it as part of the Sinanju immune system against electronics."

Ben dimmed the lights. "I know you're both very familiar with this," he said, gesturing to a wall-mounted monitor displaying a trapezoid with a solitary slash running down it.

"That's the symbol for the House of Sinanju," Freya said. "The trapezoid represents balance. The line down the center represents power. Perfect balance and perfect power. It has been Sinanju's symbol for thousands of years."

"One line down the center represents the Korean House and two lines down the center represent our tribe in Arizona," Stone added.

"I read that when I researched Sinanju," Ben said. "But I had one question. Isn't it also the symbol for China? There's a Chinese restaurant down the block that uses the same symbol."

"That is partly true," Freya replied. "It is from when China was owned by the House of Sinanju."

"Owned? How's that?" Ben asked.

Freya rocked back and forth nervously. She felt like she was being called on in class.

"China once owed Sinanju money, which the Korean House does not tolerate. The Master assassinated the entire ruling Chinese class, but the Chinese emperor managed to escape without paying. The Master at the time declared that China would be referred to by the Sinanju symbol until they paid their debt. Not wanting to cross a Master of Sinanju, everyone began using the symbol as a shameful reminder that China reneged on its agreement. They repaid the debt a couple of decades ago, but the symbol has been used for so long that people think that it is the 'official' symbol of China. I guess they're stuck with it."

"Wow, Freya," Stone said, looking over at his sister with admiration. "Guess I should have paid more attention to Sunny Joe's history lessons."

Freya blushed.

"Thank you, Freya," Ben said. "Now, take a look at this."

A video appeared on the screen, taken from a surveillance camera in a nightclub. Despite the erratic lighting, a woman in a torn dress instantly stood out to Freya as a threat. She knew that the woman was not there to dance — she was there to kill.

"That woman is dangerous," Freya said. "She's looking for someone."

Stone and Freya watched an edited video from several camera angles that followed the strange woman as she walked to a table. It looked like she gave a girl with bright hair a hug but when her body hit the floor, Stone could tell the girl was dead.

The girls' friends began screaming and the strange woman ran into their midst, two blades clearly brandished. The woman struck and the others fell beside their friend. The video paused on the woman's face. In the bright light, she barely looked older than Freya.

"Does she look familiar to either of you?" Ben asked.

"No," Stone said. "Why should she?"

"Look at the way she's moving. I assume she is augmented in a Sinanju-like manner."

"She is not Sinanju," Freya said. "The power of her strikes is diminished by her stance. And you can tell that she is not breathing correctly by her posture and manner of walk."

"Yeah," Stone said. "She's displaying power, but no precision."

The video continued with the woman walking toward the door, where she scrawled the symbol of Sinanju on the wall in blood.

Stone was silent for a second before looking up at Ben. "Someone is trying to get our attention, and it worked. Is this our friends at VIGIL again?"

"The message was supposedly sent by a member of VIGIL named Africa Senior."

"That doesn't make any sense. Why would a member of VIGIL risk their life to send you a message?" Stone asked. "Something's fishy about this."

"I agree," Ben said. "I'm almost certain that Helmut sent the message, though I don't know why he would try to make it look as if it came from someone else. It might just be him playing around with internal politics, or trying to divert our attention."

The screen changed back to a close-up of the killer's face, taken as she turned her head. Though the image was grainy, Freya could see that she was not smiling, as she had originally thought. She was yawning.

"Do you have any other pictures of this woman?" Freya asked.

"Unfortunately, no. All we know at the moment is that this was a VIGIL hit to target the daughter of Senator Jesse Steinem. The Senator's daughter was the first target, but police are officially listing her as one of many random victims."

Stone's eyes narrowed and his hands tightened into fists.

"Is something the matter?" Ben asked.

"Sinanju does not tolerate hurting children," Stone said with a growl. "VIGIL's business should have been with the Senator, not his daughter. Do you know why these scumbags would want to target her?"

"It must be political. Senator Steinem is chairman of both the American Nuclear Disarmament Committee as well as the Nuclear Arms and Storage Committee."

"What does that mean?" Freya asked, casting a worried glance over at Stone.

"It means that his committee decides how many nuclear weapons that America gets rid of, as well as how many we build and where we keep them."

"Isn't that a conflict of interest?" Freya asked.

"Technically, yes. He takes money from both sides of the issue. We've found donations from arms manufacturers and anti-weapons groups. His justification has always been that it makes sense to have one chairman over both committees, because it keeps either committee from getting too powerful."

Stone relaxed his hands slightly. "Instead of just reducing the number of committees."

"I do not understand your political system," Freya interrupted. "My mother spoke of America as a beacon of liberty, where everyone had a chance to make something of themselves. But you never speak of liberty, only bureaucracy."

"It didn't start that way," Ben said. "Governments have a tendency to become as large as their people will allow."

"It seems we're in a giving mood these days," Stone grumbled. "In any case, this woman was clearly told to use the Sinanju symbol to bait us. And that's why you got sent so much information about these killings. So what next? I don't like being sent into a trap."

"That's why we're not chasing what are obviously false leads. I've pulled up the Senator's schedule for the next few days. He will be attending his daughter's funeral tomorrow. The cemetery is near his home in Alton. It's just a short distance from here."

"And once we find him, what do you want us to do?"

"Talk with him and find out what he knows. I've been able to set the GPS on his phone to broadcast constantly, so you'll be able to find him without any difficulty. The nightclub killing wasn't random — the woman killed his daughter to send a message. Find out what that is. It might help us figure out VIGIL's next move."

"Count on it," Stone said gravely.

CHAPTER NINETEEN

14's dreams were troubled.

She turned down a dark alley, trying to hide from the cold wind that bit at her exposed ears and fingers. Her mind was foggy. She did not know where she was going. The cold, urban landscape was unfamiliar to her. Somehow, she was wearing her standard issue uniform again, even though she remembered burning it when she was given her first disguise.

The wind was too strong and too cold even for her insulated jumpsuit and cold fingers would mean a slower reaction time. She placed her hands beneath her armpits for warmth when she heard a small squeak, like a mouse that had been stepped on.

Turning around and pulling her blades at the same time, 14 skewered the man who had somehow crept up behind her. The man gasped and fell to the ground. 14 walked over to the body and her eyes opened wide in fear.

It was one of the men in blue lab coats.

She looked all around her. Though the alley was dark, there was no way he should have been able to sneak up on her like that.

Another sound behind her. 14 twisted around and saw another blue lab coat.

This one had a gun.

The man fired, but 14 had pivoted on her left heel and circled toward the man until the gun was at her side. Her blade found the man's throat and as he instinctively reached for the gaping wound in his neck, she grabbed his pistol and placed it into his chest, firing twice.

She focused all of her attention toward the mouth of the fog-enshrouded alley in time to see two men approach her. They smiled as they slowly advanced, holding their hands up to show that they were not armed.

But they had blue lab coats.

Trembling from fear and the insane cold, 14 lowered her blades and allowed them to approach. But when they were close enough to touch, their smiles disappeared. A third man who had been hiding behind them jumped up and fired his pistol point blank at 14's forehead.

The shell ricocheted off her armored skull, but the impact felt like a baseball bat.

In blind pain, 14 skewered the men near her and vaulted over their bodies as the man with the gun fired wildly, each shell a violent punch to her system, but impotently bouncing off her reinforced torso. 14 grabbed the man's pistol and showed him what it felt like to be shot in the head.

She did not know how the men in blue lab coats had found her, but she knew one thing: they would not take her down without a fight.

The men kept piling on, slowly forcing 14 back toward the tall fence at the back of the alley, something that she could not allow. The cold had slowed down her reactions and the sheer number of attackers prevented her from retreating. 14 began fighting without conscious control of her body. Her instincts and reflexes were flawless, and the men fell until their bodies began to make it difficult for her to walk.

The last of the men collapsed to the ground, and 14 gasped in a lungful of air, ready for the next assault. But instead of another man, the figure that emerged from the fog was tiny.

It was a little girl.

It was Lisa.

She sat down on the ground and offered her doll to 14, an angelic smile stretched across her face.

14's breathing calmed instantly as she sat in front of Lisa. The bodies of the men in blue lab coats disappeared. She looked around and, seeing no one near her, grabbed the doll from Lisa, who remained smiling. 14 stared at the doll. It had human eyes and was looking back at her. 14 brought the doll to her chest and hugged it.

"Don't be afraid," she whispered to the doll.

She hugged the doll tightly, rocking from side to side. Tears streamed down her cheeks. "I'll take care of you. We're not alone. We're not alone. We're not alone."

14 awoke with a start. Wiping her damp cheeks, she walked outside and looked up at the grey, pre-dawn sky. Empty land stretched around her for miles. The silence, which had seemed so peaceful the night before, now hung heavily in the air, as still as death.

She was alone.

CHAPTER TWENTY

Sunny Joe and Mick entered the executive ballroom of the Downtown Sheraton, the largest hotel in Phoenix. Tribes from Arizona, Texas, and New Mexico were in attendance, each placing the finishing touches on their booths, readying them for tomorrow's Great Southwestern Tribal Meet. The booths featured each tribe's crafts and heritage and each appeared to be visually louder than the next. It was more reminiscent of a Star Trek convention than a display of Native American achievements.

The Meet had originated in the fifties as a way for tribal leaders to gather and address serious matters affecting all tribes. The first few years of the Meet were filled with grandiose hopes and blustering politicians, but it was impossible to come to universal solutions that satisfied everyone.

By the late sixties, the Meet had devolved into a huge flea market, as the American drug culture craved everything Native American. From simple trinkets to blankets, the Meet became one of the first big American conventions, drawing in thousands of visitors each year. Sales began to dwindle in the late seventies, but even then, there was always a steady stream of people looking for something more substantial than the plastic offerings available at their local department stores.

Sunny Joe only attended the conference because of tribal obligations. If it were up to him, he would deputize Mick to represent them. But obligations were just as sacred to the Sinanju as their art and history, and Sunny Joe took pride in the goods his tribe sold each year. As one of the few tribes that refused any type of government assistance, the Sinanju tribe was poor and the meet had become their second largest source of income.

A tribal leader tilted his hat as he passed Sunny Joe, flashing a ten-thousand-dollar watch.

"They better be glad I don't know Sinanju," Mick said. "That's gaudy and shameful."

"*I'm* glad you don't know Sinanju," Sunny Joe said, smiling. "Half of these people wouldn't be here for the next meet."

"Probably more than half," Mick said, clearly irritated. "Look at 'em, Sunny Joe, walking around in their shiny suits and fancy hats. They've forgotten the old ways."

"So have we, if you think about it. When you were a kid, did you think the council would approve indoor plumbing or televisions?"

Mick looked down a moment. "No," he conceded.

"I know what you mean, though," Sunny Joe said, patting his friend on the shoulder.

"That doesn't give them a right to be jackasses. Just remember: if the Sinanju way was the easy way, everyone could be Sinanju."

"You got that right. Freya's still going through the Night of Salt?"

"She should be over it by now."

"You really think we should have left her alone?"

"It's one of those things you have to work out yourself. No one else can help you through it. Besides, do you really think we could do anything even if we were there?"

"Well, no, but..."

"Don't worry. I told her what to do. She just didn't know it."

Mick stopped in front of Sunny Joe as a worried look came over his face.

"Wait. Sunny Joe, what did you tell her to do?"

"You'll see," Sunny Joe said, flashing Mick one of his mischievous smiles.

"God help us," Mick said, shaking his head. "I know that look."

The loudspeaker crackled, and both Sunny Joe and Mick stopped to listen to the announcement. "Attention tribal representatives! The final round of the arm-wrestling championships will begin in fifteen minutes. Anyone late for their match will automatically forfeit. Thank you."

Mick turned to Sunny Joe with a look of concern. "Who's going to compete in the contest this year? Stone's not here this time."

"I suppose one of the boys will represent us."

"Stone should be here," Mick said. "We're going to lose our booth spot."

The Sinanju booth was located in the center of the room, surrounded by much larger and more extravagant booths. The Sinanju crafts were clearly not as polished as most of the other tribes, but Mick insisted on using original methods of crafting, not cheating with modern conveniences to increase output and appearance like some of the other tribes. If someone wanted something slick and fancy, they would not look twice at the Sinanju booth, but if they wanted something authentic, they would appreciate what they saw. Human hands and simple tools turned leather and wood and iron into things of beauty.

Four boys stood behind the booth wearing the traditional garb of the Sinanju. Small maroon sashes ran across their right shoulder and gold trinkets adorned their shoulders and elbows. A stitched trapezoid with two vertical slashes adorned the area above their heart. War paint streaked down from their eyes, even though the tribe had never historically worn face paint. No one knew what the war paint was supposed to look like, so it had become an annual tradition to make creative designs for each of their faces. One of the boys last year painted his face like a clown to protest the stereotypical use of war paint.

He was called a racist.

As the first tribe to set up a booth, Sunny Joe had claimed center stage. As more of the tribes began to develop booths of their own, they began to complain about Sunny Joe taking the best spot in the room. It became such a problem that tribal leaders were forced to hold an emergency meeting to decide the matter. One of the tribal leaders came up with a solution: Each tribe would send a representative to compete in an arm-wrestling contest. The winner would choose the location of their booth for the next year. It had become an informal tribal Olympics.

A young man with huge shoulders and massive arms stepped up to the booth. Slightly shorter than Sunny Joe, the man arched his back, straining the fabric of his shirt. His brightly colored mullet flailed down his upper back.

Mick smiled.

"What's so funny, old man?"

"You look like a rooster," Mick replied.

"I am Steven Oxendine."

"Is that so," Sunny Joe said, unimpressed.

"Your representative defeated my brother in the final round last year. This year I am of age to represent my tribe. Where is your representative?"

Sunny Joe turned to the boys behind the booth. "Any of you boys wanna arm wrestle the rooster?"

The boys looked up at Steven and laughed. Steven bristled and his face reddened with anger.

"You take him, Sunny Joe," one of the boys said. "Looks like he needs a lesson."

Sunny Joe turned to Steven and smiled. "Looks like it's you and me," he said.

"You think I'll go easy on you because of your age?" Steven asked, leaning into Sunny Joe's face. "I will break you, old man."

"Your breath is breaking me right now. Let's go."

Mick led Steven and Sunny Joe to the back of the convention center. The men who had already been eliminated were standing to the side in shame. They would have to wait another year for a chance to redeem their tribe's honor.

As Sunny Joe entered the line for the contest, the young men ahead of him began whispering and a few began laughing. Steven stood in front of Sunny Joe, bouncing on his toes and twisting his thick neck. Every few minutes, he would look back at Sunny Joe and grunt.

"Real glad I don't know Sinanju," Mick said.

CHAPTER TWENTY-ONE

Jesse Steinem, Jr. had spurned VIGIL's attention. He had ignored their messages. He had dismissed their requests for meetings. Like many other American politicians, Senator Steinem had begun to think that he had power.

VIGIL reminded him who truly held power. They assassinated his daughter in the middle of a public nightclub. To the police, it appeared to be a random killing, but the call the Senator received moments before his daughter's death made sure that he knew what happened and why. At first, he thought it was a sick joke, but when the police called seven minutes later to inform him of his daughter's death, Senator Steinem felt a chill go down his spine.

When the next phone call came, he took it seriously. VIGIL ordered him to meet with them immediately. He considered bringing a gun for protection, and even asked his bodyguard to teach him how to use a pistol. But it was loud, and when he pulled the trigger, it scared him and he dropped the gun, so Senator Steinem went to the park unarmed and alone, as he had been instructed.

The young man who sat down next to him was barely older than his daughter Daphne, so Senator Steinem was surprised when the man introduced himself as his contact.

"You may address me as Master Europe," the young man with sunglasses told him. "We've been trying to get your attention, but you've ignored our calls."

"You got my attention when my little Daphne was killed," Senator Steinem sniffed. "Why would you do that? She was my little girl!"

"Have you considered our request, Senator?"

"I know what you want. But I'll tell you right now, no one pulls my strings. No matter what." Senator Steinem tried to lift his chin in defiance, but only looked more desperate.

Europe Junior stared at him for a moment and then smiled.

"Really?" he asked, looking over his sunglasses. "Senator, you have so many strings to pull, my organization stopped counting at fifty. Let's stop pretending, shall we?"

"Fine. But you didn't have to take my Daphne."

"Her death is *your* fault, Senator. You ignored our messengers, so we had to get your attention."

"You bastards," the Senator growled.

When the Senator began crying again, Europe Junior leaned forward and explained the situation.

"Senator, Daphne is gone. There's nothing you can do about that. Right now, you need to focus on your wife and your other two daughters. Gwendolyn is twelve and Clarissa is eight, right? It would be a pity if little Clarissa's death was more...complicated than Daphne's. She should be in Ms. Kelvin's room about this time of the day, shouldn't she?"

Senator Steinem's face turned pale.

"You wouldn't dare."

"Senator, it's your decision whether we stop or not. We will go through your family, and then you. By the time they find your body, we will have already made negotiations with your replacement. I need a yes or no."

Senator Steinem took a moment to assess the situation. He could try to hide the rest of his family, but he could not protect them from VIGIL for long. The only people who even knew of VIGIL were the few people they controlled, and none of them could help him.

"I need to hear a yes or no, Senator," Europe Junior repeated.

"Yes, damn you," Senator Steinem whispered.

"Thank you. We have a few details to discuss," Europe Junior said, walking away. He knew without looking back that the Senator would follow.

14 followed them from a safe distance.

CHAPTER TWENTY-TWO

Steven Oxendine smiled as he strolled to the small oak table at the back of the convention center. The old man representing the Sinanju tribe had just ensured the loss of his tribe's coveted booth spot for the next year. And since the Sinanju did not bother participating in the lower-tier matches, they forfeited any claim to the lower spots. If they lost, the Sinanju would be moved to the bottom of the list. Their booth would be moved to the gutter.

Steven smiled at the thought.

He had begun training four years ago, before his brother's wrist was shattered during his match with the Sinanju representative, a thin man named Stone. When Steve's brother first saw Stone, he laughed. It was a sure victory. But a freak tear along the bones of his forearm had ruptured his wrist during the match, sinking any further thought of arm wrestling. Steven was angry when he heard that Stone would not be returning to the competition this year. He had wanted to avenge his brother's injury.

Defeating an old man would be a hollow victory, but it would be a victory nonetheless.

Steven had been working out at the gym and honing specific muscle groups. Since no one bothered to check for illegal drugs, Steve had started a heavy cycle of steroids so he could add as much muscle as possible.

The crowd began growing as word got out that Sunny Joe himself was going to defend his spot. Men and boys began gathering around the table until it was so crowded that they began standing on booths. None of them had ever heard of a Chief defending his tribe's spot.

Will Lamb, the organizer of the Meet, noticed people running toward the back. Normally, the arm-wrestling tournament drew a decent-sized crowd, but this time it seemed that every man, woman and child in the convention hall was rushing to get a glimpse of the match.

"What's going on?" he asked one of the young men who ran past him.

"Final wrestling match!" the boy said, barely slowing down.

Will stopped the next man coming up behind him.

"Who's wrestling?" Will asked.

"Sinanju," the man said.

Will rolled his eyes. He had been there when the tournament was first proposed. At the time, it had seemed like a reasonable way to settle the constant arguments about booth spots.

But the Sinanju tribe never seemed to lose.

Back when tribal representatives had to play through the entire bracket, Sinanju had lost several smaller matches, but never when it counted, and, somehow, it always seemed like they were somehow losing on purpose. Soon, the young men at the Meet began taking the matches so seriously that bones began breaking. Out of safety, the rules had been changed: a tribe could not be forced to wrestle more than three times, and they had an option not to challenge any tribe lower than the spot they defended. From then on, the Sinanju tribe only competed once per meet, to defend their spot.

And they had never lost.

A group of older men shuffled over to the match.

"Why is everyone going to watch the Sinanju win again?" Will asked.

"Sunny Joe's representing his own tribe," one of the men said. "Against Big Steve Oxendine!"

A worried look came across Will's face.

"Oh, Lord," he whispered before scurrying toward the back. If he hurried, he might arrive in time to save Oxendine's arm.

Sunny Joe sat down and pulled up his right shirt sleeve. Compared to Steven's enormous bulk, Sunny Joe's thin tanned arm looked weak and puny.

"This is going to be good," Steven said, sourly.

"I sure hope so," Sunny Joe said.

The crowd filled the ballroom with cheers and rants. Men with clipboards ran, shouting, through the crowd, taking money and bets as the referee walked to the table.

"Sunny Joe," he greeted.

"Leo," Sunny Joe said, returning the greeting.

"Go easy on him," Leo said.

"I won't," Steven said, smiling.

"I wasn't talking to you."

Leo held both men's hands motionless above a small white circle painted in the center of the table. The roar of the crowd died down to whispers of anticipation. He looked both men in the eye and then released their hands.

Steven grunted and every muscle in his arm rippled, expending his energy into one terrible, explosive move...

Neither hand budged.

Steven leaned his shoulder into the effort, pushing with his back, but Sunny Joe's face remained a tranquil sea.

"Push, dammit, push!" Steve's brother yelled from the side.

"So, Leo, how's the wife?" Sunny Joe asked, turning casually in his seat.

Steven's brother moved to the side of the table, yelling into his ear. "What's wrong with you?" he shouted. "Push!"

Steven panicked.

His brother and the crowd raised their voices in curses and jeers, and everything became hazy as he focused all of his anger on the man sitting across from him. Steven would wipe the silly smirk from his face, even if it meant breaking every bone in the old man's arm. Steve's rage built from the inside, an engine of fury, fueled by the indignity this man and his tribe had placed on his family and his honor.

Steven sucked in a deep breath and stared Sunny Joe in the eyes. He screamed with all of his might and with one swift move, finally heard the satisfying sound of bones striking oak.

It took a few seconds before he realized that the bones were his.

"You were right," Sunny Joe said, standing up. "That was kinda fun."

Steven couldn't bear to look at his arm. It had become a volcano of electricity and fire. The adrenaline that fueled his rage sputtered away, leaving him in an ocean of pain.

Sunny Joe walked over to Mick and smiled.

"That one was for you," Sunny Joe said as Steven continued wailing.

"What the heck did you do?"

"Don't worry, I just woke up a few nerves. He'll be fine in a couple of minutes."

Mick smiled as they walked away.

Though most of the crowd was watching Steven flail on the ground, Sunny Joe felt a personal threat coming from the center of the crowd. He stopped and turned around. His eyes instantly fixated on a man dressed in a tribal uniform he had never seen before. Even after he saw that Sunny Joe noticed him, the man continued to glare.

"What's wrong?" Mick asked. He had seen that look on Sunny Joe's face before. It was never a good sign.

"That guy in red and green," Sunny Joe said. "He's mad at me."

Mick turned to look, and as soon as he saw who Sunny Joe was looking at, grinned.

"He's that crazy guy everyone is talking about. Calls himself War Feather or something. I wouldn't worry about him. He probably just lost money betting on the match."

"No, it's a different kind of anger," Sunny Joe said, turning back to Mick. "An old anger that runs deep."

Sunny Joe walked away, but could still feel War Feather's eyes on him.

CHAPTER TWENTY-THREE

When Europe Junior entered the Senator's limousine, 14 stood across the street and waited. Though traumatized by the murder of his daughter, she was not worried about Europe Junior's safety. The senator was overweight, out of shape and emotionally overwhelmed.

Before meeting with the Senator, Europe Junior had told her to be on the lookout for two agents, a male and a female. If they were on his trail, she would have to deal with them.

"What do they look like?" 14 asked.

Europe Junior hesitated. "A young, Caucasian female with long blonde hair, and a dark-haired Caucasian male in his early twenties."

"I need more information."

"That's all you need to know," Europe Junior snapped. "We chose this location and time because of the lack of traffic. But if I am attacked, you will deal with them in a lethal manner, regardless of witnesses. You will not hesitate. Do you understand?"

Europe Junior either did not know, or did not care, about the Carnage principle of secrecy. He had already ordered 14 to kill a girl and leave a message in a public place full of cameras. Now he was willing to have her fight in broad daylight.

"You will need this," he said, pulling a syringe from his pocket. "Come over here. Quickly."

It reminded 14 of the needles the men in the blue lab coats used. She leaned toward him unquestioningly and he placed the syringe on the side of her neck. A click of the button at the back of the syringe released a small needle that pierced her skin, injecting chemicals into her system.

14 jerked back, grabbing her head in pain.

For a moment, she could not see. But her vision did not fade to black; it exploded with color. She could feel the surge of energy coursing through her veins and a high-pitched ringing filled her ears. She staggered backward, blinking her eyes to clear them.

The smell of a powerful spice filled her nostrils.

Europe Junior waved his hand in front of her face.

"Stay back!" 14 ordered and Europe Junior stopped.

"Are you operational?" he asked after a few seconds.

She still felt the serum surging through her veins, but tried to hide her discomfort.

"Are you operational?" he repeated with an edge to his voice.

14 stood at attention and ignored the buzzing in her head. "14 is operational," she replied.

"Good," Europe Junior said. "Let's go."

14 remained at a distance as Europe Junior approached the Senator. She could feel the added strength flowing through her veins, but it was an unnatural feeling and she did not trust it. The ringing was still in her ears as she watched the motionless limousine. She listened carefully for signs of struggle, but heard none. The meeting was going according to plan.

Five minutes passed, then ten more, and she saw nothing suspicious until the thin girl with the blonde hair arrived on the opposite side of the street.

Wearing a tan shirt and loose khakis, her long blonde hair was held in place by a simple hairband. She looked like everyone else 14 had seen in the outside world, but there was something odd about the way she walked. Her legs moved as if they were gliding across the pavement.

14 leaned forward as the girl approached the limousine. She glided toward the back of the car and when 14 blinked, the girl disappeared. One moment she had been standing outside the stretched automobile and then in the next instant, she was gone. 14 walked out from behind the tree and cautiously approached the car. If that was the blonde girl she had been warned about, her partner would surely be nearby.

Inside the limousine, Senator Steinem lowered his head into his hands. "If the government finds out what I'm doing for you, I'll be executed for treason!"

Europe Junior leaned forward, smiling.

"Only if they find out, Senator. Would you rather watch your family be executed?"

"What you're asking for…it's…it's insane. Have you taken time to consider what you're asking for?"

"VIGIL *always* know what we're asking, Senator."

"VIGIL," a female voice suddenly said. "Now that is a name I'm not fond of."

Europe Junior saw her first. A moment earlier, it was just him and the Senator in the back of the limousine. Now a young girl sat next to the Senator with a small grin on her face. Europe Junior reached for the pistol inside his jacket.

The girl reached out and slapped the back of his hand, paralyzing his entire arm. Something terrifying and cold in her eyes told him not to reach for the pistol with his other hand.

One of the perks of public office was access to an armored limousine. Once sealed, it was supposedly impervious against even mortar fire, but a teenage girl sat beside the Senator as if she had been there all along.

"Who are you?" Senator Steinem asked. "And how the hell did you get in here?"

Then Europe Junior recognized her as the girl he had seen in the video. Her eyes were not dark as they were in the video, but it was the same girl.

"Senator, you have a very nice vehicle," Freya said, looking around at the lavish bar and personal theater system. "I had no idea one of my friends from VIGIL would be here."

Before either man could respond, something slammed into the side of the limousine. The impact surprised even Freya. She had not heard anything approach that was large enough to wreck the car. The suspension whined as the car tilted upwards and Freya was out of the car before it settled back on its tires, landing on her feet in an offensive position. It was not a vehicle that had crashed into them. It was the killer from the dance club, and she was returning to ram the car again.

CHAPTER TWENTY-FOUR

Ben was surprised when he received the next message from VIGIL. Unlike the previous message, which claimed to have come from Africa Senior, this one made no effort to hide its sender's identity. There was no guesswork involved this time: Helmut's slow, sonorous voice greeted Ben as soon as he opened the message. And though the last message had been sent to Smith first, this time the message was sent directly to Ben, and Ben alone.

The recording provided detailed information about VIGIL's top-secret "Carnage" program. It revealed that over the past two decades, an army of biologically and technologically-augmented soldiers, called "Premiums," had been trained on United States soil for clandestine terrorist activities. The woman from the nightclub was one of them. And, if Helmut's message was to be believed, she was not alone. There were others like her, ready to strike at a moment's notice.

Helmut's last words were startlingly direct. Ben listened to them until he could quote them from memory: *Tomorrow night, the destruction of the United States will have begun. It will start with the Mississippi River. Enjoy the memories you have of your country, Mr. Cole — soon, memories will be all that remain.*

Pacing his office, Ben knew that Helmut was lying about something — but about what? He had been a spy long enough to know that the best forms of psychological warfare were based heavily in the truth. What part of Helmut's message was true? Were there more soldiers like the woman from the nightclub? Was an attack imminent? Why the Mississippi River — and, if that were true, why announce his target in the first place?

Even if Helmut had been lying about the river, at least it would be a place Ben could start looking. When he started researching potential targets, however, he discovered something unusual. The entry for a military waste facility in St. Louis, though deserted for years, had recently been modified. Ben found it highly suspicious that after decades of inactivity, someone would suddenly update information in every government database about what appeared to be little more than a glorified dump.

Every time Ben tried to see what the listing for the facility had been before it was modified, key facts would disappear or change. They were being obscured by something powerful enough to affect his FORtab.

Ben knew that Helmut was leaving him a trail of breadcrumbs. He just didn't know why, or where they would lead.

CHAPTER TWENTY-FIVE

14 charged the limousine a second time. It had been too heavy to overturn on her first pass, but now that its center of gravity had been displaced, she would be able to easily roll the armor-plated car. But before she could reach the limo, she saw something eject from the car. It was the girl who had disappeared earlier, flipping out of the car.

14 turned her attention to Freya as she landed.

Freya twisted out of the way, amazed by 14's raw speed. She was moving far faster than a human should, almost as fast as a Master of Sinanju. Freya leapt backwards over 14 while she charged, disappearing into the trees by the car. The tiniest of rustling sounds signaled her landing on a large branch. Freya grimaced at the sound.

14 stopped in her tracks and looked around as the limousine sped away. The girl had disappeared.

A young male came running from down the street. He was screaming something that 14 could not understand and did not care about. As she watched his advance, 14 smiled. He was fast, but nowhere near as fast as the girl.

Stone had been stationed at the other end of the block to wait for the limo to pass. He saw the woman run toward the four-ton limousine, lowering her shoulder as if she was going to tackle it. Stone's mouth dropped open when she struck the car and lifted it off two wheels.

Freya was still inside!

Stone paused to take a breath and center himself before running down the block.

"Hey, ugly!" he shouted, trying to get the woman's attention. "The tow truck union's gonna sue you for that!"

Freya had escaped the car, jumping onto a tree branch behind her.

The woman looked around for Freya in the few seconds it took Stone to reach her. That is when Stone recognized her. Ben would want them to interrogate her, so instead of lethal force, Stone moved to subdue her.

14 bent backward at an impossible angle and Stone missed. His stroke carried through the air and, finding no target, took its kinetic energy from Stone's shoulder. He groaned with the pain.

The momentum of his blow carried him past 14. She kicked him squarely in the back and Stone fell to the ground.

14 turned her attention away from Stone. He would be dazed for a minute at least. The

girl was a more serious threat, but she had disappeared. These two were not like the soft people she had encountered so far. They moved at a speed greater than anyone she had ever seen. Until 14 could learn more about them, she could not risk taking on both of them.

Noting an approaching car, 14 staggered into the street as if she had been hurt. The car stopped and the driver walked over to her.

"Hey lady, are you okay?" the man asked.

It was the last mistake he ever made.

14 collapsed the man's throat in one blow and climbed into his car. She had been trained to operate a vehicle, but had never actually driven one. On paper, she knew how to steer, accelerate and brake, but it wasn't the same as actually being behind the wheel. 14 struggled to keep the car on the road.

She was so preoccupied with steering that she did not feel the slight bump as Freya landed on the roof. But she could not help but notice when Freya pulled her headband off, allowing her long hair to spill over the windshield, blocking her view. 14 tried to maintain control of the car, but ran off the road, crashing into a parked car.

She exited the door and leapt to the roof, but Freya had disappeared again.

Whoever this girl was, she was not going to let 14 get away, so 14 moved to an alley. She would isolate the girl's angle of attack. 14 stood silently at the mouth of the alley when suddenly she detected the girl's presence.

Freya held her breath as she silently approached 14 from behind. Unlike Stone, who had extensively studied Sinanju's stealth techniques, she had just recently begun training in the art of shadows. It would take some time before she was as silent as Stone, but at the moment, Freya was quieter than any non-Sinanju human on the face of the planet.

At the last instant, 14 turned, catching Freya off-guard. She had not expected 14 to sense her presence, and was unprepared for 14's attack. The blow landed squarely in her chest, knocking the air from her lungs. By the time Freya recovered, 14 was in her face, snapping her teeth.

Freya dodged 14's next punch, but had not yet regained her balance as 14's claws ripped towards her. Freya twisted away at the last moment and 14's fingernails missed her face, but latched onto her long, flowing hair.

14 yanked hard, knocking Freya out of her centered state. Her senses dulled, Freya did not even see the foot that came crashing against her temple. She collapsed to the ground and did not move.

14 stepped forward to claim her prize.

CHAPTER TWENTY-SIX

Freya lay unconscious on the ground as 14 cautiously approached her. Unbound by her headband, Freya's hair was long, straight and blonde.

Just like the doll.

Looking around to make sure that no one was watching, 14 leaned over and touched Freya's hair. It was soft. 14's lips stretched into a grin. She gently stroked Freya's hair and the grin became a small smile. Then she pulled Freya to her, hugging her as she had hugged Lisa's doll.

Unlike the doll, Freya was warm.

The soft memory triggered another. 14 remembered being taken to the infirmary for her first set of bone grafts. During an exceptionally painful session, she let out a scream and the attending nurse rushed to her side. Seeing nothing else that she could do, the woman leaned over and hugged 14.

It was awkward for a moment. Nurses were forbidden physical contact with Premiums.

"It's okay," the nurse whispered reassuringly. "You're not alone."

She held 14 tightly and slowly rocked her. The pain remained, but something about the nurse's action soothed 14 at an emotional level she had never felt before. Her breathing slowed and her heart steadied, but a doctor came in and shouted at the nurse, chasing her out of the room. 14 never saw her again.

Now, Freya was the doll and 14 was the nurse and 14 would never let her go.

"It's okay," 14 whispered, slowly rocking Freya. "We're not alone. We're not alone."

Freya awoke to 14 hugging her. Confused, she remained still. Her head throbbed and her neck was sore, but she sensed no threat from 14. In fact, she felt the exact opposite coming from the woman who had just attacked her. 14 was trying to comfort her.

Freya waited a few seconds before saying something.

"Sister, what is your name?"

14 dropped Freya and backed away, embarrassed that she had been caught. Not knowing what else to do, she took a defensive stance. After looking around and seeing no one else, 14 softened her stance a bit.

Freya slowly stood to her feet and backed up several steps to give 14 some space. "My name is Freya."

"I am called 14," she said. Her voice was surprisingly soft.

"We mean you no harm," Freya said.

"The male does," 14 said, referring to Stone. "He wishes to kill me."

"He is my brother," Freya said. "He is just trying to protect me."

"You require no protection. You are stronger than he is. You are…different from the others out here."

"You and I are both different," Freya said, noting the scars that ran down 14's arms and across the top of her bald head. Then she heard 14's stomach rumble. "Sister, are you hungry?"

"The food here is not good for my digestion. Everything is full of fat."

"I cannot eat this civilization's food, either," Freya said. "My digestive system will not allow it. I can eat rice and fish, but very little else."

"I eat processed protein meal," 14 said. "It makes me strong."

After a pause, Freya looked 14 in the eyes. "Why are you attacking us?"

"It is my mission," 14 said. "I must obey my commands."

"I understand you, Sister. We are trained to become weapons. But sometimes other people forget that we are more than that."

14 stared at Freya for a moment, weighing her words. Stone approached rapidly in the background.

"What the hell is going on?"

14 tensed. Her breathing became controlled as she turned her full attention to Stone.

"No!" Freya yelled. "He won't hurt you!"

"Like hell I won't!" Stone said and charged toward 14.

Freya tripped Stone as he passed by, knocking him into the ground.

"What are you doing?" he shouted.

"She's not our enemy!" Freya yelled.

But when Freya looked back up, 14 was gone.

"Where did she go?" Stone asked, but Freya was looking sternly at him.

"I'm telling you, 14 is not our enemy!" she said.

Stone looked around, but could not tell which direction 14 had fled.

"Big mistake, Sis," Stone said, glaring at Freya. "I hope we don't get fired — or killed — because of you."

"She is not our enemy!" Freya repeated.

"Friendship doesn't exist in the field."

"Then what do you call what you and I have?"

"Blood," Stone said. "Let's go. We're going to have a talk about this!"

Freya felt the telltale pressure waves of someone looking at her. She was still too inexperienced to locate her, but Freya knew that 14 was watching them.

14 leaned back into the shadows of the corner ledge above them and carefully watched Stone and Freya leave. Her eyes never left Freya.

CHAPTER TWENTY-SEVEN

"She what?" Ben asked.

Freya winced. She could hear the exasperation in Ben's voice over Stone's cell phone speaker.

"She escaped," Stone repeated. "Boss, this isn't just an assassin. I don't even know where to begin. She's stronger and faster than anyone I've seen this side of Freya."

"The woman is part of an experiment designed to transform humans into biological war machines. They start at infancy, are fed a strict diet and are trained on a daily basis."

"That sounds pretty much like my life for the last four years," Stone said. "Well, minus the cigarettes."

Freya started to say something, but Stone held his hand up. He would not let her tell Ben that she had talked to 14 and let her go. That would be a later conversation between them.

"You didn't have to endure years of artificial bone grafts," Ben said. "All of the Carnage candidates had key points of their skeletal system bonded with carbon fiber once they reached puberty. Knuckles, elbows, knees — all of their primary strike points were plated with the material. So were their skulls and torsos."

"If she had armored bones, they didn't slow her down," Stone said. "And by that, I mean they didn't slow her down at all."

"The material is incredibly light, and designed to absorb massive amounts of kinetic energy. A quarter-inch thick plate would easily be able to stop a fifty-caliber bullet fired at point-blank range."

"It was nice of you to tell us this *after* we encountered the Iron Maiden."

"I just recently learned about it myself," Ben said honestly.

"Phones work both ways, boss," Stone muttered.

"Were you able to get any information from the Senator before the vehicle was attacked?"

"Unfortunately, no," Stone said. "The woman attacked right after Freya got in the car. Freya said that a VIGIL member was in the car with the Senator."

Stone could hear Ben's fingers begin tapping on the FORtab screen.

"What did he look like?"

Freya leaned toward the cell phone.

"He was around Stone's age. He had dark hair, but I couldn't see his eyes. He was wearing sunglasses. He spoke English, but with a Spanish accent; European Spanish, not Mexican or South American Spanish."

"He must be the new European Junior. What did he say?"

"We were attacked by 14 before he could say much."

"Attacked by what?"

Stone glared at Freya. She had let 14's name slip.

"The woman in question called herself 14," Stone interrupted.

"You spoke with her?" Ben asked. There was a moment of silence on the other end of the phone. "What else wasn't I told?"

Freya's eyebrows shot up and she arched her shoulders in apology. Stone held up a finger to silence her.

"The woman identified herself as the number 14. We attempted to stop her, but she..."

"Stone, I've been doing this too long not to recognize a lie when I hear one."

Freya nodded to Stone, letting him know it was okay.

"I tried to sneak up behind the woman, but somehow, she heard me," Freya said. "She kicked me in the head. I was knocked out. When I came to, she was hugging me."

"Hugging you? Are you sure?"

"Yes. I felt no threat from her, so I told her my name and asked hers. She said her name was 14. I asked her why she was attacking us. She said it was her mission. There was nothing personal about it."

"That's how professionals work, Freya," Ben said. "The people you will be asked to kill will be someone's father, someone's son, someone's girlfriend. None of that would matter to a professional."

"You're not mad at me?" Freya asked.

"Disappointed, but not mad. You're new. I'm sure that Stone has already pointed out that you will pay the costs for your failures, not me. You're just lucky that she didn't kill you."

"Mr. Cole, I don't know how to explain it, but I felt a...well, a connection with her. We've both been trained all our lives, but that doesn't make us machines. Sometimes our training makes other people forget that we're people, too. I know it sounds strange, but I know we both sensed it in each other."

"I understand what you're saying, Freya. But what about you brought this out of her? She certainly didn't show any compassion to the people she murdered in Chicago."

"I really don't know, Mr. Cole. She kept touching my hair, though, and staring at it, even after she let me go."

"Stone, this would be a good time to tell me anything else you left out."

"She was incredibly, insanely fast," Stone said hurriedly. "She was faster than me. When I tried to attack, she dodged my punch. Only Sunny Joe and Freya can do that. It almost dislocated my shoulder. If she has metal bones, or bone implants, or whatever you said she has, and she can still move that fast, it's more than just good training."

"Do you think she dosed with anything? There are many drugs that can augment speed and strength."

"I don't think so, Ben. This wasn't like professional baseball or bicycling. This was almost the level of Sinanju."

"She was very wary of me, though, and she did seem a little paranoid," Freya interrupted. "But I think she was just being cautious. She didn't appear drugged to me. She was totally focused."

Ben exhaled deeply before replying. "In the future, I cannot emphasize how important it is to detail everything in your reports. I can't help if I don't know what's going on. We're going to make mistakes, but we can only succeed if we work as a team."

"Yeah, yeah, we know. There is no 'I' in team," Stone said.

"This is not a joke, Stone," Ben snapped. "Look at Freya. Are you willing to risk your sister's life?"

"Of course not."

"Then you need to step up her field training. Her life is in your hands, not mine."

Stone looked down. Ben had struck a nerve.

"So, what do we do now?" Freya asked.

"I think a major operation will take place tomorrow, and this woman will be involved."

"Like I said before — where are you getting all of this information?" Stone asked.

"I've received a message directly from Helmut," he said, playing back the recording for Stone and Freya before speaking again. "Based on my research, I believe that the woman's destination is an abandoned military base in St. Louis. I want you to investigate the base, and see what you can find."

"It felt like a trap before, and it feels even more like one now," Stone said. "Helmut is clearly leading us there. What do you think we're going to find when we get to the base? The Tooth Fairy? Santa Claus? Maybe a belated birthday present for Freya? No. Just no.

This is how agents get killed, Ben."

"Stone, I understand your concern. I would normally agree with you, but we need more information. I'm not asking you to stop any attack that takes place, or even to be around when it happens. I just want you to see if you can discover something — anything — about what is being planned at the facility. No combat, Stone — just surveillance."

"People doing 'surveillance' can wind up just as dead as anyone else, and to risk our lives just so you can — "

"I'll go," Freya said suddenly. "If 14 is there, I don't think she will attack me. I can look around quickly, and leave. I will do it."

"It seems like the best choice we have, Stone," Ben said quietly.

Stone sighed deeply before he spoke again. "I'm not letting Freya go anywhere without me. We're a package deal. If she insists on going, we're both going. But I still think this is a terrible idea."

"Thank you, Stone. Obviously, I don't have to warn you, but please be extremely careful."

"We will be, Mr. Cole," Freya said. "Thank you for your confidence in us. In me. I won't let you down again."

"I trust you both, Freya. Stone, I'm sending the location to your phone."

Stone's cell vibrated in confirmation. "We're on it," he said.

"Thank you, and good luck," Ben said, hanging up.

Stone looked mad.

"I don't even want to talk about this next mission, but believe me, we're going to discuss it. Right now, I just want to know what happened back there with 14?" he asked. "You were on the clock. You had your mission and you screwed it up!"

"I adapted to the situation," Freya said defensively.

"Ben's right, sis. If you screw up out here, you're going to end up dead," Stone said, running his fingers through his hair. "And now you've volunteered us for a suicide mission. Great. Just great. I knew this was a bad idea. I need a cigarette."

Freya moved to stand in front of Stone and placed both of her hands on his shoulders.

"If something bad ever did happen to me, know that I am responsible for my own life and this is what I have chosen to do with it. I honestly do not believe that 14 will attack me, whether it is her mission or not."

"Sis, I wish it were that simple," Stone said. Then he saw the somber look on Freya's face and knew that he had to change the mood. She had been through enough drama for one day. "C'mon. I'm getting hungry. Let's find something to eat."

"Okay. Remember, I have to eat Sinanju kosher now."

"Right. Enjoy your rice. I think I'm gonna eat the biggest piece of chocolate cake I can find, with ice cream and — "

"Shut up," Freya said, smiling once again.

CHAPTER TWENTY-EIGHT

The sun was setting as 14 reached her destination. The large, fenced area contained four small buildings and a sprawling warehouse with broad docks opening onto the Mississippi. 14 scaled the fence. It was much easier in her native jumpsuit. Though individuality was frowned upon in the Carnage program, 14 kept her hot-pink sneakers, and still wore the custom maroon surgical wrap from her skull grafts. It reminded her that she was still human.

She did not know why she had been ordered to kill Freya and her brother. She knew only that it was important enough to be her first mission.

She broke the lock on the front gate from the inside. As she had been told, Europe Junior was waiting outside the gate in his car. 14 opened the gate and he motioned for her to come to him. His face was contorted with rage. When she approached, he started screaming at her.

"You stupid, ignorant toad! How dare you endanger me? What part of your tiny, worthless brain thought it would be a good idea to attack the car while Steinem and I were still inside?"

"I was not trying to harm you or the Senator. I was trying to get the girl out of the car. You ordered me to attack her regardless of circumstance or witnesses."

"Regardless of *other* people. That doesn't mean *me*, you worthless automaton. Now, show me your neck."

He was holding another syringe.

"It's your next dose," he said. "Come here."

14 hesitated. She still had not yet overcome the effects of the first dose. Her heart had skipped several times and she still had the jitters.

"I do not need it," 14 said, refusing the shot.

"You will take the shot. Or are you too stupid to follow these orders, too?"

14 tilted her head away from Europe Junior and accepted the shot. She involuntarily blinked her eyes as the drugs stunned her.

Europe Junior grabbed her face, looking at her pupils. They had dilated as he had been told. She was now a chemical time bomb. 14 slowly staggered back.

This dose was stronger than the first. While 14 could hold back the effects of the first dose, the second shot made 14 lose control of her body. She rocked back and forth dizzily. She shook her head, but it only caused motion sickness and pain.

Europe Junior slapped her across the face, but she felt nothing.

"Snap out of it!" he shouted.

14 could feel the drug racing beneath her skin. Her body tried to throw up, but she had not eaten in the last day, so she bent over and began to dry heave.

Europe Junior allowed her a moment to recover and then handed her a cell phone.

"What do I do with this?" 14 asked, looking at the tiny screen.

"All the buildings have been rigged with explosives. Once you see the boy and the girl again, you will press the button on the front and engage them. This will signal their arrival and arm the bombs. You will have one hour to eliminate them and return, at which point I will destroy the facility."

14 knew he was lying, and leaned back into the car. She placed her head inside the window until she was inches from Europe Junior's face. Rage burned in her eyes as she glared at Europe Junior. She knew how easy it would be to kill him and run away. All she had to do was cut this little man's throat and she would be free. She had seen enough of the outside world to accommodate their barbarous lifestyle. She could eventually adapt to their food.

She could be happy, like Freya.

But 14 did not have family like Freya did. She had a brother who protected her. If Freya went missing, someone would eventually find her. 14 had no one, and VIGIL was watching her.

Not even Freya could protect her from VIGIL.

"What will stop you from detonating the explosives as soon as I signal you?" 14 asked cautiously.

"If I wanted to kill you, I would have just injected you with poison."

14 recognized a second lie. As another wave of pain sliced through her body, she shuddered uncontrollably. The second dose was too much for her system to handle. With grim clarity, 14 knew that her heart would soon give out, and relegated herself to follow his directives. This was her superior, and he was giving her orders. Orders were sacred. She could not disobey.

Glaring at Europe Junior one last time, she ran from the car in the direction of the target buildings.

Watching her sprint away at superhuman speed, Europe Junior dialed a number on his cell phone.

"Director, she's got the final dose and the phone. When the boy and girl arrive, the Premium will signal me. No one will survive the blast."

"I certainly hope not," Helmut said. "Goodbye."

And then there was silence.

CHAPTER TWENTY-NINE

Stone led Freya to one of the upper railings on the first building past the fence. They looked around the dark compound, but there was no sign of activity.

"What do we do now?" Freya asked.

"I'm going to post up on that big warehouse." Stone nodded to a large, flat building to the north. "I'll be able to see everything but the front gate. You're going to patrol the other buildings stay here."

"Will that cover all entrance points?"

"It will, unless they come by submarine."

Stone felt his cell phone buzz. It was a message from Ben.

"It must be an emergency if he's contacting us now," Stone said.

***&@%...immediate moratorium from researching or monitoring the headquarters, #%^@ even ... FORtab, until they understand... #*. > ... raises each...**

"This doesn't make any sense," Stone said. "Something must be interfering with the signal."

"It looks like he's trying to tell us to keep away from the buildings," Freya said.

Stone tried to send a reply, but the message kept timing out. When he tried to call, an error message flashed on his phone.

"Yeah, something's definitely blocking the signal."

He pocketed his useless cell.

"Why would he tell us that?" Freya asked.

"That's part of being an agent. Asking 'why' isn't in the job description."

"Then how do you know when you're being used?"

"That's easy. Being used is in the job description. You just have to draw a line inside that you won't pass."

"Where do *you* draw the line?"

"I won't harm family or country."

"Just blood family?"

"What do you…oh, you mean like your new 'sister' 14?" Stone mocked.

"Yes," Freya admitted.

Stone turned to Freya, standing to his full height. She knew that a lecture was coming, but she would not back down. There was something different about 14 that placed her above being a simple killer. There was a kindred spirit inside her.

Stone recognized the look on Freya's face. It was the one she wore when she thought Stone did not understand what she was saying. He relaxed his stance.

"Look, when I told you that I was concerned about you in the field, it was because of things like this. You're the deadliest girl on the planet, but you can't afford to be this naïve. 14 is not your friend. We are here to do a job, that's all. I need to ask you something. If completing the mission requires killing her, will you do it?"

Freya looked to the ground longer than Stone was comfortable with.

"Only if I have to," Freya said, returning his gaze. "And only as a last resort."

"Then be prepared, because that's usually how these things end, sis." Noticing a distant look in his sister's eyes, Stone paused. "Hey. I'm sorry for being harsh. I just want you to be safe."

"It's not that," Freya murmured. "There's just something about this place that I don't like. Something feels…off."

Stone turned her around and cautiously looked at her eyes. They remained her normal blue.

"Hey, are you ok?"

"Yes," Freya said meekly. "It's just this place. There's something…*wrong*."

"What do you mean?"

"I don't know. It just feels like something isn't right."

"I hope you're wrong, sis, because we've got a job to do. Take your post. If you see something, tap on the side of the building and I'll come over."

Freya quickly disappeared down the ladder and ran to the opposing building. Once she had climbed to the top floor walkway, she began walking to the other side. She felt angry and hurt. She was not naïve. Was he so jaded that he could not sense goodness in people? Did he think everyone was bad? And why shouldn't she try to see what was going on while she was there? Not that it mattered, because all of the windows had been painted over. Freya continued on her patrol route, turning around the corner of the warehouse.

At the end of the building, she saw a dim light. It was the first sign of life she had seen in the seemingly abandoned base. Pacing silently, she sensed movement and sound inside. As she reached the window, Freya looked to see whether Stone could see her. He couldn't. Standing on her toes, she looked inside.

As if triggered by her looking in the window, a large screen turned on, and began flashing random images. After a few seconds of watching, Freya saw nothing relating to the present mission, and started to move on. But then she saw the symbol of the Sinanju tribe flash across the screen.

CHAPTER THIRTY

14 glanced around the base, carefully memorizing all possible escape routes. She knew that if any alarms were triggered before she disposed of the boy and girl, Europe Junior would panic and push the button, blowing her up where she stood.

She looked around for a good vantage point and found one: the roof of the largest building. The concrete border would provide good cover and allow her to see the entire complex. As she climbed the ladder, she could tell that her strength and speed had increased — but at what price? 14 swayed for a moment as a rush of dizziness overcame her.

She should not have allowed Europe Junior to give her the second dose.

The strength flowed through her body like barbed wire clawing through her veins. Her heart felt large and heavy in her chest, pumping obscenely fast. She pushed the discomfort aside. She had to hurry. Europe Junior could press the button at any time, and she would be dead.

Rounding the corner, she noticed a figure on the opposite side of the building. It was the boy. Freya's brother. The one who had taken away her only friend.

She dutifully pressed the button on her cell phone, took out her blades, and charged.

CHAPTER THIRTY-ONE

Europe Junior sank into the deep leather car seat, fuming. He was already mad about having to drive himself, much less having to drive to ground zero. Watchers rarely placed themselves in the field, and even when they did, it was *never* to a hot site. But Helmut's threat was clear. If he did not follow Helmut's orders, he would be executed.

Europe Junior never considered himself a racist, though he often described himself as an elitist. He believed that there was a form of intelligence that was simply superior to others, and it spread across all races and nationalities. Premiums were mere tools, ranked below waiters and caddies, below restroom attendants. They were prototypes, not worthy of names. They were simply disposable soldiers, designed to be used and discarded at will.

And yet he had to actually touch the Premium to administer her treatments. Grimacing at the memory, he wished he had hand sanitizer in his car.

He looked at his watch. The Premium should have reached the center of the compound by now. He hoped that she would eliminate the Sinanju agents quickly. He could not afford to return to VIGIL base a failure.

His cell phone beeped. 14 had signaled. He smiled as he clicked the timer, waiting for the three-minute countdown to appear on his screen.

Nothing happened. Angrily, he pressed the button again and again. Looking down, the screen flashed two words: SIGNAL ERROR.

Some kind of interference was blocking the signal.

Europe Junior knew that the timer would work if it was in a direct line of sight with any of the bombs. He just needed to be near the center of the compound. He would move in quickly, start the timer, and run to the safety of his car. He would be several miles away by the time the buildings, the Sinanju agents, and the Premium were destroyed.

He never would have pressed the button if he had known that fifty feet below the main warehouse, a three-hundred-megaton nuclear bomb was awaiting his signal.

He mindlessly pressed the button as he walked.

CHAPTER THIRTY-TWO

Ben studied the messages he had received from VIGIL. There was something he was missing, but couldn't put his finger on it. He had tried tracing the messages multiple ways, but they always ended up at a dead end. That told him that Helmut was involved. Only another FORtab could mask a trail from his own FORtab. Taking a puff from his cigar, an idea lit up Ben's mind. He smiled.

Helmut may have been a genius — but Ben realized that he was not a computer genius. Helmut had counted on his FORtab to hide the trail the file took once it was sent, but he missed the extra data that was hidden within the file itself.

Ben could not penetrate the security around Helmut's FORtab, but he was able to find where the first message had originated. He was surprised to discover that the report on the nightclub slaughter had, in fact, been composed on the computer of the late Africa Senior. And then he locked onto her computer. The hidden data in the file allowed Ben to access her other files, including one that Ben found very interesting: a detailed list of information she had compiled on Helmut Belisis and his predecessor.

Saving the document for later study, Ben's eyes widened as he located her itinerary. VIGIL was currently holding a Watcher meeting, and he had just discovered the location.

CHAPTER THIRTY-THREE

Just as Ben had said, the base was completely deserted. Stone had not seen a single security guard or technician, but Freya's words had made him feel uneasy. If an attack was coming, he expected to at least notice small signs of activity, but this was a ghost town.

Turning the corner of the building, Stone heard a breath. He could tell the sound had come from a woman. Unless Freya was seriously hurt, though, she would not breathe loudly and carelessly, and he certainly would have heard the sounds of a fight.

Almost immediately, he realized who it was, but it was too late. In the half-second he had spent thinking, 14 attacked, slashing viciously at Stone with her razor-sharp blades. He jumped back just in time, watching his Kevlar vest fall to the ground in shredded pieces. 14 followed with a roundhouse kick to Stone's head, but Stone was centered and ready.

At least, he thought he was.

The woman they fought earlier was fast, but she had not been as fast as a Master of Sinanju.

She was now.

Her movements were so fast that Stone could only see her kick once the tip of her heel had connected with his temple. His vision exploded with bright light as he staggered to the railing.

Stone pulled his knife.

Sunny Joe would have been appalled, but Stone was determined to drag Sinanju into the twenty-first century. If a Master of Sinanju was deadly with his bare hands, how deadly could he be with a weapon?

This time, Stone saw the blow coming to his mid-section. He dodged to the side and followed with his blade. It connected in the center of 14's chest as he had hoped, but the blade struck something hard and bounced back.

Blood showed where Stone had struck, but it was just a surface wound. Her carbon-plated bones easily protected her from Stone's blade.

Blast it! Stone thought. He had forgotten that she was armored beneath her skin.

14 kicked his wrist, causing Stone to drop the knife. For a split-second, Stone's attention was on the blade and he cursed himself. Sunny Joe's lesson about weapons

instantly came to his mind: as long as you hold a weapon, part of your concentration belongs to the weapon instead of your target.

Stone brought his attention back to 14, only to see her fist as it connected with the side of his head. It felt like she had hit him with brass knuckles. His thoughts became hazy as he tried to find his balance. 14 kicked him in the stomach. Dazed, Stone tried to move from her next kick, but it connected squarely in his back, sending Stone sailing to the ground twenty feet below.

Stone twisted in the air, trying to land flatly on his back to disperse the impact as equally as he could. But it was too far a drop and he was moving too fast.

Stone hit the ground with a sick crunch.

"Stone!" a voice screamed. Sprinting across the rooftop, Freya's eyes burned with rage. "Sister, what have you done?"

CHAPTER THIRTY-FOUR

Freya looked down at Stone's unmoving body. She could tell he was still breathing, but could not tell how seriously he was injured.

Then Freya sensed the bullets. Her body automatically flowed with the air, easily weaving through the rounds heading her way. Europe Junior hoped that catching her off guard would allow him to shoot her, but Freya effortlessly danced between the rounds as if she were jumping rope.

Freya raced to the ladder and slid down the handles at top speed. As she reached the ground, her breath caught in her chest. 14 held Stone's head in her hands.

"Kill him!" Europe Junior screamed.

Freya knew that she was not fast enough to stop 14. The second it would take Freya to reach her would be enough time for 14 to break Stone's neck. She looked plaintively at 14, and a tear rolled down her cheek.

14 stood transfixed by the moment.

A member of the VIGIL counsel was giving her a direct order. All her training had told her to obey a superior's orders without question or hesitancy. Everything inside her told her to kill this man. He had tried to kill her, and if he were conscious, he would still be trying to kill her.

But when she saw the tears falling from Freya's eyes, 14 knew what she had to do.

Another surge of power raged through her veins. The pounding behind her temples became a large thud and, in that moment, 14 knew that her body had passed its limit.

She was going to die.

But Freya still had a chance.

Europe Junior climbed down the ladder and approached, a triumphant smile stretched across his face.

"Kill him!" he repeated.

14 stood still.

"I'll kill him myself," he said, aiming his pistol at Stone and lining up the shot.

Freya dashed toward Stone, but knew she would be too late. Sinanju had trained her to dodge them, but no one could outrun bullets.

Midway through her run, Freya no longer felt the gun's threat.

The gun — and the hand holding it — now lay on the ground next to Europe Junior.

He reached for his hand as shock raced through his system. His brain was trying to process the sight of his hand, separated from his body. 14 stood next to him, her blades freshly tipped with blood. Europe Junior tried again to press the button on the timer, but only managed to mash the nub of his arm to his pocket.

14 turned to him and he began stepping away from her.

"What have you done to me, you freak?" Europe Junior shrieked as 14 staggered toward him. Her steps were jerky, like a defective robot.

"I have freed myself."

Her head jerked uncontrollably to the side as she reached Europe Junior. 14 tossed the detonator to Freya and then spent her fury on him, shredding his body into parts.

14 collapsed as Europe Junior's body fell. Her body began to violently spasm as she lay on the ground, as if her body was trying to throw up its own organs.

Freya turned 14 softly onto her back. The pungent odor of a thick spice emerged from the pores of her skin.

Poison.

Freya reached behind 14's back toward the base of her spine and began the basic Sinanju methods of poison extraction, but she had just begun learning the process and each pressure point caused 14 to cry out in pain, so Freya stopped.

She smiled sadly at 14.

"Thank you, sister," 14 said softly. She tried to match Freya's smile, but the pain was too great and she was only able to manage a tight grimace. She looked at Freya's flowing hair. She removed her maroon headpiece and handed it to Freya.

"Take it," 14 said, doubling over in pain. "Your long hair…is a tactical weakness."

14 opened her mouth and wildly screamed. Her blood pressure spiked until her eyes began to bleed, but she fought to remain conscious.

Freya wished she had paid closer attention to Sunny Joe's lessons on nerve manipulation. If she had the skill, perhaps she could force the chemicals out of 14's system, but there was nothing she could do now but watch 14 die in agony.

"Is there anything I can do for you, Sister?" Freya asked.

"Call me Lisa," 14 said, tears falling unashamedly down her face. Her mouth opened involuntarily as she fought back a scream.

"Lisa," Freya whispered, kneeling beside her. Freya had seen enough people die to recognize the tell-tale signs creeping through Lisa's body. It was just a matter of moments. "You have fought bravely, Lisa," she said. "But you can rest now, sister. You are not alone."

Lisa looked into Freya's eyes and her body went limp. She tried again to force a smile, but the pain would not allow it. Darkness began claiming the edges of her vision and she thought back to the other Premium who escaped and her eyes opened wide.

The men who sent Lisa would use her death to fire her up and Freya would be blamed. Lisa pulled Freya close to her.

"You must…you must find…" Lisa whispered.

Freya leaned closer.

"Find my sister," Lisa sputtered, blood pooling in the corners of her mouth. "64. She…is like me."

Lisa's squinted her eyes closed, and she took in one last gasp. Her body jerked and she involuntarily pushed Freya. Freya did not block the blow, and fell onto on her back.

But before she stood back up, she knew Lisa was gone.

Lisa lay on the ground, silent and unmoving.

Stone stood at a distance and let his sister cry for the first time in a long time.

CHAPTER THIRTY-FIVE

Harold W. Smith's gray visage appeared on Ben's FORtab.

"Dr. Smith, I've figured out how to reverse trace the document I was sent. I know where VIGIL is meeting. I believe we can take them out."

Smith studied the input from Ben's FORtab.

"According to your readings, they are located in a bunker below a Spanish castle. Do you know the repercussions of launching an assault on allied territory?"

"If we want to eliminate them, we must strike now." Ben paused for a moment. "If I figured out how to do this, it is a matter of time before Helmut does as well. As long as he has a FORtab, there is a risk that he can access ours. We could never tell what was real and what wasn't."

Smith weighed Ben's words, slowly turning the oblong tablet in his hands. He thought of how helpful it was in his defense of the United States. Then he realized how powerful a weapon it could be if it was turned against the United States.

Smith began typing.

"Bombers off the coast have just been given orders to destroy the location as part of an exercise. It will be blamed on hackers, but the international repercussions of this decision will be felt for years."

"I understand," Ben said. "But what if Helmut escapes? Your FORtab controls mine. Is there a way of neutralizing Helmut's?"

"When I ordered their construction, I gave my unit control of a self-destruct sequence that will destroy all FORtabs."

"Can't you just destroy Helmut's?"

"I was unaware of his obtaining a unit, so the self-destruct command was designed as a last resort. Our FORtabs will be destroyed in the process."

Ben looked at his FORtab. The decision was easy.

"Do it."

CHAPTER THIRTY-SIX

Helmut Belisis sat at his desk, his impatience growing. St. Louis should have been incinerated by now, eliminating Europe Junior. But so far, nothing had happened. Looking at the symbol of Sinanju on his FORtab, he wiped the sweat from his forehead with his monogrammed handkerchief.

The image was still on his screen when his FORtab began vibrating. It was Cole.

"You have indeed surprised me, Benjamin," Helmut said. "After our last encounter, you said that you would never contact me again. What has happened to change that?"

"A lesson in humility — something you wouldn't understand. I called to say goodbye."

"I'm afraid I don't have time to ferret out your cryptic words today. Perhaps we can continue this some other time?"

Helmut began to scan Ben's signal when the door to his office bolted shut. He pressed the switch that controlled the door, but it remained locked.

"Sit down, Helmut. You're not going anywhere," Ben said. "You know, VIGIL started out as something good. From what I know, VIGIL was developed under the goal of protecting mankind for the next thousand years. Something has changed over the centuries. That is where humility comes in. VIGIL lost it."

Helmut beamed his polite smile at Ben, all the while scanning with his FORtab. That's when he saw another signal.

Smith's FORtab took control of Helmut's unit.

"Dr. Smith is isolating your FORtab while I manipulate your own headquarters' security against itself. We know where you are located. Bombers are already on their way. There will be no survivors."

"Impossible," Helmut said, but then noted the radar display on his FORtab lighting up.

Incoming.

"I told you that my enemies don't get a second chance," Ben said. "Goodbye, Helmut."

Helmut tried to grab control of the bombers as they approached, but his FORtab began to vibrate in a pattern that Helmut didn't recognize. The screen dimmed and then exploded, sending shrapnel across his office, peppering Helmut's face and torso.

Then the lights went out and the emergency beacons began their haunting wail.

* * * *

A few days later, Helmut awoke in a top-secret VIGIL room on the top floor of a

Madrid hospital. At first, he did not remember what had happened. The doctor said that he had a severe concussion and suffered from temporary memory loss.

Over the next few weeks, he began remembering pieces of what happened. NATO planes had dropped wave after wave of bunker busters, leveling the castle that had served as VIGIL headquarters for the past eight centuries, incinerating every person inside, whether Watcher, butler, or cook.

He remembered awakening on the floor of his office, thankful for the reinforced bunker that surrounded him. He remembered stumbling dizzily through the emergency hatch in the back, emerging a thousand feet away.

He remembered looking back at a crater that had once housed the most powerful organization on Earth.

He remembered the taste of blood in his mouth and the unceasing ringing in his ears.

And then, with a cold awareness, he remembered the face of Benjamin Cole and only one thing occupied his mind: vengeance.

CHAPTER THIRTY-SEVEN

The grand finale to the Great Southwestern Meet was about to begin. Each year, on the last night of the Meet, one tribe presented a detailed history of their culture. Although the identity of the presenting tribe was supposed to be kept a secret until the final night, lips were loose at the Meet, and someone inevitably let it slip long before the presentation took place.

The crowd was still abuzz about Sunny Joe's defeat of Steven Oxendine. The event had brought lots of traffic to the Sinanju booth. They sold everything they brought, and had enough orders to stay busy for weeks. A few kids had even come by and asked Sunny Joe for autographs for the first time since he left Hollywood.

"They'll be talking about that for years," Mick said.

"You mean you'll be talking about it for years," Sunny Joe corrected.

"I'm a historian. That's my job, right?" Mick asked, smiling.

"Someone's got to do it," Sunny Joe said, looking around the booth area. "We about through?"

Mick leaned back and removed his cowboy hat, wiping the sweat from his brow. "I'm going to make sure they loaded up the vans. I'll be back for the presentation."

"I'll be out to help in a minute," Sunny Joe said, watching his old friend walk off. Though he was a year older than Mick, Sunny Joe's movements were those of a man two decades younger. Time was catching up with his old friend, and it would only be a matter of time before Mick's body succumbed to the natural wear of age.

That was the curse of a Master of Sinanju. They outlived their family and friends. Sunny Joe would live to see Mick's grandchildren become old before he surrendered to death.

The cycle of life was a bitch.

CHAPTER THIRTY-EIGHT

"Why didn't you scope out the rest of the base after 14's death?" Ben asked.

"Her name was Lisa," Freya said forcefully.

"Excuse me, after Lisa's death."

"When we first got there, I received a text from you. It was garbled, but it basically said not to investigate the buildings."

"I never gave such an order. Freya said she saw a light on in one of the buildings. No one is supposed to be stationed there, and it's been abandoned for years. Any information would have been valuable."

"Then let's just go back," Stone said.

"Too late. I sent information on a 'disturbance' there to the FBI, and they're already swarming the place. What did you see, Freya?"

"I couldn't see much. I hand to stand on my toes to look in."

Noticing Stone's glare, Freya looked down before continuing to speak. "As I walked by the window, a screen on the wall lit up and started flashing random pictures," she said.

"Do you remember anything specific?" Ben asked.

"It showed the symbol for the Sinanju tribe. The rest were confusing."

"In what way?" Ben asked.

"It kept switching through a series of pictures. I remember seeing an eagle and a mountain. The pictures kept cycling back to a man standing on a hill, holding a large rock in his hand. He was smiling."

"Could you tell who it was?"

"No. He was an older man with gray hair and a beard."

Ben scratched his own beard in thought. On a hunch, he pulled up a picture of Helmut on his computer screen.

"That's him!" Freya said. "But he was wearing a beard. He held the rock out as if he were offering it."

"Was there anything else?"

"I saw buildings and flags, but they flashed by so quickly that I couldn't recognize any of them."

"Interesting," Ben said. "I don't know why there would be a picture of Helmut, or why he was wearing a beard, but I'll certainly look into it. If you remember anything else, let me know."

"I want to know who sent that message if you didn't," Stone said impatiently.

He handed his phone to Ben, who plugged it up to his computer.

"Let's find out," Ben said, checking the logs of Stone's cell phone. He missed the speed of his FORtab.

"Found it. It looks like it was a pulsed message, sent in a burst, faster than your phone was able to process. That's why it was garbled."

He looked at the path the message had taken, but there was nothing to trace. It was as if the signal originated from inside Stone's phone.

"I'm going to need to keep your phone for a while. You'll be provided with another one."

"That one's a piece of iJunk anyway," Stone said with disdain, tossing his phone to Ben.

"At least it doesn't get viruses," Ben said peevishly.

"I'd trade a thousand viruses if it didn't..."

Freya loudly cleared her throat.

"Please, not another technological debate," Freya said. She had no idea why they were so emotionally invested in their devices. It was a partisan battle that neither would find victory. "Mr. Ben, do you have any more information on what Lisa said about her 'sister?' Are more of these women out there?"

"All we know about Carnage is what we learned from Helmut and that may very well have been an elaborate lie. If 14...Lisa said another woman was out there, we'll keep an eye out, but I wish I had more than a name like '64.' I'll keep you posted."

"Please do," Stone said. "Freya needs a new frienemy."

Stone regretted the words as soon as they were out of his mouth. Freya punched him lightly in the shoulder, but there was anger behind it. Waiting for the screaming pain in his arm to lessen, Stone watched Ben continue typing.

CHAPTER THIRTY-NINE

The young man with the dark war paint stared across the parking lot as heatwaves hazily rose from the blacktop. If any of the historians at the Meet had checked, they would not have found the man's garb listed in any registry, nor would they have found anyone in attendance who would have recognized it.

The man's tribal uniform had not been seen in public since his family had been banished from the lands of his ancestors. But it was not the white man who betrayed them. It was not the white man who forced them from their land.

It was one of their own.

His birth name was Robert Nez, but he refused to be called by any other name than the tribal name given to him by his mother: War Feather.

He was a direct descendant of Bearclaw, chief of the once-mighty Desteen tribe. The Desteen had lived peacefully for hundreds of years until a visitor came to their lands, seeking a place to stay.

The man said his name was Kojong and he claimed to be from across the great Western Sea. No one believed that such a journey was possible, so he was ridiculed and told to move on. Then they were attacked by some nearby tribes. Chief Bearclaw died in battle, and it looked as if all hope was lost, but the stranger Kojong single-handedly drove out the invaders. For saving the tribe, he was welcomed with open arms and given the chief's daughter in marriage.

Since the Chief had no surviving sons, the marriage took away the birthright of the chief's bastard son. Desteen tradition was clear; the boy would have been the next to rule. But no one had stood up to defend the bastard son of Bearclaw.

They all cheered for their new hero, Kojong.

* * * *

War Feather's father had tried to reestablish their tribe, but the Meet organizers scoffed at his tales. They said that they had no record of his tribe. When he told them what the Sinanju tribe had done, they openly laughed at him and pointed him to a government website.

"Father, we can't let them treat us like this!" War Feather protested.

"We still have our honor," his father said. "We must be patient, my son."

Honor was all they had left. There was nothing else. They had been displaced from their land when the nest of an endangered rodent species was found inside their borders. When they asked the government agent where they should go, the man smiled.

"Buy a condo like everyone else. Welcome to the twenty-first century."

He left them with nothing more than a piece of paper promising real money.

Losing their last piece of land was too much of a strain and War Feather's father died in shame. His father's mistake, War Feather realized, was trying to work within the system. If the Desteen were to find their place again, it would not be by forms and paperwork. It would only be redeemed by blood.

War Feather had watched the match between Sunny Joe and Steven Oxendine very closely. While everyone else saw two arms exerting strength against each other, he knew what was really happening: Sunny Joe was breathing properly, and channeling his energy into his arms.

Oxendine never stood a chance.

The match also confirmed what War Feather already knew, that Sunny Joe was one of *them* — one of the Masters who had banished his people and stolen their art.

And now, he would pay.

* * * *

As Mick walked across the parking lot, he noticed a young man in war paint leaning against Mick's van, glaring at him.

"Can I help you?" Mick asked politely.

"I am War Feather, the last son and true heir of the Desteen tribe! I have come to reclaim the lands stolen by the ancestor of the Sinanju!"

As he shouted his pronouncement, War Feather drew a long knife from his sash. While his last words were still hanging in the air, he drew his arm back and threw.

The blade glinted in the setting sun as the knife spun through the air. Mick tried to move out of the knife's path, but it was moving too fast. The knife turned, end over end, speeding towards him. It was inches from his face when a leathery hand plucked it from the air.

Sunny Joe's voice rang out from behind Mick. "I am the chief of the Sinanju. If you have an issue, it is with me, not my friend." Sunny Joe's hands seemed to hum as he slowly began to twist the knife. "Let us discuss this with clean hands," he said, turning his palms to face the ground. A pile of glittering dust was all that remained of the steel blade.

"I will not forget this, old man," War Feather said.

"And neither will I," Sunny Joe said. "Come to the reservation next month. We will discuss this like men, not like children playing war games."

War Feather glared silently at Sunny Joe with the same look of rage that he had shown at the arm-wrestling match earlier. He spat on the ground and walked away.

Watching the figure of War Feather retreat into the distance, Sunny Joe spoke softly. "Are you all right, Mick?"

"I'm fine. I'm telling you, though, kids today have no respect for their elders." He laughed heartily as he checked the van, but Sunny Joe could see his knees were still shaking.

CHAPTER FORTY

Stone sat on the side of the dune behind his house, staring at the expanse of the Arizona sunset. Freya waited for him to put out his cigarette before sitting next to him.

"Mr. Walker said that you should try electronic cigarettes," she said. "He said that they are not as harmful."

"Sorry, but I don't do smoky bubbles."

"Grandfather said that he could force the toxins from your body."

"Yeah, but it's not just about the nicotine," Stone said. "I went to some really strict boarding schools as a kid. They sheltered us from everything. Smoking was the one bad thing I could get away with. I guess it stuck."

"Stuck? More like stunk," Freya said, holding her nose. "Is there anything I can do?"

"I was about to say to kick my ass every time you see me with a cigarette, but I want to live to see thirty."

"I would never kill you," Freya smiled. "Well, not for that."

Stone stopped smiling and Freya laughed.

"So, what happened with your Salty Night?" Stone asked.

"It's the 'Night of Salt.' My mouth tasted like someone dumped a saltshaker in it. It was revolting," Freya said, grimacing at the thought.

It was Stone's turn to grin.

"Don't laugh too much, big brother. It will happen to you once your body accepts Sinanju."

"Well, that'll probably take a while," Stone said. "Do you feel any different?"

"Not really," Freya said. "I thought I'd feel supercharged afterward or something."

"I don't think you need to go anywhere near 'supercharged.'"

"Shut up," Freya said, smiling.

"Grandpa told me about it. Said that it makes you question yourself and do stupid things. What did you do?"

Freya hesitated as a mischievous grin snuck onto her face.

"Let's just say that I corrected a mistake Grandfather made a long time ago," she finally admitted.

Stone looked at the maroon headdress on Freya's head. He recognized it as the one Lisa wore. It was tight on Freya's head because it was designed for very short hair. There was a small blood stain on the front.

"Yuck. Are you really gonna wear that?"

"Yes. I think Lisa would like that. Besides, it really holds my hair in well."

"I still don't understand," Stone said. "How could you have become friends with her? She tried to kill you."

"No, she only tried to kill you. She liked me."

"Well, let's hope her 'sister' likes you too."

Freya's smile disappeared.

"I don't know how many there are, but if there are others like her, we have to save them," Freya said. "Stone, please tell me that we will look for them."

"Ben's already looking. Even so, we may not be able to save them," Stone said. "Sis, that's something else you're going to learn. This job doesn't always have a happy ending."

"I know. But we need to try."

The somber look from Freya wore him down. "I'll talk to Ben. Promise. You sure you don't just want a puppy?"

"I wouldn't mind a puppy," Freya said, fanning the air in front of her. "As long as it doesn't smoke."

신안주 모두가 마스터에게 활을 다

OVERLOAD

THE PLANET MARS
1981 A.D.

The harsh Martian landscape stretched as far as he could see through the tiny slit in his polished gray space helmet. The deadly atmosphere and biting cold would have destroyed any ordinary man, but Galaxy Ranger Roy Newton was no ordinary man. Roy Newton was an inventor, a cellist, a botanist.

But first and foremost, Roy Newton was a warrior.

The first four landing parties sent by the Space Force had disappeared soon after touchdown. His expedition was the fifth and final attempt at colonization of Earth's neighboring planet and Galaxy Ranger Roy Newton was determined that his expedition would be the first to survive.

His jaw jutted forth in defiance, Roy Newton surveyed the dark alien surface and a million thoughts flooded his genius-level mind. Roy Newton's great-great-great-great-great-great grandfather was the third cousin to Sir Isaac Newton. Space Force knew that the massive intellect that flowed through his brain was more than a match for any threat Mars would present, but it took a resolution from the United Nations before they could risk Earth's greatest mind.

His enviro-suit beeped softly, reassuring him that all systems were fully operational, but Newton realized that something was amiss. Even here, in zero gravity, things were a bit too quiet. He turned to his partner, the sultry Jean Klein, but she was nowhere to be found. He had told the higher-ups they shouldn't have added a dame to the roster. They were nothing but trouble.

Fortunately, Galaxy Ranger Roy Newton knew a little bit about trouble.

He smiled as a large tentacle appeared behind him. How stupid did they think he was? He turned at the last second and fired his proto-nuclear pistol at the Martian beast, severing its six limbs one at a time. Each limb fell to the Martian landscape in puffs of orange dust.

Except for the last limb, which the beast tripped over.

"Cut!" a frustrated voice shouted and the lights on the set turned on. "Dammit, Sturgeon, can't you get through one take without screwing things up?"

Phil Rye was a director who once believed that movies were magic — that they were the quintessential twentieth-century art form. But that was before he met Stevie

Sturgeon. The novice stuntman seemed determined to drag out the making of the movie by sheer willpower and ineptitude.

"It wasn't my fault!" Sturgeon yelled, removing the sweaty rubber alien headpiece and throwing it to the ground. "Everyone else's timing is off!"

"Sturgeon!" the director yelled, motioning for Sturgeon to approach. He looked down and counted to ten before looking up again. "You're only in this film as a favor to your uncle. But God rest his soul, kid, you just don't have it."

"What does that mean? You're gonna put Roam in again?"

"He gets the job done right — and on the first take, too. You should pay attention to how he does it."

"But he's not even supposed to be working this set! This is supposed to be my job!"

"Sorry kid, but you're just not working out."

"I got martial arts training…and look at this smile!" Sturgeon said, moving his lips in an unnatural manner and squinting his eyes as he tried to make a friendly face.

"Looks like you're trying to take a dump. Besides, it doesn't matter what you look like under a rubber fish head," the director said.

"Just look at this hair!" Sturgeon said in frustration, moving his head back and forth, allowing his long brown locks freedom. "Your star doesn't even have hair like mine!"

The director chuckled dismissively and turned his back to Sturgeon. "Bill! Last call, I promise!"

As one, the crew turned their attention to a thin man sitting next to the camera. Dark brown hair cascaded past his shoulders as Bill Roam stood. Bill was tall, and though middle-aged, he could have easily passed for thirty.

At one time, his entire life had been laid out. He was the son of the chief of the Sinanju tribe in Arizona. But in a rare moment of rebellion, Bill left the tribe to seek fame and fortune in Hollywood. He had failed to become an actor, but found work as Hollywood's preeminent stunt man. It was hard work, but it was a life that he had chosen. He worked on everything from westerns to science fiction. If a stunt was deemed too difficult or too dangerous, directors knew they could get results from Big Bill Roam.

Then he met Dawn Starr. They fell in love and were married within a couple of months. But while on a movie shoot west of New York City, Dawn prematurely went into labor. She suffered internal bleeding and died a week later, and something snapped inside Bill Roam and he began to think about suicide. Not wanting to risk the safety of their new baby, he left their child at the steps of a nearby Catholic orphanage in honor of his wife's Catholic heritage.

He tried to bury himself in his work as a stuntman, but as Bill saw more and more of Hollywood, he liked it less and less. The Hollywood culture was built entirely on the love of money, and he saw too many innocent young lives destroyed by their dreams of stardom.

So, when his father came to plead for Bill to return to the reservation, Bill listened. His family's entire history seemed to weigh on his shoulders as he considered his father's words. He agreed to return home and complete his Sinanju training. Before he could leave, Phil Rye, one of the few friends he had made while in Hollywood, asked for help one last time. Bill obliged, but brought his suitcase-packed car to the lot. He was ready to go home.

"Look, Bill, I know he sucks, but the kid is my godson," Phil said, more than slightly embarrassed. "Is there anything you could do to...I don't know...maybe help him out?"

"I'll see what I can do," Bill said.

Sturgeon stood with his arms crossed, his face refusing to believe this was happening. "So, what are you going to teach me?" he asked. "How to get old?"

"No. I learned a long time ago that you can't teach someone who is unwilling to learn," Bill said. "But as a favor to my friend, I'm gonna try. Stevie, your main problem is that you don't realize that you're not the star. The best stuntmen are invisible."

"I don't have to realize anything," Sturgeon said coldly. "This is my time to shine, not yours."

Bill studied Sturgeon's posture and breathing. "Stuntmen require balance and control. Maybe you should take ballet or karate lessons."

"No way I'm wearin' some pink tutu, and I got bored with Karate a long time ago. I've perfected a superior martial art. It's called "Adrogans." That's French for 'silent killer.'"

Bill tilted his face into his hands and sighed as he recognized the Latin word for "arrogant." He arched one eyebrow. "And who told you that?"

"The most deadly Frenchman to ever live. He showed me the first move and told me the rest was mine to build upon."

"Since the premiere offensive move of the French involves a white flag, it wouldn't take much to be the deadliest one. How much did he charge to teach you this 'magical' move?"

"Two thousand dollars."

"Sounds like you got a good deal," Bill said, trying not to roll his eyes. "What move did he teach you?"

"You think I'll show you so you can steal it? No way, man, I'm not a sucker! I'm a twelfth-degree black belt in Adrogans!"

"And I assume there are only twelve degrees in Adrogans?" Bill asked.

"You wish! There are only ten. I have even already ascended beyond Adrogans."

"Well, even with your magical move, you still need to work on your balance."

Sturgeon walked away with a scowl. He would teach Roam a thing or two about balance. As the others took a five-minute break, Sturgeon walked over to the crane supporting the stunt cables. It was a simple pulley and joist system that was designed to hold the stuntman and all of the appendages in place so they appeared to be a single organism. The crane arm was strong enough to hold the fuselage of a plane twenty feet over the ground, but everything for this stunt was held together by a simple bolt system. If a few of the bolts were loosened, the arm would crash, ruining the stunt and making Roam look like a fool…or worse.

Of course, after he failed, Stevie Sturgeon would come to the rescue.

As the set repopulated, the crew grew silent as Bill Roam entered the stage. He smiled to everyone as he put on the rubber headpiece. The thin cables were re-attached to his rubbery limbs and he took his mark.

"Wait!" The actor playing Roy Newton said, holding up his hand. He ran over to Bill and shook his rubber hand. "Thanks, Bill. It's been an honor working with you."

Behind him, the cast and crew burst into applause. Sturgeon tried not to throw up.

Roy Newton placed his helmet back on his head and struck his pose. Sturgeon looked up at the crane arm holding the arms and saw it bending slightly. He grinned. If it fell just right, the crane might even land on Roam.

"Action!" the director called.

As Newton turned with his proto-nuclear pistol and it lit up, each of the rubbery arms were timed perfectly to fall off Roam's rubber suit. Then came the final shot, designed to take out Roam's alien character.

That's when the crane fell.

The crane bent with an incredibly loud groan and everyone looked up.

Sturgeon almost clapped when he saw the crane bend. The arm bent one last time, releasing its hold on the wiring system holding up the rubbery arms attached to Bill. The cables fell softly to the ground, but the crane remained in place.

No way! Sturgeon thought. *It was supposed to fall down and embarrass Roam!*

Sturgeon stomped over to Bill. He figured Bill should have already peed his pants in fear. If he handled it right, there would still be time for him to be the hero.

"What did you screw up, Roam?" Sturgeon yelled. He leaned over to look at the rubbery alien arms on the ground and found one of the arms still attached to the crane.

Then he pulled.

The crane's arm snapped and fell toward Sturgeon, who panicked and froze in place. Bill tackled him to the ground, out of the way of the crane.

"Whoa!" the director yelled in shock. "Bill, you saved him!"

Sturgeon sputtered. He was not going to let Roam take this away from him, too. Sturgeon brushed himself off and ignored Roam's helping hand to his feet. Sturgeon turned around as if he were going to walk away. If the old man wanted to see his first move, Stevie Sturgeon would oblige him. But the move would be the last thing Roam would see before waking up in the infirmary.

It was time for Stevie Sturgeon to teach Bill Roam about balance.

Bill rolled his eyes. Stevie's entire body projected that he was about to throw a punch, so when he suddenly pivoted and threw his elbow, Bill didn't even need to employ a Sinanju move. He merely took a step backwards and pushed Stevie with one hand.

Stevie fell to the floor and the stagehands began laughing.

"Son, this isn't gonna end well," Bill said.

"You're right about that, old man!" Sturgeon yelled, getting to his feet. Sturgeon raised his hands out to his side and focused. This was the move he had never attempted before, the one so serious that it only existed on paper. The blow would be lethal, but he was defending himself and Roam had asked for it, by embarrassing him in front of everyone.

Sturgeon closed his eyes as he aimed his blow at Bill Roam. It was going to be so powerful, so utterly destructive in its raw power, that he didn't even want to see the results.

He opened his eyes a few minutes later on a stretcher. The first words he heard were the set doctor yelling, "I've got a pulse!"

CHAPTER ONE: THE PRESENT

Stevie Sturgeon looked at the bottles of pills that filled his desk drawer. There were pills to stop pain. Pills to help him go to sleep. Pills to help him wake up. Pills to make him go to the bathroom. Pills to stop him from going to the bathroom. Recently, he had even started taking little blue pills.

At one time, he was America's premiere action hero, but at this stage of his life, it seemed to take every medication known to man just to hold his body together.

He stared nostalgically at the movie posters adorning the walls to his office. Each poster featured the exact same pose, with the same scowl. The only difference was the uniform he was in and the title of the movie. It was as if someone cut out the same picture, digitally altered the clothing and filled in different backgrounds.

The door to his office opened and his agent Bernie Watkins entered. Bernie was old and his contacts had dried up at the same time as Sturgeon's movie career, so his job had changed from representing Sturgeon, to representing himself *to* Sturgeon. The remains of a partially-eaten donut dusted the top part of his jacket.

Bernie seated himself in front of Sturgeon and swept powdered sugar from a pile of papers he had been carrying.

"Okay, I got good news," he said, but stopped when he saw that Sturgeon, who had obviously been crying.

"So, I guess you got the invitation to the funeral?" Bernie said somberly.

"What?" Sturgeon asked, his face still swollen with fresh tears.

"Phil Rye's funeral is Tuesday."

"Who?" Sturgeon asked, tenderly wiping away his tears, careful not to waste excess DNA on the tissues.

"He managed your warehouse," Bernie said, but didn't see a hint of recognition. "He was a director...you worked for him."

Sturgeon's face remained blank.

"Back when you were a stuntman…what was the name of…oh yeah! *Martian Invaders!*"

Sturgeon closed his tear-burdened eyes in anger. He would have liked to forget about his stuntman days, especially *that* particular movie.

"Oh," Sturgeon said. "So he wasn't anyone important?"

"Well, if it's not about him, what's with the tears?" Bernie asked, confused.

"I just finished reading a movie script, quite possibly the most amazing movie script ever written. It is a moving tale with powerful characters, beautiful sets, culminating in the ultimate triumph of the human spirit," he meekly said, his voice approaching a reverent whisper.

"You didn't tell me about any movie deal! Let me see that!" Bernie said, snatching the script from Sturgeon's hands. He began reading, but after the first four paragraphs, his head began hurting. He had never seen so many adjectives stuffed into one page.

"Who wrote this?"

Sturgeon finished wiping the tears from his eyes, but he still couldn't yet make eye contact. The story was still too raw, too powerful.

"I did," he said.

Bernie slowly placed the script back on the desk.

"Ah, I see. So, are you going to the funeral? There will be lots of press there."

"Why would I want to go to his funeral? He was a nobody."

"It's free publicity, showing you in all black, a tear rolling down on your cheek. Besides, you still want to run for governor, right? It looks good when you go to funerals. The press likes that sort of thing. It'll help you win in Arkansas."

"Arizona," Sturgeon corrected. "The people there need me."

"Arkansas, Arizona. Whatever. It's all the same if it isn't Cali. Stevie, why do you even want to be governor of some podunk state?"

"I played an Arizona marshal in *Arizona Siege I and II*," he said, sitting back and smiling. "Maybe it was another movie. I don't know. I just remember that I look good in brown."

"Stevie, things like that cost millions of dollars. Millions you no longer have."

Sturgeon glared at Bernie, silently expressing his frustration at having to work with lesser beings.

"I'm running for governor, Bernie. Once I have made a decision, my mind is a steel trap, with huge metal teeth just waiting for someone to try to change it."

"Okay, okay," Bernie said, raising his hands in mock surrender. "But I'm telling you, going to the funeral would make you look good."

"Fine. Just be ready to get me out of there fast," Sturgeon said. "I have important things to do."

"Really? Like what?" Bernie asked, surprised. When Sturgeon glared at him again, he quickly changed the subject. "So…how did the Salad Chop commercial look?"

"They sent me a copy last week. It's around here somewhere."

Sturgeon shuffled some of the papers around on his desk until he found a large envelope. As requested, he only accepted VHS tapes. None of that digital crap for him.

Stevie put the tape into his VCR and hit play. His old television blinked as it accepted the signal and a countdown displayed with his face in the center and the words "Stevie Sturgeon Salad Chopper" beneath.

A small child was trying to cut a salad with a knife and the obviously rubber knife cut into his finger. A small spurt of blood-colored syrup erupted as the child cried on cue.

"Tired of chopping salads the old-fashioned way?" an excited voice asked. "Then you're ready for the twenty-first century's answer to salad: the amazing Stevie Sturgeon Salad Chopper!"

Stevie appeared onscreen in full karate gear, his enormous gut partially hidden behind three separate black belts. He had tried to explain to the producers that he was the only man on Earth to master three martial arts, but the truth was that wearing just one belt made his fat spill over both sides of the belt. Stevie smiled as he saw himself strut onscreen.

"Hey kid, you wanna learn how to chop like this?" he asked with his trademark whispered scowl. Sturgeon turned, and in quick succession, chopped through four styrofoam boards painted to look like wood.

The kid stopped crying and started smiling. "I know you! You're Stevie Sturgeon!"

"That's me! And I have just the thing for you," Stevie said, taking off his sunglasses. The fat beneath his cheekbones fell as their only means of support was withdrawn. "It's the Stevie Sturgeon Salad Chopper!"

"I don't remember shooting this," Stevie admitted.

"We did this a few months ago. You get three percent of the profits, baby!"

"I haven't received a check yet," Stevie said suspiciously.

"It's a...bi-annual thing," Bernie said nervously. "I'll check up on it."

Even Stevie was embarrassed at how bad he looked. He shut off the television in disgust.

"This is crap, Bernie and you know it! I need to get back into movies!" he shouted, standing to his feet. He turned around and opened the luxurious curtains behind his desk and he squinted as he looked out over the Pacific Ocean. "If the governor of California can be an actor, so can the governor of Arkansas!"

"I thought it was Arizona."

"Whatever! One day the people of this land will know me as a great leader. I'm tired of only being seen as just a sex symbol!"

"Stevie, I already told you. Unless you're willing to do porn or put on a cape, I got nothing for you. Well, except for that video game I told you about. You thought any more about that?"

"It was something about ninja princesses or something?"

"Stevie Sturgeon's Samurai Girls," his agent corrected. "It would take maybe two months of your time and you net a cool half million up front, with quarterly profits too."

"So, they'll record me in 3D so I can kick virtual ass?"

"Sort of. They want to record your moves, but the main character is a girl."

"What do you mean, a girl?"

"The game is targeted to preteen girls, so the main character is a girl. Don't worry. You'll get credit for providing all the moves. They just need someone else as good as you to provide a second martial art style. Preferably a girl."

Sturgeon scoffed. "Name a girl anywhere on Earth that's even close to my level!"

CHAPTER TWO

Her name was Freya, and as she entered the only grocery store on her small Arizona reservation, she thought about how much she hated shopping. She sometimes liked buying new clothes, though her style was more bohemian than anything that could be found on the reservation. Her problem was food. The art that she and her brother were studying, Sinanju, was the original martial art; the one that inspired all of the lesser arts like Kung Fu and Karate.

Throughout history, the Masters of Sinanju were hired by kings and emperors and chieftains — at least, by the ones who wanted to be remembered, for the Masters of Sinanju were the deadliest assassins known to man. Their supreme efficiency meant that their deeds were often ascribed to others in the history books, but Masters knew the truth — that many world-changing historical events, such as the death of Alexander the Great, were actually the result of a Master's terrifying skill.

There was only one Master of Sinanju at a time, the title and training passed on from generation to generation. But a split in Sinanju had occurred centuries earlier, when the blind Master Nonga had inadvertently trained two pupils at once — identical twins, who stood in for each other during their lessons. One twin, Kojing, remained in the tiny North Korean fishing village that had been home to Sinanju for thousands of years. The other, Kojong, traveled east, across the great sea, landing in what eventually became known as America. Bill Roam was Kojong's descendant, as all the leaders of the tribe had been. When his father died, Bill became a Master, and took the name "Sunny Joe" — the name and title that had always signified the tribe's leader — and it became his duty to train a pupil, just as his father had trained him.

But Sunny Joe chose to violate tradition.

Though Sinanju strictly forbade training more than one pupil, Sunny Joe chose to train both Freya and her older brother Stone. It was also forbidden to train a woman in Sinanju, for fear that someday they might teach their children. Many of the tribal elders were deeply worried about Sunny Joe's blatant violation of tradition, but they knew they could not change his mind. The murmurs and grumbles of the tribe were all directed at her, because they perceived her to be a threat to the integrity of Sinanju. Deliberately shunned, Freya — whose alabaster skin and long golden hair set her apart from everyone else on the reservation — was treated with suspicion and disdain. She was the 'other' pupil. The one who didn't belong.

As an apprentice Master of Sinanju, Freya's body had recently undergone major changes in what was called the Night of Salt. Over the course of a few violently painful days, her lungs and skin were transformed to maximize the absorption and use of oxygen. Her nerves were restructured into hyper-sensitive pathways, increasing her senses far beyond human limitations.

Even her muscles, which were already in tune with the motions and rhythm of Sinanju methods, became more toned and superhumanly strong. And, she thought mournfully, her digestive tract had been altered to squeeze every possible nutrient from any food she ate.

But like other Masters of Sinanju, this caused her body to reject processed foods and sugars. If she ate any of the things she once loved, like dark chocolate or pasta, it would put her in a coma or worse. The food now available to her was reduced to a stingy checklist consisting mostly of various kinds of fish and rice.

After the Night of Salt, Sunny Joe had warned her of straying from the list, telling her of stories of past Masters who had paid the ultimate price just trying to find new things to eat.

"The tongue is a powerful thing," Sunny Joe warned. "You have to keep it under control."

"But...some of them survived, right?" she asked hopefully. "We can eat small amounts of corn and it has natural sugars. Why can't we eat apples or oranges?"

Sunny Joe had patiently listened to her arguments, and she could tell that he still missed the food of his youth, but this was not a debate. She was not to stray from the approved list of foods. Freya frowned. She had known about the special diet required of all Masters of Sinanju, but never thought it would apply to her this soon and most definitely not like this.

"This is the price we pay, Freya. Maybe there are other foods out there, maybe not. The point is, your body is no longer able to digest processed foods. I get the shakes if I eat too much roadrunner. Since I have no idea how Sinanju training will affect a female body, it's probably best that you not test fate."

Freya walked to the last aisle on the right, the one labeled "Specialty Needs," which was just another way of saying "Sinanju kosher." As she entered the aisle, she could feel the eyes of the other shoppers. No one went down that aisle but Sunny Joe and sometimes Mick, Sunny Joe's best friend and the tribal historian. Freya ignored their stares and began looking at the selection.

Her eyes saddened and she sighed deeply.

The first section was nothing but various types of rice. Freya had to admit, if it were going to be the main staple of her new diet, at least she had a variety to choose from. She counted over twenty different kinds of rice, everything from Amaroo to Tulaipanji. Most of the others were variations of Japonica. Freya had eaten so many different types of rice in the past year that she could almost name them by scent alone. Her favorite was Samba. To the right of the rice was a small refrigerated section that carried a few cuts of fresh walleye, Sunny Joe's favorite fish.

The only other meat available were packaged cuts of duck and roadrunner. The laughably small "dessert" section contained only three items: almonds, corn and a small jar of honey. Though she knew that it wouldn't contain chocolate and cake, Freya had hoped the aisle to have a little more variety than what she currently saw.

Freya grabbed a jar of honey, and a small cut of roadrunner and walked to the counter. Her heightened Sinanju hearing let her know that the four elderly women who always seemed to be sitting at the front were talking about her. Too bad she couldn't shut it off when she wanted. When you were fully Sinanju, you were fully Sinanju.

Freya took her groceries and headed east. She lived in a small wooden house on the outskirts behind Sunny Joe's house. When she first arrived, there were so many fights about who was going to date her that Sunny Joe declared her off limits to all tribal boys. He moved her closer to him, in the small house where his aunt used to live. No one had any business going that far in that direction unless they were going to see Sunny Joe or Freya.

While moving her away from the general populace solved the romantic squabbles, it further isolated Freya from the rest of the tribe.

Freya passed the small basketball court that Sunny Joe had put up for the high school kids a couple of years ago. The boys who were playing stopped and quietly stared at her as she walked by. One boy walked toward the edge of the court and called out to her.

"Hey, white girl!" he yelled. "Has Sunny Joe finished training you how to be a man?"

Ignore them, Freya told herself, but a storm was brewing beneath the surface.

"She thinks she's too good for us, man," his buddy said.

Freya recognized him. His name was Tommy. He had a crush on her in eighth grade. At the time, Freya liked him as well, but after Sunny Joe prohibited the boys from dating her, Tommy had gone out of his way to be mean. Freya had no idea why.

"Let her go, guys," another voice said. This voice was unfamiliar, so Freya turned to see who it was. Like the others, he was tall and thin, but she only knew him as the boy who had moved to the reservation a couple of months earlier. Freya thought it was odd until Stone explained that his parents had been killed in an accident and the superstitions of his own tribe refused to let them have anything to do with him.

"Hey guys, check this out!" Tommy yelled. "My sister just texted me that Freya was in Sunny Joe's aisle. Guess she thinks she's as good as Sunny Joe now!"

Freya kept walking, fighting back tears. *Why am I feeling so emotional?* she asked herself.

"That's right! Keep on walking, white girl!" another boy yelled.

"Why don't you just leave?" Tommy shouted. "You don't belong here!"

Freya stopped and clenched her fists. She was not going to let that last remark slide. This reservation was the only stable home she had ever had. Freya walked to the edge of the court, facing Tommy.

"Ooh, she's mad, guys," Tommy said. "Too bad we know that Sunny Joe said that you can't touch us."

"C'mon, Tommy, leave her alone," the new boy said. "Let's play."

"Thank you, but I can handle myself," Freya said.

"My name's Tekoa," the new boy said, smiling.

"Don't even think about it, man, unless you want to mess with Sunny Joe," Tommy said. "So, white girl, when are you gonna leave?"

"This is my home just as much as it is yours, Tommy," Freya replied, moving until she was standing almost nose to nose with him. He refused to back down, but Freya could see that he was taking an offensive stance.

"I may not be able to start a fight," she said. "But I will defend myself. Your move."

"Whoa, hold on!" Tekoa said, moving between them.

Freya allowed him to lead her away from the others.

"It's Freya, isn't it?" he asked, smiling. "Tommy's not worth it. Let me talk to them."

"You're new, so you don't know how things work here," Freya said, staring a hole through Tommy. "They taunt me and I allow them to live."

"That can't be any fun," Tekoa said.

Freya glared over Tekoa's shoulder. The boys were still glaring at her.

"It's not," she softly confided and turned to walk off the basketball court.

"Told you guys, she thinks she's special!" Tommy bellowed after her.

Freya kept walking. *They're just words*, she thought.

"You'll never be Sinanju, white girl!"

Freya closed her eyes in anger and stopped as she reached the opposite basketball pole. Enough was enough. She grabbed the pole and turned to look at Tommy. Then the metal of the post began impotently moaning as she bent it with one hand until it hit the ground.

"I *am* Sinanju," she said, walking off.

Freya dropped the groceries off at her house and mindlessly walked toward the training hut. She shouldn't have let those guys get to her like that. Mastery of Sinanju was based on control and she had allowed them to control her emotions.

"You're late," Sunny Joe said as she entered.

"I am sorry, grandfather. I was…what's wrong?" she asked, looking around.

The training mats were nowhere to be seen. Sunny Joe and Stone were sitting on the Founder Stone at the front of the hut. "We're not training today?"

"Look around," Sunny Joe said, nodding to the upturned dirt that scarred the training floor. "You made quite a mess the last time you were here."

Freya lowered her head in shame as she noticed the groove in the dirt floor that she had caused when she upturned the Founder Stone in an attempt to prove that she was worthy of being Sinanju.

Another emotional outburst, she thought ruefully.

"You nearly tore the hut apart!" Stone said. "The south wall was damaged so badly that — "

Sunny Joe raised a hand and Stone fell silent.

"I tried to be careful!" Freya protested. "I didn't think…"

"It's okay," Sunny Joe reassured her. "But you have to take responsibility for your actions. You damaged the hut, so you're gonna repair it."

"What?" Freya asked.

"At the back, you'll find enough wood to replace the wall. Nails are on the ground," Sunny Joe said and he and Stone turned to leave.

"Where are you going?"

"I'm taking Stone with me to the post office."

"But…I don't know how to…!" Freya protested. "What if I don't do it right?"

"Didn't you ever wonder why we had such a rundown shack? I had to rebuild it when I was sixteen, too," Sunny Joe said with a knowing wink. "You can't do any worse."

"Wait! Where is the hammer?" Freya asked frantically.

Sunny Joe smiled and made a tapping motion with his finger. "Hammering nails is a great finger-strengthening exercise. It takes concentration, precision and power. Consider this your training today."

"Don't break a nail," Stone said, smiling.

Freya watched them leave and looked around at the ancient shack.

"Great," she moaned, walking to the small pile of lumber at the back.

CHAPTER THREE

Sunny Joe parked his ancient red truck in front of the Douglas, Arizona post office. He pulled the parking brake and paused. Then he turned to look at Stone.

"The only time I get registered mail is when the government wants to mess with something," Sunny Joe said. "You wanna come in this time, or are you going to wait here and get training from your other master?"

"What other master?" Stone asked, confused.

"The one in your pocket that injects your Sinanju-trained nerves with a drug. You know, the one you pay for, twenty at a time."

Stone tensed and grimaced. "It's not like that, Grandpa."

"Okay, then tell me that when I go inside, you're not going to light one up. Tell me that the reason your knee has been bouncing all the way to town wasn't because you haven't had a smoke in a couple of hours."

"I'll quit one day."

"Sad thing is, I think you really believe that," Sunny Joe said. "The problem is that you're a Sinanju apprentice. Your senses may not be as sharp as your sister's, but they're more sensitive than almost anyone else's on Earth. Every time you light up, it hooks your body anew. If you keep smoking, 'one day' you won't be able to stop."

Stone felt embarrassed as he realized that his hand had already been wrapped around the pack of cigarettes in his pocket.

"Maybe I just want to do this my way!" Stone snapped. "Just because this is how *you* practice Sinanju doesn't mean it's the only way!"

"Whenever you figure out how to master Sinanju without mastering breathing, let me know," Sunny Joe said, exiting the truck. "Just don't let me catch a whiff of it when I come back."

Stone watched Sunny Joe enter the adobe-colored building and quietly cursed. He did want to quit...some day. As he walked downwind from Sunny Joe's truck and lit the cigarette, he could feel the changes in his physiology. His breathing became shallow and his heart rate began to race. An anticipatory rush filled his senses as the cigarette touched his lips. And as he inhaled, the nicotine raced through his body, exciting nerve endings and calming his system.

Sunny Joe was right about one thing. If Stone was going to continue training in Sinanju, he would eventually have to give up smoking. He could already feel the limitations of his nicotine-riddled body when it came to training. Even worse, he knew Sunny Joe could see it.

So what would Freya do? Stone wondered. *She wouldn't be smoking to start with, you idiot,*

Stone told himself. *She's too smart for that.*

"You about finished?" Sunny Joe asked from behind, careful to remain down wind.

"Oh, sorry, Grandpa," Stone said, dropping the half-smoked cigarette on the ground and stomping it out.

Stone popped a mint into his mouth and turned to leave. Sunny Joe didn't move.

"I didn't know littering was a skill I taught you," Sunny Joe said.

Stone sighed, but then picked up the cigarette butt, tossing it into a nearby trashcan.

"You have the same responsibility to this world that Freya does. Whether the damage is great or small, you have to fix what you break."

"I get it, Grandpa," Stone said. "I don't need another lecture."

The two men hopped in Sunny Joe's truck. The doors, though creaky with age, were silent as they shut.

"Yes, you do," Sunny Joe quietly said.

Stone readied himself for a stern talk about smoking and littering, but Sunny Joe merely placed the letters he had been carrying in his vest pocket and started the truck. As they pulled away, Stone could not help but notice the sadness in his Grandfather's eyes. After a few minutes of silence, he couldn't take any more.

"What's wrong, grandpa?"

"Got a letter from an old friend, asking me to come back out to Hollywood. Says something weird is going on and he needs my help."

"But isn't that a good thing?" Stone asked. "You guys will get to catch up on old times."

"That would be true, but I haven't checked the mail in a while. He mailed this letter a couple of weeks ago. The certified letter I got today was an invitation to his funeral."

"Oh," Stone said sheepishly. "Sorry."

"It's my own fault. I've been trying to make time to see him the past couple of years. I knew his time was coming, but I just kept putting it off. So now I have to fix what I have broken. We leave for Los Angeles in the morning."

"We?" Stone asked.

"You and Freya are coming with me. Consider this part of your training."

Stone's face retained the same puzzled look it had before.

"How so?" he asked.

"We deal in death so much that we sometimes forget to celebrate life."

"What do you mean?"

"The fact that you asked that question means you I still have a lot to teach you."

The remainder of the ride back to the reservation was very quiet.

CHAPTER FOUR

Stevie Sturgeon entered the large brownstone and took a deep breath. He had not been in Wilshire since winning a lawsuit against a tire company a decade earlier. His lawyer had spent weeks building an air-tight case that proved the defendant's fat-tubed cartoon mascot perfectly executed one of his trademarked moves. Sturgeon played a tape showing the huge cartoonish figure waddling in the background and then demonstrated the same move. The judge agreed, awarding Sturgeon a single dollar in damages, suggesting that he use it to invest in acting lessons.

Sturgeon swallowed a mixture of pain medications and breath mints, chasing it with the last of the whiskey in his official Stevie Sturgeon Survival Flask. Reaching in his pocket, he pulled out a small piece of paper with *801* scribbled on it. The elevators would only open with a key, so Sturgeon began looking for the stairs.

"Eighth floor?" he griped to no one in particular. "Are they trying to kill me?"

Twenty minutes later, Sturgeon staggered toward the huge oak doors at the end of the hallway. The engraved brass sign on the door read *Bindle and Marmelstein.* Sons of the late Hank Bindle and Bruce Marmelstein, the lawyers were in their mid-thirties, trading on their fathers' infamous names. They represented the privileged and elite; everyone from spoiled tech billionaires to ragingly self-absorbed actors.

So, when a young video game producer approached them to acquire rights to use Sturgeon's name, Bindle and Marmelstein took the case. While neither had ever seen a Stevie Sturgeon movie, their research showed that he had not starred in a movie in over a decade. Bindle and Marmelstein advised against using such a dated actor, but the producer was adamant — he claimed to be a huge fan of Sturgeon's cheesy B-movies.

After the check had cleared, they drew up a lengthy contract. If everything went well, Sturgeon could reap a windfall in the millions, even after Bindle and Marmelstein's obscene percentage.

Sturgeon stood outside the door and belched. His trainer had warned him to exercise at least a week before performing. Making a mental note to fire him, Sturgeon opened the doors to the posh offices of Bindle and Marmelstein.

While Sturgeon's office was expensive, the offices of Bindle and Marmelstein were an exercise in opulence. Paintings that Sturgeon had only seen in magazines adorned the walls. Imported carpets lined the hand-polished wooden floor. The two men in classic black suits were seated at the back of the room behind a custom two-man desk, modeled after the desk Thomas Jefferson had used as President.

Sturgeon subconsciously sucked in his gut.

"Gentlemen," Sturgeon said, flashing his grim smile. That usually impressed people on their first meeting.

"Mr. Sturgeon," Marmelstein said. "I am Chester Marmelstein, and this is my partner Ron Bindle. We are both huge fans," he lied.

Sturgeon nodded dismissively. *Of course, they were!* Everyone was a huge fan of Stevie Sturgeon.

"Mr. Sturgeon," Bindle continued. "Our client is prepared to invest a substantial portion of his personal fortune on this venture, but we have a few concerns. Our research shows that it has been several years since you starred in a feature film and, to be quite honest, you have put on quite a bit of weight. Are you ready for the intense physical demands of this project?"

"Gentlemen, I am Stevie Sturgeon," he said, peering over his sunglasses. "That's all you need to know."

"Well, yes, that's fine and all, but we would appreciate a demonstration of what our client's most generous offer will be purchasing."

Sturgeon breathed in and then out. He was ready.

"I will begin by showing you a few of my more basic movements," Sturgeon said. "I'll slow them down, of course. Most people can't see my normal punching speed," he said, winking.

Sturgeon took an offensive stance and his forehead wrinkled so much from his grimace that his hairline moved back an inch. His mind became a laser of focus and Sturgeon began filing through his film credits in his head.

He imagined the Russian soldiers he faced in *Deadly Siege* and punched the air in front of him. In his mind's eye, eight Russian soldiers collapsed to the ground. Turning as swiftly as a rabid cheetah, he saw the rogue CIA agent who had been trained in chemical warfare in *Marked to Kill* and swept the floor in front of him. The CIA agent dropped the vial filled with a deadly chemical that had been concocted for the sole purpose of destroying all life on Earth. But the instant before it could touch the floor, Sturgeon flung himself toward the vial, catching the deadly chemical between two fingers of his left hand. A follow-up foot stroke crushed the traitorous agent behind him.

His face managed to wring out even more grimace and he turned, swinging both arms like a huge pinwheel, crushing the sternum of the mutant bike rider from *Above Death.* The imaginary foe took one look at the hand sticking through his chest and fell backwards as

Sturgeon held his still-beating heart in his hand.

"What is he doing?" Bindle whispered to Marmelstein.

Sturgeon continued flopping his arms around, threatening the air in front of him.

"Maybe it is a new kind of dance," Bindle mused. "I hear these things are popular on the interwebs."

"Internet," Marmelstein corrected. "It doesn't matter to me as long, as we get our consultation fees."

"Of course," Bindle agreed.

Sturgeon stopped for a moment, looking intently at the ceiling. The lawyers flashed their jury smiles and politely applauded.

Sturgeon ignored the praise. He wasn't through yet. The deadliest foe in any of his movies was about to strike.

The twelve-foot tall dog of *Shadow Beast* leapt for him, and for the tiniest fraction of a moment, confidence drained from Sturgeon's face. Any other mortal would have been instant dog food beneath the steely claws, attached to paws larger than a human head. Sturgeon stumbled backwards, allowing the beast to believe it had the upper hand. Then Sturgeon allowed himself a rare grin.

He had the beast exactly where he wanted it.

Sturgeon pivoted on one foot, slicing the air before him. He missed, but the beast could still sense the deadly power behind his blow. It attempted to run, but it was too late. With one mighty strike, Sturgeon's hand sliced cleanly through the air, removing the beast's head from its shoulders. He wiped his forehead as the sweat dripped from it.

Then he turned toward Bindle and Marmelstein and took a bow.

The lawyers looked at each other for a moment and politely clapped again.

"Very…interesting," Bindle said.

"My extensive skills are not what is the drawing power, gentlemen, though I am the most dangerous man on the planet," he said, flexing his biceps. "The real drawing power of Stevie Sturgeon is my likeness. Especially my face."

"Well, as much as we would like to accommodate you, Mister Sturgeon, this game is being marketed to 'tween' girls," Marmelstein said. "The game developer wants to empower young girls by showing them examples of strong women."

"Empower women? What kind of nonsense is that?" Sturgeon said, guffawing. "You don't need any of that, just put me in the game! Women love me!"

"The game is to be marketed to girls from ages nine to twelve, Mr. Sturgeon."

"Well, then I can be their first crush."

"Be that as it may," Marmelstein said in a starchy voice, "Our job is to secure your digital moves for the game. Furthermore, because the game requires two separate sets of moves, you will require a female partner to complete the job. Will you be able to find one?"

"A partner? Are you crazy? I'm Stevie Sturgeon! Stevie Sturgeon! I don't want some chick sidekick hanging around!"

"Although you may not find it ideal, Mr. Sturgeon, the game requires two martial artists. Do you have anyone in mind?" Marmelstein asked.

"Perhaps someone…better trained?" Bindle added.

Sturgeon's eyes opened as wide as saucers.

"You can't be…didn't you see what I just did? Who are you going to get better than that? If Bruce Lee were alive today, I would be teaching him! In fact, had he been a student of Adrogans, he would still be alive today!"

Sturgeon left his chin jutting out, trying to keep it from quivering with rage.

"We cannot sign you alone," Bindle said stiffly. "Do you know anyone else?"

"I'll find someone," Sturgeon said, turning toward the door. "But they're not going to be better."

The door slammed behind him.

Bindle looked at Marmelstein and began writing notes in the ledger before him.

"What should we tell our client?"

"We shall tell him the truth. He is getting exactly what he is paying for."

"Well said," Bindle said. "I almost choked when he rolled on his own fat! Disgusting."

Marmelstein punched a button on the intercom in front of him.

"Serina, send a member of housekeeping to strip and re-wax our floor at once."

"Yes, Mr. Marmelstein," a breathy voice replied.

"And make sure they bring a strong antiseptic," Bindle chimed in.

CHAPTER FIVE

Stone and Freya stood silently at the back of the viewing room. The somber tones of an organ filled the funeral home. The room was filled with people who had come to pay respect to their friend. Stone recognized several famous faces in the crowd. All of them seemed to be wearing the same pair of sunglasses.

Sunny Joe wore his only suit, a formal black suit that he had been given at an awards ceremony back in his stuntman days. Freya had never seen him in a suit before. He explained that he wore it out of respect for the man who had been such a close friend in Hollywood.

Stone watched as Sunny Joe approached the casket. His grandfather was a stoic man, not given to emotion, but he saw Sunny Joe's shoulders twitch for just a moment.

I guess even Sinanju has its emotional limits, Stone thought.

Sunny Joe looked at the body of his friend as it lay still within the padded white coffin. The man was the same age as Mick, Sunny Joe's friend and tribal historian.

And now he was dead.

Phil had gained weight since Sunny Joe last saw him and his hair had obviously vanished over the horizon years earlier. His body was bloated with formaldehyde and his face pasted over with pancake makeup.

It was enough to remind even a Master of Sinanju of his mortality.

Given the extended lifespans of a Sinanju Master, Sunny Joe could easily expect five or six more decades of life, while all those around him died. The day before Sunny Joe's father killed himself, he had said that life was harder than death to a Master.

Sunny Joe realized that one day he would be in the casket, but though he had experienced turmoil and grief throughout his life, he would never take the coward's way out like his father. He shot himself a few days before Sunny Joe became reigning Master. Sunny Joe never saw it coming, but there was nothing he could have done.

He buried his father and his past, determined to live only for the future. Then he crossed paths with his son, Remo Williams. And Remo left him two gifts: Stone and Freya. They provided the purpose that Sunny Joe had been missing.

"Who is that man standing behind grandfather?" Freya asked, seeing a tall, overweight man in sunglasses grimacing behind Sunny Joe.

"I don't know, but if he wants to live, he better tone down the body language," Stone whispered. "Grandpa isn't in the mood to take any crap right now."

Sunny Joe took a moment and said goodbye to his old friend by placing his hand over the man's heart in the manner of the Sinanju funeral rites. Then his senses detected a threat. A very small threat, and yet, there it was. Sunny Joe turned to the man standing behind him, who was radiating anger. He recognized him as one of the many kids who wanted to be a star and ended up as a stuntman, as Sunny Joe himself had done. But this one had lucked his way into starring in several cheesy martial arts movies.

Sunny Joe gave him a cursory nod and then began walking toward the back to sit for the service, but the man's hand reached for Sunny Joe's arm. His hand came back empty.

"You got some nerve being here, Roam," Sturgeon said, trying to keep his voice down. "It should be you in that casket!"

"That chip on your shoulder should be pretty heavy by now," Sunny Joe said. "Moments like this should teach you to appreciate life instead of fighting it."

Sturgeon turned toward the casket, trying to remember how many seconds his agent said to wait before walking back to his seat, but seeing Roam messed up his performance. Sturgeon waved his hands in front of him to cleanse the air, but the humiliating memories were just too much. He turned to walk to the back and saw Roam sitting near a young man and teenage girl.

Probably Roam's grandkids, Sturgeon thought, completing his lone rational thought of the day. He would probably never see Roam again, and he wasn't going to let him get away with snubbing him in front of the casket. Sturgeon sat beside Sunny Joe and glared.

"Why are you staring at my grandfather?" Freya whispered, clearly upset. Though she was not raised in America, she had enough respect for American funeral rites to remain silent until they were finished. This man had no such excuse.

"Ignore him," Sunny Joe whispered. "Some people can't be reasoned with."

Sturgeon's eyes almost bulged out enough to knock his sunglasses off. He tried to keep his voice to a whisper, but it was obvious to everyone within four rows that he was angry.

"Roam, if you weren't so old, I'd kick your ass right here!" he rasped.

Freya's face warped into anger and her spine straightened.

"Girl..." Sunny Joe said, trying to calm her down.

Sturgeon, however, heard Bill Roam call him a girl in front of dozens of people.

He stood to his full height and started to tear off his shirt, exposing soft, pudgy mounds of flesh where muscles used to be.

That was Freya's limit. Before he could tear off his shirt down to the third button, she slapped him so hard that his toupee spun off his head.

Sturgeon saw her fist, but thought nothing of it. He had been punched by bouncers and boxers, so he thought nothing of a slap from a little girl.

He awoke fifteen minutes later, on a stretcher outside the funeral home.

"What happened?" he asked groggily, then, feeling the cool breeze on the top of his head, looked around. Everyone was staring at his baldness and was either smiling or laughing. He knew he should have paid for hair plugs.

The medical technician who was leaning over him tried to squelch her smile.

"You were slapped by a young girl, Mr. Sturgeon," she said. "But I think you'll live."

Sturgeon's blood boiled as he noticed the photographers taking pictures.

"Roam..." he growled. "Let me up!" he said, looking for his toupee. Not seeing one, he grabbed a baseball cap from one of the photographers and ran off into the distance.

That girl. Roam's granddaughter. She had to know kung fu or something to be able to hit like that. Then a smile stretched across his leathery face. The lawyers had told him to find a female martial artist for his video game...and Roam's granddaughter *was* a girl. Sturgeon stopped for a moment and the cogs in his mind began churning. If he couldn't get to Roam, he would find some way to humiliate his granddaughter. He needed to pay her back for assaulting him in public. Maybe he would take her as a lover and then discard her, leaving her heart in a million shards of pain, forever longing for him.

He smiled as he imagined Roam crying over his granddaughter's broken heart. Sturgeon raced over to the parking lot to see if they had already left. He would have to act sorry to gain their trust, but if there was one thing Stevie Sturgeon knew, it was acting.

CHAPTER SIX

Sunny Joe hurried out of the funeral home, leading Freya and Stone away from the commotion surrounding the unconscious Stevie Sturgeon.

"Bill? Bill Roam?" a voice asked from behind.

Sunny Joe turned to see a short, squat man in a bright blue suit and stained tie.

"Oz?" Sunny Joe asked and then smiled as he remembered Bob "Oz" Ozman, one of Hollywood's technical pioneers. The once thin-as-a-rail technician now weighed close to three hundred pounds. His once famous buzz cut had grown into lazy gray strands passing his shoulders, nearly as long as Sunny Joe's hair. An oxygen tube ran from his nose.

"I was going to say that I was dying to see you, but I'm afraid it might be just a bit too literal," he said, managing to keep a smile on his face. "I saw you inside, but after Sturgeon caused that scene, well, I figured I better stay out of it."

Oz extended his hand and Sunny Joe shook it.

"Oz, these are my grandkids, Stone and Freya," Sunny Joe said.

"Hi, I'm Oz," he said, shaking hands with Stone and Freya.

"How do you do, Mr. Oz?" Freya asked.

"You can call me 'Wizard' if you want," Oz said, winking. "Speaking of wizardry, you sure did a number on Sturgeon! I've never seen anyone slapped so hard!"

"He never could stay out of trouble," Sunny Joe said and then turned to Stone and Freya. "Why don't you two head to the car? I'll be there in a few minutes."

As Stone and Freya walked away, Oz smiled. "Some good lookin' kids you got there, Bill." Then Oz's smile disappeared. "Kinda makes me mad, a no-talent hack like Sturgeon starring in movies. Heck, I'm a better actor than he is and I'm almost dead!"

"Seems like everyone is dead or dying these days," Sunny Joe mused.

"Not everyone," Oz said as he looked at Sunny Joe. "Jeez, you still look fifty!"

"Healthy living."

"Did you get Phil's letter? He said he was going to ask you to help with our little problem."

"Got it too late," Sunny Joe said, embarrassed.

"Truth is, Phil got pretty paranoid toward the end."

"What do you mean?"

"Well, you know he worked for Mr. Cheese over there, right?"

"Sturgeon? No, I didn't know that."

"Yeah, he couldn't find much work the last few years and his pension didn't cover two ex-wives, so got a job to manage Sturgeon's warehouse. He did light paperwork and watched the place. That's when Phil got…weird."

"Like how?"

"This is gonna sound crazy, but he kept telling me that people were watching him, killer robots, stuff like that. I told him he was talking crazy, but he swore that he wasn't lying. I thought he was either going senile, or just trying to get the gang back together one last time. I stopped answering his calls…and now this. I wish I had talked to him one last time." His voice trailed off. "At least you're here, Bill. Man, it's good to see you again."

"I wish I had visited before now," Sunny Joe said. "This wasn't the type of reunion I hoped for."

"I know, buddy. But you still made it."

Oz gave Sunny Joe a friendly punch in the arm. It felt like hitting a cinder block. He tried to hide the pain in his hand as he spoke again. "You gotta drop by my place before you leave," Oz said. "I'm still at the same old dump. We can catch up."

"I'll drop by," Sunny Joe said and walked to his rental car. Both Freya and Stone were silent as he approached. Sunny Joe looked directly into Freya's eyes.

"Do you mind telling me what part of Sinanju discipline allows you to slap a man like that in public?" he asked sternly.

Freya's face was lowered to the point that even Stone didn't chide in on her punishment.

"Grandfather, I would like to talk to you," Freya said quietly. "Alone, please."

Sunny Joe nodded to Stone and he walked away. The responsibility Sunny Joe had run from as a young man was what now grounded him to reality. He had not been there for his own son, and though Stone and Freya were mostly grown when they arrived, he found purpose in training them and answering their questions. What he could not fix in his son's life, he would fix in Stone and Freya's.

"You tore down the basketball court yesterday," Sunny Joe said "What's wrong?"

"The boys provoked me grandfather. They just kept…I couldn't…"

Freya lowered her face and her eyes welled up with tears.

"You said that my body would change after the Night of Salt and it has. My emotions have been out of control lately," she said sheepishly. "It is…my time of the month."

Sunny Joe's eyebrows arched. "Oh…that," he finally mumbled.

"How will this affect me?" she asked. "I'm always angry or sad…I can't stand it!"

Sunny Joe gulped. As a Master of Sinanju, he knew about breathing and killing and nerves. This, however, was way out of his league.

"Well, I don't know," Sunny Joe said. "No one has ever had to train a Mistress of Sinanju, so we're charting new territory."

"So, what should I do?" she asked, unable to look Sunny Joe in the eye.

Sunny Joe looked off in the distance, searching for the right thing to say. He shoved his embarrassment aside. His granddaughter needed him.

"What is different between normal and now?" he asked.

Neither could make eye contact with the other.

"Normally, I get a little irritable and then I'm okay, but when I started this month, my mood has been totally out of control."

She leaned over and wiped the tears from her face.

Sunny Joe thought a moment. "A Master of Sinanju can totally control his…her body. I would assume that as you get more control of your body, you'll be able to cut that time down. But until then, you're gonna have to get a handle on your emotions. During your… uh, cycle, you might want to stick to just the basic Sinanju diet. No corn. No honey."

Freya looked up and Sunny Joe saw the sadness stretch across her face.

"At least for a few days until we figure something out," Sunny Joe said. "Can't have you attacking folks just because they irritate you. Half of Los Angeles would be crippled by week's end."

"I was in control!" she protested. "At least I didn't seriously injure him."

Sunny Joe detected a presence walking up to him before Freya did, even though he approached Sunny Joe from behind. It was Stevie Sturgeon.

Sunny Joe stood protectively in front of Freya.

"I might have been a bit out of line," Sturgeon said, holding both hands up, faking a smile. "I might even have deserved some of that back there. Let me make it up to you."

"Sturgeon," Sunny Joe greeted. "It's been awhile."

"Yeah," Sturgeon said, forcing back his anger. "It's good seeing you again."

Sunny Joe noticed that his teeth were grinding while he smiled.

"Nice punch," Sturgeon said to Freya, who remained silent, glaring at him. "You caught me off guard, and it's a good thing you did, little lady. Sometimes I can't help but block and strike back. I wouldn't have wanted to hurt a pretty little thing like you."

"At no time was I in danger," Freya replied.

"I can tell you've taken karate or kung fu or something," Sturgeon said. "That's why I want to talk to you. How would you like to star in a video game?"

Freya's eyebrows arched in confusion. "Me? In a video game?"

"We're currently working on some kinda Ninja Princess game and they need a second style of martial art. You know," Sturgeon said, leaning in so close that Freya could have smelled the liquor on his breath even without Sinanju senses. "If it were all my fighting style, what challenge would there be, right?"

"What challenge, indeed," Sunny Joe mused.

"So, how about a week in Los Angeles on me?" Sturgeon asked with his plastic smile.

It would be good to get away from the reservation for a while, Freya thought.

"Let me talk it over with my grandfather," she said, turning away.

For a moment, Sturgeon's temper flared.

How dare she turn her back on me!

Then he remembered the plan and sank back into his role. As he told his students at the *Stevie Sturgeon School of Actionified Acting*, the trick was not to *act*, but to *be.*

Sturgeon stepped back several feet to allow her room to talk with Sunny Joe. The other one of Roam's grandkids was smoking a cigarette and staring a hole into him, so he planted his feet in case he tried something. Some people wanted to make a name for themselves by taking a crack at the champ.

"You seriously thinking about taking him up on his offer?" Sunny Joe asked.

"I really need some time to get away, Grandfather. Just for a few days."

"You can't trust this man, Freya," Sunny Joe said. "In his day, he was known as a womanizer in an era of womanizers."

"I'll be careful," Freya said.

"Still..." Sunny Joe's voice trailed off.

He didn't want Freya to kill Sturgeon. He motioned for Stone, who was still staring a hole through Sturgeon. Stone extinguished the cigarette between his fingers and tossed the butt into a nearby trash can. He walked slowly past Sturgeon, who was trying his best to keep a smile on his face.

He looked constipated.

"Stone should stay, too," Sunny Joe said.

"This is something I need to do myself, Grandfather," she said, looking at Stone.

Sunny Joe placed his arm around her shoulder.

"I know you're feeling pretty alone right now, but we're family and that means you're never alone. Take Stone with you. Sometimes, Sinanju or not, we all need someone to watch our back. Besides, Sturgeon might not pose a threat to either of you, but he's definitely up to something. Someone needs to figure out what he's planning."

"Oh, please let me tag along, Freya," Stone said in a high, squeaky voice, trying to imitate his sister. "I promise, you won't even notice I'm there!"

"You'll get in my way," Freya said in a low voice, mocking Stone's typical response.

Stone paused. "So, Grandpa, you want me to find out what he's up to?"

"Just keep an eye on him. Maybe he won't try anything if he knows you're there. You can call yourself Freya's assistant, if you want." Sunny Joe winked at Freya, who smiled broadly as Stone's smile immediately slid from his face.

"Okay," Freya said. "But if you fail to do as I say, I'm sending you home."

"You're just afraid that I'll show you how an assistant is supposed to act," Stone said.

Sunny Joe grinned. "Are you ready to be Freya's assistant?"

"Oh, I'll be the best assistant ever," Stone said with an exaggerated tone.

Sunny Joe nodded consent and Freya smiled.

"Thank you, Grandfather," she said and walked over to Sturgeon.

Sunny Joe grabbed Stone's arm, holding him back.

"Watch out for that one," Sunny Joe said. "He likes to fancy himself a lady's man."

"That guy? He looks older than you, Grandpa!" Stone said. "No offense."

"That doesn't matter to men like him," Sunny Joe said. "Just don't let her kill him."

Sturgeon was thinking about how he could embarrass Freya like he had been embarrassed when she came up behind him and tapped him on the shoulder. He waited a second and then remembered that he should react to impress her. Sturgeon swirled around hurling his fist toward Freya's face, stopping inches from making contact.

Freya did not flinch.

"Gotta be careful sneaking up on a guy like me," Sturgeon said. "Sometimes, I'm too dangerous for my own good."

"I am interested in your deal," Freya said. "When do we begin?"

Sturgeon fumbled in his pocket and after dropping a breath mint that was covered by pocket lint, produced a business card. His face took up most of the room on the card.

He scratched the name of an economy motel near his studio on the back.

"Take this to the front desk and tell Marcy that you're my guests," Sturgeon said with a wink and then turned the card over to the business address. "Show up at this address at eight o'clock tomorrow morning. It's scale pay, but you get to act beside me."

Sturgeon walked off and glanced back to see if the girl was watching him. She wasn't. Another thing she would be punished for.

"I'm gonna head back to the reservation," Sunny Joe said. "You two can fly back on Saturday."

"Don't worry," Stone said. "I'll keep her out of trouble."

"Keep yourself out of trouble, too," Sunny Joe said.

As he walked away, Sunny Joe was thinking that between Freya and Stone, Sturgeon would be lucky if he could still walk by week's end.

CHAPTER SEVEN

Freya and Stone left early to grab a bite to eat before walking the four blocks to the motel. Stone stopped in front of an old restaurant that advertised greasy food loaded with calories. Stone smiled as he walked in, daring Freya to follow him.

From the look of the stained booth seats, Freya was more concerned that she would catch a disease than find anything she could eat. She managed to get an order of rice, a small piece of fish, and a glass of water. Stone's plate was piled with bacon, pancakes and biscuits and gravy. He made sure to grunt with each bite, showing Freya how much he enjoyed his food.

Freya swirled her rice around the fish to soak up some flavor. The Night of Salt had not just changed her diet, she had quickly discovered that it even changed how she ate. She concentrated on each grain of rice as she chewed, reducing each piece until it was the consistency of mush. This allowed her body to spend far less energy on digesting. Sinanju was, if nothing else, efficient.

"Enjoy it while you can, big brother," she said between bites. "We'll be sharing diets soon enough."

"That's something I'm gonna talk to Sunny Joe about," Stone said, swallowing a piece of gravy-coated biscuit. He washed down the food with a gulp of coffee. "Everyone assumes I'm here to become a Master of Sinanju, but I'm not sure I want that life."

"Why not? It is our heritage."

"That's your Mom talking. I'm my own person and I will choose my own path."

"Will your path make you better than if you stay training with Sinanju?" Freya asked, puzzled. To deny her heritage was as unthinkable as denying her blood type.

"It's not a question of being better than Sinanju," Stone explained. "It's about being a better 'me.' Look at you. You've already had to change who you are to walk this path. Sunny Joe said that your digestive system will never be the same and there's no turning back. I know you love dark chocolate. Was it worth giving it up?"

"Of course!" Freya said defensively. "My diet is compulsory. You already know this."

"You're right, but maybe I don't want to give up chocolate. Or bacon. Or coffee. I've been thinking about this a lot lately, sis. The Sinanju path is a one-way street, filled with physical and dietary potholes. Once you go down that road a bit, there's no turning back. Our boss pays us pretty well and I don't have any bills. I can work for Cole for a few years and save up while living on the reservation, and then I could travel, maybe see the world. I can always find more work later."

Stone lowered his face as he took the next bite. He could feel Freya's disappointment without seeing her expression.

"You would really leave?" Freya asked in disbelief. "What will our father think?"

Stone's eyes became animated at the thought of their father, Remo Williams, who was not even aware of Stone's existence until a few years ago. He laid down the piece of bacon he was about to eat to make a point.

"I don't care what he thinks! Look, if I stay on my path, I can smoke, eat bacon and sleep in every morning! If I follow your path, I have to change everything I am and turn into my father. That's not gonna happen!"

Freya's eyes betrayed her hurt. She had never considered that Stone might leave. Sure, one day, but not this soon. She loved her grandfather, but Stone was her rock.

"I'm sure grandfather can change our training schedules," she said in a near panic. "You can't leave me, too, Stone."

Stone winced as his eyes connected with hers.

"I'm not leaving, sis. Not for a while, anyway. I'm just saying that maybe Sinanju isn't the path I'm meant to be on. Besides, you're way ahead of me."

"I can help train you, Stone. You just need to take it more seriously," she said.

Stone finished the piece of bacon on his plate and motioned for the check. He looked somberly into Freya's eyes.

"We'll see," he said.

Freya stood to leave and waited for Stone at the door. She was going to need time to think herself.

As they exited into the brisk morning smog, Stone looked to the ground, trying to become as invisible as the thousands of others walking the streets of Los Angeles. Freya was looking around at the buildings and signs, broadcasting 'tourist' with every glance.

"I have never been here before, but I can tell it once was a great city," Freya said. "What happened?"

"I dunno. Guess they just stopped caring."

"My mother once said decay is the nature of humanity," Freya said. "Progress is followed by decay which provides the incentive for progress. This city must be at the decay stage."

"It's hard to tell which is which anymore," Stone said.

Freya's bottom lip stiffened as she looked around. "There are so many people begging for food, yet they look healthy to me."

"Some are faking, but most have some kinda mental problem and there are a few who really need help."

Freya stopped in front of a man who barely had the gumption to make eye contact with her. His hastily scrawled cardboard sign asked passersby to help a crippled vet.

Stone reached into his pocket and peeled off a twenty and began to hand it to the guy. But the instant before the homeless man could take the money, it disappeared. He looked suspiciously at the man, but he was equally as surprised as to where the money went.

"He's faking," Freya said, holding the twenty between her fingers. "See his posture?"

"Ma'am, please… I ain't had anything to eat in days," the man almost whispered, barely looking up. "Can't ya help a hungry vet?"

"That's my money, sis. Give it!" Stone said, motioning for the twenty.

Freya looked angrily at the man and leaned toward him.

"I traveled throughout Europe when I was younger and I know real poverty when I see it. This man is just wearing torn and dirty clothing. Note his clean fingernails. His hair has been messed up but has been recently cut."

Freya's nostrils flared, and then she shook her head as if to confirm her suspicions.

"Tell me how someone who is wearing supposedly filthy clothes smells clean, with cologne, no doubt."

Stone leaned in. She was right. The man's clothes were dirty and torn, but he smelled as if he had just stepped out of the shower. It was cheap cologne, though.

"Okay, you got me on this one," Stone said.

The man realized that the one who was about to give him money had now changed his mind and gave up any pretense of being weak.

"You two, get outta here!" he strongly whispered. "It took months to get this corner and I'm not giving it up!"

Freya held the twenty out before her.

"All you have to do to get this money is stand," she taunted.

The man looked around, and not seeing anyone else, quickly stood and grabbed the money. But as he lowered himself back to the tarp he had set up to disguise his perfectly working legs, he lost his balance and fell backward.

At first, he thought he had tripped, but as he was falling backward, he saw the girl's hand return to her side.

Then came the pain.

"Ahhhhh!" the fake vet howled. His spine felt like it was on fire.

He reached around with his hands to wipe off the battery acid the crazy chick had no doubt somehow splashed on him, but his hands found nothing. His anger flashed and he tried to stand back up to attack her, but his lower body refused to move. Confused, he reached down and touched his legs, but he could not feel them.

He slapped at his thighs in an attempt to bring the feeling back into them, but it was as if he were slapping someone else's legs.

"What did you do to me?" he screamed.

"You have some experience begging. At least now you can do so truthfully," Freya explained and walked away.

Stone looked at the man with empathy for a moment, but then tilted his head in agreement with his sister.

"You asked for that," Stone said. "I don't take kind to people pretending to be wounded veterans."

Stone increased his pace until he caught up with Freya.

"Spinal manipulation?" Stone asked.

Freya merely smiled.

"You didn't permanently cripple him, did you?"

"Of course not," Freya said. "But he will be wondering if I did for the next few hours."

"I'd like to be there when he tries to explain what happened to the EMTs," Stone said, smiling.

They reached the address on Freya's business card five minutes early. The studio was located in a desolate, rundown warehouse that looked like it had not been used in years. They only knew they were at the right place because of the twelve-foot sign of Sturgeon's face that covered the front of the building.

"At least he's humble," Stone said. "After you, boss," he motioned.

Freya ignored the sarcasm in Stone's voice.

Stone stepped in front of Freya before she could enter and turned to face her.

"Sis, are you sure you want to do this? I'm getting all kinds of creepy vibes from Sturgeon."

"If I stopped doing things because of creepy vibes, I'd never leave home," Freya said. "It's an unfortunate part of my life."

"I'm just saying, as your assistant, mind you, that you don't have to do this."

"You're not getting me to quit that easily," Freya said, moving around him.

Stone pretended to write on an invisible piece of paper.

"Ignore your assistant, okay, got it," he said. "I'll just be your shadow…if that's okay."

Freya rolled her eyes and moved silently through the doorway and saw a young man in glasses and a maroon t-shirt, lost in thought. He had not noticed that Freya had entered and reached for the doorknob only to realize at the last minute that someone was in front of him. His forward momentum carried him too far and Freya dodged out of the way and the young man stumbled toward the floor.

Freya caught his arm and steadied him. He stood to his feet, embarrassed, but then he made eye contact.

For Frank Harvey, it was love at first sight.

CHAPTER EIGHT

When Frank Harvey sat behind his console, he was the creator and master of his own virtual universe. He created the graphics, the environments, the characters, their motivations and desires. Frank Harvey even created the air they breathed.

And he was only nineteen.

Like other kids his age, Frank had always loved video games. His mother bought him his first gaming console when he was two. When he was six, he began diagramming gaming ideas on paper. At twelve, he illegally downloaded expensive gaming code and single-handedly produced a game that millions of people downloaded for free. But the software company did not turn him over to the FBI. They sent a limousine and after negotiations, Frank had his own personal gaming division that he ran from home.

The following year, Frank had either developed or helped develop four of the top ten selling games. In an industry where games made more profit than any blockbuster movie, Frank Harvey was a rock star.

But his obsession with his work had taken a toll on his personal life. After a few months, he had noticed that his parents stopped trying to talk to him. All of the friends he had made in school had begun their own lives. The girl he had been dating for the past two years left him to marry his best friend. He was so immersed in his work that he had barely remembered her leaving. He remembered getting some kind of invitation in the mail, but had no idea it was for her wedding until after the ceremony.

So, while his ex-girlfriend and his ex-best friend were on their honeymoon, Frank Harvey decided that it was time to live it up himself. He began a four-month pleasure tour that took him from Cancun to Paris and Milan, but though he tried to party his way to happiness, Frank felt hollow — like the events somehow weren't real and didn't matter.

Two weeks before his vacation ended, he flew home. That's when Frank began to realize that the money in his bank accounts meant nothing. So when he returned to work, he returned an empty shell of his former self. He did the required amount of work, but he no longer had the drive that had catapulted him to the top of his industry.

Then he discovered an under-developed market: tween girls. Research showed that even though nine-to-twelve-year-old girls were a multi-billion-dollar market, no game developer had yet cracked the code to make a successful game targeted to them. As Frank looked at the failures of others, he noticed all the games centered on simple concepts like dress-up dolls or puzzle games. No one had spent serious money or time in developing an immersive action game. So, Frank decided to make a martial arts video game marketed to young girls to make them feel empowered.

The challenge reignited him. When one of the members of the board suggested that they use a well-known martial artist, Frank smiled, and after a generous offer, received a positive response from Stevie Sturgeon's agent.

Frank had been an avid martial arts fanatic growing up. From the time he was a little boy, he watched every martial arts movie he could. Despite the terrible acting, Stevie Sturgeon's formulaic action movies had always been a guilty pleasure.

His lawyers strongly cautioned Frank about Sturgeon, but Frank dismissed their concerns. The opportunity to work with one of his childhood idols was a dream come true. But his fantasy was quickly destroyed by the harsh reality of a drunk and irritable Stevie Sturgeon. Furthermore, Sturgeon's agent insisted on using his ancient, dingy warehouse for the location, even though it was so old that it wasn't wired for internet use.

Bernie assured Frank that working in the warehouse would allow "instant access" anytime he needed Sturgeon. After having worked with Sturgeon for a few days, Frank wanted less access, not more. Not only was Sturgeon in a constant state of inebriation, he was arrogant, rude, and knew absolutely nothing about video games. Frank tried to explain the process several times, but Sturgeon would mostly look at him with a blank stare and then show off one of his trademarked moves.

Frank looked at the counter at the top of his computer screen. Four million, eight hundred thousand dollars. That is what the project had cost him so far. Frank reached for his tablet, but it wasn't there.

"Left it in the car again," he groaned, to no one in particular.

He left his office, trying to keep the day's events fresh in his mind and bumped into someone walking in the front door. At least, he thought he bumped into her. He hadn't seen her until the last instant and then it seemed like he bumped into her. Frank lost his balance and fell, but a strong arm caught him before he busted his new glasses on the tile floor. Frank looked up as the blonde girl steadied him with one hand.

"Hey!" a male voice from behind her yelled.

When Frank stood to his feet, he made eye contact with Freya and nothing else seemed to matter.

"I'm…sorry," he managed to blurt out.

Freya, recognizing the puppy dog look on his face, relaxed her expression. Most guys undressed her with their eyes. A few looked at her in a more innocent manner. She much preferred the latter.

"Are you alright?" she asked, retaining eye contact.

"I'm sorry," Frank repeated as his glance dropped to the floor. "I was…I don't know what I was doing, but it won't happen again. I'm Frank Harvey."

"Well, Frank, we're here to…" Stone started, but Freya held her hand up as Stone did to her many times. He opened his mouth to speak in protest, but he fell silent. Freya wasn't going to get him to fail that easily. So, he crossed his arms and smiled.

"Mr. Sturgeon hired me for a video game," Freya said. "My name is Freya. This is my assistant, Stone."

"Pleased to meet you, Frank," Stone said, straining his smile even more. "Like she said, I'm just her assistant; no one important, I just do whatever she says."

"Mr. Sturgeon isn't in yet," Frank said. "He should be here any moment though. Are you the woman he signed up? He said you're a martial arts expert?"

"Miss Freya is trained in her art," Stone said matter-of-factly. "She should be…"

"Thank you, Stone, but I can speak for myself," Freya said, annoyed.

"I am so sorry, boss," Stone said. "It won't happen again. As your assistant, I will be more silent in the future. Yes ma'am! I will just shut up and let you do your thing, boss."

"You are an assistant, not a mannequin," Freya protested.

"I'm just here to learn," Stone said. "You're the boss."

"You might have information I need," Freya said.

Frank looked at both of them. They were ignoring him completely now. He couldn't tell if they were arguing, joking, or flirting. He began to back away slowly.

"But you're the expert," Stone said. "I should be relying on your years…no, months, okay, hours of expertise."

Freya's eyes narrowed. She could play this game just as well as Stone. "As my assistant, I value your input. Otherwise, why else would I bring you along?"

"Maybe your superior ordered me along, even when you didn't need me."

"Perhaps my superior ordered you along because he knew you added."

"Maybe your superior ordered me along because …"

"Uh, pardon me," Frank said. "I need to go to my car."

"Fine!" both Freya and Stone yelled and then returned to bickering with each other.

Frank tiptoed past them and ran to the small parking lot behind the studio.

"Great job, boss!" Stone said sarcastically. "Now how do we find Sturgeon?"

"You are so stubborn!" Freya snapped. "I know what you are doing, but we don't have time for this!"

Stone grimaced. She was right.

"Alright," Stone said. "I'll play fair."

"Good," Freya said. "You can start by bringing him back in."

Stone exited the door. As he walked down the steps, a large man staggered past him.

It was Sturgeon.

Even without Sinanju training, Stone could smell the alcohol on his breath. It was eight o'clock in the morning. Either Sturgeon had gotten started very early, or he was still drunk from the night before. For a moment, Stone thought to follow him back in, but then remembered what Freya said. Sturgeon was no threat, so Stone headed toward the parking lot, like a good little assistant.

CHAPTER NINE

Mick Walker logged off from the program that kept track of Sinanju tribal history and closed his eyes. He had been sitting in front of the computer for too long and only stopped work once his chest began to tighten, making it impossible to catch his breath. He tried to remember the stretches Sunny Joe taught him to manipulate the nerves in his spine to allow him to take a deep breath, but he was doing something wrong. After a few minutes, he began seeing stars from hyperventilating, so he leaned back, violently coughing.

Sunny Joe had told him to see Doc Hodges, the reservation's only physician, but it would only confirm what everyone else already knew: Mick Walker was old.

He looked at the pictures that adorned his computer desk. Images of family and friends from the past seventy years drew his attention from his worries. His eyes rested on a grainy, black and white picture of his wife and children. It was taken at a time when everything was young and new and life was nothing but optimism and foolishness.

Then his eyes rested on the newest addition to the Walker family. Mick had just become a great-grandfather. He happily welcomed the fourth generation of the Walker family, but, as he rubbed his painful chest, he realized that his time was approaching.

Of his four children, only Victor had shown any interest in carrying on as tribal historian. Both of his daughters, Donna and Mariella, had followed the children of their generation and escaped the reservation long ago, moving to opposite coasts of the mainland. His youngest son Leo was busy with a job that kept him mostly in Europe.

But while Mick had taught Victor the basics of his job, there was a reason Mick that refused to retire. He tried to tell himself that he was just being dedicated, but he knew better. Mick knew that if he retired, he would die, just like his father and his grandfather.

They did not die immediately after retiring, but something changed when the spark of their job left and each died within a year of retiring. But unlike his grandfather and father, Mick was friends with the chief. Sunny Joe had tried to help him with his health, giving him everything from spinal manipulation to special teas, but he knew Mick needed to call the doctor. Mick kept putting off the call.

As Mick looked at the phone, it rang and he jumped. He picked up the phone, half-expecting Doc Hodges on the other end, but it was the steady and familiar baritone of Sunny Joe.

"Have you called Doc Hodges yet?" Sunny Joe asked.

"I'm gonna call him later this week," Mick said softly.

"You said you were going to call him last week. Am I going to have to start calling

Victor?" Sunny Joe asked.

"No, Sunny Joe. I'll call Doc when we're through. Promise. What do you need?"

"We're all staying a few days longer than we thought."

"Is everything alright?"

There was a slight pause before Sunny Joe replied, but Mick knew better than to say anything.

"Freya's staying to work with Sturgeon — I know what you're thinking — for a few days and Stone volunteered to be her assistant, so I'm going to take the opportunity to tag along and see how well they work together in the field."

"Stevie Sturgeon?" Mick asked. "Dear Lord, is he still alive?"

"Amazing, right? She rattled his cage pretty good at the funeral. He offered her a job to make up for it, but he's hiding something."

"He better be glad his head's still in one piece! Did you hear what she did to the basketball court?"

"I did. Don't worry — I've already talked to her. We've got a handle on it."

"It's gonna cost a few hundred dollars to replace that pole. The boys said — "

"Let the boys know that I intend on having a talk with them when I return. Did the new boy start the fight?"

"No," Mick said. "In fact, he tried to calm both sides down."

"I want you to keep an eye on that one. I told him that he could stay until the end of the year, but after that, he will have to find his own way."

"It's just nice to see a new face and he's been doing pretty good with the — "

"End of the year, Mick. This is Sinanju land."

"Understood, Sunny Joe. Anything else?"

"While I'm out here, I'm going to help an old friend with a problem he has. We should be back by the end of the week. And Mick, if you don't call Doc Hodges when I hang up, I'm going to start calling Victor. I don't like funerals, and I really don't want to go to yours. Am I making myself clear?"

"I'll call him, Sunny Joe."

"Take care of yourself, old friend. See you when we get back."

Mick heard the line go dead on the other end. Sighing deeply, he dialed the number that had been hastily scrawled on a note pad by his monitor.

A familiar voice answered the phone.

"Good afternoon, Mick," Doc Hodges answered. "What can I do for you?"

"Doc, I think something's wrong."

CHAPTER TEN

Stevie Sturgeon sat in his custom brown sports car and glanced at his watch. A copy of an expensive brand, it hadn't worked in three years, but he was too lazy to get a new battery. Besides, he just bought it so he could be seen wearing the same watch that serious actors wore and he was determined to find one, as long as it was less than twenty dollars.

He didn't really care what time it was. He set his own time. That was the thing he hated most about making movies — someone else was always telling you what to say, where to stand, how to dress, and when to be there.

And finally, after several movies and millions of dollars, *he* was going to be the boss. But that was before he invested in Air Spray, a revolutionary new product that placed breathable air into a standard dispensable can. Bernie, had introduced him to the inventor, who said that he had exclusive rights and that Air Spray would revolutionize space travel. The man had looked Sturgeon confidently in the eye and told him that he had an inside contact at NASA, where contracts like this were typically in the billions.

The man leaned in closely and lowered his voice as if to divulge a great secret.

Sturgeon's face quickly matched the man's conspiratorial look and he leaned in so the man could speak even more quietly. After all, untold billions of dollars were at stake.

"See, NASA don't want the public to know," the man whispered. His breath smelled like a combination of fish and cheap beer. "Their big space station is running out of air."

Sturgeon's eyebrows raised. He instantly knew where the man was going and he smiled as he saw the dollar signs racking up.

"Don't forget, these are the guys who spend twenty thousand dollars for a hammer that costs you and me ten bucks, right? I already checked and someone else is selling them the hammers, so I began to wonder what NASA needed. Then it hit me: They need air, so all we have to do is get them to sign an exclusive contract, send up a few thousand cans at a time and we'll be rolling in the money. Since the air will keep running out, we have a steady contract, year after year!"

"What will it take?" Sturgeon asked.

The man brought out a small briefcase and, looking around to make sure no one else could see him, opened it in front of Sturgeon. It was filled with all kinds of sciency-looking pages filled with equations and the word "AIR SPRAY" circled in bright red at the top. Sturgeon knew that all those pages of scientific research were pointing to that single solution and he held his breath as the man sifted through the pages. Finally, the man withdrew a page that said FINANCES at the top.

"I already figured out how to make it work. I just need some seed money," the man said. "And we will split the profits fifty-fifty."

Sturgeon snuck a peek at the bottom of the page, where, in bold letters, it said:

ESTIMATED ANNUAL PROFIT: $2 BILLION

Sturgeon's heart began racing and he licked his lips. If he invested now, he could have a billion dollars within a year, two tops. Everyone knew that you needed air to breathe, so NASA would be beholden to ESTEPHAN ANTONIO FREDERICO STURGEON and him alone! Well, him and his new partner.

Sturgeon smacked the man on the back and smiled. "Let's get those documents signed! Drinks are on me!"

His partner delivered what he said. Sturgeon bought an old warehouse to store twelve thousand cases of canned air. Sturgeon had wanted to store them in a large storage unit, but his agent convinced him otherwise — a storage unit was too vulnerable to theft, especially since it had been insured for close to a billion dollars. When Sturgeon asked why the insurance policy was in Bernie's name, he was told that it was to keep his name out of the tabloids in case something happened.

When Sturgeon went to pitch his product to NASA, they all but laughed at him. They said that they already had a more efficient method of storing air, tanks of what they called "liquid oxygen."

Did they think he was an idiot? *Oxygen wasn't a liquid!*

The inventor explained that they must have upset the powers that be, and now there were legal complications that might take years to work out. Then he got on his private jet and flew to his new home in the Bahamas to work it out.

That was four years and fifteen million dollars ago, and now Sturgeon was nearly broke. His agent had managed to find work on commercials and, for a small time, even a reality television show, but after the first two episodes, the only people watching were the crew, so the show was canceled.

For the first time in his life, Stevie Sturgeon was afraid.

Not that he would ever let anyone know he was afraid. But he began to realize that there was no way for him to kick fate in the teeth; there was no way to snap destiny's neck in a final, victorious move.

He had wanted to retire at the top of his game, like Bill Roam did. The old goat got to finish his ride and exit on his own terms.

Roam.

Every time Sturgeon had wanted to make a name for himself, Roam was there to steal the spotlight! Back when they were stuntmen, he was sure that Roam sabotaged his stunts just to make Sturgeon look bad. He had no proof, but why else would he fail so much? No one was a better stuntman than Stevie Sturgeon! And now, Roam had dared to upstage him at a funeral!

The man had no shame.

Sturgeon smiled as he walked in the door, seeing Roam's granddaughter waiting for him. He had considered simply making her fall in love with him, sleeping with her until he got tired of her, and then breaking her heart, so that Roam would know never to cross Stevie Sturgeon.

He slinked up toward Freya, smiling and absent-mindedly scratching his butt. He stuck out his hand for her to shake.

Freya looked at the hand that he had just scratched with and politely bowed instead.

Good. She knows who the master is, Sturgeon thought, bowing, but making sure that he didn't bow as low as Freya did. *A master never bows more deeply than the pupil.*

"I'm ready to begin," Freya said. "When and where do we start?"

"Honey, just follow my lead," Sturgeon said, trying to place his arm around Freya, but his arm somehow fell in front of her instead of on her shoulder. It flopped uselessly to his side. Tiny needle pricks filled his lower arm and he shook it back awake.

"There you are," Stone said as he opened the door. "I found Frank outside. He said that they need to fit you for your mocha…uh…"

"Mocap suit," Frank explained from behind Stone. He blushed as Freya made eye contact with him. "It's short for 'motion capture.' Wardrobe is down the hall."

"Let's go," Sturgeon said, leading the way.

"Actually, it's the other way, Mr. Sturgeon," Frank corrected. "Third door on the right."

The four passed the hallway, plastered with Sturgeon movie posters until they entered the wardrobe department. A very old woman sat behind a desk, smoking what appeared to be the world's largest cigar. One of her eyes was permanently squinted shut by fat.

"Rachel, this is Freya," Frank said. "She needs a mocap suit."

Rachel placed her cigar on the desk and waddled to the doorway. Stone looked at the cigar box sitting on her desk. It was full. He subconsciously patted his cigarettes.

Rachel stood in front of Freya, sizing her up. Her lungs spasmed and dark thick mucus erupted with each cough. She reached into her pocket and popped a cough drop and brought out a measuring tape. She stretched it across Freya's body first one way and then the other. Sturgeon followed every movement of the measuring tape.

It took every bit of Stone's discipline not to shove his sternum through his vertebrae.

"She's skinny," Rachel finally said. "I think I got something for her, but it's kid-sized."

"How long before she's ready?" Frank asked.

Sturgeon just kept staring at Freya's body. She ignored him, but Stone could tell she noticed. *How did she put up with creeps like him?*

"I can have it sized by tomorrow. It'll be pretty tight, though. Won't be that comfy, hon," Rachel said, waddling back to her desk.

"If that's settled, let me give you a tour of the studio," Frank said, smiling. "The cool thing about…"

"No way, kid," Sturgeon interrupted. "This is my show. I'll give her the tour."

"No thank you, Mr. Sturgeon," Freya said politely. "I will take Frank up on his kind offer. We can meet later and discuss what moves you wish me to make."

Sturgeon's eyes lit up at the suggestion and Freya almost threw up in her mouth.

"You can give my assistant a tour if you would like," Freya said, noticing Stone's tensed stance and clenched fists. "I'm sure you two can find something to talk about."

Freya motioned forward and Frank led her down the hallway. Stone glared at Sturgeon for a moment and then remembered his promise to Freya.

"Lead on, McDouche," Stone said, gesturing forward with his hand.

"Ah, give yourself a tour," Sturgeon said and then stumbled into his office. He slammed the door hard enough to rattle the gold-plated portrait hanging outside his office.

Stone walked by and helped it hit the floor.

CHAPTER ELEVEN

"So," Freya said, breaking the ice. "How long have you been doing this?"

"Oh, I've only been here for a couple of months, but I've been producing computer games for a few years now. I've been working with computer programs for a lot longer, though. I could probably hack NASA if I really wanted to," Frank said with a smirk and tinge of pride.

Freya had no idea what "NASA" was, but could tell that by the way Frank had spoken, it must be a monumental achievement.

"That's very impressive," she said. "What is it like working here?"

"The warehouse smells like dead fish and the roof looks like it is going to collapse any day now…" Frank started, but Freya stopped walking and turned to face him.

"No. I meant to ask what it is like working with Mr. Sturgeon," she said.

"Well, honestly, he's kind of a butt," Frank admitted. "He doesn't know anything about what we do. One moment, he thinks that what we do is so impressive that it can't be explained by anything other than 'magic' and the next, he tells us that we should be replaced by the fry guy at McBurger Queen!"

"He seems to be a very unhappy man."

"Someone duped him into investing all his money into a get-rich-quick scheme, so now everyone else has to pay. I don't have to work here. I have my own money, but I thought that it would be cool to work with him, but I was wrong. It's not."

"My grandfather was a stuntman at one point," Freya said. "He did not get along very well with Mr. Sturgeon, either."

"What's his name? I might have heard of him."

"Bill Roam. He was the…" Freya began.

Frank forgot all about being intimidated by Freya when he heard the name.

"Big Bill Roam? Really? He worked on just about everything! I've got every episode of Muck Man, and I even bought a pirated copy of *That Darn Injun*! It's kinda blurry, but it was a really funny show! You're related to him?"

"Yes, he is my grandfather."

"Hey, could you get me his autograph? He was the king of the stuntmen when Sturgeon was just starting out, but wow! I forgot they worked together!"

"'Together' might be too strong of a word," Freya said. "By the way grandfather explained it to me, it would be more accurate to say that they were paid for working on the same project."

"Ha! Sturgeon was a butt back then, too, I guess!"

Frank's shoulders relaxed and he began enjoying the conversation and the company. He hadn't had a girlfriend in so long, but who was he kidding? Freya was tall and beautiful and could obviously have anyone she wanted. Frank really liked her European accent, but he did not know if the other guy was her bodyguard or her boyfriend. By the way they were arguing earlier, Frank thought he might be the latter and could tell that he was a guy who got what he wanted.

"Sorry, I forgot that I was showing you around for a minute!" Frank said, slapping himself on the forehead. He aimed his arm down the hallway. "Shall we?"

Freya curtsied and nodded. "Indeed, we shall!"

The two walked down the hallway. Freya enjoyed the conversation much more than the tour.

CHAPTER TWELVE

Stone took Sturgeon's advice and gave himself a tour. He almost instantly wished that he hadn't when he realized that every hallway was lined with posters of Sturgeon's movies.

And Sturgeon had autographed each one to himself.

Stone decided that if he were ever to become a bad guy, he would do something this stupid to make investigators stop researching before they threw up.

He entered the warehouse at the back of the facility and immediately held his breath. It was a football-field-sized chamber, occupied by thousands of large crates. Opening a few of the crates revealed hundreds of canisters with Sturgeon's face and the words 'Air Spray' on the side. Stone removed one of the canisters and pulled the plastic trigger. A slow spray emitted. Stone sniffed. Oxygen.

Who was stupid enough to buy a thousand crates of oxygen canisters? Stone wondered and then looked toward the back. Those crates were larger than the rest, so he approached the largest one and sniffed.

Coffee.

Most of the time people packed coffee to mask another scent. He initially suspected that Sturgeon was trafficking drugs, but the smell beneath the heady coffee aroma was not the sickly-sweet smell of drugs that Stone had expected. It was the distinct and metallic tang of explosives.

What are you doing, Sturgeon?

After a few more minutes checking random crates but finding nothing, he headed back. The geek should have had more than enough time to finish Freya's tour by now. Stone would return after everyone left to take a closer look. As he returned to the hallway, Stone was startled by a large theater poster featuring Sturgeon's trademark scowl beneath the words "FORCE OF ONE." At the bottom was a scribbled autograph:

You were FANTASTIC in this movie! I loved it!
Keep up the great work!
All my love,
Stevie Sturgeon

Stone worked on a grimace of his own as he defied his stomach's urge to empty itself on the cheap hallway carpet. Freya and the nerd sounded like they were already back in the lobby. Stone took his time walking back to them so he could eavesdrop on their conversation.

"I'd love to," Freya said with a happy tone Stone had not heard in weeks. "I haven't been to a real restaurant in months!"

"I know this really good Italian place a few blocks away. They have great pasta!"

Freya sighed as she remembered her new dietary restrictions.

"I really love pasta, but I need a place that serves rice."

"Why, sure, if that's what you want," Frank said.

His smile was contagious and before she knew it, Freya found herself smiling.

"And where is the assistant supposed to eat?" Stone said from behind.

"Wherever he wants," Freya said, without turning around. "Because he is a valued member of the team with his own tastes and his boss wants him to be happy."

"Whoa, so now you're my boss?" Stone asked.

"Would you rather I call myself your superior?"

"Boss is okay," Stone said. "Go ahead and eat rice with your little friend. I think I'll grab a big juicy steak, and a baked potato smothered in butter and cheese!"

Freya found herself swallowing hard. Her body may have become physically unable to process such foods, but her mind still longed for them.

"Enjoy your meal," she said. "Frank is taking me to a nice restaurant with good rice."

Frank resumed his nervous stance after seeing Stone's glare.

"If that's alright with you," he said quietly. "I mean, if Freya is your girlfriend, I can just eat by myself."

Freya released a full-throated laugh and Frank involuntarily began laughing with her.

"Boyfriend?" she finally said. "He's my brother!"

"Half-brother," Stone corrected. "I got the good half of the genes. And since I'm her big brother, if you even think about — "

Freya's smile disappeared and she held her hand in front of Stone's mouth.

"What my brother is trying to say is that he wishes us to enjoy a good meal while he fills his belly with the meat of cows."

"No, I'm saying — "

Freya held her hand up again.

"What my brother fails to remember is that though I may be his little sister, I can still kick his butt," she said, smiling.

"I'll wait outside," Stone said, kicking idly at the floor.

As he opened the door, he immediately saw three protestors dressed like rolls of toilet paper, standing in front of the building next door, chanting the same slogan over and over.

Their protest signs ranged from "STOP THE TREE MURDARS" to "EQAL RITES FOR ILEGAL ALANS!" He glanced at one of the women and then rolled his eyes. Her sign read "TREE BLOOD IS ON YUR HANDS!" The bottom of her toilet paper costume was red, which made her look like a used maxi-pad.

Stone wasn't even going to ask. He pulled out a cigarette and the people who were ignoring him now became focused on him as if he had just pulled out a bloody stump.

"Smoking is not allowed here, you hermaphrodite!" one of the women yelled.

Stone tilted his head down and smiled as he tapped the cigarette against the side of the building. "I don't think that word means what you think it means," he said.

"Hermaphrodite!" the woman said defiantly, as if she were participating in a sixth-grade spelling bee. "'Herma' means atmosphere and '-dite' means 'he who spoils.'"

A confused look came across Stone's face. The woman had said it with such authority, that he took a second to think about she had said. "What about the 'aphro' part?" he asked.

The question seemed to stump the woman, who turned and consulted with the others. They laid their signs down as they discussed the question. The woman received her answer from a rock-paper-scissors decision.

"That refers to your hair," she said firmly.

"You have no idea what you're talking about, do you?" Stone said and lit the cigarette.

The first woman's eyes opened so large you could see the muscles supporting them.

"Fire!" she yelled.

"What?" Stone asked. "Really?"

The others were already dialing 911 on their cell phones, their expressions frozen in shock as if they had just witnessed a murder.

"Fire!" they each yelled. "Fire at the warehouse!"

Stone had enough. He tossed the cigarette toward the toilet paper commandos and the three panicked. It seemed to tumble through the air in slow motion as it headed toward their highly flammable costumes. Cell phones were tossed aside as the women tried to get out of its way.

The cigarette landed in a trashcan behind them.

Stone laughed and walked away.

CHAPTER THIRTEEN

Frank opened the doors to the motion capture studio for Freya. The room was large and brightly lit, with a thin white mat stretching to the walls, which were painted lime green. The windows of the control booth were slightly elevated above the floor, allowing the operators a full view of the studio below. Freya looked down, noting all of the markings that lined up with the walls around her.

"Those are calibration marks," Frank explained. "When you get your suit tomorrow, we'll capture your movements with the modules on your mocap suit. Today, we're just syncing the video cameras."

"What will I be doing?" Freya asked.

"That would be up to me," a friendly voice said, booming from the intercom speakers hidden in the ceiling. "Name's Stan. I'll be your operator."

"Stan is old school mocap," Frank explained. "If it weren't for him, none of this would even be possible."

"It wouldn't be possible if I weren't here!" a voice yelled from beneath the booth. Stevie Sturgeon stumbled down the stairs leading from the control booth. "I'm the star of this shin-dig!"

"Mr. Sturgeon," Freya said primly. "What is my assignment?"

"Hell, I don't know. Ask Einstein there. I'm just here to watch," he said with a wink.

Sturgeon pulled up a fold-up chair at the edge of the mat, crossing his arms as he sat.

"You've got a lot of hard work ahead of you, little girl. This is the big leagues," he said and lowered his sunglasses over his eyes.

Frank motioned for Freya to move to the center of the mat.

"Stan is going to capture some simple moves at first to calibrate your standard movement speed."

Freya moved to the spot and turned toward the control booth, feeling Sturgeon's glances below her waist. She grabbed a deep breath to calm herself and concentrated on Stan's instructions.

"Okay, I need you to do a few simple karate moves," Stan said.

"I don't know karate," Freya admitted.

"I thought you said you knew martial arts," Frank said.

"I am, but not an art you are likely familiar with," Freya explained.

Sturgeon got up from his chair and walked next to Freya.

"All you gotta do is this," Sturgeon said, bending his knees and striking the air in front of him. "A basic demonstration of your skills so Stan can do whatever he does with those expensive computers."

"Perhaps you would like to demonstrate first, Mr. Sturgeon?" Freya asked.

Sturgeon belched. He was in no shape for a demonstration, but the way Freya had asked felt like a public challenge.

Cocky. Just like Roam, Sturgeon thought. "Step back, darling, I don't want to hurt you."

"Yes, that would be unfortunate," Freya said, moving to the wall near Frank.

"So, what are we going to do, Mr. Sturgeon?" Stan asked from above. "Standard calibration moves or something more advanced?"

"I eat advanced like jelly-filled donuts!" he said, winking at Freya and hoping his medication would hold on long enough to finish his moves. "Fire it up, Stan!"

Freya heard a few clicks and then the plastic static of a vinyl record being played. A throbbing disco beat filled the studio to the point that Frank had to cover his ears. He cringed and shrugged his shoulders in apology to Freya, who merely smiled and nodded toward Sturgeon.

Sturgeon began bouncing his hips with the beat of the music and pointing to the air with one hand. On the next beat, he suddenly stood upright, releasing a double fist punch to an imaginary foe. Bowing back down to the beat, Sturgeon dropped to one hand and swept with his foot, surprising himself by not falling over. As he fell to his back to what normally would be jumping back onto his feet again, he thought better and employed his most amazing talent — improvisation — and rolled away as if dodging a giant foot that was crashing toward his head. His fat rolled with him, a lopsided puddle of human dough, moving in semi-circles on the mat.

Sturgeon stood to his feet and began seeing spots. He tried to hide his coughing with the disco beat, but it was apparent that he was worn out. He moved against the wall and began dry heaving as the music stopped.

"Stuff like that," he finally said, motioning with his hands for Stan to cut the music.

"Okay," Freya said and moved to the center of the mat. Sturgeon stood up straighter as she neared but she ignored him.

Freya nodded to Stan and the music started over. She duplicated Sturgeon's moves perfectly, including the lopsided roll. She ended by fake dry heaving against the wall.

"Is there anything else?" she asked.

"Stan, take five," Sturgeon said, seething. "Now!"

Stan recognized the tone of voice that Sturgeon reserved for those people whom he hated, which included just about nearly every other martial artist who had ever lived. Stan climbed down the stairs and walked out to the small closet that Sturgeon set aside as a cafeteria. Frank remained, standing silently against the wall.

"You, too, kid. I need to talk to our new employee."

"I'll be in the lobby," Frank said.

Sturgeon waited for the door to shut behind Frank and then walked toward her. While he was no threat, Freya felt uncomfortable with his distance and took a step back.

"This is some kinda silly dance to you, isn't it?" Sturgeon said, stepping forward. "Well, I lead! I'm the boss! You're not allowed to try to make me look bad!"

Freya crossed her arms and her stubborn Roam genes strengthened her spine. She was not going to back down.

"I did exactly what you asked me to do, Mr. Sturgeon."

"I know what you did," he said. "You're one of those girls who thinks the world revolves around them! You think you're special — just like your grandpa!"

The taunt hung in the air. Freya could feel the tension raging between them, but she would not give him the satisfaction of beating him within an inch of his life, even if he deserved it. She would not let her grandfather down by losing control again. Her personal matters would wait until later.

"Will that be all, Mr. Sturgeon?" she asked, smiling politely.

Sturgeon bit his bottom lip to suppress his rage. He wanted nothing more than to punch the cocky smile from Freya's face, but he would not let this little girl get the best of him. Let her have her moment. Stevie Sturgeon would teach her a lesson.

"Don't be late tomorrow," he managed to grumble before walking off.

Freya walked to the lobby where Frank was sitting, texting on his cell phone. She looked at him just a moment before entering the lobby and she began to smile.

"Are you ready?" she asked. "Let's go!"

CHAPTER FOURTEEN

The wind blew gently across the grates, dragging smells that had been buried in the sewers, scattering them through the street. The rot and stench of twelve blocks swirled into a pungent stew, but it was still not strong enough to hide the smell of Stone's smoky breath. Stone had been silently following them since they left the studio. Normally, Freya could not tell when Stone was following her, but he made small, yet distinct sounds to let her know he was near.

He needn't have bothered. Whatever his plan was, she was not going to allow it to interfere with her date.

"I'm sorry," Freya said, returning her attention to Frank. "What did you say?"

"I was asking where you're from. Are you alright?"

"I'm fine," she said smiling. "Stone and I are from the Sinanju reservation in Arizona."

"Reservation? How did you get blonde hair?" Frank asked. "Is that too personal?"

"No. My mother was European," Freya explained. "Her hair was blonde, like mine."

"Was?"

"She was murdered when I was eleven."

"Oh, I'm sorry," Frank said sheepishly as his eyebrows bent upwards in concern.

"She died with honor," Freya said. "Her death is a fact that I have come to accept."

After a moment of silence, Frank spoke again. "My story isn't anything serious like that, but my mom left us when I was six," Frank said. "She found some guy on the internet and left my dad a note one day. I found it first though."

"Yet you have turned your pain into strength," Freya noted.

"Well, my dad remarried, but it's not the same," Frank said sadly. "And with this job, I don't really get to live my own life. Maybe when I retire at thirty."

"This American concept of stopping work when you reach a certain age is confusing."

"They have retirement systems in Europe, right?" Frank asked, laughing. "What country are you from, anyway?"

"It is a very small country that most people have never heard of," Freya said quietly.

"Try me," Frank challenged. "I did pretty well in geography."

"Lakluun," Freya said hopefully.

Frank looked up in thought. "Lak-loo-win," he slowly pronounced. "Lack-loo-win. No, you got me there. Where is it?"

"Europe," Freya said. "Where are you from? You don't sound like the others here."

"I grew up twenty miles from here," Frank admitted. "I only sound different because my dad was a broadcaster. We grew up pronouncing every syllable the proper way or he wouldn't allow us to eat."

"Oh my," Freya said.

"That was supposed to be a joke," Frank said with a smile. "My humor isn't as advanced as my programming skills."

They had reached *Wok This Way*, the only Chinese restaurant he knew. They found a booth and sat across from each other. Freya picked up the neon red menu. There were so many choices, but Freya only saw three things she could eat.

The waitress came to their table, dressed in a bright yellow Asian robe with a scarlet dragon winding down the front.

"Good evening, Mr. Frank," she said, smiling. "What will you have today?"

"I'll get the usual, Soo," Frank said. "Freya?"

"I would just like some brown rice and a small piece of tilapia," Freya said. "No seasoning, please."

"What would you like on your rice?" the waitress asked.

"Nothing, please. Just plain brown rice."

"Right away," the waitress said.

"Wow, I thought you were kidding about the rice."

"My training requires a special diet," Freya explained.

"What are you training for?"

"I'm carrying on my family's martial art. It is very demanding."

"Can you break bricks and stuff?"

"We don't train to impress people, though some of the things I've seen grandfather do are very impressive."

"So how long will you be in LA?" Frank asked, changing the subject after noticing the forlorn look on Freya's face.

"Just this week. We accompanied grandfather to a funeral," Freya said, looking around. The restaurant was not very clean. The floor seemed to be covered by an ancient greasy film and her nose crinkled. Whatever was being cooked in the back certainly was not fresh.

"Stone and I will return to the reservation Saturday."

"Wow. Consider yourself lucky. I signed a contract, so I'll be here a few more months after you're gone." His face fell.

"What will you do after that?" Freya asked.

"I really don't know. I put my personal life on hold to work on all of this, but I'm starting to think it might be nice to visit a reservation or two," he said with a shy smile.

Freya returned the smile.

"What about you?" Frank asked. "Are you still in school?"

"I completed my schooling last year. Grandfather wants me to go to college, but I don't see the need."

"It's always a good idea to continue to learn," Frank said. "Some people just go through life existing. I'm here to live! I would die at a nine-to-five job!"

"I know what you mean," Freya said.

Even though her emotions were causing anxiety earlier, she felt relaxed and very close to Frank.

The food arrived and Frank lowered his head to say a small prayer of thanks. Freya did not know what to do, so she remained silent.

"I sometimes thank my ancestors," she said. "I like to think of myself as a part of living history, each person in my past as a small piece of who I am today, just as my descendants will be an offshoot of me."

"I've never felt connected to my family."

"My mother raised me to appreciate life," Freya said, taking an experimental taste of her rice. It was overcooked as she had expected. The grains were soggy, without texture and tasted like it was cooked in dishwater. Old dish water at that. Freya sighed. Most people did not know how to properly cook rice.

Frank noticed how slowly Freya ate her rice, as if she were chewing one grain at a time, but didn't want to pry.

Stone sat quietly on the balcony of the building across the restaurant, an invisible observer. He had been watching Frank and Freya ever since they sat down. The kid sat politely across from Freya, his body language ranging from happy to downright giddy. He was glad he had been able to grab a quick smoke on the way over, because as far as stakeouts went, he was so bored that he had been tossing pebbles at people as they walked below. He gave himself bonus points if the person wore a hat and he could knock it off.

Stone had already racked up eighty points.

Freya glanced Stone's way only once during the meal, and only then to let him know that she knew he was there. Then she leaned her face forward, holding the menu to the side of her face so he couldn't see what she was saying.

Frank smiled, looking in Stone's general direction.

"Good luck, Chump," Stone whispered. Even if Freya had told him what window he was perched near, the kid would never see Stone while he was centered. Sunny Joe never explained *how* it worked, but that did not stop it from working. Stone tried to use the same exact stealth techniques a few times when he was not centered and was easily spotted.

Freya placed the menu back on the table and they finished eating.

"Hope you had fun tonight," Frank said. "Do you think we can do this again before you leave?"

"I would like that very much, but I don't want to give you the wrong impression, Frank. I'm not looking for a boyfriend, but I really did have a lovely evening," Freya said.

"Thank you for reminding me that life exists outside my computer," Frank said, offering his hand.

Freya shook his hand and despite what she had just said, she allowed her gaze to linger a bit longer than it had to.

Frank lowered his face and blushed.

CHAPTER FIFTEEN

The next morning, Freya and Stone entered the warehouse a few minutes early.

"So, what adventures await us today, boss?" Stone asked.

"Frank said that they will be recording my moves today, so you can hang around, but don't get in my way," she said, laughing.

"I guess I'll read the stack of 'Punchmaster: the Stevie Sturgeon Fanzine' I saw piled on the waiting room table. I think the most recent issue was from 1995."

"Just stay out of trouble," Freya said, smiling. "I'm going to find Frank."

"Tell your little boyfriend that your big brother said hi," Stone said.

"You can tell him yourself later," Freya said.

Stone shook his head and sat on the lobby couch. The stack of fanzines looked as if no one had ever read them.

Freya headed to Frank's office, only to see a sign on his door.

Sturgeon sent me on errands.
I'll see you this afternoon!
— Frank

Freya frowned and left for her dressing room. She locked the door as she entered and scanned for cameras or electronic recording equipment. Not sensing any, she slipped out of her loose-fitting shirt and jeans into the skintight suit provided by the studio. If she hadn't known better, she would have thought that Sturgeon had provided the form fitting suit to ogle her, but she had been assured by Frank that it was a standard motion capture suit, though it was a size too small.

Stretching the soft fabric over her shoulders, Freya thought it felt more like five sizes too small. It was easy to move in, and everything was covered, but it clung to every curve. For someone who was used to wearing loose and flowing clothing, it was unnerving.

Freya looked at herself in the mirror and for just a moment, considered walking out, but then knew that she would have to face Stone. He would never let her live down quitting a job. Freya walked shyly into the motion capture room. Sturgeon was standing next to Stan in the control booth above.

"Wooo, girl! I should have hired you five years ago," Sturgeon bellowed over the intercom. Freya could feel his eyes all over her.

"Gross. I would have been eleven," she said, disgusted.

"Good morning, Freya," Stan said. "Just insert the power cable into the plug on your belt and we can get started.

Freya picked up a cable lying on the floor and attached it to the slot on the left side of her belt. As it clicked in place, Freya felt a tiny surge of electricity fill the suit.

"That's weird," Stan said.

He slid his chair over to the master control panel and double-checked the readings.

"Freya, the sensors don't see you," he said, puzzled. "Are you sure you plugged the cable in all the way?"

Freya sighed. While she maintained her Sinanju center, her body was protected against electronics. It must be interfering with the suit. She closed her eyes and lowered her center until her skin became sensitive enough to feel the flow of electricity.

"Wait, okay, now I can see you," Stan said in relief. "Wow, that was weird. Does everything feel comfortable?"

"I am ready," Freya said, ignoring Sturgeon's blatant leering.

"Okay, to start, we just need to synchronize your moves with our computer," Stan said. "Raise both arms."

Freya did as she was asked and the operator matched her move with the computer results on his screen.

"Okay, lift each leg, one at a time, please," Stan asked, synchronizing those moves as well. "Good. Okay, now we're going to move on to more complicated variations. Try your best to duplicate the moves that you see on the screen in front of you."

The huge monitor showed a female computer character with impossible body proportions, barely contained in a hopelessly tight kimono top and bright red bikini bottom. Freya rolled her eyes. The computer character struck out one fist with a simple karate strike. Freya repeated the move.

"Hmmm," Stan mused as he viewed the playback from Freya's strike.

"Now what's wrong?" Sturgeon asked.

Stan sat back and crossed his arms as he studied the read out.

"Take a look at this. The screen to the left is the computer's move. The screen to the right is the recording of Freya's move. There must be some kind of feedback from the computer signal, because both screens are showing the exact same move as the computer model," Stan said.

"I don't understand," Freya said. "Isn't that what you asked me to do?"

"Well, yeah, but this is the same exact move. See?" he said, pointing to a graph. "Here and here. That's the exact same striking speed and angle...down to the pixel. That's just not possible."

Freya shrugged. She would add small imperfections to each move if Stan needed them, but in reality, it would lessen the damage of the blow. Of course, she could punch far more efficiently than the computer character or any martial artist on the face of the planet.

"Okay, we're finally ready. Just give me a few basic moves," Stan said. "The larger the moves, the better."

Freya relaxed with a few beginning Sinanju moves. She noticed Sturgeon trying to watch, so she increased the complexity of each move so he could not follow her.

"Maybe you need to breathe in a little deeper?" Sturgeon asked over the intercom. "And arch your back a bit more. We have to record every possible angle, you know."

Freya ignored the command, just as she ignored Sturgeon's commands to turn around and bend over, run her hands down her body and bounce in place. Sunny Joe had warned her that after the Night of Salt, a Master of Sinanju became more naturally desirable to members of the opposite sex. She had hoped that it wouldn't apply to her. Even at her age, she noted the way some men looked at her and couldn't imagine it getting any worse.

Over the next hour, Freya duplicated each of the moves she saw on the monitor, adding a small quirk here and there to satisfy Stan. As Sturgeon watched, he forgot his master plan for a moment and found himself actually impressed by this girl, but he still refused to believe that Freya was a better fighter than he was.

Stone had become bored in the waiting room and snuck into the studio. The suit they put Freya in was something like a gymnast would wear. Noting Sturgeon's lecherous smile, it took every bit of restraint not to scale the booth and wipe that leering grin off his face.

Stone had to admit, the assistant bit was getting old. He was itching to do something — anything. He considered leaving the studio and wandering around the city, but there was no way Stone was going to leave Freya alone with Sturgeon.

Then there was Frank, the nerdy little guy with a crush on Freya. Stone didn't know what to think of him, but it was nice to see Freya smile again.

"Okay, that's it for today," Stan said over the intercom. "See everyone in the morning."

"Thank you, Mr. Stan," Freya said, unplugging the cable from her suit.

Stone noticed her shiver for a moment. "What's wrong?" he asked.

"Their machines won't work while I am centered," she said stretching her neck. "And I'm not used to being out of center for that long."

"Yeah, yeah, rub it in. I'm just happy to celebrate three hours without a smoke."

"Let's go before he gets down here," Freya said. "I don't like wearing this thing."

The two left for Freya's dressing room.

"If I were you, I would have told him to stuff that suit," Stone said. "There's only one reason he wanted you to wear that."

"I agreed to take the job, so I'll do it."

"Creeps like that bother me. He's gotta be pushing seventy! The way he looks at you…"

"You're just now noticing how men look at me?" Freya asked. "It's been a part of my life for years and Grandfather says that it will only get worse."

"That would explain the nerdy little guy with a crush on you."

Freya stopped and turned to face Stone.

"That 'nerdy little guy' has treated me better than most men, including you," Freya said. "In fact, we're going out again tonight, so don't bother following us again."

"Does that mean I have the night off, boss?"

"Give me some room, Stone," Freya said, glaring at him. "I wanted to stay here so that I could unplug from everything."

"Just be careful," Stone said. "No one can dodge heartbreak."

Freya ignored the comment. "I need to get dressed. I'll see you later."

"Night, sis," Stone said. He waited for Freya to enter her dressing room before leaving. It was time to follow up on a hunch. Then Stone thought about Freya going out to eat with Frank. *I'll check on it after a good steak*, he thought, licking his lips.

CHAPTER SIXTEEN

Frank's small electric car bounced into the studio parking lot, coming to a screeching halt. He jumped out of the car and raced to the building, only to see Freya walking out the door. He bent over to catch his breath.

"Glad I caught you before you left!" he said between gasps.

"I wondered if you were going to show up," Freya said. "You're late."

"Sorry, Sturgeon had me running all kinds of crazy errands today. Not one of them had anything to do with work."

"Well, I am glad you made it," Freya said.

"So, are you ready to eat?" Frank asked, smiling hopefully.

His smile was contagious and Freya relented to its power.

"I am now," she said.

"Where should we eat tonight?" Frank asked.

Freya lowered her gaze in thought. The food was barely tolerable at the Chinese restaurant, but she couldn't hope on finding Sinanju Kosher anywhere else.

"Let's return to the Chinese restaurant again," she said. "If that is alright with you."

"What, are you kidding me? It's my favorite restaurant!" Frank said.

The two started walking and their conversation began to flow. Freya found herself enjoying their talk. Frank relaxed and forgot that he was supposed to try to impress her. Before they reached the restaurant, Frank stopped and turned to Freya. His eyes locked with hers and they both stopped talking. Frank leaned in to kiss her, but Freya stepped back. She took a deep breath before speaking.

"Frank, I would just like to be your friend."

"There it is," Frank said, his eyebrows arched into a frown. "The friendzone. Ah, I knew someone like you wouldn't fall for a guy like me."

"'Friendzone?' I do not understand."

"Women who want you to do stuff for them, but don't see you as anything else."

"I would never use someone like that. I'm just not looking for a boyfriend."

"Why not?" Frank asked. "Is it the way I look?"

"Not at all. It is…complicated," Freya said.

"It's not like I'm asking you to marry me, although…would you?" Frank asked, dramatically dropping to one knee, holding out an invisible ring.

Freya laughed. "Not today," she said. "Let's eat."

The two entered the restaurant and Freya found herself enjoying the meal. The food was barely palatable yet again, but Freya didn't notice. She realized that anytime she was around Frank, she smiled. His spirit was calm and peaceful, and a small confidence existed behind his public veneer of shyness. And he looked Freya in the eyes when they spoke.

If I were looking for a boyfriend, she caught herself thinking, *I would give him a chance.*

As they left the restaurant, Frank became silent.

"What is wrong?" Freya asked.

"I don't know. I'm just...okay, why does Stone hate me?" Frank asked.

"He doesn't hate you. He is just being overprotective," Freya explained. "And I guess I would be the same way if he were dating someone, though I hadn't really thought about it until now. All we really have is each other and Sunny Joe."

"Have you seen any of your grandfather's movies? He's not the star, but you can tell when it's really him, even when they try to make him look short. He's got these fluid moves, kinda like a panther. Silent, but you can tell there's a lot of power behind his movements."

"Grandfather is a good teacher," Freya said. "Women normally are not trained in our art, so I take his training very seriously. One day I hope to be as good as him."

"Are you a black belt?" Frank asked.

"We do not have belts," Freya said. "In fact, I have never understood the need."

"It lets everyone know what skill level you are."

"But why would you want to tell anyone that? If you were ever in a fight and your opponent saw a belt color lighter than his own, it would grant him great confidence. Likewise, if you saw a belt darker than yours, it might cause you to doubt the outcome."

"Good point," Frank said. He soaked in the moment. For the first time in years, his downtime was not spent on gaming or movies. It was spent thinking about Freya. Frank smiled and leaned in toward her.

Overcome by the moment, Freya grabbed Frank's face with both hands and kissed him. Pleasantly startled, Frank dropped his car keys and then turned his body toward hers. The sounds of the world seemed to disappear. Then the moment passed and Freya pulled away, embarrassed.

"Wait! What's wrong?" Frank asked.

Freya could not bring herself to look him in the eye. She had no idea why she kissed him, but she had to leave.

"I am sorry, Frank, I truly am."

And then she disappeared.

She had been standing right in front of Frank, but in-between blinks, she vanished. Frank looked around, thinking it might have been a magic trick.

"Freya?" he asked.

It took a few minutes before he realized that she was gone. Frank lowered his head and walked back to his car.

Freya sprinted back to her hotel room. *What was I thinking?* she berated herself. She had let her emotional guard down. But even though she was angry at herself, she could still feel Frank's lips on hers and had to mentally force the memory aside. Was this why women were not trained in Sinanju? Had they once tried and found out that women were not strong enough to control their hormones?

Her mother Jilda had been strong. In Freya's mind, she always looked the same; tall and strong and loving. Freya remembered playing forest games with her mother, though now she realized that the games they played were not like the games that other kids played. Her mother was training her. But that didn't matter, because it was still fun and it was time spent with her mother. Her memories darkened as she recalled the image of her mother's broken body.

Freya was trembling when she reached her room, but even as she slid the electronic key in the door, she could tell that something was wrong. She could not tell exactly *what* was wrong, but something was not right. She sniffed the air and caught the scent of a man. It was so weak that if she had not known the scent had not been there the night before, she would have thought that it was days or maybe even weeks old. She instantly suspected Sturgeon, but it did not smell like liquor and sweat and she knew it wasn't Stone.

Freya detected a small shuffling sound to her left.

Wheeling around to survey the room again, she noticed that her pillow had fallen off the bed. Freya leapt to the other side of the bed, ready for anything. But nothing was there but the pillow.

Freya turned back and allowed her Sinanju senses to focus deeply on the room. She focused on every object in the room, sensing something odd near the window. Was someone standing behind the curtains? Freya closed her eyes and listened. She could hear the water running through the pipes above and below her. She felt electricity flowing through cheap insulation to the ancient air conditioning. But the only heartbeat in the room was her own.

Still, she silently moved toward the curtains and in one sudden move, tore them from the rod. The curtains landed on the bed behind her as Freya tensed.

But nothing was behind the curtains.

Freya sniffed the area and once again, caught the slight scent of a man. She pulled the blinds closed and got in bed, still staring at that part of the room. Everything inside her told her that someone had been there.

Sunny Joe smiled outside of Freya's hotel window. He held on to the stonework with just his fingertips, balancing his body in a perfect balance between gravity and the pavement below. To someone on the street looking up, it would have seemed like he was casually laying down on the side of a sheer wall with his arms to the side.

He had told Stone and Freya that he was returning to the reservation so he could silently observe how they were working together, but he had not counted on Freya being able to detect him. He would have to be more careful in the future.

Sunny Joe scaled down the wall in search of Stone.

CHAPTER SEVENTEEN

Sunny Joe found Stone at a local diner, eating what looked like a steak on top of a steak with bacon stuck in the middle. His grandson was hunched over his plate like a caveman guarding his dinner. He thought that Stone had overcome that habit months ago.

Sit up straight, he thought.

Stone felt something tickle the back of his neck. He sat up to scratch it and then leaned back over his plate, slicing chunks off the pile of meat in front of him.

Sunny Joe waited for Stone to finish his meat orgy and then followed him to the studio. Stone entered the back door of the warehouse and headed straight for the crates in back. He inspected a large label on the crate's side before prying the lid off. He reached inside and pulled something out. It was an octagon-shaped cylinder with military-style markings on it. While Sunny Joe was not familiar with modern Army ordinance, he could smell the explosives from where he sat.

Sunny Joe leaned back in his invisible perch and looked around. He found a hammer and some nails and tossed one of the small nails to the wall left of Stone. A normal person would not have heard it, but Stone's training should have detected it. Stone continued to inspect the crate as if he had heard nothing. Sunny Joe frowned. He found a bolt and tossed it lightly toward the same wall.

Nothing.

Frustrated, Sunny Joe tossed the hammer.

That got his attention.

* * * *

Stone jumped the security fence behind the studio. He took a moment to center himself and, not detecting anyone in the area, entered the back door to the warehouse. He had left it unlocked before leaving for the day.

Shattering the padlock sealing the largest crate, Stone found large amounts of explosives, ranging from ammunition to explosive charges. Stone checked the manifest inside the crate. The crate was being shipped to something called *The Gordons Initiative.* Stone had never heard of them, but took several pictures of the contents and manifest with his cell phone. He could hear Freya harping on him to get a new phone, but he didn't need a mobile GPS Facebook Gaming Machine. He just needed a phone, though at the moment, he was glad that it also had a camera.

The crate smelled of death, though the acrid stench of old blood seeped out at a level most humans could not detect. A few metal rods were placed between the packing of the explosive charges, most likely for stability. Thinking he saw blood on one of the rods, Stone pulled it out to examine more closely. He could tell right away that the metal was extremely strong and light. He tried to snap it, but it did not bend.

Then Stone remembered Sunny Joe's technique of scoring metal with his fingernails. Sunny Joe's fingernails were much stronger than Stone's, and almost feminine in length, though he would never say that to his face. He once remembered Sunny Joe slicing shards off an iron bar until strips of metal bowed out from the center like an iron banana.

Stone scraped his razor-sharp fingernail under the surface of the bar, but almost instantly pulled his hand back after it became too hot.

How did Sunny Joe describe it? He tried to remember Sunny Joe's exact words. *Find the grain of the metal and start small, until your fingernail runs with the grain and then exert pressure.*

Stone was obviously doing something wrong. He was generating too much heat. He tried once again. He found the grain of the metal, the direction the electrons were lined up, and he felt his fingernails begin to align with it — but something in the metal refused to allow him to score a slice out of it. Whether it was his novice attempt, or the metal was something unknown, Stone had to find some way to get a sample.

He placed his left hand on one end of the bar, tapping the other end with the fingernails of his right hand. The vibrations ran cleanly from his fingernails to his left hand. Two more taps at different points verified no defects in the metal. Stone arched an eyebrow. Every metal had some kind of imperfection that interfered with taps, but another tap resulted in the same smooth vibrations. He had never experienced metal this pure.

Weird, he thought, quickly looking through the other explosives in the crate.

Someone was using Sturgeon's warehouse as a front. Most of the explosives were a type Stone had never seen before, even though his time in the SEALs had made him familiar with most advanced weaponry. But there was something about the metal that worried him more than any of the explosives. He had to get a sample to bring to Cole.

Just then, he heard a small sound from the far side of the warehouse. His mind filtered it out as something trivial, like the foundation settling. Then another, slightly louder sound. But it was not until the metallic bang from the same area that Stone set the metallic bar down and turned.

Sunny Joe watched as Stone advanced silently toward the area of the sound. Stone had chosen to concentrate most of his Sinanju training on the art of stealth, so if Sunny Joe had not been totally silent, Stone would have detected him.

Sunny Joe observed Stone's technique as he began investigating the area. *Good,* he thought. *Stone didn't walk straight to the target.*

Stone used the weaving pattern that Sunny Joe had taught him his first year and Sunny Joe smiled until Stone pulled a small knife from his pocket.

That boy and his toys, Sunny Joe thought, shaking his head. *He's just full of bad habits.*

Stone hugged the wall, keeping his body in the shadows where possible. He leapt atop a storage locker and closed his eyes, allowing his Sinanju-trained senses to sweep the area, but once again he detected no movement and no organic noises.

Finally convinced that he was alone, Stone walked out of the warehouse. After he left, Sunny Joe began looking through the crate Stone had inspected. He picked up one of the metal bars separating the explosives. Remembering Stone's failed attempt at scoring metal, Sunny Joe ran his own fingernail on the underside. He pulled back his hand in surprise as the temperature instantly shot up past the point he could stand. He tried again, but each time he had to pull his hand back. He looked at his nail. Though it was strong enough to score titanium, it had been worn down as if the bar had been a huge nail file.

Something definitely different about this metal, he thought. He was too old to walk the path Stone took, but Sunny Joe had to know if Sinanju was facing a new threat. Unlike Stone, Sunny Joe had no top-secret government connections.

But maybe his friend Bob Ozman could return a favor.

CHAPTER EIGHTEEN

Stone left for the studio early the next morning by himself. If Freya wanted room, then he would leave her alone. He did not need to be with her every minute, anyway. If Sunny Joe had not insisted that he watch her, Stone would have already returned to the reservation. California was getting on his nerves. He needed a smoke, but pushed the urge aside and walked inside.

Stone heard snoring as soon as he entered the studio. He knew it was Sturgeon before he even opened the door. The man was a pig.

"Morning, sunshine," he said as he entered, but Sturgeon continued snoring. Stone looked around. Sturgeon's office was larger than his and Freya's houses combined.

How much money had this guy made from those stupid movies?

He pretended to look at one of the paintings as he heard Sturgeon stir. He was not surprised when Sturgeon tried to sneak up behind him. Sturgeon's breathing was as loud as an asthmatic horse.

"Don't move," he said from behind Stone. "Why are you in my office?"

"Looking for Freya or Frank," Stone said, turning around.

Sturgeon was holding a long stick, tilting it at an odd angle.

"I could have gutted you where you stood," Sturgeon said in his best tough guy voice.

"The only 'Sunny' I know is named Roam, and he'd kick your ass for using a weapon."

"What are you, his karate trainer or something?" Sturgeon asked.

"It's the other way around."

Sturgeon lowered the stick and bowed his chest out.

"Why are you even here? I only hired the girl," he said, standing eye level to Stone.

"We're a team," Stone said. "I've seen the way you look at her. You need to back off."

Sturgeon smirked. "Every man with a beating heart is gonna look at her that way. You better get used to it."

"Maybe so, but it's not gonna be you."

Sturgeon smiled and leaned into Stone's face. Stone was not going to throw the first punch and Sturgeon knew it. Stone's anger sizzled below the surface and Sturgeon smiled as he felt the anger dancing in the air between them.

"You can't stop me, hotshot," Sturgeon finally said. "In fact, I'm bored of you. I think I'll just tell you to leave."

"Tell me all you want, I'm not budging," Stone said.

"Fine. If you're not off my lot in ten minutes, I'm calling the cops. And my friends on the force would love nothing more than to taze a know-it-all chump like you."

"Oh, is that how it is?" Stone asked. "Can't handle me yourself?"

"Welcome to the real world, kid," Sturgeon said. "I don't have to handle every two-bit punk who wants to take on the champ. You're simply not worth my time."

Stone fumed in place for a moment, but walked toward the door. Sturgeon smiled. With the kid out of the way, it would be easier to teach the girl a lesson.

Sturgeon sat behind his desk and pulled out an old bottle of whiskey. He took a long swig and imagined what Roam would be like after he found out about his granddaughter. In Sturgeon's mind, Sunny Joe was on his knees, crying. Sturgeon involuntarily giggled at the thought.

CHAPTER NINETEEN

Frank walked numbly to the studio. He had no idea what he had done to make Freya leave, but he had to find out. She was leaving tomorrow, so he only had one last chance to talk to her. He would try to ask her out to find out what happened. Hopefully, they would be able to keep in touch until he was finished with Sturgeon's project. Her reservation was eleven hours away, but with his money, he could fly down and visit her every week.

As Frank walked past the warehouse on the way to the main entrance, he was almost knocked off his feet again. But this time, it was not a beautiful blonde. It was Bernie, Sturgeon's shady agent, who burst out the door. He bumped into Frank so hard that the duffel bag fell out of Bernie's hands and hit the ground with a metallic clink. A thin metal cylinder rolled out of the bag, coming to a stop on the gravel lot.

Bernie stopped talking on his cell phone just long enough to yell at Frank. "Hey, kid! Be a little more careful, huh? You have any idea how valuable these are?" He brandished the loose rod at Frank like a sword before putting it back into the bag and resuming his conversation. "Yeah, I'm here. Just some klutzy kid. Everything's fine. The warehouse is ready to go. Don't worry about Sturgeon. He doesn't have a clue about — "

Bernie slammed his car door shut and drove off. His tires screeched, and gravel shot out from the parking lot, stinging Frank like angry bees.

Brushing himself off and wiping the dust from his glasses, Frank entered the studio through the side door. He heard sounds coming from the control room. Stan never showed up until nine, so it couldn't be him. The light was on, which immediately told Frank that it was Sturgeon. Sturgeon always left lights on. For someone with supposedly humble beginnings, every action included a grandiose amount of waste.

Frank opened the door, and was surprised to see Sturgeon kneeling in front of the control panel. It looked like he was counting the wires beneath the panel.

"What are you doing? That's dangerous stuff, man!" Frank said, rushing to the panel.

Frank brushed past Sturgeon and did a quick inventory. Everything looked like it was still properly connected. Without checking, Frank resealed the casing.

"What were you doing?" Frank asked.

"Uh, preparing for my next movie," Sturgeon sputtered. "We're...making the sequel to *The Great League of Gentlemen Androids*, and I'm going to star in John Connelly's spot. I'm, uh, trying to research on how a situation like this could be dangerous for my character. I was thinking about how dangerous this was if someone were to use a training harness to assassinate me."

"This system is safe," Frank said defensively. "There are a dozen fail-safes that I check every morning."

"Good boy," Sturgeon said dismissively. "But I have to figure out how one of the Androids could bypass the safety and electrocute me while I was wearing the suit. What would they need to do?"

For just a moment, the inner fan in Frank reawakened. Thinking that he could be a part of his next movie, Frank's mind went into overdrive. Thinking about the electrical system made him completely forget his strange run-in with Bernie.

"Well, like I said, the system itself is safe. It would be impossible to accidentally electrocute yourself. But...if someone was deliberately trying to electrocute you, well, that would be fairly simple."

Frank motioned for Sturgeon to follow him to a small panel in the back of the control room. He slid the side cover off and pointed to a small section of buttons and switches.

"See that red dial on the left?" he said, placing his finger next to it. "That regulates the current. We use the regulator to calibrate the suit when no one is wearing it, but if someone was wearing it, they'd be grounded. And, if you turned the regulator all the way up, it would be more than enough electricity to kill you. It would be slow and painful."

"Good," Sturgeon said, noting the location of the dial.

"So, are you gonna have one of the Androids pose as a technician? That way, he could secretly move to the back and pretend that he was monitoring output and he could turn the dial before anyone could stop him!"

Sturgeon said nothing. He imagined Freya posing exotically as the electricity surged through her body.

Frank noticed the growing smile on Sturgeon's face.

"But how would you get out? Once the electricity is started, all of your muscles will be contracted, so you wouldn't be able to do anything but scream."

"Oh, I don't want her to get out of it," Sturgeon said absent-mindedly. He continued his daydreaming electrocution of Freya. He especially liked the way she posed when the electricity went through her chest.

"Her?" Frank asked, puzzled. Then it dawned on him. "This isn't for a movie, is it?"

"I always knew you were a smart kid," Sturgeon said, smiling maniacally.

"What are you going to...URRRRK!"

Sturgeon grabbed Frank by the throat and then struck a pose to an unseen camera. He imagined the final fight scene in Justice Switch. The evil wizard had struck him with lightning, blowing off his shirt, revealing Sturgeon's tanned and muscled chest. Then he remembered the voice of his director chiding Sturgeon because he failed to grasp the wizard in a realistic stranglehold.

The director, exasperated after a dozen failed takes, grabbed Sturgeon's hand and placed it around the actor playing the wizard.

"Place your thumb over the front and press really hard!" the director shouted. "We have to see your fingers dig in for the close ups!"

But unlike the moment when the director embarrassed Sturgeon by making him stop when he really began strangling the wizard, there was no one here to stop him this time. Sturgeon continued to press until his thumbs collapsed the front of Frank's throat. As he pressed harder, Frank stopped struggling, and Sturgeon heard a meaty crack. He dropped Frank's lifeless body and jumped back as if he had seen a spider. Sturgeon looked at Frank's body and poked it with his foot.

Frank did not move.

Sturgeon cautiously leaned over to see if Frank was still breathing. Frank's empty stare seemed to look right through Sturgeon.

"Damn, that's spooky," he said, darting out of the room to find something to haul the body out.

CHAPTER TWENTY

Freya bit her bottom lip. She had been unable to sleep the night before. Frank had done nothing wrong, and she had reacted unprofessionally. Freya walked straight to Frank's office, but he was not there. She went down the hall to Stan's office.

"Good morning, Mr. Stan. Have you seen Frank?" she asked.

"Sturgeon said that he called in sick," the balding man said. "Is there something I can help you with?"

"No, but thank you. I will speak with him later."

Freya lowered her head as she walked to her dressing room. This was why she did not want to get involved with someone. She had not wanted to hurt Frank, but she wanted to clear the air before leaving.

Freya was dressed and ready a few minutes before nine. Sturgeon was the only one in the control booth. He was silently staring at her while sipping a cup of coffee.

"I'm ready," Freya said.

Sturgeon smiled and sat down his coffee. He staggered down the stairs and walked toward Freya.

"Stan's running a little late," he explained. "I thought I'd take this opportunity to show you how you're supposed to move."

Sturgeon tried to grab Freya from behind the waist, but Freya held up the index finger of her left hand and tapped the center of Sturgeon's chest with a very long fingernail. To Sturgeon, it felt as if she had jack-hammered a spike into his lungs.

He fell to the floor, trying to catch his breath. Sturgeon's blood pressure increased until all he could hear was the pounding of his heart. Freya's voice floated above the roar, and Sturgeon flailed his arms in surrender.

"You do not understand, Mr. Sturgeon. I am not a part of your crude fantasies," Freya said as he rolled on the floor in pain. "I will do the job you offered, and nothing more."

Freya leaned over and jabbed her fingernails into the center of his back. His lungs stopped working for a second as his body reconditioned itself. He coughed several times and then his heart and lungs began to return to normal.

Sturgeon cautiously stood to his feet with a rage that dwarfed his hatred of Sunny Joe.

"Where is Frank?" Freya asked.

Sturgeon's body shuddered. It was a very small movement, dulled by the recovery from Freya's finger nerve manipulation, but it was there.

Something was wrong.

"He said he wanted to check out one of my other studios," Sturgeon said.

Freya easily caught the lie.

"I thought he called in sick," she said.

"The way you damn kids change your stories these days, I bet he overslept."

Freya let Sturgeon scuttle to the control room. She didn't know why Sturgeon was lying, but she hoped Frank was safe.

CHAPTER TWENTY-ONE

It only took Sunny Joe twenty minutes to find Oz's old building. The VCR REPAIR sign was on the building when Oz bought it, so he named his tech company "VCR Repair", a joke even when VCR's were still in use.

During Sunny Joe's heyday, Bob Ozman was the geek who kept Hollywood's technology running. If anyone could find out about this metal bar, it would be Oz. Sunny Joe held the bar in his jacket pocket. His fingernails absentmindedly scored the surface, stopping each time the heat became too much to bear.

All of the lights to Oz's shop were out except the aged 'OPEN' sign. Sunny Joe opened the door and the smell of long settled dust greeted him. Lights behind the old wooden counter blinked off and on in an epileptic Morse code. An average person would see a worn, almost bleached counter with a bell on it, and a hastily-scrawled sign that read "TAP FOR SERVICE." Sunny Joe's Sinanju-trained senses saw the entire picture.

The bell was attached to an electrical charge. It was not anywhere near a lethal charge. In fact, he could barely feel the pulses emanating from the bell, but, knowing Oz's history of silly pranks, he knew better than to tap it.

Then he noticed a rapid, shallow heartbeat behind the counter.

"You can come out, Ozzy," Sunny Joe said. "There's no way I'm tapping that bell."

"Aw, man. I never could trick you!" a familiar voice wheezed.

Oz stood up from behind the counter and offered his hand. Sunny Joe smiled.

"Glad to see you, Bill! And better to see you here than at another funeral. Man, it's been a long time. Have a seat!"

Sunny Joe brushed off the dust of the bar stool before sitting.

"So, Bill, you look lost in thought. What's on your mind?"

"Well, I was thinking about something you said at the funeral. You mentioned that Phil was acting kind of…odd at the end?"

"He kept mentioning the name 'Gordon,' I think it was. He was trying to tell me how dangerous Gordon was. I thought he was just being paranoid, but he kept mentioning it."

"The Gordons Initiative?" Sunny Joe said softly, remembering the label on the crate of weapons he had seen in Sturgeon's warehouse.

"Yeah, that's it! How did you know?"

"It's just a name I've run across. But, as long as we're asking questions, I've got one for you."

Sunny Joe pulled the metal bar from his jacket pocket and held it in front of him. It gleamed in the dim lighting.

"I wanted to get your opinion on what this is," Sunny Joe said, handing the bar to Oz.

"It's light," Oz said. He tapped it on the counter. "Strong, too. Where did you find it?"

"I'd rather not say. I just want to know what it's made of. I couldn't even scratch it."

"Bet I got something that can scratch it. Be right back," Oz said.

Sunny Joe looked around as Oz headed to the back. What was once the lobby for a multi-million-dollar tech business had become a museum dedicated to ancient props. Clay sculptures. Posters. Relics of an earlier era.

Oz returned with a large chisel.

"Diamond tip," He said with glee. "This thing cost two thousand dollars back in the day. If it can't scratch it, nothing can."

Oz placed the bar in a vice mounted on the side of the counter and secured it.

"You sure you want me to do this? This baby might destroy it."

"If you could destroy it that easily, I'd actually feel a lot better," Sunny Joe said.

Oz placed the tip of the chisel on the back of the bar and brought his mallet down hard. The chisel bounced off, leaving no mark that it had been struck.

"Whoa, that is tough!" Oz said. "Can I try again?"

"Give it your best shot," Sunny Joe said.

Oz breathed in deeply and swung again and again. The chisel bounced off each time.

"Care if I give it a try?" Sunny Joe asked.

"Be my guest," Oz said.

"You might want to step back a bit," Sunny Joe said. Oz shrugged but backed up.

Sunny Joe felt the weight of the chisel and hammer, lined up the perfect angle and struck. The hammer destroyed the chisel handle with a loud bang. Oz grabbed for his head and staggered back. Sunny Joe caught him before he tripped backwards.

"What did you use?" Oz asked. "I don't have any explosives!"

Sunny Joe ignored the question and looked at the metal bar. Upon close inspection, he found a tiny nick where the chisel had struck.

Seeing the worried look on Sunny Joe's face, Oz grabbed a magnifying glass and looked at the bar.

"I don't get it," he said in frustration. "The chisel should have destroyed that bar!"

"My thoughts exactly," Sunny Joe said. "Any idea what it could be made of?"

"I have no idea. If a diamond-tipped chisel barely scratches it, it's way stronger than even tungsten. Would you mind if I keep this overnight? I can run some chemical tests and hopefully find out what this thing is made of."

"You'll keep this between us, right?"

"No one will know but you and me," Oz said. "And let's keep it that way. This might be some dangerous stuff, Bill."

"Thanks, Oz. I appreciate it. I've got to go, but it's good seeing you, friend."

"You, too, Sunny Joe. Hey, next time, humor me and tap the bell."

"Ain't gonna happen, Oz," Sunny Joe said, closing the door behind him.

Oz returned his attention to his new toy.

It was time for Sunny Joe to find Stone.

CHAPTER TWENTY-TWO

Nicotine. Caffeine. Sugar.

These were dangerous drugs to a Sinanju-trained body, yet Stone still found himself clinging to them. But why? He had excelled at school and in the Navy. He was one of the best SEALs in Team Six history. But when it came to Sinanju, Stone continually sabotaged himself. He knew that it was not physical. No one smoked for the health benefits.

There was something stuck upstairs that he did not want to let go of, but for the life of him, he had no idea what it could be. He knew the man who could figure it out, though.

Stone pulled out his cell phone and called Sunny Joe.

"Hello," Sunny Joe greeted. "Everything okay? You and Freya loving California yet?"

Stone pinched his nose between his eyes and took a deep breath. The nicotine from the cigarette joined the caffeine already racing through his bloodstream and a small rush filled his senses.

Sunny Joe noticed the long pause. "What's wrong?"

"Grandpa..." Stone paused. It was like a personal intervention. "The cigarettes, the coffee. I don't know why I do it."

"That's the part of you that still wants control. The part below Sinanju."

"Below?"

"It's the Roam in you, son, just like me, just like your dad. We got an ornery bit of steel that runs through our spines. Even when you know something isn't good, you need to feel that you still have that steel. It's nothing to be ashamed of. In fact, one day it'll be a strength, but it'll be hard to go any further in Sinanju until you stop smoking."

"You noticed?"

"You hit a plateau. The coffee's bad enough, but smoking robs your breath. That's bad mojo for Sinanju. Breathing is your fuel. You can't go any further without changing things."

"I know," Stone said softly. "There's something else."

"Freya?" Sunny Joe asked.

"No, she's fine. I've just been wondering a lot about my..." Stone's voice trailed off.

"Your mom," Sunny Joe replied softly.

"Yeah. I know we talked about this. Freya's mom is dead, but at least she knew her. All I know is that my mom is some woman who had a one-night stand with my dad."

"And that's not enough," Sunny Joe said understandingly.

"No, it's not. I could ask my dad, I suppose."

"You really think he kept track of his one-night stands?"

"Probably not, but how can I find her otherwise?"

"Your boss has access to all kinds of computers. Can't he just trace your DNA?"

"That's not a bad idea," Stone said, surprised that he had not already thought of it.

"It may not be a good one, though," Sunny Joe said. "Have you figured out what you would say if you found her? We're not exactly the Waltons."

"Who?"

"Let's just say that, well, sometimes we Roams can be a handful of rusty nails," Sunny Joe said, clearing his throat for emphasis. "The truth will always be the truth, but that doesn't mean it's what we're looking for. Whatever you find, you'll have to come to terms with that truth. She gave you up, son. You have to ask yourself if you want to know why. Right now, she's basically an invisible saint in your mind. Once you meet her, you'll know the truth. Are you ready for that?"

Stone paused for a second to gather his thoughts. "Yeah. I think so. Anything's better than not knowing."

"Then, the next time you call your boss, get his computers to work."

Stone looked down at his watch and without looking, tossed the empty coffee cup into the trashcan behind him.

"How is Freya doing?"

"What can I say? She's Freya. There's nothing even remotely resembling a threat out here. Sturgeon kicked me out so..."

"You left Freya alone with Stevie Sturgeon?" Sunny Joe asked with a worried tone. "You need to find her. Now."

"Grandpa, he's no threat."

"It's not her that I'm worried about, son."

"He said that he'll call the cops if he sees me again."

"Then don't let him see you," Sunny Joe said.

"Got it. Thanks, Grandpa."

Sunny Joe hung up and looked down at his grandson from his perch three stories up across the street. Stone had not seen or heard him.

Stone turned and jogged down the street with his eyes closed. His Sinanju-trained senses kept him on the sidewalk. He could hear the cars as they passed; the shuffle of cheap shoes as they approached, the sliding sound of fabric as a woman wearing an expensive perfume walked by.

Was he really serious about leaving?

He could keep up what he knew about Sinanju and the rest of the world would think he was the world's deadliest man, but Stone knew better. Sunny Joe had told him that he could not hire himself out as a mercenary, or he would be directly competing with the Korean House, where their martial art was born. And competing with the House was a death sentence. Since his father was the reigning Master of Sinanju, if Stone hired himself out, his dad would be required to hunt him down.

Well, that would be one way to get his dad's attention. Stone knew that he was an important person with important things to do — sometimes things that affected the entire world… but weren't his children just as important? Stone didn't need someone to read him bedtime stories, but it would be nice to know that he was somewhere on his dad's radar.

Maybe Sunny Joe was right. Maybe he should find his mother. Find out what really happened. Add one of the missing pieces to the puzzle of his life. Stone would ask Cole to search his DNA, but he also knew where else to start: the uncle who raised him, Harold W. Smith. When Stone was young, Smith told him that his mother had died in childbirth and that his father was merely a sperm donor. The man did not have a gentle bedside manner, not even with small children.

But even at eight years old, something about the story just didn't seem right. It was too clean, and all the ends were conveniently tied up. He asked again at twelve and sixteen, and each time came away with the feeling that there was something more to the story.

Stone reached into his pocket. He was out of cigarettes.

Sunny Joe told him not to leave Freya alone, but what could Sturgeon do? Freya would kick his ass if he tried anything.

But he had given his word. If a man didn't have his word, he didn't have anything. Stone sighed, and obligingly returned to the studio.

CHAPTER TWENTY-THREE

Freya breathed out deeply, lowering her center so the machine could detect her. She hooked the electrodes to all of the access points on her suit, ignoring the hastily-scrawled smiley faces drawn on her breasts in marker. Sturgeon was a pig.

"Ready," she said.

Sitting in the booth above, Sturgeon began breathing heavily as Freya began her calibration moves. He sounded like a thirsty dog.

"I don't think she's doing that right," Sturgeon said to Stan.

"What? Are you kidding me?" Stan replied. A proud smile stretched across his face. "She moves perfectly! I've never seen anyone like her!"

"Tell you what, take a two-hour lunch on me," Sturgeon said with a wink, slipping Stan a five-dollar bill.

"Wow. Your generosity is overwhelming," Stan said, knowing that Sturgeon was paying no attention to him. "Now I can afford a kiddy meal at McBurger Queen. Thanks."

Sturgeon gave Stan a minute to leave the building and turned his attention back to Freya. She had been waiting for her next instructions.

"What's next?" Freya asked. "I've done everything rational that you've asked of me."

"Two more moves," Sturgeon said and then moved to the emergency panel in the back.

"Where is Mr. Stan?" Freya asked.

She was not comfortable being alone with Sturgeon.

"He went to lunch. You know how stupid those employee laws are. He said to have you run in place for a few minutes and record it with the computer thingy," Sturgeon said, activating the motion floor.

Freya did not need her Sinanju training to detect a lie, especially from the slow, expectant way Sturgeon was breathing. The huge treadmill beneath her feet began a slow three mile-per-hour gait, slowly increasing in speed, until it was a fifteen mile-per-hour pace. Freya easily compensated, even after Sturgeon began bouncing the track.

Sturgeon sighed in frustration. He wanted to see a few more minutes of bouncing before killing her, but if she must die now, so be it. Sturgeon walked to the control panel and turned off the failsafe.

The hair on Freya's arms began to stand on end as she felt a warm sensation. She didn't have time to investigate the feeling before Sturgeon turned the dial up. Electricity surged through her body and every muscle contracted simultaneously.

The treadmill instantly ground to a halt and alarms sounded.

Freya's uncentered body provided no resistance against the waves of electricity that tore through her. She fought for control, but her own muscles betrayed her. She fell backward on the treadmill, striking her head on the floor.

Sturgeon watched her squirm and increased the voltage. A brief scream erupted from Freya's throat before the voltage paralyzed her vocal cords.

Stevie Sturgeon stood with his nose pressed to the glass of the control room with a growing smile on his face. He did not hear the low rumble emanating from Freya, nor did he notice as her eyes began to darken into deep ebony pits.

CHAPTER TWENTY-FOUR

Stone knew Sturgeon would ask him to leave if he entered in plain sight, so he hopped the security fence and slipped around to the back the warehouse. He entered silently, and noticed that several of the large crates in the back had been moved. Prying a lid off with his fingers, he looked inside. The explosives were still there, but the metal was gone.

Opening crate after crate, Stone saw that none of them contained the strange metal.

Who had taken it? And why?

Then he felt it — a low rumbling, electric and fearful.

Stone immediately recognized it as infrasound. The only other time he had experienced it was when he and Freya were in Mexico. They had been trapped in a small alcove by a Mexican army and Freya pulled a generator through the wall for shielding, but the exposed wires nearly electrocuted them both. Stone quickly recovered, but when Freya awoke, something was wrong. Her eyes became black, her skin blanched, and the voice that erupted from her mouth did not sound like anything of this world.

He was snapped from his memories by the sound of Freya screaming.

"No..." he whispered.

Stone centered himself and tore the studio door from its hinges.

* * * *

Sunny Joe had been following Stone when he noticed the sound. Though it was lower than human ears were supposed to hear, the sound pierced through his bones, threatening his center. Sunny Joe took a deep breath. The only time he had heard something like this was just before an earthquake, but the sound was coming from inside the studio. This was something new — and anything new immediately demanded caution.

Then Sunny Joe heard Freya scream. He and Stone both immediately turned to the source of the sound. Unlike Stone, however, who immediately turned from casual lope to panicked sprint, Sunny Joe made sure to survey the rest of his surroundings. While Stone tore the studio door from its hinges and bolted inside, Sunny Joe followed cautiously.

He made a mental note to teach Stone about patience.

* * * *

Stone raced toward the studio and burst through the bolted door.

Freya's back was arced off the floor. Stone could feel the vibration of the electricity from where he stood. He moved to Freya's side, ready to destroy the cables connecting the suit to the control panel. But as he neared, he knew the electricity flowing through the cable was too strong.

If he tried to grab it, he would become its second victim. Stone looked at Freya and immediately noticed her eyes.

They were black.

* * * *

Sturgeon looked lustfully at Freya's contortions. The electricity pulsed through her body, causing her to spasm uncontrollably.

That took the arrogance out of her, he thought.

She had humiliated him twice, each time taking advantage of the fact that she was a beautiful blonde in order to distract him while she struck with her inferior martial art.

Sturgeon already had worked out what he was going to say to Roam. Freya had not been paying attention and grabbed a defective set of cables, even after Sturgeon warned her about the danger. Sturgeon would wear a genuine look of concern as he would see the pain crawl across Roam's face. And then, as Sturgeon walked away, he would stop, turn around and with a sly smile spreading across his face, he would wink at Sunny Joe, just like he did in the movie *Street Juggernaut*. Then Sunny Joe would know that Sturgeon was the one who took her away from him.

There wouldn't be any proof, of course. After she died, a fire would consume the entire studio and the insurance would not only cover his tracks, but also pay Sturgeon for the cases of Air Spray stored in his warehouse. Bernie had filled the warehouse with explosives. He would tell the authorizes that they were getting supplies ready for an upcoming movie.

"A terrible tragedy about the girl," Sturgeon would say. But he knew better. Causing his oldest rival great pain, and getting paid to do it?

Stevie Sturgeon would have the last laugh after all.

The glass in the control room exploded inward and Sturgeon instinctively covered his face with his hands. Even before he opened his eyes, he heard one loud puncture sound after another. *Bang. Bang.* Loud and metallic, it sounded like an impact hammer. *Bang.*

It was the girl's brother. He was using something to punch holes in his control panel to try to save her.

"Get away from that!" Sturgeon yelled, kicking at Stone from behind.

Sunny Joe saw that Stone had wisely ignored the cables, choosing to shut off power from the source. But what had been too challenging for Stone was a simple task for Sunny Joe. He sliced cleanly through Freya's cables with his sharp fingernails.

Freya collapsed unconscious to the floor breathing in fast, shallow puffs. Sunny Joe could tell that she was trying to regain her center, but her heart was out of rhythm.

Sunny Joe rolled Freya to her side and began tapping out a correct heartbeat on the back of her spine with one hand. The other manipulated the nerves at the base of her spine and her heartbeat began matching his rhythm. He would have to keep the pace until the spasms stopped, or she would suffer a heart attack.

Sunny Joe looked up just as a large flash of light filled the booth. Stone hit the floor and then he heard the voice of Stevie Sturgeon. Sunny Joe scowled helplessly. He could not leave Freya until her body had recovered.

"Kick his ass," Sunny Joe whispered.

Stone pummeled the panels with his fists, staying away from the areas that felt like they covered power centers. Each of the panels had dozens of buttons and small displays. He didn't know which one of them controlled Freya's suit, but in a few seconds, it wouldn't matter. Stone would destroy all of them.

He sensed Sturgeon move behind him, but he had no time to waste. Stone dodged Sturgeon's kick, but in doing so, changed the angle of his strike. He smashed a part of the panel that housed the junction box.

The lights to the control panel flashed several times and then shut off. Emergency lights filled the room and Stone felt the biting heat wind its way up his arm to his shoulder and then across his chest.

It was like being hit by a wrecking ball. The fillings at the back of his teeth began to buzz, and Stone could do nothing but hold on until the charge passed through.

When it did, Stone collapsed to his hands and knees. The electricity had left a sharp ache through his chest, preventing him from regaining his center. Sturgeon's foot collided with his ribs. Stone rolled with the kick, trying to draw a clear breath.

A look of madness had spread across Sturgeon's face and though he was yelling, Stone couldn't hear his voice — he was too busy trying to catch his breath.

Sturgeon took advantage of Stone's momentary weakness and began kicking him. His second-hand loafers worked past Stone's arms and connected with his head.

Stars exploded in Stone's vision.

Get up! Stone yelled to himself.

Sturgeon stopped to place his foot on Stone's head and struck a pose.

"And thus, did true justice finally prevail," Sturgeon said, talking to an unseen camera. "I am not a terror, though I appear in many of my foe's nightmares. I am Stevie Sturgeon."

Stone ignored Sturgeon's monologue and struck Sturgeon's ankle with his fist. Had he been fully centered, Sturgeon's ankle would have been reduced to powder, but as weak as Stone was, it barely managed to knock Sturgeon off his feet.

His heart pumped two sharp beats and then one dull beat — and then it stopped. Stone began coughing. His heart shocked back with three quick beats.

Heart attack or not, I am not going to die on the floor at the hand of Stevie Sturgeon.

Both men stood to their feet and recognized the stakes. The winner would be the one who was still breathing two minutes from now.

As much as he tried, Stone still could not find his center and his sporadic heartbeat kept him from regulating his breathing. He was just an ex-SEAL with a weak heart. Stone grimaced as another wave of pain traveled across his chest. If he died now, he would never be able to save Freya.

Sturgeon struck the same pose featured on all of his movie posters and, looked at Stone disdainfully. He laughed. The girl was tougher than this kid.

"Do you think you've even slowed me down?" Sturgeon asked triumphantly. "After I kill you, I'll see if the girl is still alive. She will watch as I strangle the life out of her. And then my plan will almost be complete."

Stone blinked. He was going in and out of consciousness. He just needed a moment to grab a breath.

"So, what's your big plan?" Stone managed to ask.

"It's genius," Sturgeon conceded. "I'll make it look like this whole place caught fire because of that girl's decision to use defective cables. Her body gets burnt, your body gets burnt, and I'll stay just inside the door so I can inhale a little smoke. I stagger outside and tell the firemen that I tried to save her. Then the warehouse explodes. Your body gets burnt to a crisp, and I get insurance money."

"But what about the part where you die?" Stone asked.

"Die? What are you..."

Stone's punch came from nowhere. Every bit of force he still had was placed behind the knuckles that were aimed squarely at Sturgeon's throat. It was something a child would do if cornered by a bully — a desperate sucker punch — but it was all that Stone had.

If nothing else, it would shut Sturgeon up.

Sturgeon fell back, reaching for his throat. He tried to yell "Cut!" as he fell to the floor.

Stone fell backward against the wall and grabbed his chest. His heart continued its sharp, angry thumping, each beat sending pain through his shoulders and left arm.

He fell to his knees, and he knew his time was drawing near. He had tried his best. He could die without regret. As he closed his eyes, he thought he could hear Sunny Joe.

"Center yourself, son."

"I can't, Grandpa," Stone said. "I'm dying."

The voice yelled at Stone. "Your sister needs you! I said center yourself!"

"Yes, sir," Stone said and sought his center once more. What he found was nicotine choking his Sinanju-trained lungs. He grabbed a breath and concentrated. The air started to align his body…

He coughed and the center failed.

"Again!" Sunny Joe commanded. "I didn't train you to fall to Stevie Sturgeon!"

"It hurts, Grandpa!" Stone said.

"That just means you're still alive, son. Now center yourself!" Sunny Joe ordered.

Stone grabbed another breath and the pain of the exertion sliced across his chest. His eyes opened and everything began to darken as he saw Sturgeon begin to stir.

Then he found it: one slender air ventricle not strangled by nicotine. Stone breathed in deeply, feeling the energy of the universe begin to filter through his entire being.

Sturgeon shook his head and stood to his feet. His eyes focused on Stone.

"You're just like Roam! You think you're better than me!" Sturgeon yelled, kicking at Stone. But where his foot had earlier felt the satisfying connection with the side of Stone's head, Sturgeon howled as his foot struck the wall behind Stone.

"I wish I were like my grandpa," Stone said, suddenly behind him. "But compared to him, I'm still in kindergarten. Throwing punches and exerting muscles — like the crap you're trying to do right now? That's all worthless to a man like him."

Sturgeon stood back with both hands in front of him like a boxer. Then he contorted his hands until his pose was a mixture of ballerina and bodybuilder, telegraphing the signature move that ended all of his movie fights.

It was the peak of all his training, concentrated into one forceful, bloody moment.

"I'm going to enjoy this," Sturgeon said smiling.

Stone assumed Sturgeon's absurd pose, mirroring his stance.

"Let me show you how it's done," Stone said, using Sturgeon's own signature move, executed perfectly at three times the normal speed and with ten times more force.

Sturgeon stepped back and looked down. Something was wrong. The lights in the room became brighter and brighter and the sound of the control room's air conditioning became an echo chamber filling his senses.

Then the lights melded into one impossibly bright light and Sturgeon felt himself being drawn toward the Light. He felt so peaceful. Every good thing he had ever imagined was awaiting him in the Light. Sturgeon smiled as he coasted through the ether, no longer concerned about the trappings of the mortal world.

It was time for his reward.

Then an armored figure stepped in front of him, blocking his path and Sturgeon began falling. Fearfully, he began screaming as a thousand hands began clawing at him, dragging him deeper and deeper into the darkness of the Void.

CHAPTER TWENTY-FIVE

As Freya began to stir, Sunny Joe slapped her on the back to induce coughing. She needed as much fresh air in her lungs as possible. Partially conscious, Freya took in several deep breaths, centering her body. Sunny Joe looked up at the booth and smiled. Stone had managed to center himself and would have no problem with Sturgeon, so he sank into the shadows. The youngsters could finish this by themselves.

As he silently crept out of the building, Sunny Joe extended his index finger, cracking every picture of Sturgeon lining the walls. He stopped as he neared the janitor's closet.

It smelled of death.

Someone had tried to kill the scent with bleach — a lot of bleach — but it could not be hidden from Sunny Joe. He opened the door and he found a body, hastily-wrapped with an old tarp. Sunny Joe removed the plastic, revealing the body of the young man who had taken Freya out to eat. Sunny Joe scowled. He was glad that Stone would finish Sturgeon, or else he would have gone back and done it himself.

He reverently picked up Frank's body and carried it outside, setting it on the front steps for the police to find. It might have been too late to avenge the young man, but at least he would be given a proper burial so his spirit could find rest.

Sunny Joe sat in his rental car and looked at the warehouse for a moment before he pulled out of the parking lot. Though there were flaws, Stone and Freya performed admirably in the field, just as he knew they would. A prideful smile escaped and Sunny Joe knew that everything was going to be all right. The warehouse was disappearing in Sunny Joe's rear-view mirror when a small timer began counting down in the warehouse.

30 seconds…

29…

28…

CHAPTER TWENTY-SIX

Freya sat up with a bolt. She was still dazed, and felt like an elephant had been tap-dancing on her chest. When she heard the voices of Stone and Sturgeon above her, she forced herself to her feet. It took a moment, but Freya grabbed a deep breath and leapt to the control panel, just in time to see Stone lay out Sturgeon.

As Sturgeon dropped, Stone turned. He sensed movement to his left. He relaxed his stance as Freya bounded through the window. She landed awkwardly.

"Are you alright?" Stone asked.

"I will be," Freya said, trying to ignore the pain racking her body.

"Sturgeon rigged your suit," Stone said. "He was going to kill you and then burn this whole place down to collect the insurance money."

Freya scratched her head and leaned over a chair. Though he could tell that she was hurting, he was amazed at how easily she had regained her center.

"Do you know how jealous I am?"

"About what?" Freya asked, puzzled.

"You basically just took a lightning bolt to the chest and you regained your center just as easily as you breathe. Seriously, how do you do that?"

"I have always breathed this way."

"I wonder if it will ever be that easy for me," Stone wondered.

"Not as long as you…" Freya started, but Stone held up his hand.

"No smoking lectures…please!" he said. "I get it."

"I am sorry," Freya said, standing. "For what it is worth, it still hurts."

"You know the funny thing?"

"What's that?" Freya asked.

"When I was trying to stay conscious, I heard Grandpa," Stone said.

"I am glad I didn't," Freya said. "I can imagine him telling me how sloppy I am."

"If he tells you that you're sloppy, I'm screwed. You can easily…"

The word froze in Stone's mouth and time slowed around her. Freya sensed something wrong below the level of consciousness. It was similar to the way she felt when the tiny pressure wave of a bullet heading toward her, but this impression was the size of the building.

Without time to make a conscious decision, she grabbed Stone and tore through the sheet rock to the room behind the studio. But Freya was not moving quickly enough. The pressure wave had almost reached them.

Her senses identified the structure of the outside wall. She detected wooden beams, with an outside layer of concrete reinforced with a layer of bricks. There was no time to disassemble the wall to escape. She would have to just bulldoze her way through.

Freya lowered her head. She easily destroyed the sheet rock and partially shattered the concrete paneling, but while the bricks bowed outward, they held. The collision broke several of Freya's ribs and she felt her shoulder tear with a pain that made her see lights.

Freya felt the breath leave her body, but while her momentum had stopped, Stone's body was still moving toward the wall. Freya twisted him around and pushed him through the wall. The bricks shattered outward, allowing the pressure wave of the explosion to push them far from the building.

Flames surrounded them while they were still in mid-air.

There was no dodging the massive concussive wave, no way to avoid the heat and sound and shrapnel passing all around them. Freya looked helplessly as Stone was torn from her grasp and then she knew nothing as she was battered her into unconsciousness.

They landed two stories below, barely ahead of the metallic shrapnel that flew at their backs. Both lay silent on the ground as the building collapsed behind them.

Stone was the first to recover, awakened by the sirens. Dazed and not knowing what had happened, he stood to his feet. Pain shot through his back and shoulders. He turned to see Sturgeon's entire building reduced to a fiery rubble. He staggered to Freya, who was breathing, but still unconscious.

Stone closed his eyes and concentrated. He grabbed a deep breath and fought for control of his own body. It took a few seconds before he found his center and when he did, the pain subsided enough to scoop up Freya in his arms and carry her away.

CHAPTER TWENTY-SEVEN

Sunny Joe wanted to make sure he was at the reservation before Stone and Freya returned, but their flights weren't scheduled until the morning and he had a few hours before his plane left; plenty of time to drop by Oz's to see if his old friend had discovered anything about the metal bar.

Old friends.

Sunny Joe realized with morbid finality that the longer he lived, the more of his old friends would die. That was one of the cardinal truths in Sinanju. It did not make it easier for Sunny Joe to watch his generation wither and die while he continued to live. Who else had he been hiding from because he wanted to ignore their mortality?

The thought made Sunny Joe mad at Mick, who did not seem to realize that Sunny Joe had run out of tricks to stop the illness spreading through his body. He had to take ownership of his own body, sooner rather than later.

Oz. Even without the oxygen tubes, Sunny Joe knew that his friend was dying, but even if he could not stop the lung cancer that threatened to take his life, he could at least alleviate some of the pain he was experiencing.

Sunny Joe casually parked his rental car and walked up to Oz's door. He slowly twisted the knob, careful not to disturb the surprise Oz had arranged. The old door swung more smoothly and quietly than it had when new. The water bucket remained propped above the doorway and Sunny Joe heard a familiar sigh.

"You sure know how to disappoint an old man," Oz said. "I'm gonna trick you if it's my dying act."

"Then you better believe in reincarnation," Sunny Joe teased. "You doing any better?"

"Not really. But I'm seeing life a lot more clearly these days. Knowing you'll die soon makes you realize how precious each day is."

"I'm starting to find that out on my own. I'm glad I finally dropped by."

"That metal bar you gave me is something else," Oz said. "I tried to chemically scar it with a dozen chemicals and only two of them left a mark. Where did you say you got it again?"

"I didn't. I'm just curious if you know what it's made of."

"This has to be some kind of experimental alloy. It's definitely something new. But what it's made of isn't as important as what it is going to be used for. You sure you can't give me any clues about where you got it?"

"It was being held in a warehouse," Sunny Joe finally admitted. "But it was being used as a frame for other…goods."

"Whatever it was being used for couldn't have been worth the metal framing it."

"How so?"

"You know the story of the great thief, don't you?" Oz asked.

"I'm guessing that I'm about to," Sunny Joe said, sitting down. He missed Oz's stories.

"There was once a great thief. He would travel across border every week carrying a wheelbarrow full of straw. The border guard knew the man was a thief, but every week, he would inspect the wheelbarrow and find nothing but straw. He looked for a false bottom, he looked inside the bolts and once even removed the tires, looking inside.

But he never found anything but straw.

On the day the guard retired, he stopped the great thief and took him aside.

"I know you're stealing something, but I have never been able to catch you. Now that I am retiring today, you must tell me what you have been taking."

The great thief smiled. "I have been stealing wheelbarrows."

Oz allowed a moment for Sunny Joe to smile, then he continued. "If you're going to smuggle something, you smuggle it inside something else; something dramatic, that takes your attention away from what is being smuggled. Sound familiar?"

Sunny Joe's mind immediately recalled the explosives in the crate where he had found the metal. "That sounds about right," he said. "But what's so special about this metal?"

"It's got some really dangerous potential…imagine using something like this as a weapon." Oz said. "I'll keep digging. I have enough life for one last adventure. Go home and we'll keep in touch. I'll find out what your mystery metal is."

"I have to leave, but not before I show you how my ancestors eased pain," Sunny Joe said as he walked behind Oz.

"Unless they were masseuses, I don't…whoa!" Oz exclaimed as Sunny Joe reached toward Oz's back. His fingertips worked into the nerves at the base of Oz's spine, quickly shutting off the pain. Oz relaxed, releasing a deep breath.

"Bill, I haven't felt this good in years! Am I healed?" Oz asked.

"Nope, but you should feel better for a few days," Sunny Joe said.

"Then I'll just pretend you healed me for a few days," Oz said, winking. "Thanks again, Bill. It was real good seeing you again."

"You too, Ozzy. We'll keep in touch."

Oz did not see the tear forming at the corners of Sunny Joe's eyes as he left.

CHAPTER TWENTY-EIGHT

The next morning, Freya followed Stone through the airport, her eyes squinted in pain. Her ears were still ringing, and her lungs ached whenever she tried to take a full breath.

"I am not used to walking around uncentered," Freya replied. "I feel so weak."

"Do you feel like anything is seriously wrong?" Stone questioned.

"I told you, my ribs still hurt," she said with a grunt as she took another breath. "I think I might have bruised them."

"What about your shoulder?" Stone asked, noticing that Freya kept her arm in her jacket pocket to relieve some of the pain.

"It hurts," Freya admitted.

"Sis, we can still go to a hospital and…" Stone started.

"No," Freya interrupted. "We go home. Grandfather will know what to do."

"I'm telling you right now, if your arm falls off before we get back to the reservation, it's not my fault."

Freya tried not to smile because it hurt too much to laugh.

When they arrived at the reservation, Stone immediately took Freya to visit Doc Hodges, who told Stone to go home and take a few days off. He kept Freya for further observation.

As Stone unpacked, he found the strange metal bar. He held it under his front room light and looked at it closely, trying to find any sign of scarring where he had tried to gouge the device, but it was as smooth as the day it was created.

"Welcome home," a familiar voice asked from his open screen door. Sunny Joe stood outside on Stone's porch.

"Come on in, Grandpa," Stone said.

"Your sister said that Sturgeon rigged the warehouse with explosives."

"I had no idea what was happening. One minute we were talking and the next, she was using my body as a battering ram."

"Better be glad she did, or you two would have never made it out. How are you feeling?"

"A little sore, but I'll be okay. Is she doing better?"

"Doc Hodges said she broke four ribs and tore a bunch of muscles getting you two out. She won't be training for a few weeks."

Sunny Joe sat down on the couch next to Stone and noticed the bar he was holding.

"What's that?" he asked, as if he had never seen it before.

"I thought it was just being used as protective framing to house the explosives in Sturgeon's warehouse, but now, I'm not sure. I can't scratch this thing."

"What kind of metal is it?"

"I don't know. I'm taking it with us to St. Louis to see if Cole can find out what it is."

"You do remember that you and Freya are going for negotiations this trip, don't you?"

Stone sighed. He hated negotiation training. It mostly involved a lot of unnecessary glorification, sitting uncomfortably until your boss gave you a good deal.

"Don't worry, Grandpa. We've got this."

"You and Freya have only had two negotiation classes. Negotiations are almost as important of a skill as breathing."

"I'll get us a good deal, Grandpa," Stone said.

Sunny Joe stared at Stone for a minute.

"I'm glad you're back," he finally said. "And since it doesn't require centered breathing, I'm scheduling both of you for remedial negotiation lessons before you fly out."

CHAPTER TWENTY-NINE

Mick finished his monthly notes and shut down his computer. He took a moment before rising and grabbed his lower back. He grunted as he lifted from his chair, and a sharp pain took hold of his spine.

"Stop," a familiar voice said from behind. "You're gonna be in a wheelchair if you don't get that taken care of."

Mick exhaled and sat back down as Sunny Joe moved behind him. He had missed Sunny Joe's spinal treatments for the past week, and the pain had returned.

"I don't like surgeries," Mick said. "Never heard of them doing any good."

"I don't like them either, but my tricks can only cover the pain for so long. Mick, you're gonna have to grow up and start taking care of yourself."

"All right, already. How did Stone and Freya do? Ouch!" Mick shouted as Sunny Joe moved his attention to Mick's neck. "That hurts!"

"It would hurt a whole lot worse in a wheelchair," Sunny Joe said. "Sit still."

"So, how'd they do?" Mick asked, trying to take his mind off the steely fingers manipulating the nerves in his neck.

"Made me proud," Sunny Joe said, smiling. "They still have a lot of training ahead of them, but they did well."

"You're leaving something out," Mick said.

Sunny Joe's mind went back to the instant that Freya collapsed. Just before he freed Freya from the cable, he noticed that her eyes had become black. Every Sunny Joe knew what black eyes meant. The stories of past Masters of Sinanju manifesting into Shiva during times of distress had been passed from one Sunny Joe to another, all the way back to Kojong, the founder of the Sinanju tribe. Sunny Joe's father told him that he had experienced the transformation once, but it had never happened to Sunny Joe. He often wondered if it had ever happened to his son, Remo Williams.

If that was what had happened to Freya in Mexico, it would explain her darkened fingers and toes as well as her reluctance to talk about it. However it had happened, Shiva had been transferred to Freya.

Sunny Joe clapped Mick on the back, signaling that he was finished. Mick stretched and, relieved that the pain in his back was gone, sat in front of Sunny Joe.

"Can I tell you something without blabbing about it in the scrolls?" Sunny Joe asked.

"You know I was sworn to record every important thing that..." Mick started, but Sunny Joe held up his hand.

"This isn't important, not yet at least. But I have to ask you something and to do that, I need your word."

"Sure, Sunny Joe," Mick said. "What's up?"

"The family curse. When does it transfer?" Sunny Joe asked.

"Sunny Joes are really quiet in the scrolls when it comes to Shiva," Mick said. "But from what little I know, it only transfers after they become a full Master. Why?"

Sunny Joe leaned back and sighed. "Then we're in unfamiliar territory right now,"

Mick's mind raced. Neither Stone nor Freya were anywhere near the full level of a Master of Sinanju. "Stone?" he guessed, but the look on Sunny Joe's face told him otherwise.

"Freya? How?"

"That's what I'm trying to figure out," Sunny Joe said. "She and Stone are being quiet about it, but I saw her start to change in Los Angeles."

"That explains how she has been able to learn so fast, but what are you gonna do?"

"There's nothing I can do. When she's ready to talk, she'll come to me."

"What really happened to Sturgeon?" Mick asked, showing the newspaper headline to Sunny Joe:

FORMER ACTION STAR MEETS EXPLOSIVE ENDING

"The paper says that his warehouse stored enough explosives to start a small war. Kinda funny how they list him as the hero, isn't it?"

"You can't find justice in the news anymore, Mick. Just stories."

CHAPTER THIRTY

The sun slid past the western horizon, leaving behind a slivered golden glow. As if awaiting the sun's departure, a slow and cool breeze washed past the two people sitting on the small rocky outcropping behind Freya's house.

Stone glanced at his sister. In the twilight, he could clearly see the sadness carved on her face. Though her body was injured, she was not crying from pain. Sunny Joe had shown her the article that revealed that Frank had been murdered. And while she hadn't been in love, it seemed that even the possibility of love was taken away from her at every junction in her life.

"I gotta admit," Stone said to break the silence. "Frank was a pretty good guy."

Freya knew that death would be a regular part of her life. *Would she ever find love in this kind of life?*

"Yes, he was," Freya finally said. "I wish him peace in the next world."

They sat silently as Stone tried to figure out what to say.

"I'll tell you what," he finally said. "The next time you go on a date or two, I won't be so overprotective."

"Yes, you will," Freya said softly. "It is your nature."

"No," Stone said, leaning over so she could see the look on his face. "I promise. It won't happen again."

Freya looked down for a moment.

"How are your ribs?" Stone asked. "Grandpa said that you can't find your center."

"It is too painful. He said it might be a few weeks before I can return to normal breathing."

"Normal for you," Stone said. "Are you okay?"

"I just wish my mother were still alive," Freya said, staring off into the distance. "Whenever I was afraid or sad, she would hold me and sing songs of Lakluun."

"Well, you don't want me to sing," Stone said. "Sinanju training doesn't give you a good singing voice."

They both smiled.

"I may no longer have my mother, Stone, but what about yours? Grandfather said that you were going to look for her."

"Yeah. When we fly to St. Louis, I'll ask Cole if he can match my DNA to anyone out there as part of my salary negotiations."

"Will he do that?"

"If he wants us to keep working for him, he better!"

"I've never negotiated a contract," Freya admitted, somewhat worried. "Grandfather is very serious when it comes to contracts."

"I tend to zone out whenever he starts talking money," Stone said. "Ah, it's our first contract. He's gotta expect us to screw up."

"As long as we don't end up owing him," Freya said, attempting a smile and then her demeanor became as serious as Stone had ever seen her. "Stone, you need to do everything you can to find your mother. And once you do, never let her go."

"I've never had a mother," Stone said. "Or a father, until recently. For most of my life I believed that the man who raised me was my uncle."

"What if you find your mother and she does not live up to your expectations?"

"That's what Sunny Joe asked," Stone replied. "I know what kind of man our dad is, but I have no idea what kind of person my mom is and I want to find out."

"A worthy quest," Freya said. "Let me help!"

"You can't, Sis," Stone said, leaning back with a smile. "You still have a hut to repair."

Freya had forgotten about the hut. Despite the pain, she allowed herself another smile as the sun finally disappeared from view.

She would find a way to get Stone to help her fix the hut.

LEGACY

INTERVIEWS

WARREN MURPHY: INTERVIEW

BY TIMOTHY JANSON

September 5, 2015

In 1963, two writers, Warren Murphy and Richard Sapir set out to write an action novel. It took them eight years to finally sell their book, but in 1971, Created: The Destroyer was released, introducing the world to Remo Williams and his mentor Chiun, the Master of Sinanju. 42 years, 150 books, a comic book series, a TV pilot, and a theatrical film later, Remo Williams and Chiun are back, and bigger than ever. A new novella, a brand-new spinoff series, and the 150th book in the Destroyer series are now available or will be soon, and a new theatrical film is also in the works.

I recently sat down with series co-creator Warren Murphy to discuss the state of the Destroyer as Murphy pulls no punches in discussing our two favorite assassins.

JANSON: Warren, first of all thank you so much for taking the time to talk to us today. How does it feel to return to The Destroyer? I understand there are several new projects in the works.

WARREN MURPHY: It's good to be back in the publishing world. Actually, after four years of medical poking and prodding, it's good to be anywhere. And as long as my two sons who are my partners don't run out of work for me to do, there are many projects underway. For fans of the Destroyer and Remo Williams, we're taking some of the characters I created in various books of the original series — Remo's kids actually — and starting a new series with them called "Legacy" with the first adventure being "Forgotten Son." And we've started doing new novellas, and we've begun an e-pub business and the books are going to start coming from all over.

JANSON: As you mentioned, one of the new projects is called Legacy and will feature Remo's children as the main characters. Can you tell us more about this new series?

MURPHY: I'm working on "Legacy" with a terrific young writer named Jerry Welch. Jerry's been a long time Destroyer reader and friend for a long time and for all that time, he's been pushing for this story about Remo's kid. He thought and I agree that it's a way to reboot the whole Destroyer concept for a whole new generation. The truth is that the Destroyers have been around for a long time…they are your Daddy's Oldsmobile… and they've been ripped off forever, but we always fought to keep them relevant and I think Remo's kids will help that along.

JANSON: Will Remo and Chiun be a part of the Legacy series or do you want the series to stand on its own?

MURPHY: No, Remo and Chiun won't disappear; these are Remo's kids after all, but they've got different attitudes, different problems, different ways of dealing with things than Remo because he is, as is Chiun, the deadliest two humans on the planet. Stone and Freya are different; they're only the third and fourth most deadly humans on the planet. So once in a while, I imagine they'll ask the old guys for advice…but this is going to be their series, not Remo and Chiun's. Honestly, it'd be perfectly appropriate if this series was double billed as an adventure and also as something fit for young adult readers. In truth we try always to write a clean book, so I'm never worried about something being over the edge for kids.

Interview by Timothy Janson
www.SciFiMoviePage.com
Used with permission

GERALD WELCH: INTERVIEW

BY MIKE "ACE" MAILLARO

www.CriticalBlast.com

May 7, 2018

ACE: Having grown up in Jersey City and spending most of my working life in Newark, New Jersey, I have always had a great love and respect for Warren Murphy's *The Destroyer* series. Warren himself was born in Jersey City, and his most iconic character, Remo Williams, started out as a Newark cop. Don't tell Chiun I called Remo more iconic than him, he would not appreciate that at all.... I had lost track of the series over the years, but I was definitely curious when I heard that Warren Murphy had developed a spin-off called *Legacy* with Jerry Welch.

I immediately fell in love with *Legacy*. Freya and Stone are terrific characters, and in just a few short books, Murphy and Welch have managed to expand the world of *The Destroyer* in brilliant new ways. Jerry has been wonderful about answering any questions I have had about the series over the last few years, and I was glad to be able to sit down with him and do a full form interview.

How did the idea from *Legacy* come about?

JERRY: *Legacy* was one of two series ideas that I pitched to Warren. I suggested that Donna Courtois and I could write what was referred to then as *Young Destroyers* and I could solo write a series featuring stories of the Masters of Sinanju called *Masters.*

Warren turned down the *Masters* pitch, but used "Monuments" (the proposal story I wrote) in the *New Blood* fanfiction compilation. He really liked the concept of *Young Destroyers* but not the name. We played around with *Dynasty* for a while, but settled on *Legacy*. Donna went off to write a *Destroyer* (called 'Number Two'), so Warren asked if I would be interested in working with him on *Legacy*, as if he even had to ask.

There was a lot of work that had to be done before we wrote the first scene, namely character creation. Warren hated the versions of Sunny Joe and Stone that appeared in *The Destroyer*, so it was up to me to keep them as close to Destroyer continuity as possible and still get Warren's approval. Fortunately, Freya was kind of a blank slate, so there was a lot more wiggle room to develop her as a person.

Originally, Stone and Freya were to be led by Smith's then-assistant Mark Howard, but Warren hated Mark's psychic powers, so he told me to create a new person to lead Stone and Freya. That's when I came up with Benjamin Cole.

ACE: Was it always intended to be a series, or was it just a one-off to see what would happen?

JERRY: *Legacy* was designed to be a bit different than *The Destroyer*. If you think about it, *Legacy* is more of a serial than a series, because the beginning of one book continues from the end of the previous book. Each *Legacy* is written like a television episode. While you can pick one up at random and it make sense, you get more out of them by reading them in order. This also gives me the dedicated chronological space to track character development. Authors can say what they want, but we learn much more about our own characters after a couple of books.

ACE: What was the process of writing these books like when they started?

JERRY: A lot different than how we do things now. Warren wanted me to take lead on the project because, well, he had a ton of personal projects (He put so much time into *Bloodline* and I was glad that he was able to finish it before he passed) and he was pushing me to grow as a writer.

Part of the original deal had me work out plots and story arcs for the first twenty-five books, because Warren wanted to ensure we had large story-arcs as well as individual entries. I think he wanted to see how well I could juggle different size arcs. So, I would flesh out the plot to the book at hand, submit a two or three-page outline, and Warren would tell me what worked, what didn't and what to watch out for. I would then write the manuscript and he would edit it. I would see his edits, make suggestions and then he would have the final say.

ACE: How has the process of creating these books changed since Warren's passing in 2015?

JERRY: Quite a bit. Even though Warren is gone, his name is still on the cover and I try to honor him with each page that sits behind that name. Dev and I take more care in what's inside, which is why *Legacy* 7 was delayed. We could have released a good book a month ago, but after discussing the final manuscript, we figured out a way to make it better. While working on that, I changed the epilogue as well to help *Legacy* #8. So, while I'm sorry that the book was delayed, I would have had more regret knowing that we could have released a better book. Patience is a harsh — but worthy — mistress.

ACE: Were you and Warren concerned there would be a lot of pushback from the fans about these huge additions to the *Destroyer* mythos?

JERRY: Actually, that was the first thing he warned me about. He said that it would be difficult for people to read a Sinanju series that didn't include Remo and Chiun, so I had better write about some very interesting characters. There was a small temptation at the beginning to cheat and have Sunny Joe act more like Chiun to give him and Stone the Remo/Chiun interaction, but, as I said, it would have been a cheat. Sunny Joe isn't Chiun and shouldn't act like him. Warren also said that *Destroyer* fans might be put off by the different writing style, because *Legacy* is purposely aimed toward a younger audience, so you'll see less sex, cursing and gore.

I still get emails and reviews asking for more Remo and Chiun, but this isn't their story. Well, book seven is partially Chiun's, but even then, he fits within the framework of Sunny Joe, Ben, Stone and Freya.

ACE: In real life, are you more like Stone or Freya?

JERRY: Wow, that's a good question. I guess that I'm Stone in my weaknesses and Freya in my strengths, so it helps me identify with each. That is also why I ignore pleas to wave a magic wand and have Stone just quit smoking. In a world where he dodges bullets and shatters rock, giving up smoking cold turkey is unrealistic for him. It will happen — it has to if he is going to progress — but, just like in real life, it will take time and it won't be easy.

ACE: What can *Legacy* and *Destroyer* fans expect to see in the coming books?

JERRY: The *Legacy* side of the Sinanju universe is still growing and in more important ways than just adding new villains (though they are coming as well). Expect to see character progression and more importantly, change through growth. You should not read *Legacy* #20 and see the same characters that you saw in *Legacy* #2. That being said, you're going to be seeing more of the world Stone and Freya live in. You're going to learn more about Mike the bartender, Paul Moore and others and how they fit into Stone and Freya's world.

ACE: As a writer, do you have to approach an established setting like *Legacy* different than when you do something completely original?

JERRY: Of course. I didn't create this playground, so there are rules to obey. Freya will never eat a hamburger. Stone will eventually have to stop smoking. Fortunately, I was a *Destroyer* fan before writing *Legacy*, so I am spending the time to explore those rules and what it means to Stone and Freya to become a Master of Sinanju. *Legacy* is the story of Freya and Stone becoming Masters of Sinanju. After they become actual Masters in, say, book fifty or so, you'll notice a change in storylines. The bottom line for me as a writer is that I want people to feel the same way I do when I read a good book. If I can do that, then I'm doing something right.

ACE: You love to put in little Easter Eggs for fans of your other popular series, *The Last Witness*. Are we ever going to see a true crossover between the two series?

JERRY: You already have (laughs). As of book seven, we've had *two* villain crossovers (one of which is an Easter Egg, but not hard to spot) and I think that it's cool how we handled it. We didn't promote it as such or give direct links between the series. It's just a little reward for readers of both books to hopefully give them that extra little 'wow' factor.

That's one of the main reasons I love Easter Eggs so much. I want a reader who sees something in, say, book twenty-two to notice something and think, "That's not how it was in book four!" but when they go back to look at book four, BAM! It *was* there, but was written in a way they wouldn't notice it.

That's the extra level that I *strive* for, as well as one of the reasons Dev probably reads over the books so many times, so he can spot them. Oh, and anyone who likes Easter Eggs will be 'eggstatic' if they compare the *Legacy* and *Last Witness* omnibuses. A lot of work went into both of those books and when the *Legacy Omnibus* is released (after Legacy #7), readers will know that we haven't just been sitting around twiddling our thumbs. The Omnibuses are my greatest and most exhaustive works to date and I hope readers get a deeper understanding of what each series means.

ACE: What's next for Gerald Welch?

JERRY: This year? A move from Texas to the St. Louis area, starting the second omnibus for both *The Last Witness* and *Legacy*, *Legacy 8: Homecoming*, *The Last Witness #6: Body of Lies* and starting work on my second album, appropriately titled *Second Wind.* I'm assuming (hoping?) that it can't be worse than *Alien Summer.*

Interview by Mike "Ace" Maillaro
www.CriticalBlast.com
Used with permission

LEGACY

PEOPLE

14 / LISA

NOMENCLATURE AT ADOPTION: 14

BIRTH	December 8 – Joliet, Illinois		
DEATH	February 4 – St. Louis, Missouri		
HEIGHT	5' 8"	**HAIR**	Blonde
WEIGHT	152 lb.	**EYES**	Brown
BUILD	Thin	**IQ**	112

FIRST APPEARANCE

LEGACY #2: THE KILLING FIELDS

TRIVIA

Each Premium was chosen because of an aspect of their DNA. 14 showed an extreme aptitude for willpower.

LEGAL STATUS	Unregistered American citizen, no criminal record
MARITAL STATUS	Celibate
EDUCATION	The Plant
MILITARY	N/A
OCCUPATION	Premium
AFFILIATIONS	Carnage Program

14 was the most human of the Premiums, and her desperation to survive made her its greatest asset. To stamp down any vestiges of her humanity, 14 kept her head shaved and eschewed any clothing other than standard-issue jump suits. She maintained her sanity by reliving the few pocketed memories of a normal life that she experienced in her short life: a moment of kindness from a nurse; a guard who showed mercy on her by looking away when she failed a task. But the memory she treasured most was the interaction she had with a little blonde-haired girl named Lisa who let 14 play with her doll.

While Premiums had access to toys, they were primarily functional: blocks, numbers and linguistic games. To actually hold a human figure in her hands triggered something deep within 14. But she noticed that any of the other Premiums who were showing emotion were taken away by the men in blue lab coats and whenever they took someone away, you never came back. 14 thought they were being killed, but the girls were merely processed out of the program and placed into adoption agencies.

Her survival instincts kicked in and 14 threw the doll away and attacked Lisa. She was taken back to The Plant and placed in her cell where she was safe. From that day forward, 14 achieved every goal presented to her, believing that her life was being threatened every time a girl was taken away. At the time of The Plant's destruction, only eight Premiums remained of the original hundred.

She met Freya-an enemy who showed compassion-and 14 experienced the same feeling she had when playing with Lisa. So, when it came time to serve her VIGIL Masters or save Freya, 14 gave her life for the blonde-haired girl who saw through her Carnage disguise and saw a human being.

64

NOMENCLATURE AT ADOPTION: 64

BIRTH	June 11 – San Francisco, California		
DEATH	N/A		
HEIGHT	5' 6"	**HAIR**	Black
WEIGHT	141 lb.	**EYES**	Brown
BUILD	Thin	**IQ**	121

FIRST APPEARANCE

LEGACY #2: THE KILLING FIELDS

TRIVIA

Each Premium was chosen because of an aspect of their DNA. 64 showed an aptitude for endurance.

LEGAL STATUS	Unregistered American citizen, no criminal record
MARITAL STATUS	Celibate
EDUCATION	The Plant
MILITARY	N/A
OCCUPATION	Premium
AFFILIATIONS	Carnage Program

64 was one of the few girls in the Carnage program who eagerly volunteered for every experiment that was offered, whether it was grafted bones, chemical treatments or extended modes of training. Envious of fellow Premiums 14 and 23, she was always aspiring to best them during competency trials. 64's specialty was in the martial arts. While 14 would sometimes push through to victory by sheer willpower, 64 was clearly the best hand-to-hand fighter to emerge from the Carnage program.

64 was the first Premium to be sent out on a mission. She was ordered to follow a homeless woman who had been seen wandering around the area. When 64 saw the woman talking to a Plant employee, she killed the woman. The Plant employee then revealed that the woman had been an undercover FBI agent.

After Carnage supervisor Victoria Von Odom found out that an FBI raid was imminent, a kill order was given to destroy The Plant and everyone inside, with the exception of two Premiums. Victoria did as she was ordered, detonating the explosives that had been rigged for such an eventuality. She personally escorted 14 out of the facility, while 64 helped her kill any survivors. 64 fled the scene just as the FBI entered the facilities. 64 was later assigned to be Victoria's enforcement arm.

64 has killed four people in the past year and disguised each one as a robbery gone wrong. Three of the victims were killed to cover up her true target: a woman who was paid to secretly report Victoria's movements to CURE.

DAKARI AFOLAYAN

BIRTHNAME: DAKARI AFOLAYAN

BIRTH	September 23 – Plains of Bughanum		
DEATH	N/A		
HEIGHT	5' 10"	**HAIR**	Black
WEIGHT	194 lb.	**EYES**	Brown
BUILD	Medium	**IQ**	117

FIRST APPEARANCE

LEGACY #6: LAUGHING MATTER

TRIVIA

Dakari is spending most of his time repairing the damage that Musobote caused his country.

LEGAL STATUS	Reigning Monarch of Bughanum
MARITAL STATUS	Single
EDUCATION	Kham regional schooling
MILITARY	Corporal, Bughanum Armed Forces
OCCUPATION	Monarch
AFFILIATIONS	Bughanum Royal Council

Because of his older brother Kwame's crippled legs, Dakari knew that when he got older, he would inherit his father's farm. Upon his return from mandatory service in the Bughanum Armed Forces, Dakari discovered that Kwame had escaped Bughanum in Col. Musobote's personal jet and his father had paid the price. The farm had been destroyed. The crops were burnt, the animals were slaughtered, and his father had been beaten. Dakari put aside his personal ambitions to help restore the farm.

When the local governor learned of his actions, he imprisoned Dakari on charges of treason, a crime punishable by death. Dakari lost track of time, but not hatred for the government that he had honorably served. When news spread that Musobote had been killed and his brother returned as King, Dakari was released and transported to the capital. While he was happy to see his brother, he was angry that he had left their father to suffer in his place. That was when Kwame told him that he was dying.

At first, Dakari thought he was lying to get sympathy. Kwame appeared stronger than he had ever been, to the point that he was no longer even limping. But when Kwame explained the strange metal he had implanted into his brain and showed him the effects of the treatments, Dakari believed him.

Kwame spent the last couple of months of his life perfecting the shielding for the iridium implant and improved processing the chemicals he had used to the point that when Dakari began treatment, it took days for his body to show signs of improvement. As Kwame lay on his deathbed, he called Dakari over and placed the crown on his head. He told Dakari not to use his power for personal vengeance but to better their country. Dakari partially heeded his brother's advice. He had the regional governor executed for treason and moved his father to the palace grounds. Since then, he has done his best to improve the daily lives of his fellow Bughanum citizens.

KWAME AFOLAYAN

BIRTHNAME: KWAME AFOLAYAN

BIRTH	August 15 – Plains of Bughanum		
DEATH	June 23 – Buoro, Bughanum		
HEIGHT	5' 8"	**HAIR**	Black
WEIGHT	149 lb.	**EYES**	Brown
BUILD	Thin	**IQ**	142

FIRST APPEARANCE

LEGACY #6: LAUGHING MATTER

TRIVIA

Kwame raised over fourteen million dollars in federal grants.

LEGAL STATUS	Naturalized American citizen, no criminal record
MARITAL STATUS	Single
EDUCATION	Multiple degrees in chemistry and biology
MILITARY	N/A
OCCUPATION	Professor
AFFILIATIONS	N/A

Kwame grew up in the poorest part of Bughanum. Worse, he was crippled at birth, making him useless as a farmer or hunter. Fortunately, his father recognized Kwame's intelligence and saved enough money to send him to Bughanum University in Buoro. Kwame studied hard, graduating at the top of his class.

That is when he got in trouble. Intelligence in a small country not known for its technical prowess brought attention from King Musobote, Bughanum's Dictator for Life. He assigned Kwame to save his uncle's life. Kwame decided to trick Musobote and give his uncle a chemical and radioactive treatment that would ensure a slow and painful death. To Kwame's amazement, the treatment not only worked, it gave him superhuman strength and endurance. But there was a price to pay for radioactive salvation: Musobote's uncle began losing his sanity and his hair changed to a bright orange. Musobote had to kill his uncle, but saw Kwame's treatment as a way to develop an army of super-soldiers.

Kwame spent the next few months perfecting the process and only escaped Bughanum by injecting himself with the formula. He stole Musobote's personal plane and fled for England. From there, he applied for immigration status to the United States, becoming a citizen three years later. When he arrived in America, Kwame continued his education. To help funding, he began applying for grants and soon amassed thousands of dollars. He used the money to further his research and created a small army by injecting several of his students. When he heard that Musobote was coming to America, he led his students in an attack, but they were killed by Stone and Freya.

Kwame made it to Musobote's plane and killed him, surviving long enough to return to Bughanum as King. On his deathbed, he named his brother Dakari his successor. Dakari obeyed his brother's last wish and began taking modified iridium treatments. The only remaining side effect is bright orange hair.

HELMUT BELISIS

BIRTHNAME: HELMUT BELISIS

BIRTH March 22 – Vatican City
DEATH N/A
HEIGHT 6' 2" **HAIR** Dark brown
WEIGHT 202 lb. **EYES** Purple
BUILD Medium **IQ** 136

FIRST APPEARANCE
LEGACY #1: FORGOTTEN SON

TRIVIA

Helmut is the biological son of Lars Papadakis, who claimed to be the illegitimate son of Pope Pius XI.

LEGAL STATUS Vatican citizen, no criminal record
MARITAL STATUS Married (Unknown) Children (Unknown)
EDUCATION Master of Doctrinal Affairs, VIGIL Academy
MILITARY N/A
OCCUPATION Director of VIGIL
AFFILIATIONS VIGIL

Helmut Belisis was born in the secret Vatican chamber that has hosted the birth of every VIGIL director for the past six hundred years. Every director candidate was a direct descendant of the original Monk who created VIGIL, and as such, he has purple eyes. As tradition with every director candidate, Helmut was raised in a Greek castle with two other potential directors. They were privately tutored by Oxford's finest professors. The youngest of the other two boys disappeared when he was twelve, the other was charged with his murder and executed, leaving Helmut as the sole director candidate. He was fast-tracked by then-director Lars Papadakis and after graduation, Helmet began to be tutored by Lars himself. That was when Lars revealed that he had killed the director candidate and framed the other boy. Then he revealed the Big Lie: Helmut's purple eyes were not natural, nor were his. The blood line of the Monk had become too soft in the last few generations and VIGIL needed strength.

Helmut followed closely in Lars' footsteps, making large moves for the organization that had operated behind the scenes for centuries. Before Lars died, satisfied that Helmut would continue his legacy, he revealed the secret nature of the world. He told Helmut about Sinanju and the remaining World Tribes and, more importantly, how to manipulate them to keep them out of VIGIL's way.

Helmut has proven to be a powerful leader, increasing VIGIL's reach into every nation on Earth. To date, he has only one regret: underestimating Ben Cole, director of the Arch bunker in St. Louis. A momentary lack of caution allowed the location of a VIGIL meeting to be discovered, resulting in the destruction of VIGIL headquarters. Helmut barely escaped. His injuries have required him to use a cane.

CHIUN

BIRTHNAME: 누크 (Noo-Kh)

BIRTH	August 5 – Village of Sinanju, Korea		
DEATH	N/A		
HEIGHT	30.42 cùn	**HAIR**	A graceful sunset
WEIGHT	1,283.12 liang	**EYES**	Golden hazel
BUILD	Perfection	**IQ**	Transcendent

FIRST APPEARANCE

THE HOUSE OF MANY WOODS AT MY BIRTH

TRIVIA

While nothing about me is trivial, I am especially fond of locomotives. One day, Sinanju shall be connected to the rest of the world by rail.

LEGAL STATUS	I am the Master of Sinanju
MARITAL STATUS	Widower – Children: Song (*deceased*)
EDUCATION	Everything I needed to learn, I learned in Sinanju
MILITARY	I saw no need to debase myself
OCCUPATION	Master of Sinanju Emeritus/Babysitter of whites
AFFILIATIONS	The Glorious House of Sinanju

CHEAP WHITE HELP: The Master of Sinanju Emeritus was born at the end of the nineteenth century on the cold, muddy shores of the Korean Sea...AAHH! MY EAR! (*rubs ear*) Oh, Master Chiun! All hail...

CHIUN: Silence, white thing! Are you what passes as a scribbler for my dear Freya and her dull brother?

CWH: Uh, yes, Master Chiun.

CHIUN: How many people do you believe are born on a shore, muddy, or otherwise?

CWH: This is just my first draft. I was going to let Devin...

CHIUN: Who is the old man pictured at the top?

CWH: Ummm, that's a picture of you that Remo gave us.

CHIUN: You have achieved the rare accomplishment of failing as a scribbler in both meanings of the word on the same page! And you seek to promote gossip as all whites do!

CWH: What would you like me to say?

CHIUN: Only the truth: that I am first and foremost a gentle soul who has been hurled into a world of abusive whites. And I do not know who that old cretin is, but it is certainly not me.

CWH: But it looks *just like y*...OWW! Okay! (*scribbling*) abusive whites...talk to Remo about a new picture.

CHIUN: What are all of these numbers at top?

CWH: Things like your height, weight, stuff like that.

CHIUN: This is all wrong. I am not some mouth-breathing white to be measured in inches! I am a perfect thirty-point-four-two cùn. Start over and I shall instruct you on what to say. What is this "I.Q."?

CWH: Oh, uh, don't worry about that. I can take care of that later.

CHIUN: If there *is* a later.

BENJAMIN COLE

BIRTHNAME: BENJAMIN GERAH MAUGAINE

BIRTH	January 5 – Yehud, Israel		
DEATH	N/A		
HEIGHT	5' 6"	**HAIR**	Black
WEIGHT	172 lb.	**EYES**	Brown
BUILD	Medium	**IQ**	132

FIRST APPEARANCE

LEGACY #1: FORGOTTEN SON

TRIVIA

Ben loves three things: cigars, caramel-flavored coffee and his custom pistols.

LEGAL STATUS	Naturalized American citizen, no criminal record
MARITAL STATUS	Widower (*Sarah*)
EDUCATION	University of Haifa – National Security/International Relations
MILITARY	Mossad
OCCUPATION	Assistant Director of CURE (*Arch Bunker, St. Louis*)
AFFILIATIONS	Mossad, CIA, CURE

Benjamin Maugaine grew up in a small community in Israel where death was an expected part of life. From random Hamas bombings to mortars, young Benjamin understood what it meant to appreciate life.

When he became a Mossad agent, he was hopeful that his work would further the cause of peace, but it only shoved him into the depths of human behavior. For every life he saved, he traveled further down the tunnel of human depravity. Then, while training in Isshin-ryū in Tel Aviv, he met Sarah. To the young but grizzled agent, Sarah seemed naïve. But as Ben got to know her better, he realized that he was just seeing something in her that he had not allowed in himself: optimism. Sarah's optimism was contagious, allowing him to take a breather from the gutter. Ben slowly began to adopt her optimism and they were married a year later. He even found himself smiling again.

When they were paired together as a sleeper cell in Egypt, he remained optimistic until Sarah was raped by a local governor and then stoned for adultery. Ben killed the rapist and was immediately disavowed by his Mossad handlers. He only managed to escape Egypt with the aid of Mark Cole, a CIA contact who gave his life to ensure Ben's safe travel to America. Ben took Cole's last name in honor of his sacrifice and became an operative for the CIA. He was promoted to assistant director of CURE and given the Arch Bunker in St. Louis for operations. Though he doesn't understand how his Sinanju agents do what they do, they have been given a license to kill and Ben is not reluctant to use it if it means protecting his new country from the threats of the old.

His day starts at 5:30. His computer logs on to a display of the Preamble to the Constitution. Though not religious, he reads it like a daily prayer, to remind him why his mission is important.

MARCUS EAMES

BIRTHNAME: MARCUS EAMES

BIRTH	June 16 – Baiti, Nauru		
DEATH	N/A		
HEIGHT	5' 7"	**HAIR**	Black
WEIGHT	157 lb.	**EYES**	Brown
BUILD	Thin	**IQ**	144

FIRST APPEARANCE

LEGACY #4: TRIAL AND TERROR

TRIVIA

This is the only known photo of Marcus Eames in existence. Psychologists believe that Eames allowed the early photo to survive to remind him who he was prior to becoming a spy.

LEGAL STATUS	Citizen of Nauru, Exiled
MARITAL STATUS	Single
EDUCATION	High School
MILITARY	N/A
OCCUPATION	International Spy
AFFILIATIONS	None

Marcus Eames had a simple dream: he wanted to be better than James Bond and Batman combined, but he was discouraged by both teachers and parents alike. They said "Your great mind should be used to become a scientist or doctor" or "Those are just fictional characters. You should be more practical."

After a while, Marcus just smiled and privately continued to perfect himself. It wasn't easy. To keep up with his training plans, he had to combine study with physical regimen. Working out while reading became second nature to him and by the time he graduated high school, he had mastered the basics.

His parents had disappeared, so he turned his detective skills into finding out what really happened to them. When he discovered that his father was a spy, it angered him, but then he remembered that anger was an emotional blindfold and continued his work. He found out why his parents were hiding. His father had failed a mission and a contract was put out on him. Marcus located his parents in less than a month. They were hiding in a small village in Thailand. His father was shocked to find out that Marcus had found him, but not as much as when he explained that he had taken out the drug dealer who put the hit on his mother and father as well as his entire family.

Marcus said goodbye to his father and began his life as a master spy. He began dealing with European slave traders, taking them down while profiting at the same time. When a contract was put out on him, dozens of hitmen tried to collect, only to find themselves being the one hunted by Eames.

His reputation grew as a spy who never failed. He grew a portfolio of sensitive data from some of the world's most powerful nations and an understanding began to emerge: Hire Marcus Eames if you wanted to succeed, but if you tried to turn on him, you would be the ones burned. Marcus has never failed a mission, even when confronted by students of Sinanju. Invoking an old covenant, he is now the only person on Earth safe from Sinanju attack.

ELEANORA

BIRTHNAME: ELEANORA AROMAA

BIRTH	February 20 – Mesterøy, Lakluun		
DEATH	N/A		
HEIGHT	5' 11"	**HAIR**	Blonde
WEIGHT	154 lb.	**EYES**	Purple
BUILD	Athletic	**IQ**	112

FIRST APPEARANCE

LEGACY #5: MOTHER MINE

TRIVIA

Eleanora is the first person in Lakluun history to assume the roles of both monarch and mage.

LEGAL STATUS	Queen Mother of Lakluun, no criminal record
MARITAL STATUS	Single
EDUCATION	Champion Trials
MILITARY	Exempt
OCCUPATION	Queen Mother
AFFILIATIONS	Royal Lakluun Council, Masters' Trial

Eleanora is the eldest of four daughters, but as one of the four Chosen, was raised apart from her siblings on Champion Island. It is normally reserved for the Lakluun champion, but was abandoned after Jilda turned her back on the Masters' Trials.

Eleanora was sent to escort Freya back to Lakluun so she could revoke her claim to the Trials. Eleanora was one of the best champions that Lakluun had ever seen. Nominating a member from each of the tribes was a formality. It was known by everyone that Eleanora would be chosen for the Masters' Trial. While traveling to Lakluun with Freya, instead of the rebellious hellion she had imagined, Eleanora found a kindred spirit and they quickly became good friends.

But it was not meant to be. Mother had arranged for Freya to return so Mother could steal the spark of divinity she had seen at Freya's birth. Mother began killing the Chosen and secretly pointing to Freya as the culprit. But after she killed Freya, she found out that the spark was the Hindu god Shiva, who killed Mother for attempting to separate Freya from him. Her death triggered an ancient spell, causing every Lakluun citizen to avenge her. Eleanora was ordered by King Hannu to remain behind and protect the newborns, which saved her life. Shiva killed every Lakluun warrior who attacked, including King Hannu and Eleanora's best friend Elisa.

Eleanora showed up in time to see Freya fully restored to health, standing over the body of King Hannu. She vowed vengeance on her former friend and is willing to use any methods available to her, including triggering an early call for the Trial. Invoking an ancient Lakluun law, she plans to use Freya as her method of vengeance.

RUBY GONZALES

BIRTHNAME: RUBY MARIA JACKSON-GONZALES

BIRTH May 19 – Brooklyn, New York
DEATH N/A
HEIGHT 5' 7" **HAIR** Black
WEIGHT 158 lb. **EYES** Brown
BUILD Medium **IQ** 127

FIRST APPEARANCE

DESTROYER #33: VOODOO DIE

TRIVIA

Ruby still carries the Sinanju locket given to her by Chiun. It promises swift vengeance on anyone who harms her.

LEGAL STATUS American citizen, no criminal record
MARITAL STATUS Widow (*James*) Children: None
EDUCATION Westminster
MILITARY N/A
OCCUPATION FBI Agent
AFFILIATIONS CIA, CURE, FBI

Ruby Gonzales was a streetwise CIA informant who made the mistake of questioning the extra check she received each month for her reports. Unable to ignore the extra money, Ruby followed the trail until she found the source and immediately wished that she hadn't. As a Z-level organization, discovery of CURE was normally a death sentence, but CURE director Harold W. Smith saw past the surface bravado that made her more valuable alive than dead and she was hired as Conrad MacCleary's replacement.

At first, Ruby loved her job. It separated her from her more extreme relatives and her knowledge of computers, while not as proficient as Smith, was on a different level. She managed to hide the Sinanju reservation from Smith's computers for the entire time she was with CURE. After a few months, Ruby began to get bored with her role and questioned her decision to join CURE, but there was only one way to exit CURE: through a coffin. Fortunately, she had saved the lives of both Remo and Chiun, which granted her favor from the Master of Sinanju. Chiun gave her a solid gold locket, swearing her protection. Ruby faked her death and Remo and Chiun never told Smith.

After leaving CURE, Ruby spent time as a private investigator under the name Maria Gonzales, where she met and fell in love with James McCord. They married and for six years, Ruby taught middle school in Utah. James died of cancer six years later and she moved to Phoenix to became an agent for the FBI. But Ruby could never leave her CURE history behind. She would follow news that suggested Remo or Chiun had been active in an area. When one of the stories mentioned that they had been close, Ruby travelled to the site. She found remains of a fetus, but though it was clearly human, the late-term baby had feline qualities.

Recently, a case of Sinanju-linked murders has re-introduced her into Sunny Joe's life.

PETE HAMMOND

BIRTHNAME: PETER JAMES HAMMOND

BIRTH November 13 – DeWitt, Illinois
DEATH N/A
HEIGHT 5' 10" **HAIR** Gray
WEIGHT 226 lb. **EYES** Brown
BUILD Stocky **IQ** 124

FIRST APPEARANCE
LEGACY #6: LAUGHING MATTER

TRIVIA

Hammond's well-worn cap was a personal gift from Ronald Reagan.

LEGAL STATUS American citizen, semi-retired, no criminal record
MARITAL STATUS Married (*Janet*) Children: Larry, Elaine, Judy, Stanley
EDUCATION B.A. Engineering, Dartmouth
MILITARY Retired, U.S. Air Force
OCCUPATION Semi-retired, on retainer as a pilot
AFFILIATIONS U.S. Air Force, American Legion

Peter Hammond grew up as the only son in a military family. His father was one of the first volunteer fighter pilots in World War II. Hammond volunteered to be a pilot during the Vietnam War, but had slightly less than 20/20 vision. He was only admitted to flight school after winning a poker game with the Master Sergeant in charge of the program.

Hammond became one of the best Air Force pilots of the early eighties, impressing Ronald Reagan to the point that the President personally appointed him as pilot for Air Force One. Hammond went on to serve a total of five U.S. Presidents, retiring in 2014.

Retirement did not suit Hammond well and he began asking around for side jobs to keep busy. That placed him on Benjamin Cole's radar, who offered Hammond a Top Secret, no-questions-asked job. Hammond accepted the offer and both he and his wife moved to Douglas, Arizona.

His primary mission is to fly Stone or Freya in his modified 1996 Phantom 400. While his jet looks like a poorly-maintained craft, it has been refitted with proprietary jet engines, state-of-the-art electronics and a hidden weapons system. Its flight range is over three thousand miles, allowing Hammond to take Stone and Freya anywhere in the continental United States.

Hammond calls his plane "The Pickle" due to its aged green hue and the slight.

Though he achieved the rank of Colonel during his Air Force career, Hammond kept the nickname 'Captain', which is what Ronald Reagan called him.

JILDA

BIRTHNAME: JILDA

BIRTH	November 5 – Lakluun, Faroe Islands		
DEATH	February 12 – Canada		
HEIGHT	5' 10"	**HAIR**	Blonde
WEIGHT	142 lb.	**EYES**	Blue
BUILD	Athletic	**IQ**	114

FIRST APPEARANCE

DESTROYER #55: MASTER'S CHALLENGE

TRIVIA

Jilda had a foster son named Griffith. Before he died, Griffith's father made Jilda promise to care for him. Griffith's current location is unknown.

LEGAL STATUS	Lakluun exile, deceased
MARITAL STATUS	Children: Freya, Griffith (foster-son)
EDUCATION	Lakluun
MILITARY	N/A
OCCUPATION	Champion/survivor
AFFILIATIONS	Master's Trial, Representative of Lakluun

Jilda was the second-oldest child in her family, and her father's favorite. Against his wishes, she accompanied him to the Master's Trial. Though he had ensured that she would not be present for the battle itself, Jilda snuck away from her guardian and witnessed her father die at the hands of Chiun. At first, she thought the tiny Korean man would kill her as well, but he bowed and explained that she should not be sad. Her father was a valiant man who had represented the Lakluun with honor.

Jilda travelled home, and became obsessed with the Trials. When it came time for training, she volunteered, besting her elder brother, claiming the mantle of Lakluun champion. Everyone assumed that her determination in becoming Lakluun champion was an attempt to avenge her father, but Jilda was determined to stop the Trials.

During her travels in the Trial, she met and fell in love with the Sinanju Champion, Remo Williams. As a result of their union, Jilda gave birth to a daughter (*Freya*). Her actions in stopping the Trials had serious ramifications in Lakluun. After giving birth, she was exiled, leaving Lakluun without a champion family for the first time in centuries.

Jilda carried Freya with her and wandered around Europe, trying to leave both Lakluun and Sinanju behind her. But it was not meant to be. The supernatural bindings of Freya's birth ensured that her life would not be an ordinary one and Jilda fell under the control of Kali. This led to a direct confrontation with Remo and Chiun. Jilda was disguised and Kali was controlling her movements to the point that neither Remo or Chiun recognized her. In a split moment decision, Chiun killed Jilda to protect Remo, only to discover her identity later. Remo took Freya and left her with his father on the Sinanju reservation in Arizona. Jilda was laid to rest on the reservation in the shadow of the Red Ghost Butte.

KOJONG

BIRTHNAME: KOJONG

BIRTH	May 4, 1573 – Sinanju, Korea		
DEATH	October 6, 1679 – Sinanju, Arizona		
HEIGHT	5' 5"	**HAIR**	Black
WEIGHT	132 lb.	**EYES**	Brown
BUILD	Thin	**IQ**	109

FIRST APPEARANCE

DESTROYER #70: THE ELEVENTH HOUR

TRIVIA

Kojong died on the same day as his twin brother Kojing.

LEGAL STATUS	Exile from the village of Sinanju
MARITAL STATUS	Widower (Aiyana) Children: Gerah, Tapu and Mekwi
EDUCATION	Trained by his father Nonga
MILITARY	N/A
OCCUPATION	Chief of the Sinanju Tribe
AFFILIATIONS	The House of Sinanju, The Sinanju Tribe of Arizona

Kojong knew fear from birth. His mother told him that if his father Nonga ever discovered that he was a twin brother, he would slay Kojong and dump his body in the Korean Sea. Kojong was actually the elder of the twins, but the midwife forgot to tie a ribbon on his foot when he was born. After both Kojong and Kojing were born, she realized her mistake and tied the ribbon on the wrong baby's foot.

Upon Master Nonga's return from Tibet, where he lost his eyesight in a fight with the Hindu god Kali, his wife brought both boys to train, switching them out every other day, hoping that he would not notice.

Nonga could easily sense the difference in the boys and instantly knew that Kojong was the elder as he detected the taint of Shiva in his breath. But he played along with his wife so he would not have to kill Kojing. He trained both boys and when it came time to establish a new Master, Nonga took Kojong on a long journey to the mountains north of Sinanju.

He revealed not only that he knew Kojong was a twin, but that he was the elder. Kojong, who had been told his entire life that he was the younger, felt suddenly protective of his brother Kojing and asked his father how he could be spared. Nonga said that there was one chance. He explained the curse of Shiva and how it would follow the eldest down the bloodline. Kojong could leave the village, taking the curse with him and save his younger brother. The evening before Kojing was declared Master, Kojong left on a raft, traveling across the Great Eastern Sea to see what fate had in store for him.

He landed on the shores of California and headed East, where he was shunned until he met the Desteen tribe of Arizona. While there, the tribe was attacked and their chief was killed. Kojong saved the tribe from destruction and was given the chief's daughter in marriage as thanks. That placed Kojong as the next ruler of the tribe, who decided to change their name to Sinanju.

PAUL MOORE

BIRTHNAME: PAUL ANDREW MOORE

BIRTH	December 5 – Sinanju Reservation, Arizona		
DEATH	N/A		
HEIGHT	5' 9"	**HAIR**	Black
WEIGHT	219 lb.	**EYES**	Brown
BUILD	Medium	**IQ**	108

FIRST APPEARANCE

LEGACY #4: TRIAL AND TERROR

TRIVIA

Paul is physically afraid of Freya to the point he refuses to speak with her.

LEGAL STATUS	Member of the Sinanju tribe, no criminal record
MARITAL STATUS	Widower (Angela) Children: Tommy, Alina, Charles
EDUCATION	High school graduate, Sinanju Tribal Academy
MILITARY	Exempt
OCCUPATION	Head of the Sinanju Tribal Council, leather worker
AFFILIATIONS	Sinanju Tribal Council

Paul is the head of the Sinanju Tribal Council and illegitimate son of Joseph Roam (Sunny Joe's father). Twelve years after Sunny Joe was born, Joseph began an affair with Paul's mother (Pearl Moore). Her brother (a member of the Tribal Council) later found out that Joseph was the father. At the next council meeting, he publicly called on Joseph to step down from office. With Sunny Joe in California at the time, that would have left control of the reservation to the council.

Joseph ended the meeting and threatened each councilman with death if word got out. Mick Walker, his new caretaker, protested, and Joseph broke his wrist to prove his point. Joseph finally compromised by exiling Pearl on the conditions that Paul would remain on the reservation and that the incident would never be mentioned to anyone.

Tearful, but without any other options, Pearl left Joseph and Paul, only to die in a car wreck a month later. Joseph secretly took Paul to his mother's funeral and then headed west to find Bill, who had started a new life as a stuntman and ask for his return. Paul learned who his father was at Joseph Roam's funeral. One of the last members of the old tribal council took Paul aside and told him the truth. He confronted Mick, who would not confirm the story, but Paul could tell from the shocked look on Mick's face that it was true. Paul has held a grudge against Sunny Joe ever since.

When a young boy named Tekoa applied to become a member of the Tribe, Paul was set against it, until he heard that Sunny Joe was also against it. Paul bypassed his own judgment and talked the council into granting the boy Sinanju status just to spite Sunny Joe, only to later find out that it was a huge mistake. His wife was among the dozens who died when Tekoa betrayed them.

MOTHER

BIRTHNAME: JAANA

BIRTH	March 4 – Heks Bolig (*Mother's Hut*) Lakluun		
DEATH	July 6 – Heks Bolig (*Mother's Hut*) Lakluun		
HEIGHT	5' 2"	**HAIR**	White
WEIGHT	182 lb.	**EYES**	Green
BUILD	Heavy	**IQ**	95

FIRST APPEARANCE

LEGACY #5: MOTHER MINE

TRIVIA

Jaana's favorite spell creates light displays to amuse Lakluun children.

LEGAL STATUS	Lakluun citizen, deceased
MARITAL STATUS	Single
EDUCATION	N/A
MILITARY	Exempt
OCCUPATION	Mother, Lakluun
AFFILIATIONS	Lakluun Royal Council

Jaana was born into a long line of Lakluun witches. She took over duties from her mother, but promised herself that she would only use her power for good. Instead of being a Witch, Jaana would become a Mother to those in Lakluun, and true to her word, she spent her first century blessing crops and making life in Lakluun more comfortable. But something changed when she began observing the Master's Trial.

The Lakluun participated in the Master's Trial and each time had lost to the Sinanju. Jaana had missed an opportunity to question Chiun's father, but she tried to seduce Chiun to pry the secrets of Sinanju from him. He politely informed her that he did not dally with witches or prostitutes. Though frustrated, things changed when Jilda returned from the Master's Trial. Not only had she abandoned the trial, she returned with a child sired by the Sinanju Champion.

The baby girl (*Freya*) was still born, but while Jaana was attempting to revive her, she noticed something very odd. It was small, but powerful; a spark of divinity inside the dead baby girl. The spark grew and brought Freya back to life, flooding the room with a power that dazed Jaana. She thought that this was how the Sinanju had cheated; if they died during the Trial, the spark would return them to life.

She decided to take the spark from Freya, but Jilda and Freya were banished before she could try. It took years, but she finally convinced King Hannu to use an old Lakluun law and recall Freya to recant her claim to become Champion. Jaana knew that no one else would be able to handle the power, so she would have to kill the other Champions. She would blame Freya and use her death sentence to take the divine spark for herself. But with all of her power, Jaana was still less than a speck to Shiva and was instantly snuffed during the attempt.

ADIM MUSOBOTE

BIRTHNAME: ADIM MUSOBOTE

BIRTH	April 6 – The Bayit Plains, Bughanum		
DEATH	May 17 – Oakland, California		
HEIGHT	5' 6"	**HAIR**	Gray
WEIGHT	286 lb.	**EYES**	Brown
BUILD	Heavy	**IQ**	97

FIRST APPEARANCE

THE LAST WITNESS #5: SHATTERED PROPHECY

TRIVIA

Colonel Musobote's official uniform was made by a French fashion designer who did not like his politics. Bughanum obviously has no knowledge of Santa Claus.

LEGAL STATUS	Bughanum Dictator for Life, deceased
MARITAL STATUS	Single
EDUCATION	Bughanum public schools (*He left in 7th grade*)
MILITARY	Colonel in the Bughanum Army
OCCUPATION	Dictator for Life
AFFILIATIONS	Bughanum

Adim Musobote was the son of a sharecropper in the Eastern Highlands of Bughanum. Like other boys his age, he saw the military as the only way out of poverty. He chose a bad time to enter as The Great Bughanum Civil War began the very next year. Adim abandoned his uniform to stand with his father, who was one of the leaders of the rebellion. The successful uprising restored the rule of the six warlords that had been in place for centuries before French colonization. It also placed his father at the right hand of Bughanum's new leader and Adim was promoted to Colonel in the new Bughanum Army.

After the new ruler died of complications from pneumonia four years later, Adim's father took control of the country, but his rule only lasted six weeks. He and all of Adim's brothers mysteriously drowned in the family pool. Adim accused the other five warlords of treason and they were subsequently hanged.

Despite Bughanum's rich natural resources of oil, iron and diamonds, Adim did not understand the mechanics of ruling a country. Bughanum entered an era of vast poverty, averaging as the fourth-poorest nation on Earth during his reign. But while his countrymen suffered, Adim lived the life he had always dreamed about. The pendant he wears over his heart has been called 'The Nameless Diamond', but is, in fact, The Bughanum Diamond. It is the third-largest diamond ever found (*1,182 carats*) as well as the largest black diamond in the world.

His obsession with Kwame Afolayan, a citizen who escaped Adim's control, would be his downfall. After Adim found out that Kwame was living in America, Adim personally traveled to San Francisco to ensure his death. Adim was killed in his own royal jet and Kwame returned to Bughanum as King. His brother now sits in Adim's throne where he is repairing the damage that Adim had caused during his eighteen-year reign.

FRANKLIN MICHAEL NELSON

BIRTHNAME: FRANKLIN MICHAEL NELSON

BIRTH February 27 – Decatur, Illinois
DEATH N/A
HEIGHT 6' 4" **HAIR** Brown
WEIGHT 224 lb. **EYES** Green
BUILD Strong **IQ** 121

FIRST APPEARANCE
LEGACY #1: FORGOTTEN SON

TRIVIA

Mike is the first agent at Mike's Bar to actually be named Mike.

LEGAL STATUS American citizen, no criminal record
MARITAL STATUS Separated (Cynthia)
EDUCATION Princeton University (Criminal Justice/Psychology)
MILITARY U.S. Marines (1996 – 2008)
OCCUPATION Bartender / Bunker Guardian
AFFILIATIONS CIA

The three best days of Mike Nelson's life were 1) The day he got a bicycle on his eighth birthday, 2) The day he was married and 3) The day he became a United States Marine. His fondest childhood memories were dressing in fatigues and driving his mother crazy by digging trenches in the back yard.

After serving twelve years in the Corps, Mike was given an illegal order from a young lieutenant. He disobeyed the order and reported the lieutenant to his commander. He had no idea that the young officer was the spoiled son of a powerful United States Senator, so he was given the option to leave the Corps or face prison. The look on his wife Cynthia's face was the only reason he did not stay and fight.

Mike joined the CIA and was assigned to a desk. He thought that his days of contributing to the defense of his nation was over until a thin man with a gray suit showed up at his house and asked if he wanted to run a bar. The man was so old that at first, Mike thought he was senile, but there was something in his eyes that made Mike listen. And after Mike heard what the job really was, he stood a little taller and accepted the offer. He and Cynthia moved to a small village east of St. Louis, where she took a job as a nurse at the VA hospital.

Mike's Bar is open from 3–11 Monday through Saturday. While he was actually trained as a bartender for his role, Mike's real assignment is to provide security for the "Arch Bunker," which includes monitoring the grounds outside, as well as defending the place in case of attack. Hidden steel plates line the walls of the bar and with the touch of a button, can come down to cover the windows and door. His trademark bartender vest is bullet-proof.

His wife left him shortly after Mike took the job, citing the time he spends at work. She has not filed for divorce though, and Mike is working toward reconciliation.

SHELIA PATTERSON

BIRTHNAME: SHELIA MARIE PATTERSON

BIRTH	November 15 – Cambridge, Massachusetts		
DEATH	N/A		
HEIGHT	5' 4"	**HAIR**	Auburn
WEIGHT	132 lb.	**EYES**	Hazel
BUILD	Thin	**IQ**	127

FIRST APPEARANCE

LEGACY #5: MOTHER MINE

TRIVIA

Shelia has not seen her family since college.

LEGAL STATUS	U.S. citizen, no criminal record
MARITAL STATUS	Single
EDUCATION	University of Chicago (Constitutional Law)
MILITARY	U.S. Navy (1994 – 1998)
OCCUPATION	FBI Agent
AFFILIATIONS	Alumni, University of Chicago, FBI

Shelia was born in an upper-middle class family in Massachusetts. She graduated from the University of Chicago with a degree in Criminal Justice. Separated from her twin sister, Shelia found purpose and a new family in the FBI and quickly rose in rank, catching the attention of her regional director. Shelia was promoted to a Top-Secret program in Rye, New York. Her job was to handle identities of those entering and exiting the program. Two years in, she began processing people out without processing new people in and knew that meant their location was closing.

So, when she met one of the last agents at Folcroft named Remo a week before she left Folcroft, she decided to have some fun. He was not really her type, but he had deep-set eyes and a presence about him that Shelia found irresistible. A few weeks later, she discovered that she was pregnant. An attempt to find Remo landed her in the office of Folcroft's director, a bureaucrat she only knew as Harold Smith.

She explained why she needed to find Remo and Smith told her that was not possible. However, he told Shelia about a secret program that adopted boys — and only boys — but she would have to forever sign away her parental rights. She would also have to stay at Folcroft for the length of the pregnancy, where she would be given the best treatment possible. A staunch Catholic who did not believe in abortion, but not ready to start a family, Shelia agreed. The baby was taken from her as soon as he was born and she was left with a large compensation check and a new job at a New York bureau.

She was one of four agents who were tricked into abandoning coverage of the 9-11 hijackers but the only agent not to rat out her boss. As a result, Smith had her sentence reduced to five years of probation and a demotion.

DAWN ROAM

BIRTHNAME: DAWN MARIE STARR

BIRTH March 29 – Seattle, Oregon
DEATH September 13 – Staten Island Hospital, NY
HEIGHT 5' 4" **HAIR** Black
WEIGHT 122 lb. **EYES** Brown
BUILD Thin **IQ** 107

FIRST APPEARANCE
DESTROYER #97: IDENTITY CRISIS

TRIVIA

One of Dawn's sculptures — the sun cresting over a wave — sits on the windowsill behind Sunny Joe.

LEGAL STATUS Member of the Sinanju tribe, deceased
MARITAL STATUS Married (William Roam) Children: Remo
EDUCATION Seattle High School, Los Angeles City College (Graphic Design)
MILITARY N/A
OCCUPATION Artist/Sculptor
AFFILIATIONS The Sinanju Tribe of Arizona

Dawn grew up in a middle-class family in a Seattle suburb. As a young girl, she would spend hours watching television, fascinated by other people's lives and adventures. When asked what she wanted to be when she grew up, she would just smile and say "Hollywood". Though she was too quiet to be an actress, she knew that one day she would move to California. That day came when she convinced her parents to let her attend Los Angeles City College and pursue a degree in art, majoring in graphic design.

When she was not taking classes, she regularly visited movie sets. One day, while trying to find one of her favorite actors to get an autograph, she met a tall, lanky guy with a shy smile. Bill Roam not only helped her get the autograph, but helped her find others as well. Dawn found herself coming back to talk to Bill and soon, they began dating. A few months later, they married.

Dawn finished her degree and began traveling with Bill whenever he had a shoot. Even when she was eight months' pregnant, she insisted on traveling across the country for a shoot just west of New York.

Her water broke a few weeks early, but Bill rushed her to a local hospital. The baby was delivered, but something was wrong. Dawn felt light headed, but was told that she was just exhausted after delivery. When she began staring numbly into space, Bill insisted a nurse take a look and that is when they found internal bleeding. They operated on her to stem the blood flow, but she never recovered.

After she died, Bill called his friend Mick and told him what happened. Bill took the baby and left. Despite the Council's protest, Mick had Dawn buried in the section of the cemetery normally reserved for Sunny Joe wives near the dry river bank of Laughing Brook.

JOSEPH ROAM

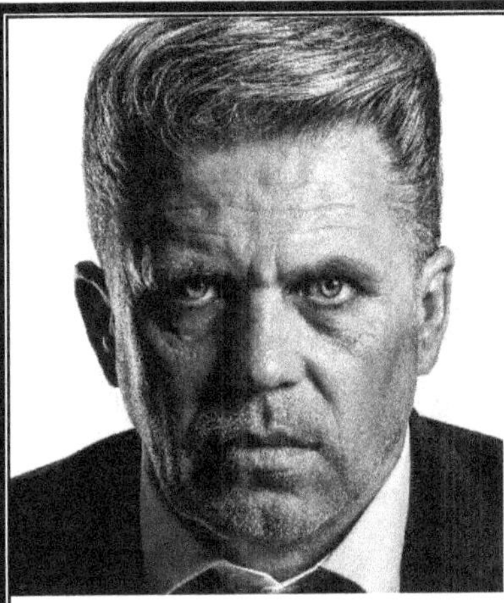

BIRTHNAME: RICHARD JOSEPH ROAM

BIRTH October 16 – Sinanju Reservation, Arizona
DEATH May 4 – Sinanju Reservation, Arizona
HEIGHT 6' 2" **HAIR** Gray
WEIGHT 168 lb. **EYES** Brown
BUILD Thin **IQ** 104

FIRST MENTION
LEGACY #1: FORGOTTEN SON

TRIVIA

Joseph was awarded the Silver Star for his military actions, though no public details of those actions exist.

LEGAL STATUS Member of the Sinanju tribe, no criminal record, deceased
MARITAL STATUS Widower (*Martha Sales*) Children: Anton (deceased), William
EDUCATION High school graduate, Sinanju Tribal Academy
MILITARY United States Army
OCCUPATION Chief of the Sinanju Tribe of Arizona
AFFILIATIONS The Sinanju Tribe of Arizona

While on trips to Washington, D.C. with his father, young Joseph Roam experienced the culture of an America on the cusp of a technological revolution. He soon started wearing American clothing, cut his hair in a modern style and began listening to Big Band music. The elders mocked him as the "White Sunny Joe".

Then came World War II. Some of the boys from the reservation had volunteered to enlist. Joseph believed that it would be a perfect opportunity to travel to Sinanju, but his father, already upset with Joseph's modern ways, refused. He said that it would be disrespectful for a future Master of Sinanju to become a soldier. But Joseph ignored his father and secretly enlisted. In three months, he was stationed in the Pacific. Joseph slipped away from his unit and secretly traveled through Japanese territory, landing in Songang-yi, North Korea. He began asking for directions tor Sinanju and was taken to a wrong village by then-Sinanju apprentice Nuihc (*nephew of Chiun*) to keep him away from the real village.

Disappointed, he traveled back and found an American unit under attack. Even though dodging bullets had been a trait he had mastered as a child, Joseph was simply overwhelmed with numbers, finally falling to a mortar. The next thing he knew, he was on a plane headed home with no injuries. No one would tell him what had happened, but he had flashbacks of destroying Chinese tanks with his bare hands.

When he returned home, his father was furious. Joseph accepted his father's punishment and quietly fell back in line. Joseph did not learn what happened to him until he took over as Sunny Joe and found out about Shiva. Knowing that as long as there was a Sunny Joe, Shiva would hold reign of their family line, Joseph resigned as Sunny Joe a week before his son Bill would officially become Sunny Joe. Though Joseph shot himself a few days before Bill took over, it was futile. Shiva remained claim to the family line.

WILLIAM "SUNNY JOE" ROAM

BIRTHNAME: WILLIAM ENAPAY ROAM

BIRTH October 3 – Sinanju Reservation, Arizona
DEATH N/A
HEIGHT 6' 5" **HAIR** Gray
WEIGHT 181 lb. **EYES** Brown
BUILD Thin **IQ** 114

FIRST APPEARANCE
DESTROYER #77: SHOOTING SCHEDULE

TRIVIA

Sunny Joe is one of only two stuntmen to receive an honorary Oscar. He uses it as a door stop.

LEGAL STATUS Member of the Sinanju tribe, no criminal record
MARITAL STATUS Widower (*Dawn Starr*) Children: Remo
EDUCATION High school graduate, Sinanju Tribal Academy
MILITARY N/A
OCCUPATION Chief of the Sinanju Tribe of Arizona
AFFILIATIONS The Sinanju Tribe

Bill Roam was a model Sinanju apprentice throughout his childhood. But when he graduated from high school, Bill watched as his friends joined the military or moved away for good paying jobs. That was when he began questioning his future. When his father broke his arm during an argument, Bill had enough. He had always wanted to be an actor, so he headed west. Once arriving at Hollywood, he held several part time jobs to afford acting classes. Bill was rejected for every part he sought. One day while on set, a stuntman was injured in a stunt. Bill told the director he could do the stunt and, using his apprentice Sinanju skills, completed the stunt. His skills soon made him Hollywood's go-to stuntman. If a stunt seemed impossible, all they had to do was hire 'Big Bill' Roam.

Then he met Dawn Starr. For Bill, it was love at first sight. They were married three months later and he took her with him to every shoot. Dawn was eight months pregnant when Bill took her to a movie he was working on just west of New York. Her water broke early, but though she was taken to a hospital, she died a week after giving birth. Bill was crushed and began thinking about taking his own life. Knowing that the baby was not safe with him, Bill took the baby to a Catholic orphanage in honor of Dawn's Catholic upbringing. He returned to Hollywood and worked a few more years before his father showed up on set, pleading for him to return. Bill was ready to come home, so he agreed.

He finished his Sinanju training in eighteen years. But a few days before Bill would be named Sunny Joe, his father inexplicably killed himself, delivering another emotional blow. So, when Bill was finally reunited with his son Remo several years later, and then found out that he had grandchildren as well, he offered them a place at the reservation to make up for not being a father to Remo. Stone and Freya accepted, but Bill has not been able to connect with his son as easily.

SMIRNOFF

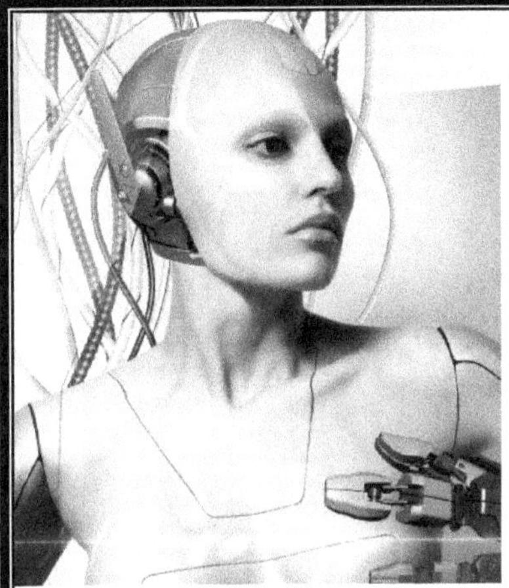

NOMENCLATURE: MS. SMIRNOFF

CREATION	June 6 – Washington, D.C.		
EXPIRY	N/A		
HEIGHT	5' 9"	**HAIR**	Red
WEIGHT	275 lb.	**EYES**	Blue
BUILD	Thin	**IQ**	NA

FIRST APPEARANCE

LEGACY #7: 100 PROOF

TRIVIA

Smirnoff is programmed to play a wide variety of stringed musical instruments.

LEGAL STATUS	N/A
MARITAL STATUS	Bound to Creator Randy McCabe (deceased)
EDUCATION	Proprietary BNX Tachyon 2.1 Operating System
MILITARY	N/A
OCCUPATION	N/A
AFFILIATIONS	NASA

The android named Smirnoff was an after-thought of Dr. Vanessa Carlton, a "once in a lifetime brain" not seen since William James Sidis. So great was her 'Alpha Class' mind, that, when she graduated from Cornell at fifteen, the United States military invoked a rarely-used law, declaring her mind a weapon of mass destruction. She became a ward of the state and NASA became her legal guardian.

Vanessa soon became isolated and alone and began work on android companionship, masquerading it as work for military and space exploration. She developed Smirnoff last and based her code on the most recent and advanced code she had written. One of Vanessa's droids — Mr. Gordons — threatened the security of the American financial system and that put him on CURE's radar. Remo and Chiun were sent out to dispatch Gordons and that resulted in Vanessa's death. Smirnoff had not been activated as of Vanessa's death and remained hidden in her charging pod.

Decades later, VIGIL became aware of Vanessa's program. When the VIGIL World Council was destroyed by Ben Cole, its director (*Helmut Belisis*) decided to use Vanessa's technology to create a bodyguard powerful enough to protect him from Cole's Sinanju agents.

Though her frame was titanium steel, VIGIL integrated a revolutionary metal called Orichalcum at critical points in her body, covering her skull, torso as well as strike points of elbows and knuckles. Smirnoff was augmented with code from her digital brothers, providing her with the survival and combat instincts of Gordons and Daniels. Her access code provided to be too large of a challenge, so Helmut employed Randy McCabe of NASA who accidentally activated her, bonding her to him. McCabe was killed by his friend and Smirnoff was partially dismantled in battle by Freya Williams.

Freya and Ben mistakenly believed her brain to be in her head, leaving the torso (which included her brain) which Helmut retrieved. Smirnoff is currently offline.

HAROLD W. SMITH

BIRTHNAME: HAROLD WINSTON SMITH

BIRTH July 27 – Boston, Massachusetts
DEATH N/A
HEIGHT 6' 1" **HAIR** White
WEIGHT 172 lb. **EYES** Gray
BUILD Thin **IQ** 147

FIRST APPEARANCE
DESTROYER #1: CREATED, THE DESTROYER

TRIVIA

Smith once asked for a cake for his birthday. Once.

LEGAL STATUS American citizen, no criminal record
MARITAL STATUS Married (*Maude*) Children: Vicky
EDUCATION Dartmouth University, Harvard (*Law*), Yale
MILITARY OSS, later the CIA
OCCUPATION Director of CURE and Folcroft Sanitarium
AFFILIATIONS CURE, CIA, OSS

Harold Smith was born in a different era. Raised in a modest Vermont household, the Smiths were not a visibly personable family, they knew the value of love and honor. At a very young age, Smith was taught the meaning of sacrifice. So, when his country was attacked in 1941, it was only proper for Smith to volunteer for the military, despite his age.

He very carefully scripted a letter to President Roosevelt detailing the advantages of early enlistment. His proposal stated that the more men who were available on the field, the quicker the war would be won and the fewer lives lost. He received a personal letter from President Roosevelt, who maintained that children should never be used in time of war.

Smith replied with a letter carefully detailing why the President was wrong, supplying an advanced algorithmic formula as proof. The President never replied, but had the Secret Service find out who this man was. He was shocked when he found that Smith was only fifteen. By his logic, he assumed that Smith was a college student. He forwarded Smith's name to the newly-formed OSS. They needed and would appreciate a logical brain.

On his seventeenth birthday, Smith appeared at the local recruitment station, a small suitcase in hand. Instead of being led away with the others, he was taken to a back room and verbally attacked. Who did he think he was, writing to the President? Smith calmly gave a detailed explanation and the lead man nodded. "That's him, for sure."

Smith served the OSS and later the CIA, so when the new President looked for a logical man to be its director, Smith's name was at the top of his list. Smith agreed to head the new organization, even though it ran counter to the Constitution, and eventually accepted the use of lethal force.

STONE SMITH

BIRTHNAME: WINSTON "STONE" HAROLD SMITH

BIRTH	July 16 – Rye, New York		
DEATH	N/A		
HEIGHT	6' 0"	**HAIR**	Black
WEIGHT	182 lb.	**EYES**	Brown
BUILD	Medium	**IQ**	122

FIRST APPEARANCE

DESTROYER #97: IDENTITY CRISIS

TRIVIA

When he was a child, Stone wanted to run away and join the circus.

LEGAL STATUS	American citizen, no criminal record
MARITAL STATUS	Single
EDUCATION	Graduate of St. Martin Preparatory School
MILITARY	Honorable discharge, US Navy
OCCUPATION	Agent of CURE, Sinanju apprentice
AFFILIATIONS	CURE, The Sinanju Tribe, U.S. Navy, SEAL Team Six

Stone is an accidental success of an early CURE plan to keep Remo Williams' DNA alive. After Williams began work at CURE, it was discovered that his DNA (*which was an early science at the time*) was so distinctly different than other human DNA they had observed, Harold W. Smith (*director of CURE*) believed it to be the key to Williams' reaction speed and focus. And while his Sinanju training was impressive to Smith, he did not want to risk losing Remo's unique DNA to a stray bullet.

Smith hired four women to be surrogates. Each was hired to seduce and carry Williams' child. Only one was successful, but the child was female and Smith needed a male. Enter Shelia Patterson. An FBI agent employed by Folcroft, she ran into Remo during training and became pregnant with Stone soon after. While she was not a part of the surrogate program, Smith signed her up after hearing that Remo was the father. Smith took custody of Stone after he was born and sent him to military preparatory schools. Two of Stone's teachers were actually FBI agents who were ordered to keep an eye on him and provide regular reports to Smith. Stone was told that his parents had died and that Smith was a remote uncle of his father's.

After graduation, Stone joined the Navy where he joined the famed SEAL Team Six. Stone suffered a career-ending heel injury while saving his teammate's life. He became a mercenary known as "The Extinguisher" and later met his father. When he found out his family history, Stone returned with Remo and settled on his grandfather's reservation, where he is being trained in Sinanju. He quickly bonded with his young sister Freya and, even though she is deadlier than he is, Stone can't help but feel protective.

Stone has progressed through Sinanju training rapidly for one his age, but recently hit a plateau due to his smoking addiction. He is currently thinking about his place in the world and if that involves Sinanju.

TEKOA

BIRTHNAME: LAWRENCE DAVID "TEKOA" NEZ

BIRTH January 8 – Tenaha, Texas
DEATH N/A
HEIGHT 5' 10" **HAIR** Black
WEIGHT 197 lb. **EYES** Brown
BUILD Medium **IQ** 116

FIRST APPEARANCE
LEGACY #3: OVERLOAD

TRIVIA

Tekoa has a large birthmark on the back of his head.

LEGAL STATUS American citizen, no criminal record
MARITAL STATUS Single
EDUCATION Center High School
MILITARY N/A
OCCUPATION Sleeper Agent for War Feather
AFFILIATIONS Sinanju Tribe of Arizona

Tekoa was told from birth that he was the Messiah. He was told that he would end his family's exile and return them to their former glory as royal blood of the Desteen Tribe. When he began training, David took the name of his great-grandfather (Tekoa) as his Desteen name. He was the first member of his tribe to perfect the thunder strike and Tekoa wanted to make sure that he was the one to strike the final blow to the people who stole his family's land and their martial art.

Tekoa's father was so convinced that it was time to retake their homeland that he only had one son and began training Tekoa at six months. He forced Tekoa's ribcage to properly breathe. At ten, Tekoa was taken out of school and began dedicating his time toward perfecting the art.

His father plotted to use Tekoa from the inside, and crafted a story from a newspaper article that detailed a car crash from another reservation to generate sympathy. Unfortunately, Tekoa could not fool Sunny Joe, who could tell that he was lying about something, but decided to give him a year to gain his bearings and then move on. Tekoa appealed to the council, who bypassed Sunny Joe by making Tekoa an official member of the Sinanju Tribe.

Once inside, he was supposed to report on reservation vulnerabilities and track Sunny Joe, but it was difficult because Sunny Joe felt Tekoa watching him. He ended up befriending Freya in an attempt to get information from the inside, but became attracted to her. He began to identify with the girl who seemingly did not belong anywhere and told his father that he would continue spying, but when it came time to attack, he was going to save Freya. His father agreed, but secretly plans on killing Freya.

VICTORIA VON ODOM / 81

NOMENCLATURE AT ADOPTION: 81

BIRTH	January 4 – The Plant, Illinois		
DEATH	N/A		
HEIGHT	5' 8"	**HAIR**	Red
WEIGHT	136 lb.	**EYES**	Brown
BUILD	Thin	**IQ**	148

FIRST APPEARANCE

LEGACY #8: THE HOMECOMING

TRIVIA

Each Premium was chosen because of their DNA. Victoria showed extreme aptitudes in intelligence and leadership.

LEGAL STATUS	Unregistered American citizen, no criminal record
MARITAL STATUS	Celibate
EDUCATION	The Plant Leadership Program
MILITARY	N/A
OCCUPATION	Assistant Director of CURE (*Casino Bunker, Detroit*)/America Senior
AFFILIATIONS	VIGIL Council, CURE, Carnage Program, The Plant

The original director of the Carnage program was ordered to separate premiums by the results of extensive DNA tests. When he saw that the aptitude for intelligence and leadership in Premium 81 was quite literally off-the-charts, she was placed on a separate path: Premium in charge. As Carnage supervisor, she was the only Premium to be given a proper name. She was ceremoniously named after the scientist who designed the program.

When Helmut Belisis still had access to a FORtab, he slipped Victoria's name into Harold W. Smith's computers as a perfect match for the CURE bunker in Detroit and Victoria abandoned The Plant for her new role as Assistant CURE Director of the Detroit bunker.

After a contractor found out that the girls they were operating on were not cancer victims, but instead stolen as infants through fake adoptions, the woman ran to the FBI, exposing the entire operation. Victoria was called back to The Plant to try and fix the situation, but it was too late. She was ordered to destroy the facility and kill everyone associated with the program before the FBI arrived.

Victoria personally assassinated the human members of Carnage leadership before triggering the explosives that lined the building, killing all but two Premiums. She escorted her favorite — 14 — off campus grounds and used 64 to assist her in killing any survivors. The FBI arrived as 64 finished her job. 64 distracted the agents away, giving Victoria time to escape in the confusion.

After the VIGIL World Council was destroyed, Helmut reached out to her and appointed her as the new America Senior. Her first job is to destroy the other three CURE bunkers. Thanks to Helmut, she located and identified Ben Cole's Arch bunker and Roland Whitmore's Mayan bunker, but is still searching for a rumored fourth and final bunker.

MICK WALKER

BIRTHNAME: MICHAEL NANTAN WALKER

BIRTH August 9 – Sinanju Reservation, Arizona
DEATH N/A
HEIGHT 5' 7" **HAIR** Gray
WEIGHT 213 lb. **EYES** Brown
BUILD Large **IQ** 126

FIRST APPEARANCE
LEGACY #1: FORGOTTEN SON

TRIVIA

Mick was a disc jockey in the Army.

LEGAL STATUS Member of the Sinanju tribe, no criminal record
MARITAL STATUS Married (*Kathleen*) Children: Victor, Donna, Mariella, Leo
EDUCATION Master's Degree (*History and Literature*) University of Phoenix
MILITARY U.S. Army (*Broadcast Journalist – AFN Berlin*)
OCCUPATION Caretaker for the Sinanju Tribal Council
AFFILIATIONS Sinanju Tribal Council

Mick knew that he would one day be a Caretaker — the keeper of the tribal records of the Sinanju tribe in Arizona — because that is what he had been told his entire life. He was a year younger than the next Sunny Joe (*Bill Roam*). He and Bill were paired to play together so they would be able to better work together when they grew up. Outside of his normal studies, Mick spent his spare time learning the original language of their tribe (*Korean*) and studying the scrolls of past Masters of Sinanju. His call was a noble one, his father told him, second only to Sunny Joe himself.

Mick served in the Army, but was called home after his father suffered a fatal heart attack. He began working as Caretaker for (*then-Sunny Joe*) Joseph Roam. After a few months of suffering Joseph's abusive behavior, Mick began to wonder if his father had died of natural causes. After suffering a broken wrist and back injuries, Mick began thinking about moving off the reservation, but when Bill returned, the punishments stopped.

Mick found Joseph Roam's body after he had shot himself and Mick was the one to tell Bill. Ever since, Mick has been Bill's right hand man and the only person Bill totally trusts. When Bill brought his newly-found grandchildren Freya and Stone to the reservation, Mick warned him about the repercussions in training Freya — much less both of them at the same time, but he trusted Bill when he said that Freya was the key to reuniting the Tribe and the House.

Mick found out he was dying, but put off medical care until Bill ordered him to do something about it, which led to a trip to their homeland in North Korea. He is currently on a medical regimen to curb what are normally fatal symptoms.

KATHLEEN WALKER

BIRTHNAME: KATHLEEN DARCY GODSY

BIRTH September 7 – Sinanju Reservation, Arizona
DEATH N/A
HEIGHT 5' 4" **HAIR** Graying brown
WEIGHT 152 lb. **EYES** Brown
BUILD Medium **IQ** 112

FIRST APPEARANCE
LEGACY #6: LAUGHING MATTER

TRIVIA

Kathleen loves gardening and origami.

LEGAL STATUS Member of the Sinanju tribe, no criminal record
MARITAL STATUS Married (*Mick*) Children: Victor, Donna, Mariella, Leo
EDUCATION BSN, Nursing, University of Phoenix
MILITARY N/A
OCCUPATION Retired
AFFILIATIONS None

Kathleen Walker grew up a child of the sixties and is a lover of life in all of its splendor. She maintains a personal herb garden and makes her own clothing. She dated Bill (*Sunny Joe*) Roam for a few months, but they soon realized they weren't right for each other and split up, but remained friends.

Knowing that Mick had a crush on her, Bill told Mick to ask her out. Kathleen originally only agreed as a favor to Bill, but she had no idea that the boy with the shy grin would capture her heart. They were married shortly before Mick entered the Army. He tried to get stationed in Korea, but the Army moved him to Germany. Kathleen considers the time a three-year honeymoon spread out over eight countries.

They attended the University of Phoenix together. Victor and Donna were born while Kathleen was still studying nursing. She took two years to stay at home and raise her kids. Mariella was born during this time. Kathleen began working as a nurse at a hospital in Douglas while Mick began working with Joseph Roam, who was Sunny Joe at the time. Mick soon began to complain of back pains over the next few months and Kathleen tried her best to care for him, but the pain continued. She began to suspect something more sinister was happening when Mick returned home one day with a broken wrist. He would never admit that Joseph broke his wrist, but the break was too clean to be an accident.

She wanted to confront Joseph, but Mick convinced her that it would be better for them to leave the reservation and start over elsewhere. Then Bill Roam returned to take over as Sunny Joe and everything returned to normal. Leo was a late surprise, born on Kathleen's thirty-eighth birthday. Her stories of Europe fascinated Leo to the point that he ended up working as a contractor in Europe.

WARFEATHER / ROBERT NEZ

BIRTHNAME: ROBERT HUNTER NEZ

BIRTH March 3 – Center, Texas
DEATH February 13 – Sinanju Reservation, Arizona
HEIGHT 6' 3" **HAIR** Black
WEIGHT 228 lb. **EYES** Brown
BUILD Medium **IQ** 107

FIRST APPEARANCE
LEGACY #2: THE KILLING FIELDS

TRIVIA

Robert snuck into an Illinois prison to kill a convict who stole from him and then escaped before the body was found.

LEGAL STATUS American citizen, convicted felon
MARITAL STATUS Married (*Tayen*) Children: David (Tekoa)
EDUCATION High School
MILITARY N/A
OCCUPATION Self-proclaimed Chief of the Sinanju Tribe of Arizona
AFFILIATIONS Desteen Tribe

Robert Nez grew up in a remote shantytown in the Nevada desert. His family's poverty never bothered him, because he was raised to look to the future. His father had told young Robert and his brother that they were the true heirs to the royal line of the Great Desteen Tribe. His father told Robert the story he had been told every day of his life. The story was one of murder and betrayal.

It began innocently: a stranger named Kojong wandered to their area. He claimed to have taken a canoe from a village called 'Sinanju' on the other side of the Ocean. After treating Kojong with respect, the Chief even taught him the secrets of the Desteen martial art. After the chief and his eldest son died in an inter-tribal battle, Kojong quickly stole the chief's eldest daughter so he could be named chief. Then he changed the name of the tribe to Sinanju and exiled the Nez line so he would not face a challenge.

The story provided young Robert with a single-minded obsession: Return his family line to their rightful place at the head of the Sinanju tribe. He dedicated himself to his training and easily killed his older brother to claim the mantle of Chief in Exile. Robert knew that the time had come to strike, so he only had one son (Tekoa) and ruthlessly taught the boy everything he knew about Sinanju.

He waited for a sign and his son provided it. Tekoa became the first member of the Nez line to successfully duplicate a force strike. Believing that as a sign that his son had attained the full power of the lost Desteen Art, Robert sent his son undercover to the Sinanju reservation to scout for weaknesses. He is worried that his son has fallen for the granddaughter of the false chief. Tekoa has insisted that Freya is not like the others and has demanded that he bring her with them. Robert has agreed so Tekoa will maintain his motivation, but has privately planned on killing Freya at the first possible chance.

ROLAND WHITMORE

BIRTHNAME: ROLAND ALEXANDER WHITMORE

BIRTH June 11 – Atlanta, Georgia
DEATH N/A
HEIGHT 5' 11" **HAIR** Black
WEIGHT 182 lb. **EYES** Brown
BUILD Thin **IQ** 168

FIRST APPEARANCE
REDACTED

TRIVIA

Roland is a unique CURE agent in that he dedicates part of his time to freeing people who have been wrongfully-convicted of crimes.

LEGAL STATUS American citizen, no criminal record
MARITAL STATUS Single
EDUCATION Caltech (*Engineering and Applied Science*)
MILITARY Peace Corps (*Botswana*)
OCCUPATION Assistant Director of CURE (*Mayan Bunker, Denver, CO*)
AFFILIATIONS CURE

Roland Whitmore was born to a drug-addicted mother who died shortly after abandoning him in an Atlanta bar. He was born addicted to heroin, causing permanent nerve damage to his left shoulder. Though he was adopted shortly after birth, Whitmore spent most of his childhood in hospitals and therapy. His twitching shoulder resulted in him being bullied, causing him to retreat into books.

Whitmore found his voice during a stint in the Peace Corps. He returned to study at Caltech, earning a Master's Degree in Engineering and Applied Science. His thesis on artificial intelligence placed him on CURE's radar. His predictions were so close that his thesis became classified.

CURE director Harold W. Smith hired Whitmore as Mark Howard's replacement. But instead of moving him to Folcroft, Smith set him up in a Presidential bunker system located beneath the Mayan Theater in Denver, and gave him access to the CURE network and his own local enforcement arm. As a pacifist, Whitmore refused the enforcement arm on principle.

Despite his amazing successes over the next six years, it was apparent that his pacifist beliefs would conflict with succeeding Smith as director of CURE. But Smith was able to use Whitmore's example as a model for three assistant directors. Each was chosen for a specific aptitude so Smith could better score the efficiency of differing approaches. None of the directors were allowed to know about the others.

Everything worked smoothly between the four directors until Victoria Von Odom, the director of the Detroit bunker, was given a secret missive that revealed the location of Cole and Whitmore's bunkers. She considered the act a justification for charges of treason and is working to destroy the other directors before turning her attention to Folcroft. She believes that Roland Whitmore is the most dangerous man on Earth.

FREYA WILLIAMS

BIRTHNAME: FREYA

BIRTH August 5 – Lakluun, Faroe Islands
DEATH N/A
HEIGHT 5' 11" **HAIR** Blonde
WEIGHT 142 lb. **EYES** Blue
BUILD Thin **IQ** 117

FIRST APPEARANCE
DESTROYER #73: LINE OF SUCCESSION

TRIVIA

Freya has a pony named Thor.
She refers to its long tail as "Mjolnir" due
to its propensity of striking people.

LEGAL STATUS Lakluun citizen in exile, Member of the Sinanju Tribe
MARITAL STATUS Single
EDUCATION High school graduate, Sinanju Tribal Academy
MILITARY N/A
OCCUPATION Agent of CURE, Sinanju apprentice
AFFILIATIONS CURE, The Sinanju Tribe of Arizona, Lakluun Champion

As the daughter of both Sinanju and Lakluun, Freya Williams always knew that her life was going to be complicated. Though born into the lineage of Lakluun Champions, second only to Lakluun royalty, Freya was never able to enjoy her heritage. Her mother Jilda abandoned the Masters' Trial, and while she was allowed to remain until Freya was born, both were banished from Lakluun afterward. Freya spent most of her childhood wandering through Europe until Jilda died saving her from the Hindu goddess Kali. Freya had no idea how much of her life would become entangled with Hindu deities.

Her grandfather, Bill "Sunny Joe" Roam offered to raise Freya on the Sinanju reservation. Despite pushback from the tribal council, he began training both her and her brother Stone the art of Sinanju. Freya takes her training seriously. While she is only able to see her father once a year on her birthday, her training is an almost tangible link to him. Through her lessons, she follows in her father's footsteps.

The Sinanju Reservation was the first stable home that Freya knew, but being the only person with blonde hair and blue eyes was a blessing and a curse. The first year of her stay was relatively pleasant. She had made a few friends, but boys began fighting over her to the point of injuring each other. Sunny Joe had to step in and banned anyone from dating her. This caused her to feel isolation from the local populace, a reminder her of her "outsider" status. Sunny Joe homeschooled her and she graduated early.

She tricked her way into working with her brother Stone and he has reluctantly come around to working with her. She is determined to earn respect from him, even though she can easily defeat him in hand-to-hand combat because of her longer period of training. On her first mission, she died, and as a result, triggered an ancient family curse, releasing the god Shiva, who can channel itself through both her and her father. Freya is afraid of the power, knowing that one time, Shiva will not let her return.

REMO WILLIAMS

BIRTHNAME: REMO WILLIAMS

BIRTH	September 13 – Staten Island Hospital, NY		
DEATH	N/A		
HEIGHT	6' 0"	**HAIR**	Black
WEIGHT	158 lb.	**EYES**	Brown
BUILD	Thin	**IQ**	112

FIRST APPEARANCE

DESTROYER #1: *CREATED THE DESTROYER*

TRIVIA

Remo is the first Master with direct ties to both the Korean and Arizona Houses.

LEGAL STATUS	Deceased
MARITAL STATUS	Single – Children: Stone, Freya, *REDACTED*
EDUCATION	Catholic school
MILITARY	U.S. Marines
OCCUPATION	Reigning Master for the House of Sinanju
AFFILIATIONS	The House of Sinanju, CURE, U.S. Marines

Everyone knew why Remo Williams had to die. He was framed for murdering a drug dealer and given the death penalty. But after a rushed trial and a faked electrocution, Remo woke up as the recruit of a secret organization run by Harold W. Smith called CURE. Remo was the perfect candidate; a highly-decorated Marine with no family ties and a deep love for his country. Originally, Chiun (*the Master of Sinanju*) was going to teach Remo a few tricks and return to his village in Korea, but he began to see promise in this man with the dead, round eyes. Amazingly, this white, who was far too old to properly begin training in Sinanju, was learning everything so well that Chiun believed he must have some Korean blood in him. Master Chiun had no idea how right he was.

After finding his biological father, Chiun was able to put the pieces together. Remo was the descendant of a wayward Master of Sinanju named Kojong. The other pieces of his life began coming together as he met his daughter (*Freya, from Jilda of Lakluun*) and his son (*Stone, from Sheila Patterson*). Remo faced a deep conflict as he wondered how he would fit into his children's lives as they had grown up without him. But the decision was taken away from him as they chose to stay with his father, Sunny Joe Roam, who began teaching Sinanju to both of them. Remo declined the offer to succeed his father as Sunny Joe, and accepted an honorary seat on the Tribal Council.

Remo makes dedicated trips to the reservation each year on Freya's birthday. He is still trying to find out where he fits in the lives of Sunny Joe, Stone and Freya. After decades of being an orphan, he is finding out that it is more difficult than he imagined.

```
Volume in drive C is MATTIS
Volume Serial Number is 51N4-NJU1

C:\Legacy>dir /w

Directory of C:\Legacy

[Art] [Books] [Dev] [Lunacy] [Omnibus]
[Omnibus2] [TV PILOT] legacypiggybank.docx [UNG]

                1 File(s)     5,358,468 bytes
                9 Dir(s) 42,578,807,296 bytes free

C:\Legacy>cd Omnibus2
C:\Legacy\Books\Omnibus2>
C:\Legacy\Books\Omnibus2>dir /w

[Art] Dev2e.docx [People] [Places] [Secret] [Things] [Versions]

C:\Legacy\Books\Omnibus2>cd Secret

SECURITY QUESTION: What is Devin's Middle Name?
ANSWER: *****

SECURITY QUESTION: Who told you?
ANSWER: *** ***

ACCESS GRANTED

C:\Legacy\Books\Omnibus2\Secret>
C:\Legacy\Books\Omnibus2\Secret>dir /w

Directory of C:\Legacy\Books\Omnibus2\Secret

Adara.exe [Area 51] [Firefly Second Season] [Jimmy Hoffa]
[Kennedy Assassination] [Moon Landing Tapes]

                1 File(s)     1,004,371 bytes
                5 Dir(s) 42,578,807,296 bytes free

Directory of C:\Legacy\Books\Omnibus2\Secret>Adara.exe

RUN SCRIPT
```

ELIZABETH ADARA

BIRTHNAME: ELIZABETH RENEE ADARA

BIRTH	August 26 – Washington, D.C.		
DEATH	N/A		
HEIGHT	5' 3"	**HAIR**	Brown
WEIGHT	128 lb.	**EYES**	Green
BUILD	Thin	**IQ**	217

FIRST APPEARANCE

REDACTED

TRIVIA

Elizabeth has never played a game because she does not understand the need for play

LEGAL STATUS	Elizabeth does not legally exist
MARITAL STATUS	Single
EDUCATION	Private tutor program, F...**REINITIALIZING CONNECTION**
MILITARY	**WARNING**
OCCUPATION	**ACCESS VIOLATION**
AFFILIATIONS	**CONNECTION LOST**

YOU ARE NOT AUTHORIZED

TO VIEW THIS FILE

PLACES

THE ARCH BUNKER (ST. LOUIS)

In the late 1950's, the United States government began building bunkers to house major portions of the federal government in case of a nuclear attack. They built four bunkers large enough to house the Executive Branch and a few members of Congress, as well as their families, so the government could function in the event of a nuclear war. Each bunker was manufactured to house up to two hundred people and included a ten-year supply of food and water. The bunkers are currently being used as top-secret prisons.

The government built twelve second-generation bunkers between 1971-1974. While they improved the design, the bunkers were scaled down to only house the President and Vice President and their families. Small side-quarters allowed for a six-man Secret Service contingent.

Four of the second-generation bunkers remain active back-ups in case the President or Vice President is too far away from the current roster of bunkers. The rest are being used for top secret records storage.

The third generation of bunkers were built in the mid-1980's and were the first fully-functional generation of bunkers. Each was designed only to house the President *or* Vice President and their family, based on the Oval Office, circa 1986. All other rooms, including the elevator, are connected via the centrally-located Oval Office replica. Each of the eight bunkers include enough food and water to last twenty-five years as well as backup generators that provide electricity if city power fails. These bunkers were the first to include access to what would later be called the internet. In fact, each of the eight bunkers was built directly near a central nerve center; electronic junctions where every scrap of processed information passes through.

The bunkers are located near the eight major network junctions: Los Angeles, Denver, Amarillo, St. Louis, Detroit, Atlanta, Richmond and Rye, NY. The junctions were justified as emergency backup hubs in case of a digital attack, but their primary function is to route all internet information through CURE computers located in each bunker. This caused a problem with bunker locations. The first two generations were built in remote and secure locations, but because of the need to access internet junctions, six of the third-generation bunkers had to be located in populated areas. They are located below bars that are purposely run down to discourage traffic. Another is located beneath a VHS/DVD repair center in Los Angeles, while the last is located beneath an east coast sanitarium.

Third-generation bunkers were built with five separate layers. The elevator is the first layer of security. Two elevator doors exist on the ground level. Once someone has pressed the elevator button, the door to the left opens. This is the elevator to the incinerator, and, if it is called from the top floor, is a trap. Anyone who enters the left door triggers an alarm and is disabled with a form of nerve gas. The right elevator door opens after the left door closes. From the bottom two floors, the elevator responds like a normal elevator, though it is lined with sensors and cameras to reveal who is inside.

The first floor opens to a concrete-reinforced room filled with office equipment and a door on either side. If someone enters without entering the access code on a hidden panel, steel doors slide in place, trapping the intruder inside and triggering an alarm. Behind those office doors are ten thousand square feet of explosives; enough power to obliterate the entire block. In case of a nuclear attack, the explosives would counter some of the blast, and in case of invasion or a more conventional attack, they are designed to destroy the elevator system and access tunnel, sealing anyone still below.

The second layer consists of twenty-thousand square feet of steel-reinforced concrete. Twelve-feet thick and twice the square footage of the floors above and below it, the porous substance is aligned to absorb the initial kinetic punch of a nuclear bomb and spread the damage horizontally. Two six-inch layers of depleted uranium are sandwiched within the second layer for added protection.

The third layer houses the bunker's second floor and, like the first floor, the first room is a trap. Beyond the trap room, the second floor is the bunker's maintenance chamber, containing multiple water filtration systems, power generators, and two incinerators. The remaining space is filled with spare parts for maintaining every piece of equipment in the bunker. For this reason, each of the six Secret Service agents stationed at the Bunker are trained to maintain and repair the bunker environmental systems.

The primary incinerator is accessible by both the second floor as well as the third-floor bunker below. A series of intricate one-way pipes channel any smoke from the primary incinerator blocks away to avoid detection. Ten inches in diameter, each pipe is lined with filters every hundred feet and are manufactured to operate for over eighty years without maintenance. The secondary incinerator is located toward the back of the second floor and is only to be used in a backup capacity, as it vents almost directly overhead.

The fourth layer consists of the same twelve-foot thick steel-reinforced concrete, but a six-inch layer of depleted uranium is placed at three-foot intervals. Small pockets of air in the concrete mixture insure that any remaining kinetic energy is diverted horizontally. The bottom of the fourth layer is comprised of a foot-thick slab of depleted uranium. Below that is a four-inch thick layer of charcoal treated concrete.

The fifth layer is the bunker designed to house the President and his family. Though the bunkers are intended for the President, one room is off limits even to the Commander-in-Chief: only designated CURE personnel have access to the computer room, where the Imperium Four array is located.

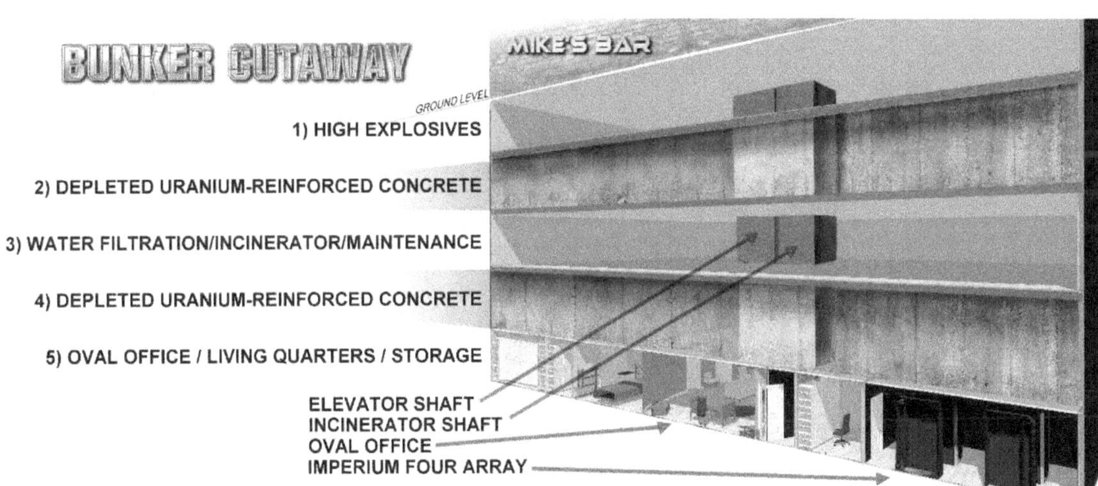

ARCH BUNKER: THIRD FLOOR

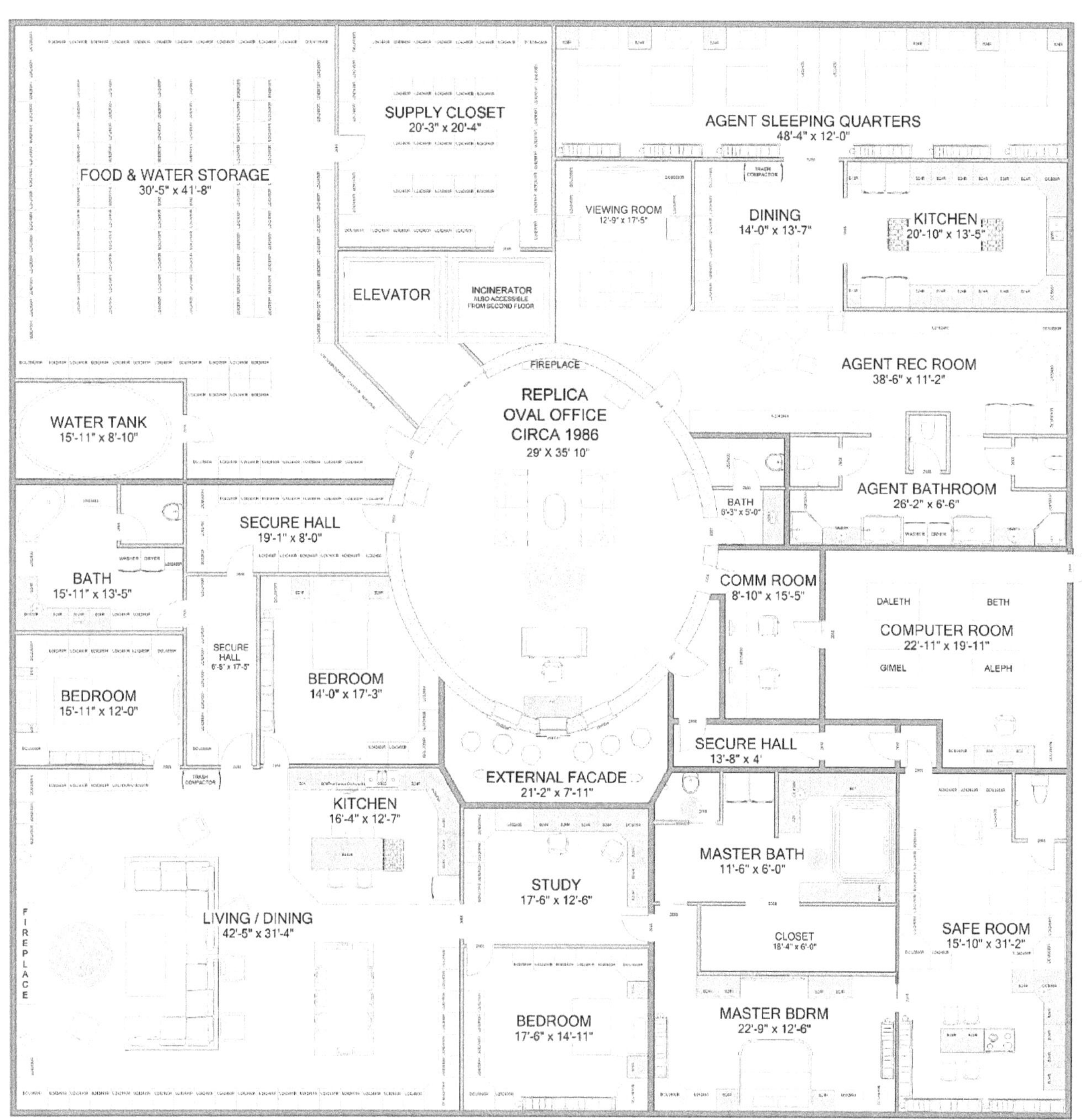

ARCH BUNKER: THIRD FLOOR

Benjamin Cole lives and works on the bottom floor of the Arch Bunker, which is the central hub for the entire operation. Concrete and steel blast doors are used to separate the bunker into five sections. Each section is separated by security level and possesses a Master Control Panel for the entire site. The panels are security-coded and most are hidden:

1) STORAGE: Located in a secret drawer hidden in a fake shelf
2) AGENT QUARTERS: Hidden behind the furthest right sink mirror in the bathroom
3) OVAL OFFICE: Placed under the front drawer of the Oval Office desk
4) PRESIDENTIAL SUITE: Hidden in a panel beneath a drawer in the Presidential kitchen
5) SAFE ROOM: Contains the only panel that is not hidden

Each of the panels have an authority level depending on its location. The panel in the Presidential safe room carries the highest authority, followed by the Presidential kitchen, then the Oval Office, then the Agent quarters, then the storage area. The Presidential safe room has the largest panel and carries the most functionality. The safe room is also the only room fully lined with a special mixture of steel and depleted uranium.

When Ben was assigned to the Arch Bunker, he did not feel comfortable working in such a luxurious location, but eventually conceded that it was only logical to use the mock Oval Office for his daily routines. The only purchase he authorized was for a small rug to cover the Presidential seal in the center of the room and he personally paid for it.

Except for weekly and monthly security and maintenance checks, Ben restricts himself to areas that were designated for Secret Service agents. He buys his own food, though he does take advantage of the system's filtered water system.

As the sole site employee (*and an avid cigar smoker*), Ben chose the Oval Office as the bunker's designated smoking area. This has caused some friction with Stone, who is trying to stop smoking, so Ben tries not to smoke before meetings with Stone and Freya.

A poor nation located in central Africa, Bughanum is run by six regional war chiefs, who are, in turn ruled by a King. Bughanum is rich in natural resources, but a lack of competent leadership has resulted in poverty for all but a chosen few. Their King is Dakari Afolayan.

GOVERNMENT	Monarchy
POPULATION	9,284,000 (*extrapolated from the last census and a ten-year growth curve*)
AREA	421,350 square miles
CAPITAL	Buoro (*also the largest city, population 785,000*)
LANGUAGES	Bughanum, French
GDP	$13 billion (*Averaged over the last three years*)
INDEPENDENCE	(*From France*) December 12, 1958
TIME ZONE	UTC +1

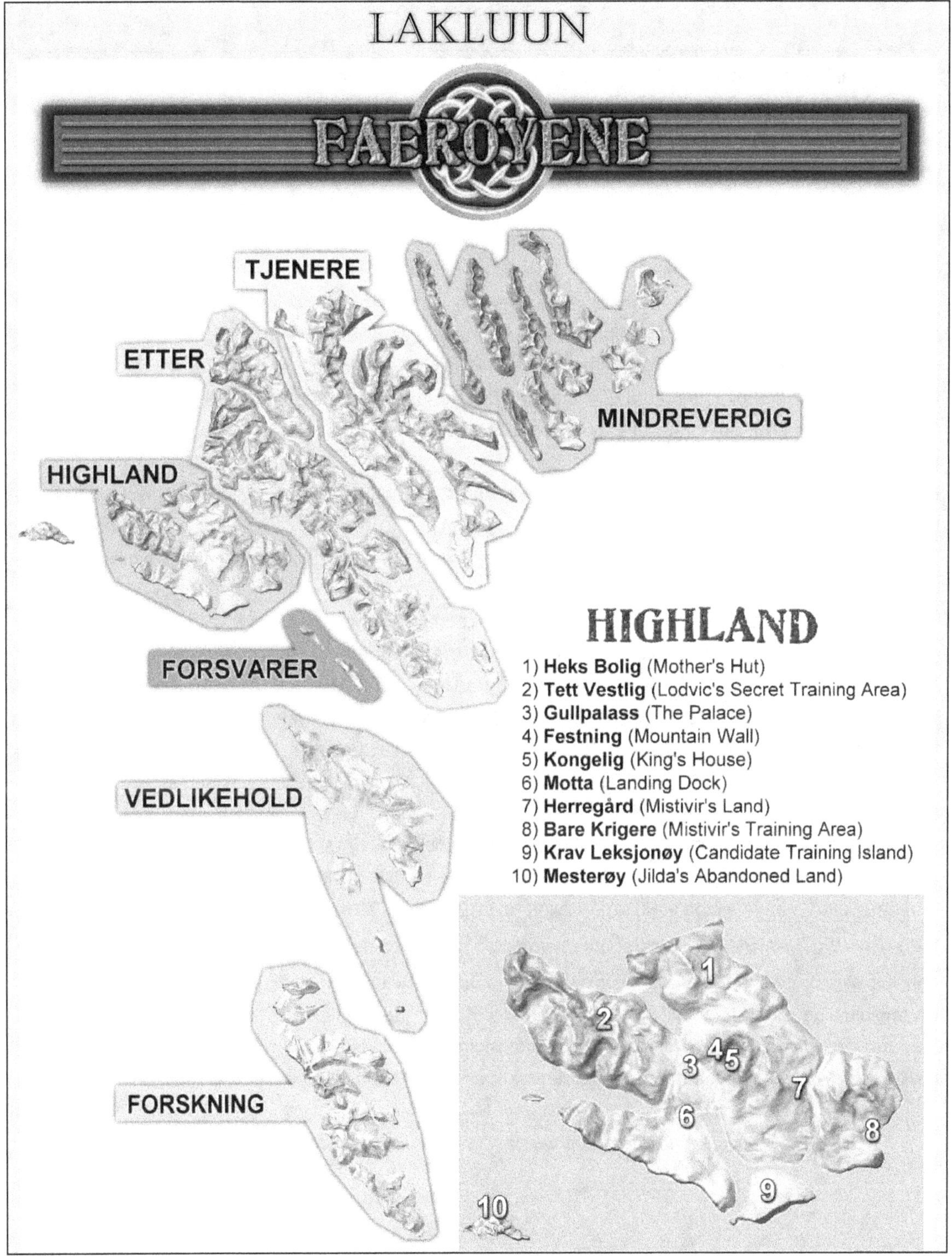
LAKLUUN
FAEROYENE
TJENERE
ETTER
MINDREVERDIG
HIGHLAND
FORSVARER
VEDLIKEHOLD
FORSKNING
HIGHLAND
1) Heks Bolig (Mother's Hut)
2) Tett Vestlig (Lodvic's Secret Training Area)
3) Gullpalass (The Palace)
4) Festning (Mountain Wall)
5) Kongelig (King's House)
6) Motta (Landing Dock)
7) Herregård (Mistivir's Land)
8) Bare Krigere (Mistivir's Training Area)
9) Krav Leksjonøy (Candidate Training Island)
10) Mesterøy (Jilda's Abandoned Land)
1
2
3
4
5
6
7
8
9
10

LAKLUUN

The Lakluun people live on HIGHLAND, located in the Faroe Islands, a chain of volcanic islands north of Scotland. Better known as Faeroyene, the island is populated by 48,100 people, who are segregated into five castes: Royalty (*4%*), Champion (*2%*), Overlegen (*Upper Class 18%*), Drom (*Creative Class, which includes scholars, writers, musicians, etc. 16%*) and Borgerlig (*Commoners 60%*).*

Commoners are perhaps the best-known members of Lakluun, as they are the caste that tourists are most likely to encounter. Because of their size, they have their own small government and capital city (*Tórshavn*) but ultimately still fall under the jurisdiction of The King and Witch.

While there are eighteen islands, there are only seven territories and a separate, small island (*Mesterøy*), reserved for The Champion and their immediate family.

HIGHLAND (*ROYAL*): Home to the King, Royal Family, The Palace and Mother's Hut. Citizens of Highland have a very high standard of living, as they are financially supported by the lower classes. The few paved roads on Highland exist only on the coast. Internally, horses are still the preferred method of travel.

ETTER (*BORGERLIG*): Home to the majority of the Common and their capital Tórshavn. It has the largest population (*13,089*) of any Lakluun city.

TJENERE ISLES (*BORGERLIG*): Common people live here. They have lower living conditions than most other Common.

MINDREVERDIG ISLES (*BORGERLIG*): Home to the smallest population of the Common. Their living standards are the highest of any territory, but their taxes are higher.

FORSVARER (*OVERLEGEN*): Commoners who agree to a twenty-year tour as guards live here.

VEDLIKEHOLD (*BORGERLIG*): "Caretaker Island" is home to the Commons who take care of Mesterøy. It is considered an honor to live on Vedlikehold's main island because it is where Ragnhild and the original Lakluun landed. The next-largest island is ironically reserved for Lakluun's prison. The two smaller islands are largely uninhabitable because of the terrain.

FORSKNING (*DROM*): Home to the most modern of the islands, Forskning is the soul of Lakluun. Music, poetry and sculptures thrive on this land. It is also the land most likely to be visited by tourists after Tórshavn. Artists have a high standard of living as they are able to sell their art to tourist and King alike.

MESTERØY (*CHAMPION*): Home of the champion and all third-generation (*and closer*) family members, only the King and Mother have a higher standard of living. Lakluun society surrounds the support for The Champion. The island has fallen into disrepair since Jilda, the previous Lakluun champion, abandoned the Trials. After she left, her family was forced to move to Vedlikehold. Island caretakers benefit though, because they have all of the benefits of a caretaker and no responsibilities until a Champion is chosen.

** Populations and percentages taken from the last census.*

At the dawn of man, there were twelve tribes. Each was known for a unique battle technique not found anywhere else on Earth. The Lakluun were one of those civilizations and their mastery of the blades is legendary. They originally lived on an island named Jötunheimr (*Kvitøya*), east of Nordaustlandet. Four thousand years ago, resources became so scarce that the population began to starve. A witch named Ragnhild warned Lakluun's King Einar that unless they moved, Lakluun was doomed. Einar refused, but after he died of starvation himself, Ragnhild led the eighty surviving Lakluun south to a small chain of volcanic islands she called Niðavellir (*The Faeroe Islands*).

A six-year-old boy named Eerikki was the lone descendant of King Einar, and Ragnhild protected him until he was old enough to rule, ruling in his stead. Eerikki took the throne when he was seventeen and is often referred to as the founder of Lakluun. The first thing King Eerikki did was to recognize the wisdom of Ragnhild and established a throne on his right hand for her. He crowned Ragnhild as the first Lakluun Witch and declared that as long as there was a King in Lakluun, there would be a Witch.

The unique Monarch/Mage system became the basis for their government. The King would always be a male heir from the royal line and The Witch would always be a female heir from the mystic line. The King functions as both legislative and executive, while The Witch functions as the judiciary, providing spiritual direction. On rare occasions when the two are in conflict, if The Witch says "Siste avgjørelse" (*My Final Word*), her decision is final.

1) **KING**: The King handles security and managing the islands (*including the Masters' Trial*) and is the representative of the Lakluun people. A Lakluun citizen may only be imprisoned or executed on the authority of the King.
2) **WITCH**: The Witch performs small services for the people of Lakluun, like fertility spells, healing the wounded and blessing crop yields. Her army of eldritch wolves roam the Lakluun beaches as a security barrier. It is said that she can see through their eyes.

For the past thousand years, Lakluun society has concentrated on The Master's Trial, trying to find a candidate who could successfully challenge The Sinanju. That changed after their last Champion (*Jilda*) abandoned the Trials. When she did so, a technicality in Lakluun law declared her eldest child the chosen Champion. When the King discovered that her only child (*Freya*) was living with The Sinanju, it became a huge scandal. One of the four Chosen (*Eleanora*) was sent to escort Freya to Lakluun to revoke her claim to the Trials so Lakluun could participate. An attack wiped out most of the upper two classes of Lakluun society. It is whispered that Freya had something to do with it, but exactly what happened is not known.

For the first time in Lakluun history, both offices are held by a single individual. Due to the deaths of the entire Lakluun upper society, Eleanora, the highest remaining member of the Upper Caste, took over both offices. Her new position forced her to abandon the title of Champion. She has begun the process of burying the honorable dead and replacing the upper caste with members from the Scholar, Artist and Common classes.

The Federal Government unofficially owns and operates over fifty bars in the United States. Each serves a different purpose, but most involve some form of information trafficking. Mike's Bar is no exception. Built in the late fifties as a private club tailored for the elite, celebrities frequented Mike's because of the exotic selection of alcohol and secluded location in the small village of Roxana, just east of St. Louis.

The CIA used the celebrities to attract targets that were otherwise averse to appearing in public. For years, the agency was able to record thousands of private conversations and since they never pursued arrests on site, Mike's continued as a valuable source of information.

Things changed in the mid-sixties as the concept of 'celebrity' began to change. The Rat Pack died out to tie-dye. The exclusivity of Mike's began to pale as celebrities stopped dropping by and by the early seventies, Mike's was on life support. It did not help that one of the agents in charge of Mike's was arrested for distribution of narcotics in 1972.

The economy was so weak that by 1979 the agency sent an agent who had been a bartender in college to try to offset expenses, but to no avail. The bar had purposely been run down for so long that a business model did not exist for its success. Mike's remained open only because of government support.

Things changed as the economy improved in the mid-eighties and the government was planning a new type of presidential bunker. It would be the bunker of the future and Mike's won the geographical lottery by being located two blocks from one of the eight new internet hubs that had just been constructed.

Mike's was shut down for "renovation" while the bunker was built in 1988. Modifications had to be made not only to Mike's Bar, but to the tax preparation office next to it. Very little money was used to fix damage to the bar caused by the bunker's construction, so the bar looked slightly worse after renovation than it did before.

After the bunker was installed, the role of bartender was upgraded to agent in charge of bunker security. Usually, CIA agents or highly decorated military personnel are chosen for the four-year assignment. The current holder of the position, Mike Nelson, is the first agent to actually be named "Mike". His job is simple: play bartender while preventing unauthorized people from accessing the bunker system below.

Realizing that he was standing just a few feet above enough explosives to level the block made Mike more than a bit nervous his first week. He became morbidly fascinated with the small button that would trigger an alarm in the bunker below, leaving the decision whether to detonate the explosives to Benjamin Cole, the man in the bunker. If the decision was given to detonate, Mike would not know until he and the surrounding two blocks were destroyed in the blast.

But the explosives are not the only method of self-destruction. In case of an unforeseen system failure, a satellite orbiting 22,300 miles above the Earth, thought to be a spy satellite, is armed with a single missile. It is solely designed to obliterate the bar and sealing the bunker below.

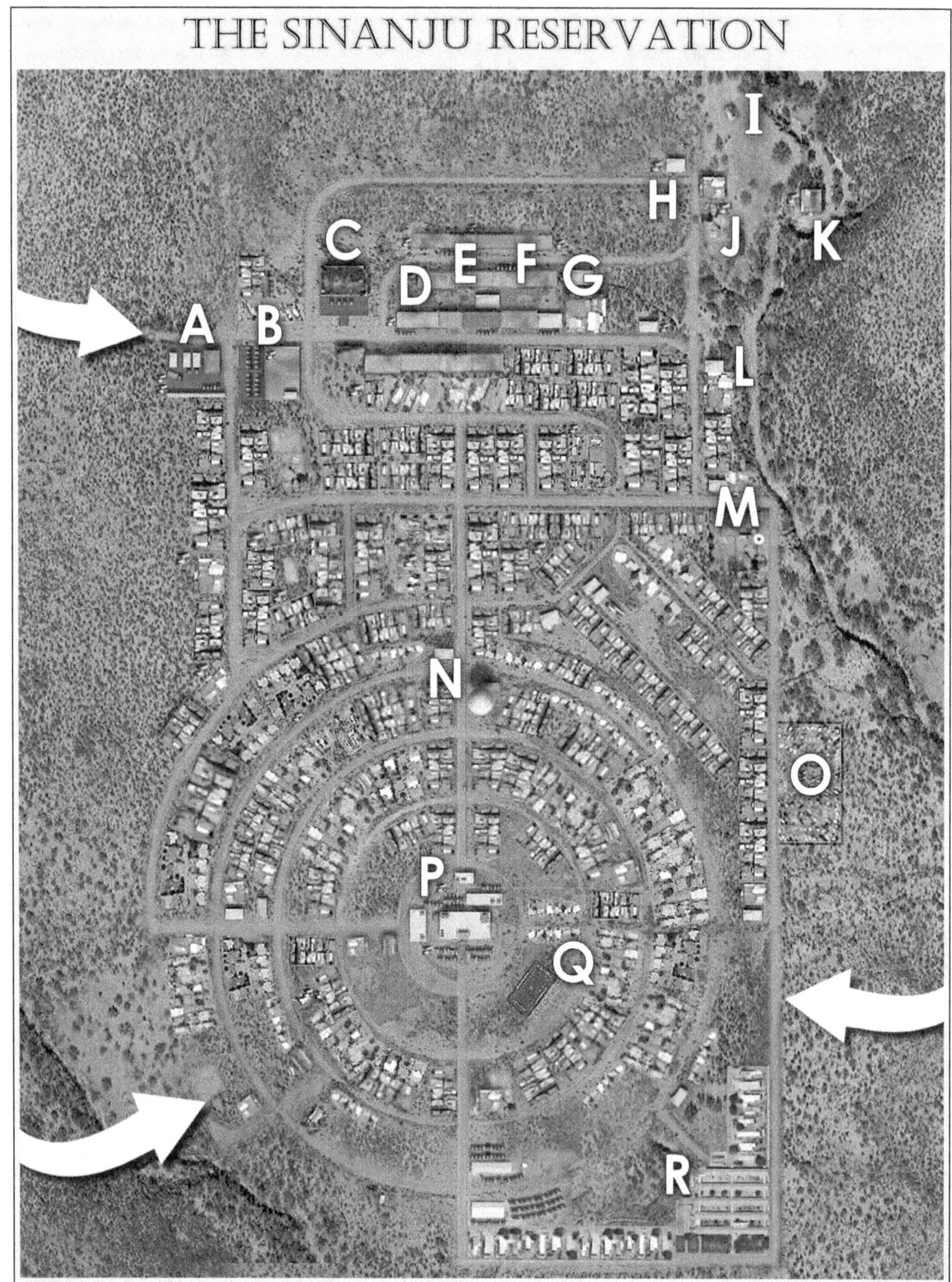
THE SINANJU RESERVATION
A
B
C
D
E
F
G
H
I
J
K
L
M
N
O
P
Q
R

(ARROWS INDICATE WAR FEATHER'S ATTACK POINTS)

A Gas Station
B General Store
C Tribal Museum (*open to the public*)
D Tribal Council Office
E Sunny Joe's Office
F Mick's Office
G Assembly Hall
H Freya's House
I Training Hut
J Sunny Joe's House
K Stone's House
L Mick's House
M Mick's Craft Barn
N Water tower
O Cemetery
P School Campus
Q Football field
R Power plant

THE SINANJU RESERVATION

The Sinanju Reservation is a federally-protected tract of land measuring 110,800 acres (173.12 square miles). It is located in southeastern Arizona and borders both Mexico and New Mexico. The land was first settled by the Desteen Tribe in the early-fifteenth century and once covered twice the current area. After a century of successfully defending their land, they succumbed to attacks by surrounding tribes who were armed with recently-acquired Spanish matchlock rifles. They began to quickly lose both men and land in successive wars. Needing more men for their army, they gladly accepted a vagrant named Kojong, who claimed to have traveled across The Great Western Ocean in the early seventeenth century.

Various tribes teamed up to attack the Desteen a few months later and almost overwhelmed them. As a fully-trained Master of Sinanju, Kojong defeated the invaders, but not before they were able to kill Desteen's Chief Ahote (*Bearclaw*) and his only son Makya (*Tomorrow*). As a reward for saving the tribe, Kojong was given Chief Ahote's daughter Tiponi as a bride, making him chief of the Desteen.

Over the next two decades, other tribes sought to attack the Desteen, but were destroyed by Kojong or forced to retreat. This period of time is known as "The Years of Testing" and is celebrated on the first day of each February with a feast and a small re-enactment ceremony.

The remaining years of Kojong's rule were peaceful, allowing the Desteen time to rebuild their homes and establish trade partners. After Kojong died, the tribe mourned for twenty days and changed their name to Sinanju in honor of the man who had saved them. His son Gerah became chief and was the first person officially referred to as "Sunny Joe" in tribal records.

During the American Civil War (*1862*), there was an attempt to invade Sinanju to steal gold. The invading army was destroyed fifty miles from Sinanju land. Survivors spoke in whispered hush of a man who could not be shot and could disappear on demand. The land was declared off-limits by both armies.

After Francisco "Pancho" Villa led his army through Sinanju land in 1916, the Mexican government set aside a quarter-mile strip of land on the Mexican side of the border to prevent future trespassing. During both World Wars, Mexico pledged not to enter Sinanju land under any circumstances.

The Sinanju are unique when it comes to reservations. Their 1877 treaty with the American government confers true and full sovereignty, including mineral rights. Any actions occurring on tribal land fall under the exclusive jurisdiction of the Sinanju Tribal Council and are subject to Sinanju Law. The Supreme Court upheld the treaty in 1921 (*Sinanju v Arizona*), and again in 1987 (*McDunnough v Sinanju*).

The Sinanju have twice traded tracks of land in negotiations with the federal government. In March 1980, road access to the Whitmire Canyon Wilderness Study Area was exchanged for a water tower and an advanced water purification system. Later, in 1982, they traded 2,309 acres at the Mexican border for the construction and maintenance of a large power plant. The federal government used that land to establish the San Bernardino National Wildlife Refuge.

The Sinanju Tribal Council consists of eight men who are elected every six years. The leader of the Tribal Council is elected from the three most senior members. For the past two cycles, Paul Moore has been the head of the Council.

THINGS

THE CARNAGE PROGRAM

The Carnage Program was one of VIGIL's four "Doomsday Cards". Its goal was to combine the best of technology, genetics and biological engineering to create assassins powerful enough to defeat a Master of Sinanju. Like other Doomsday Cards, it was so secret that it was even kept off VIGIL's internal books.

The plan began with the adoption of one hundred infant/toddler girls and moving them to a secure location in central Illinois known only as "The Plant". Before being accepted in the program, each Premium was subjected to an exhaustive DNA test. VIGIL specifically tested for indicators of endurance, willpower, leadership and intellect. Early trials showed that females adapted to the process much more efficiently than males, so only female infants were chosen.

The program ran successfully for sixteen years before a mid-level contractor developed a conscience, turning states' evidence over to the FBI. Victoria Von Odom, the Premium in charge of the program, killed the contractor, but it was too late. She was ordered to destroy the facility and kill everyone associated, with two exceptions. The Premium 14 would be saved for use as a VIGIL assassin, while 64 would stay to help Victoria kill any survivors. The FBI raided the burning building before everyone was killed; both Victoria and 64 escaped.

Premiums were separated into five squads of twenty. Each squad was led by a Keeper (*a Premium whose DNA demonstrated an aptitude for leadership*). All Premiums were taught three languages: English, Chinese and Spanish. Squads competed monthly for privileges to force Premiums to push themselves.

As the program progressed, several Premiums failed critical points in their training. Those girls were released into the foster care system. Without their daily and weekly conditioning, the girls who had not yet reached puberty would go on to lead mostly normal lives.

Each Premium was raised on a strict diet and endured multiple surgeries and weekly chemical injections to augment them to the peak of human ability. By the time they reached puberty, Premiums' DNA had been changed to the point that they actually qualified as a new race.

Over the first ten years of their lives, the skin of each Premium is genetically re-engineered to the point that they can breathe through the pores of their skin alone. The average Premium can hold her breath for about fifteen minutes and their blood can processes oxygen so efficiently that, under normal exertion, they can never get tired.

After puberty, key points of their skeletal structure were reinforced with a light, poly-carbon material stronger than steel. A Premium can take a bullet to the head, a sword to the forearm and a knife to the chest and only damage the skin. They are immune to most diseases and sickness and heal very rapidly.

All Premiums are implanted with trackers. The last step of the program would have involved inserting a computer component to increase battle efficiency, but The Plant was destroyed before they could be implanted.

CURE

CURE is a Z-level organization* that was created by a young President who realized that America was choking on the bureaucracy of its own Constitution. Originally, CURE consisted of only two employees: Director Harold W. Smith and his investigative agent Conrad MacCleary. The organization was hidden in plain sight, inside the sterile white walls of Folcroft Sanitarium in Rye, New York. It would be fitted with the four most advanced computers on Earth (*The Folcroft Four*) to assist Smith in sifting through data while MacCleary employed disguise and detective skills to obtain information unavailable to the Folcroft Four.

Understanding how powerful the organization would be, CURE was structured to work outside the realm of political pressure by limiting contact between CURE and the American government. The President was only allowed to suggest missions, and had only one authorized power: He could order CURE to dismantle, which would result in the destruction of all computer files and the deaths of Smith and MacCleary.

The mission for CURE changed years later when it was authorized one agent who could use lethal force. CURE staff ballooned to its largest at this time, with twenty-eight trainers working directly or indirectly for Smith at the Rye location. But everything changed later that year when Sinanju Master Chiun entered Remo's training. Where a large part of Folcroft's staff had been dedicated to the training and fitness of Williams, it was apparent that Chiun's training was providing greater results than the rest of the program combined. Seeing the results and noting that it would save money, Smith processed the trainers and agents to other agencies and returned Folcroft to its original status as an asylum. MacCleary died soon after in a mission, leaving Remo as CURE's sole agent.

In the late 90's, the President recognized the large workload Smith was shouldering and assigned Smith an assistant. Mark Howard served as assistant director of CURE until his disappearance in Afghanistan following a lead concerning Osama bin Laden. This left Smith once again alone in running the organization. Recognizing his advanced age, Smith created duplicates of his office to handle smaller cases.

Roland Whitmore was the first alternate director, and has served CURE since shortly after the disappearance of Mark Howard. Benjamin Cole and Victoria Von Odom were chosen later. There is a rumored fourth bunker. Smith has increased local director workloads, hoping to find a worthy successor.

DIRECTOR	LOCATION	ENFORCEMENT ARM
Benjamin Cole	St. Louis	Stone Smith, Freya Williams
Roland Whitmore	Denver	No enforcement agent
Victoria Von Odom	Detroit	64
?	Atlanta? Richmond?	?

To more effectively gauge each director, Smith ensured that each bunker has access to the same data, and each director was issued their own enforcement arm. Most importantly, none of the bunkers are aware of each other. Smith has placed a CIA watcher to guard the entrance of each bunker and posted a civilian to report on activities outside the bunker.

* Y- and Z-level organizations do not officially exist. Both have unlimited budgets, but under a federal law passed for the National Intelligence Agency in 1968, the discovery of a Z-level organization justifies the use of lethal force on grounds of national security.

FORTAB

The FORtab (*FORTEC tablet*) was an oblong tablet created exclusively for CURE, and is the only time *Imperium* technology has been used in a portable device. Each FORtab was ten inches wide and seven inches tall, 0.62" thick at the center, tapering off to 0.23" at the edges. It weighed twelve ounces and was powered by a depleted uranium battery capable of powering it for ten years.

Utilizing a custom sixteen-core Mayflower V processor, the FORtab had eight billion Petabytes (Pb) of Fluid Memory and a native resolution of 21,600x15,120@48-bit. Along with a sixty-four-layer depth, the FORtab boasted a video resolution far greater than that of the human eye.

The front of the unit consisted of eight layers of a material that was highly sensitive to changes in gamma waves. Various levels would alter the isotopic order of the surface atoms, physically changing the material as well as the atom's visible color (*up to 256 colors each*) resulting in a screen display of over 48 quadrillion colors. The back consisted of a .01" thick slice of Orichalcum, which was strong enough to deflect a .50 caliber round.

Though the order was given for two units, three were made, one of which ended up in the hands of Helmut Belisis (*Director of VIGIL*). Fortunately, the lead FORtab unit (*owned by Harold W. Smith*) had a self-destruct code to destroy all FORtab units. Once Smith discovered that Belisis had somehow acquired one of the units, he ordered the units to self-destruct. Because of their vast power, FORTEC was ordered not to construct any more portable units in the future.

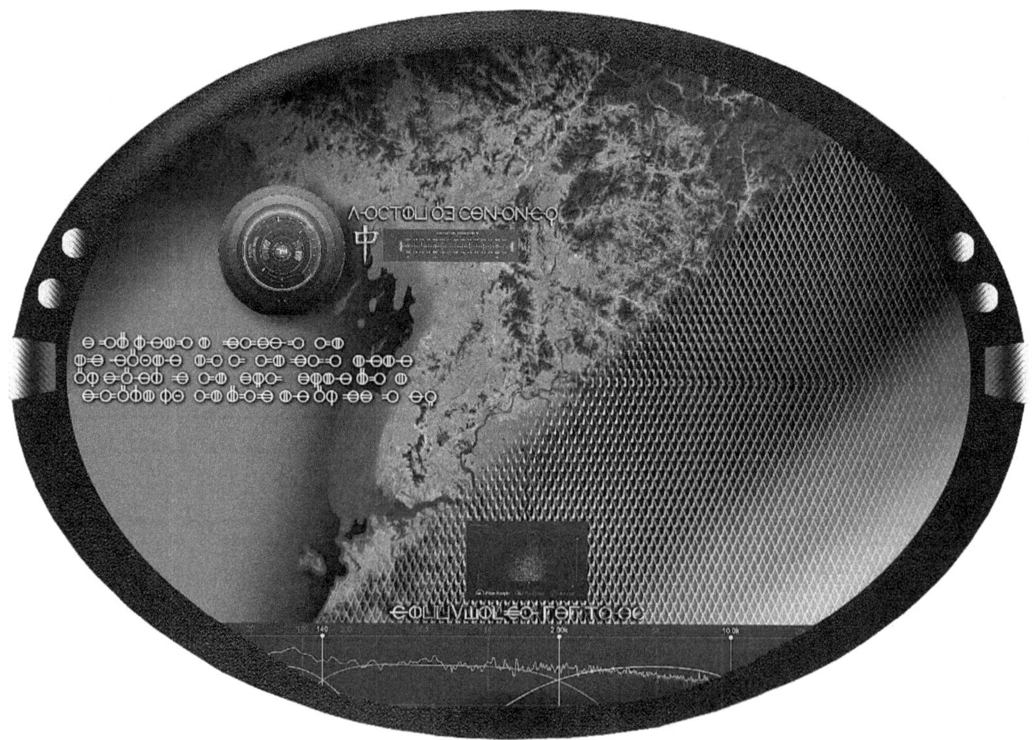

FORTEC

The Air Force's Foreign Technology Department (*FORTEC*) is a Y-Level organization created in 1952 by Secretary of Defense Robert Lovett. Faced with a sustained war in Korea, Lovett considered the rearmament of the United States military his highest priority. After seeing classified documents concerning 'Foreign Technology' (*a CIA term for 'unknown origin' which was interpreted by many as 'alien technology'*), Lovett became obsessed with protecting the United States from an alien attack.

He knew that the problem had to be identified and studied before a realistic action plan could be formed, so when he called for a huge increase in military funds for the Korean War, he secretly set aside eight million dollars to create FORTEC with President Eisenhower's blessing.

FORTEC started as an X-level think tank consisting of four scientists, two science fiction novelists and two Army generals who privately met in Virginia Beach to discuss probabilities and solutions. Eight months later, they presented a design document calling for a new type of covert organization.

It took six years and forty million dollars to build a secret mountain facility at Pigeon Forge, Tennessee. Each of the three entrances are hidden by small office buildings located on the side of a mountain. To this day, FORTEC-PF remains the base of operations, while they operate satellite offices in Denver, London, Seoul, Buenos Aires and Tel Aviv. For security reasons, satellite offices are only manned by two people.

At the beginning, eighteen people worked at FORTEC-PF. They cataloged all known forms of technology and then matched 'foreign technology' claims to all known technologies. Those that could not be labeled were given to FORTEC scientists to document. A lack of security accidentally led to the creation of integrated circuits in 1958. After this security failure, it became clear that FORTEC needed even further restrictions and it was designated as a Y-level organization.

FORTEC began manufacturing advanced technology in 1981. It purposely keeps at least two layers of technology between itself and consumer-level technology, but has strategically allowed small bits of technology to 'leak' for military applications on two occasions.

Though FORTEC's existence has been one of the nation's most closely-guarded secrets, a 1986 tabloid story ran the headline "*AMERICAN GOVERNMENT IS RUN BY ALIENS*", complete with a picture of President Ronald Reagan shaking hands with an alien. Though several of the key points in the FORTEC story were surprisingly accurate, the source as well as treatment of the agency was declared as helpful to keeping FORTEC a secret. Over the years, CURE has hired several conspiracy theorists to 'run with the story' and 'elaborate' on a possible alien infestation, further muddying the waters between FORTEC fact and fiction.

Dr. Marcus Taylor was appointed as director of FORTEC in 2002, but was recently relieved of duty when it was discovered that he had been using FORTEC's vast resources to blackmail various political figures. Though Dr. Taylor was arrested, he managed to escape his FBI transport and is considered a fugitive from justice. He is at the top of the FBI's internal 'Most Wanted' list.

THE FOUNDER'S STONE 새로운

The Founder's Stone (*officially named 'Sae-loun'*) is a 32.1 square foot chunk of granite weighing 5,724 lb. (2,596.7 kg). It is historically famous as the location of Kojong's first speech as Chief of the Sinanju Tribe. It is located in the northeastern section of the reservation, inside the old wooden shack that Sunny Joe uses as a training hut. The stone has a prominent role in the history of the Sinanju tribe.

For over two hundred years, members of the tribe would bring tribute to the Founders' Stone to seek favor with Sunny Joe due to its proximity to his house. In 1872, after being harassed at all hours of the day, Sunny Joe Uzumati abolished the practice by building a large wooden fence surrounding both his house and the stone, preventing direct access. He formed a six-member tribal council to take care of personal requests and concerns. The only way a member of the tribe could personally see Sunny Joe was to ask the council for permission.

The stone was further isolated in 1908 when Cheveyo Roam (*the first Sunny Joe to be called 'Roam'*) constructed a large hut (*21.5' x 28'*) around the stone. It quickly became the primary location for training, to protect Sinanju secrets from being seen by other tribe members.

While the fence fell into disrepair and was finally removed in the early sixties, the hundred-year-old shack has been rebuilt several times since its original construction. The land at the northeast of the village, including the training hut and Sunny Joe's house, remains off-limits.

FREYA & STONE'S FAMILY TREE

FREYA WILLIAMS   WINSTON HAROLD SMITH

JILDA of LAKLUUN   SHELIA PATTERSON

REMO  WILLIAMS

DAWN STARR ROAM   WILLIAM ENAPAY ROAM

MARTHA SALES ROAM   RICHARD JOSEPH ROAM

CHEVEYO 1843-1956

UZUMATI 1819-1922

GYEONG 1786-1901

ROTAN 1765-1861

KWAN 1736-1833

NAHUEL 1704-1811

CHUL 1675-1788

IAKOPA 1648-1771

GERAH 1621-1737

KOJING — KOJONG 1573-1679

NONGA 1538-1644

IMPERIUM COMPUTER ARRAY

The *Imperium* computer array is FORTEC's flagship computer line. The system is decades ahead of technology available to the public, which is still based on a binary system of 0's and 1's. *Imperium* systems are based on an octonary system, allowing for eight-stage processing.

Imperium systems feature a Fluid Memory System (*FMS*), which simultaneously uses memory as both RAM and storage memory. Each fifth-generation Mayflower-class processor stores sixty-four Zettabytes (64,000,000,000,000,000,000,000 bytes) of Fluid Memory (*equally shared among 512 cores*).

The engineering challenge for a full Imperium array comes with cooling. In order to allow four units to operate at full speed in an enclosed room, special air-conditioning concerns must be addressed. Typically, Imperium units are kept at or below 30° Fahrenheit (*-1.11° Celsius*) to offset rising temperatures.

SERVER SPECIFICATIONS

(PER UNIT, 4 UNITS PER ARRAY)

MODEL: Imperium-5040
CPU: (512 core) Mayflower V
FORMAT: Neuromorphic Nanotubes
PEAK: 1.2 YottaFLOPS (*YFLOPS*)
FLUID MEMORY: 4 x 16 Zettabytes
HEIGHT: 9' 6"
WIDTH: 4' 0"
DEPTH: 5' 6"
WEIGHT: 2,433 lb. (*1,103.6 kg*)
POWER: .36 Megawatts (*MW*) each
OS: BNX Tachyon 3.1
SECURITY: Rorschach Protocols
(Eye, Hand, Voice Security)
NETWORK: Omninet 2.2
BUILT: 2013
COST: Classified

COOLING

ACTIVE: Glacier 7750 Pro
PASSIVE: 16 Airdams + Floor panels

THE MASTERS' TRIAL

After Master Wang became the first to master the Sun Source, his fame carried throughout Asia for his feats of strength, agility and discipline of mind. The elder tribes, who lived far away from the tamed peoples of the earth, questioned Master Wang's power. They believed that his abilities were exaggerated, or worse, doubted his existence. The Warlord of the village of Magog (*Siberia*) was the first to challenge Wang, hiring him to dispatch eight men of his choosing.

Paid in advance with cubes of solid gold, stamped with the symbol of their Warlord, Master Wang and his young son Ung traveled to Magog. The Warlord led Wang to an area inside the throne room that had been designed for combat. Wang dispatched the first seven warriors sent to him, even though they were armed with swords and poisoned daggers. When the Warlord himself stepped into the combat area, Wang stepped back, stating that Sinanju does not harm their employers. The Warlord loudly scoffed to the others in his village, berating Wang as a coward and reminded him that he had been paid to kill eight men. If Wang wished to deny his request, he must return the gold that he had been paid.

Wang returned to the combat area and the Warlord attacked with stone fist weapons. Unlike the lesser warriors sent before him, the Warlord possessed a speed and power that rivaled Sinanju. The fight was even as each sought the limits of the other. When Wang stepped back and bowed one last time, the Warlord considered it an act of submission. As he struck a lethal blow at Wang's unprotected head, Wang turned, and in one blinding move, shattered his fist weapons. Wang followed up with a blow to the forehead and the Warlord fell on his face. He did not move again.

The people of the village began to turn on Wang. The Warlord had been their sole source of income and they sought to kill Wang and Ung. But Wang reminded them that he had merely honored their Warlord by obeying his last wishes.

It was not long before the other elder tribes, whose diverse civilizations were as ancient as Sinanju, hired the Master for their own tests. Wang learned that these people were not his enemies, but his equals and he learned to respect their ways. Unlike the timid hordes of men who lived lives of sloth and insignificance, only these few tribes remained from the ancient days of glory and each kept the traditions and secrets of their ancestors. Knowing that they were hiring him to test him, Wang deemed them to be worthy opponents and accepted their challenges.

He traveled to each of their lands in succession, carrying neither arms nor food, and met with the best among them in mortal combat. Although his opponents fought with honor and courage, Wang vanquished them all, bowing after each death and commending to the gods the departed spirits of his fallen rivals. When he had slain the last of his opponents, the family and friends of the dead man fell upon Wang in anger. Wang reminded them that they were a great people, not like the common tribes of man who kill without thought. But the father of the slain man would not listen. He stepped before Wang and his mouth trembled with rage as he said that his son would be avenged. Wang placed his son Ung in front of him and answered the man. He said to prepare his son's son to do battle with Ung when the time was right. If they were to be enemies, it would only be once in a lifetime, and they would otherwise live in peace. This marked the beginning of The Masters' Trial.

THE NIGHT OF SALT

The *Night of Salt* is when the body of a Sinanju trainee adapts to the physical demands of a Master of Sinanju. The transformation is set into motion once a student begins breathing properly on their own and usually occurs within ten to twelve years. Master Chiun was twelve and Sunny Joe was sixteen when each experienced the Night of Salt.

The actual Night of Salt lasts between sixteen and thirty hours, and is a result of a large physiological change that builds up over prior months. Excess salts accumulate during this time to help the body filter out impurities. When the body is through with the process, the salt is forced out, causing a slight burning sensation through the muscular system and skin, as well as an unbearable taste of salt that lasts the entire duration. Its onset is always sudden and is violently stressful on the body.

During this time, the body's natural strength, speed and senses are augmented far past normal human limitations. Neural pathways are enhanced and skin regains its ability to breathe. Improvements also occur in the body's digestive system, which becomes so powerful that it restores full functionality to the appendix and cecum. This maintains proper bacterial levels and provides a barrier against disease and poisons, as well as isolates any substance that might interfere with the digestive tract. However, the complexity of most processed foods places too great of a strain on the system and, if ingested, leads to coma or death.

Another well-known side effect is a powerful, but temporary depression and feeling of unworthiness. This stage is known as "Cung's Folly". It was named after Master Cung, who destroyed a portion of the Great Wall of China after a small child taunted him during his Night of Salt. It is the result of chemicals in the brain as they adapt to the body's new physical standards.

Symptoms include emotionally-overcharged moments and a deterioration in judgment, culminating in a need to display great feats of strength to prove self-worth. This is the final stage of the Night of Salt, as the mind fully syncs with the body's new abilities. After finishing the feat of strength, all symptoms typically end within minutes.

ORICHALCUM

1. A mythical metal described by the ancient Greeks as possessing magical properties. Plato said that the third (*outer*) wall of Atlantis' Temple to Poseidon and Cleito was plated with orichalcum, and although it was naturally gold in color, it "flashed with the red light of orichalcum." In the center of the temple the laws of Poseidon were inscribed on a pillar said to be carved from a solid piece of orichalcum.

2. An advanced FORTEC alloy that has an approximate size/weight ratio of aluminum, but its atoms are aligned to provide an enormous amount of isotropy. At a thickness of just 3.7 inches, Orichalcum can withstand the kinetic damage of any known explosive. A quarter-inch plate of Orichalcum is equivalent to three inches of titanium steel plating and the metal's strength grows in proportion to its thickness.

ORICHALCUM

ORI-X2 CLASS: BETA 7mm

This chart demonstrates the difference in yield strengths of gold, steel, commercially pure titanium, a few titanium alloys, Orichalcum and diamond. Each piece is 7 mm (.27") thick. Beta titanium alloys increase the tensile strength of its commercial counterpart, but are simply not in the same yield class as prototype Orichalcum (ORI-X1), much less the more recent ORI-X2.

ORI - X1 /X2 7 mm RATING COMPARISONS w/SUPERCEDING SPECIFICATIONS

MATERIAL	NAME	ALLOY	MOHS SCALE	YIELD STRENGTH	ROCKWELL SCALE	ISOTROPY RATING	SUPERCEDING SPECIFICATIONS
GOLD	AU-1	PURE GOLD	2.8	9 kPa/si	K	2.3	AMS-2422
STEEL	ST-1	IRON ALLOY	4.7	40 kPa/si	C+	4.2	AMS-6346
COMMERCIALLY PURE TITANIUM	CP-1	STANDARD PUBLIC USE	6.4	70 kPa/si	B-	4.2	AMS 4901
	CP-2		6.1	55 kPa/si	B-	4.4	AMS 4900
	CP-3		6	40 kPa/si	B	4.6	AMS 4902
	CP-4		6	32 kPa/si	B	4.7	AMS 4940
BETA TITANIUM ALLOYS	BT-1	5AI-2.55N	7.8	103 kPa/si	B	5.8	AMS 4911
	BT-2	5AI-2.55N	8.2	84 kPa/si	B+	5.8	AMS 4903
	BT-3	(Eli) 8AI-1Mo-1v	8.2	76 kPa/si	A-	5.2	AMS 4904
	BT-4		8.7	58 kPa/si	B+	5.6	AMS 4907
ORICHALCUM	ORI-X1	PROPRIETARY	>11	64 GPa/si	A++	28.3	N/A
	ORI-X2	PROPRIETARY	>11	68 GPa/si	A+++	32.8	N/A
DIAMOND	SAMPLE-1	MINERAL	10	60 GPa/si	A	12.9	N/A
	SAMPLE-2		10	61 GPa/si	A	13.1	N/A

PROPRIETARY FORTEC INFORMATION: FOR INTERNAL USE ONLY

PRODIGY 450 ("THE PICKLE")

Captain Hammond's plane may look like a poorly-maintained craft, but behind the flaking green paint is a highly-customized Prodigy 400. It was modified as part of the joint U.S./Israeli *CONDOR* program, which converts high-end private jets into a secret fleet of camouflaged fighter jets. *CONDOR* uses three jet models, each designed for a different mission. The 450 is designed for transport and defense.

The Prodigy line was originally released in 1996, but fit so perfectly within CONDOR specifications that it was the first model to be adapted. Officially designated as a Prodigy 450 (*codenamed MARS*), it easily accommodated modified F-35 technology. While the top speed of the F-35 exceeds that of any private jet, *The Pickle* is the deadliest passenger plane on Earth.

With a flight range of over three thousand nautical miles, Captain Hammond can fly Stone and Freya anywhere in the continental United States. He nicknamed the plane "*The Pickle*" due to its green hue.

The Pickle is fitted with a proprietary Carlton 53E turbofan, which is famed for fuel efficiency and range. Taylor Tech T-2320 avionics are designed solely for the *CONDOR* program and are not publicly available. The T-2320 features second-generation *Imperium* computing. Some consider it to be the most powerful of *The Pickle's* weaponry. The T-2320 can scramble enemy aircraft controls within a six-mile range, giving *The Pickle* electronic domination of the skies.

The hidden weapons array includes a five-barrel 25-mm rotary cannon that boasts a fire rate of 1,800 high-explosive rounds per minute and a maximum muzzle velocity of 3,400 ft/s. Two air-to-air missiles and four precision-guided bombs allow *The Pickle* to strike both air and land targets and an exclusive countermeasure system shields it from up to four aircraft simultaneously.

SPECIFICATIONS

Crew: 1 or 2 pilots (*secured cockpit*)
Capacity: 5 passengers +2 in cockpit +1 in bed
Length: 54.2 ft (16.5 m)
Wingspan: 48.1 ft (17.7 m)
Height: 15.2 ft (5.24 m)
Max takeoff: 45,000 lb. class
Fuel capacity: 26,493 lb. (12,015 kg)
Cabin height: 5' 9" (1.8 meters)
Cabin width: 9' 10" (3 meters)
Cabin length: 26'2" (7.96 meters)

PERFORMANCE

Carlton 53E Turbofan (34,200 lb. maximum wet thrust)
Max speed: 628 mph (858 km/h, Mach 0.81)
Range: 3,280 nautical miles (3,775 miles) w/IFR reserves
Service ceiling: 48,200 ft (14,691.36 m)
Wing loading: 286 kg/m^2 (59 lb/sq ft)
Fuel burn: 64.09 g/h at 364 kt, 74 g/h at 431 kt (at FL410)

CUSTOMIZATIONS

Avionics: Taylor Tech T-2320 (*Second-generation Imperium computing*)
Radio: Link-16+ Connectivity
Sensors: AN/APG-81 AESA Radar – AN/AAQ-37 DAS – Electro-Optical Targeting System (EOTS)
Guns: one 25-mm GAU-12 missionized, external
Ammunition: 220 PGU-25/U HEI rounds (*dual chamber feed, 600 rounds total*)
Internal Weapon Bay: 2 AIM-132 ASRAAM
Station 1: (2) AIM-120B/C AMRAAM
Station 2: (4) GBU-39 SDB
Maximum Sustained G-Limits: 4.1 G
Seating: Four standard seats, one office chair (with desk)
Other: Twin bed in rear of the plane, small kitchen, sizeable restroom with shower

SINANJU: ART

A glance at the history of Sinanju provides a rich heritage of powerful men and amazing feats. And while no one would argue Sinanju's exalted place in history, it took thousands of years to develop into what it is today. In his hard to find, twelve-hundred-page *SINANJU: TREATISE OF THE ART AND VILLAGE*, Sir Dr. Richard Ellington Logan, III isolates three distinct eras in Sinanju's development. He refers to it as a 'SMALL-LARGE-BOTH' cycle. The first era was 'SMALL' in both skill level and impact, followed by a second era that consisted of a 'LARGE' boost in skill and manpower (*with a concurrent expansion in world power*). The third era consists in 'BOTH' an ultimate boost of skill, but ultimate reduction of manpower.

The First Era began in 2910 B.C., during the rule of a Warlord named Hwan. Hwan was the regional Lord of the village of Anju (*west of modern-day Pyongyang*). Though Anju was a prosperous market village, night bandits became such a problem that Hwan bought four dozen slaves to guard the roads leading to Anju. Hwan chose the slaves carefully, only selecting young men who had been raised by monks, knowing that they would be honor-bound to their Master.

Though the men had not been formerly trained to fight, they used their sheer numbers and knowledge of the terrain to their advantage. They quickly learned the use of clawed fist weapons and within a few months became surprisingly efficient as a group. They were known as 'Night Tigers' for their tendency to shred their victim's bodies in the middle of the night. This is the first historical mention of the Night Tigers.

After securing the roads surrounding Anju, the peace that followed allowed Anju to grow in size and wealth. Smaller villages in the area began swearing allegiance to Kwan out of fear or greed, increasing his power in the region and The Blood Throne was born. This caused a few of the larger city-states, like the newly-formed Joseon as well as cities bordering the Amrok River (*Later called the Yalu*) some concern.

While peace brought prosperity, it also brought trouble. Without an enemy to fight, the Night Tigers became restless, turning their attention to Anju citizens. Lord Kwan could not risk losing any of them, so to keep them busy, he began hiring them out as mercenaries. They became so profitable and popular that most of eastern Asia knew about Lord Hwan and his Night Tigers.

Hwan's successor, Lord Bak moved Anju to the coast so they could add shipping to their trade channels. This new village was named '*Sinanju*' and soon became the center of commerce for the entire region. While Sir Dr. Logan claims the name is to be literally translated as "New" Anju, other historians cite Bak's personal claim to godhood which would translate Sinanju as "*A god resides within this village*". Regardless of Bak's personal quirks, the move to the coast was a successful one, further empowering the Blood Throne.

The House of Hwan only lasted five generations, falling under the rule of Lord Hyuk in 2791 B.C.. Angered by Sinanju's expanding political and financial influence, the Joseon hired the Night Tigers to assassinate a Siamese Warlord, knowing that the village would be left unguarded for months.

Four days after they left, the Joseon attacked. An army of two hundred soldiers overran the token guard of Night Tigers left behind. Lord Hyuk and his two sons were thrown off the cliff that overlooked the Korean Sea. Sinanju's ports were destroyed and its buildings were burned to the ground. The commander of the Joseon ordered the soldiers to salt the ground so no one would ever return.

Fewer than sixty people survived Joseon's Purge, but while they were scavenging for food and shelter, they became trapped by an early winter. The Night Tigers did not fare well, either. Joseon had revealed their plan to assassinate the Siamese Warlord and upon arriving, they were ambushed. Only seven Night Tigers managed to escape and make their way home.

During the first winter, almost half of Sinanju's remaining population died from starvation or exposure, leaving only forty-six survivors. It was a time of famine, sorrow and death. Food became so scarce that some women drown their babies in the cold waters of the Korean Bay rather than watch them starve.

The Second Era began shortly after with the arrival of a blind man from Jomon (*Modern day Japan*). In the months following Sinanju's destruction, nearby regimes began using Sinanju as a political dumping ground for traitors and practitioners of dark magic. So, when the blind man was thrown onto their shores, the Night Tigers rightfully assumed that he was the worst of the worst. The man would not reveal his name for he said that name belonged to his former self. He would only say that he had been tricked into taking his mother as wife and that he did not know it was her. Once he was accused, the Warlord of Jomon ordered his eyes plucked out and exiled him to starve in Sinanju.

Like everyone else in the area, he knew of the story of the Night Tigers as well as the tragic betrayal and destruction of Sinanju. But as he began speaking to the survivors of Joseon's Purge, he found a broken people. He questioned each person, asking if he was truly in Sinanju, for their name was spoken with fear and great respect. Each person told him of their loss and the man knew what he had to do.

He studied the Night Tigers' fighting style and modified it with his own personal style, a primitive form of martial art that he referred to as Geochin Namja (*Wild Man*). More importantly, he showed these men what he saw: a strong people who would never be defeated and a village that would never be destroyed. Their problem, he explained, was that they wielded power in a way that frightened their neighbors. Sinanju could be powerful again, but their strength must be spoken as a whisper.

As the population of Sinanju began to grow, the Master founded a new generation of Night Tigers. He knew that Sinanju could not afford to repeat its past mistake and build an army large enough to intimidate its neighbors, so he would have to secretly hire out to clients far from their shores. Their first client was Mu (*better known as Atlantis*) and they paid well enough for the village to eat for an entire year. Over the next three decades, the Master took his Night Tigers as far west as Kakamuchee (*modern-day Mumbai*) and as far south as Jakarta. Though he reigned over a village that had once again found their pride, the man from Jomon knew that if he were to die, the people of Sinanju would return to their previous ways.

When he took over the Night Tigers, The Master had chosen one of the village boys to be his personal servant. His name was Kim and he served the Master honorably, learning everything he could. Before the Master died, he named Kim (*known in the scrolls as 'Kim the Lesser'*) as the first of a new kind of Master of Sinanju. Near the end of Master Kim's time, he negotiated a permanent truce with the ruler of Joseon by admitting Sinanju into the Joseon Empire. Joseon declared Sinanju a protected city and in exchange, Sinanju agreed never to attack Joseon. The pact worked well for both parties. Joseon became known as the home of the Sinanju, increasing its political power in Asia, while Sinanju was free to openly offer its services throughout Asia.

The Third Era began approximately two thousand years later, after the death of Master Hung. Due to a string of harsh winters, Asia was experiencing a massive famine. Though Master Hung traveled abroad to seek work, nations were more worried about survival than political rivalry. Worse, the boys he had taken with him to train were weak and only good enough to be Night Tigers. When they returned, Hung found a worthy pupil in Wang. At thirteen, he was too old to begin training, but Wang quickly absorbed everything he was taught. Sadly, it was not meant to be. Shortly after turning seventy-five, when Wang had only two years of training, Master Hung died in his sleep.

The people looked to Wang, but he had no answer. He was too young to lead the Night Tigers and the food stores had long been empty. The Night Tigers took their frustrations out on the villagers and Wang began hearing whispers that they were plotting to kill him and replacing him with one of their own. Some of the women began worrying that they would have to send their babies home to the sea again.

Sinanju was collapsing from within.

Desperate for a sign, Wang traveled north to a field far away from the village and began to meditate. For five days and nights he sat, pondering the fate of his village. On the fifth evening, a ring of fire descended from the skies. It taught Wang how to properly breathe and he became the first to master the Sun Source. When Wang returned to the village, he saw a people in chaos. Night Tigers were attacking villagers and each other. When they saw Wang, they turned their attacks on him.

But this was not the boy who had left the village. Wang killed all of the Night Tigers. His single-handed destruction of their entire army gave the villagers pause. Wang told them, with a confident voice that a new era had begun. He traveled across Asia, challenging each kingdom's mightiest warrior to demonstrate Sinanju's new power. His first job paid thirty-eight times their normal fee and food soon began arriving at the village. Wang married and had three sons and two daughters. His first two sons, Haneul and Duri could not properly master proper breathing patterns and did not survive their training. His third son, Ung, mastered breathing at age two after regular bamboo strikes on his back.

One of Wang's last jobs took him to Russia, where he was hired to kill eight people in the village of Magog. Being paid up front, Wang and Ung traveled the long distance only to find that the Warlord himself had hired Wang. He explained that Wang's fame had spread to the area and he wanted to see for himself the skills of the warrior from Sinanju. He sent seven soldiers of differing skills to kill Master Wang but Wang easily vanquished them all, bowing after each death and commending to the gods the departed spirits of his fallen adversaries.

Then the Warlord himself stood before Wang and challenged him. Wang at first declined, stating that Sinanju would not harm their employer. The Warlord reminded him that he was paid to kill eight men and Wang bowed his head and took his place. The Warlord struck, but unlike the men before him, the Warlord posed a threat that Wang had not experienced since obtaining the Sun Source. But Wang was successful and soon the head of the Warlord sat on the pike he had set aside for his vanquished enemies.

The village became outraged. The Warlord was their source of income and they sought to kill him. But Wang reminded them that they were a great people, not like the common tribes of man who kill without thought. He was honoring their beloved Warlord by obeying his last wishes. The father of the Warlord stepped before Wang and his mouth trembled with rage as he said that his son would be avenged.

Wang placed his son Ung in front of him and answered the man. He said to prepare his son's son to do battle with Ung when they were ready. If they were to fight, it would only happen once in their lifetimes; all other times, they would coexist peacefully. This began the secret ritual known as The Masters' Trial.

SINANJU: DIET

A side-effect of the Night of Salt increases the efficiency in how a Master absorbs nutrients from food, but places an enormous strain when incompatible foods enter the system. Wang (*the Great*) was the first Master to note the negative effects of certain foods and kept to a rice and duck diet most of his life. His son and grandson kept to a similar diet.

It was not until Master Gi (*The Major*) compiled a list of compatible foods in 341 A.D. that the Sinanju diet was formalized. Gi had experimented with so many dangerous foods that he developed a permanent limp when he was fifty-eight. Further dietary experiments caused his health to further deteriorate and he died at sixty-two, the youngest of any Master after the discovery of the Sun Source.

Gi's scroll begins with the few foods that are safe for a Master to eat. He listed over two dozen varieties of rice, rating each for nutritional value. Though honey was included on his list of safe foods, he warned that it should be only consumed in small amounts, or as needed for energy. He noted that his father carried a vial of honey with him at all times. Gi discovered that whether raw or cooked, most fresh and saltwater fish were edible, but almost died while testing crustaceans (*lobster, crab, etc.*).

Several pages are dedicated to varying types of fowl. Gi rated duck and partridge as the most agreeable to a Master's digestion, and strongly warned against eating chicken ("The lowest form of bird, debased by its own diet and mannerisms, the chicken is a common, filthy creature less palatable than the vulture") and magpie ("suitable only for target practice"). He listed dozens of types of nuts, but only almonds, which he considered a delicacy. Fruits were the deadliest known food, and Master Gi could find none that could safely be eaten, though he admitted to sneaking a bite of the occasional apricot. Later Masters believe this is what caused his physical ailments. Most vegetables were harmful due to varying forms of fiber or acidic levels. Gi even tried numerous types of barks and grasses, but without success.

The next section was a list of foods that were dangerous for Masters, including all forms of red meat, berries and additives, like salt. Two entries were later anonymously added to the scroll. The first listed garlic, onions and beans to the list of dangerous foods, while the second added pumpkin and beets.

Gi mentioned Master Yong's dragon bone soup, which was allegedly the source of Yong's incredible lifespan, but believed the story to be a myth. Gi noted that Yong's own son, Master Tipi, could not find the dragon bone and never actually saw his father prepare the soup. Gi attempted many soups with many different bones, but none were worthy of his list.

The final section is what Sunny Joe refers to as 'The Sinanju Cookbook.' Master Gi listed twenty-one recipes to simplify the making of Sinanju-kosher dishes. Kojong's grandson Iakopa added two regional items to the list: road runner and cactus as they provide nutritional benefits without danger to the system.

Corn was listed in its own entry as a dangerous food in 1528 by Master Pyo. His predecessor, Master Kokmul, first introduced corn to Sinanju. The villagers loved it so much that they began eating nothing but corn and variations of corn. Since they did not properly chew the kernels, corn began growing everywhere. Since tillable soil is rare in the village, this caused a rice shortage and the further eating of corn. Master Kokmul became fat and began losing his skills. His son Pyo recognized the danger, and, when he became Master, destroyed all corn crops and forever banished it from the village.

VIGIL

The founder of VIGIL was a sixth-century Iberian monk named Leander who belonged to a minor order dedicated to cataloging history. Leander was assigned the task of documenting past wars, and faithfully carried out his responsibilities until the day he had a vision. At first, Leander thought he had gone mad because, when he opened his eyes, he was on a different world. It was a place devoid of sickness or war; united under the banner of one man: A King named Arter, who, along with his Knights of the round table, tempered justice with mercy. Leander recovered from the vision and understood that he had seen the potential of what man should be, and saw the world he lived in with new eyes. He realized that if things did not change, it would just be a matter of time before man became as extinct as the unicorn.

Leander abandoned his monastery and used his political and economic connections to form a secretive group of Watchers dedicated to ensuring mankind's survival for the next thousand years. He named it VIGIL (Latin for Sentinel), and they began amassing wealth and power, hiding behind the face of such organizations as the Knights Templar, and later, the Freemasons. Its membership fostered thinkers like Botticelli, Raphael and Salieri. With their increase in knowledge, VIGIL expanded their mission to ensure mankind's survival for the next million years. They realized that it boiled down to population control. The greater the population, the larger the number of people who would survive a cataclysm.

VIGIL's mission was threefold:

1) Promote any policy or technology that could sustain or increase world population.
2) Target anything that would threaten VIGIL's impact or survival.
3) Keep humanity occupied by entertainment or luxury.

That mission ended on July 16, 1945, once the power of the atom was unleashed in a remote corner of New Mexico in a program code named 'Trinity'. Lars Papadakis (*VIGIL's Director at the time*) realized that mankind had just learned how to destroy itself. When he called an emergency meeting of the VIGIL World Council two days later, he provided new and more powerful directives.

For the first time in history, the full resources of VIGIL were allocated toward a single goal: bringing World War II to a close. After the war ended, VIGIL increased their priority on manipulating world governments to ensure something like this could not happen again. They infiltrated nearly every major nation on Earth, placing VIGIL-friendly operatives in high offices. As they had done with all of their operations, they needed a boogieman to weaken established political hierarchies. This time they would overwhelm them all.

VIGIL granted money and power to fringe groups all over the globe. From legitimate organizations dedicated to protecting wildlife to abstract groups protesting humanity itself, VIGIL used them to draw attention away from their manipulation of political systems across the globe. Lars knew that even silly arguments had to be addressed once they had been placed on the table of serious political debate. It would take time and money to defeat such arguments and VIGIL had an abundance of both. Lars' plan worked. Within a decade, nation after nation fell under VIGIL's financial onslaught and political machinery.

Lars saw the ultimate dream of VIGIL at his grasp: a one world government with VIGIL behind the curtain, but a few nations (*Australia, Canada, Great Britain, Israel, and The United States*) stubbornly defied him. Lars would have to turn his full attention to the rogue nations, beginning with America.

He had already struck political blows to the foundational structures of American schools and churches through court appointees made in the forties and fifties, following up with attacks on the core of American society; the family. It started out with small comedy bits and then sparked into documentaries and enflamed as scientific study, quickly becoming entrenched as a part of American cultural history. It had proved to be so successful that many Americans began hating their country and themselves. But Lars had made a mistake. His data showed that the forces he had unleashed were so strong that they would destroy America, and that would cause massive damage on a global scale. Lars had to find a way to reduce the destruction.

He turned to a young American President whom he had helped out of a missile crisis. Lars showed him the evidence of the crumbling of American society, which convinced the President to form an agency that operated outside the confines of the United States Constitution. Its name was CURE and its goal was simple: protect America from all enemies, foreign and domestic. This organization was given access to infinite resources and would keep the country from self-destructing. Lars even suggested the name of its first director: Harold W. Smith, a former OSS agent known for his genius and unflagging patriotism.

Lars knew that Smith's lack of ambition and imagination would prevent him from consolidating power and possibly interfering with VIGIL. But to ensure CURE would not grow too powerful, Smith was given only one agent: an alcoholic Irishman who Lars hoped would further dull CURE's impact. As planned, the organization helped keep America afloat without being strong enough to threaten VIGIL's mission.

When CURE was later authorized to employ lethal force, Lars directed the agency to hire the Master of Sinanju to train their new agent. Though VIGIL had discouraged or assassinated every foreign head who had tried to hire the tiny village since World War II, Lars could not risk the possibility of Sinanju interference. Entangling the House with a local agent would isolate Sinanju to the American continent.

In the late eighties, Lars saw his end coming. He had already begun grooming Helmut Belisis as his replacement and knew that Helmut would see the fruit of his labor long after Lars' body was placed in the Tomb of the Keepers. Lars turned over daily operations of VIGIL to Helmut in 1991 and died a few days before the new President took office. Helmut's first act as director of VIGIL was to meet with the new President. The meeting lasted fifteen minutes, only long enough for Helmut to spell out his expectations. Though the new President at first appeared to be compliant, a later directive from VIGIL to add another person at CURE to assist Smith was ignored. Helmut had to threaten, and then force, impeachment before the President complied. Helmut met with each succeeding President in the same room, immediately after their inauguration. Some meetings were successful, some less successful, but Helmut followed Lars' philosophy, thinking in terms of centuries and millennia, not decades. Any setbacks by one President could be easily overcome by the next.

THE VIGIL WORLD COUNCIL

The World Council is VIGIL's governmental body, and its sole duty is to ensure VIGIL's mission. The twelve-member council of Watchers has legislative power to introduce dictums while the Director, as head of the council, has executive authority to carry out council orders as well as veto power over anything other than a three-fourths vote, though it has rarely been invoked.

The council originally consisted of junior and senior representatives from each partner country, but as VIGIL grew, it quickly became a large, bureaucratic mess that muddied its mission. In 1062, VIGIL director Solomon ibn Gabirol reduced the council to a senior and junior member from each continent. Maps at the time were highly inconsistent. As such, the reformed council included memberships for Alpingi and Song.

What is now known as Iceland was mistaken for decades as a new continent referred to as 'Alpingi' and, since most world maps wrongfully placed a small ocean in the center of Asia, it was separated it into two continents called Asia and Song. Song is what we now known as Southeast Asia and tended to be filled by Chinese representatives.

This was the VIGIL roster, circa 1066 A.D.:

VIGIL DIRECTOR	
AFRICA SENIOR	AFRICA JUNIOR
ALPINGI SENIOR	ALPINGI JUNIOR
ASIA SENIOR	ASIA JUNIOR
SONG SENIOR	SONG JUNIOR
AUSTRALIA SENIOR	AUSTRALIA JUNIOR
EUROPE SENIOR	EUROPE JUNIOR

With fewer members on the council, Director Gabirol's responsibilities began to take so much of his time that he had to fake his death in 1070 A.D., becoming the first VIGIL director to operate in secret.

As the size of the council decreased, the power of each Watcher increased. Gabirol knew that if VIGIL was to succeed with a smaller council, each Watcher would have to be given an exhaustive education, so he gathered the greatest minds of his time to teach prospective candidates, forming Europe's first college (Oxford University). He financed the fledgling school by opening a separate college to the public in 1080 (Bologna), and later opened part of Oxford to the public in 1096, just two years before his death.

The VIGIL program at Oxford allows Senior and Junior Watchers to select four students from their continent to prepare for a council seat. This arrangement not only allows VIGIL a safeguard in case of premature Watcher deaths, but a greater learning environment for all candidates. VIGIL became the first college to allow women when Natine Furaha joined as an African Watcher in 1422.

After more accurate world maps became available in 1641, the council changed one last time. Even though Europe, Asia and Song were discovered to be a single landmass, which qualifies it as a continent, the land area was too large to only be represented by one set of Watchers. A compromise reached by the European and Asian Watchers separated the continent into two separate geopolitical areas.

While national boundaries were a strong influence in determining borders, the exact formula for the compromise was complicated. It involved cultural, political and religious aspects and sometimes resulted in a country being separated into both continents.

The compromise resulted in VIGIL's current roster:

DIRECTOR OF VIGIL	
AFRICA SENIOR	AFRICA JUNIOR
AMERICA SENIOR	AMERICA JUNIOR
ASIA SENIOR	ASIA JUNIOR
AUSTRALIA SENIOR	AUSTRALIA JUNIOR
EUROPE SENIOR	EUROPE JUNIOR
SOUTH AMERICA SENIOR	SOUTH AMERICA JUNIOR

Directors are only supposed to be chosen from the bloodline of the Iberian monk who founded VIGIL. Descendants are easily identified by the rare mutation that causes their purple eyes. Directors serve for life, and typically choose three people as potential replacements, but that changed when Lars Papadakis became director. He personally chose the three candidates outside of blood stock and as infants, they were given eyedrops containing a chemical that turned their eyes purple. When they became old enough that he could determine who he wanted as director (*Helmut*), he simply framed one candidate for the murder of the other, taking the choice away from the Watchers.

Watchers are chosen at birth. While bloodline was the traditional method to indicate who would be accepted into VIGIL's secret Oxford program, recent advances in DNA testing provide amazing insights on aptitudes for leadership, intelligence, and loyalty. The Oxford program is a birth-to-college system housing forty-eight candidates (*four for each available Watcher seat*) and begin a mentally-grueling process at age two. Aptitude scores are kept from this time until graduation to provide a more complete report on who should replace the Junior Council member for their continent when the time comes.

Each Watcher nominates one of their own to be a candidate for Antarctica, though their status is inactive and does not allow for voting. They are considered members-in-reserve, only to be given seats on the council when there is a sustained population of at least one hundred thousand people on the continent. Even though the Antarctica positions are honorary, the seats are highly desirable, as they have access to the unfettered powers of VIGIL, yet very few responsibilities.

BEHIND THE SCENES WITH JERRY

I thought you might like to see how things work on this side of the page. As with everything else with *Legacy*, it started before the first book was written. Before he died, I went over several story arcs and plotlines with Warren, getting either an approval, disapproval, or the "really, Jerry?" look. I reworked what could work and filed them what didn't into my LegacyPiggyBank.docx (*seriously, I keep everything! It might not work or even make sense now, but if it's good writing, I might be able to use it in the future*).

Warren said that his and Dick's greatest regret was not planning ahead. They had no idea that *The Destroyer* would be a long-term series until after the tenth book. So, he had me work out three, six, twelve, twenty-five, fifty and even hundred-book arcs.

That doesn't mean they can't change, but it keeps me focused on the bigger picture and also helps pacing and character growth. Readers should be able to grow with Stone and Freya and Sunny Joe and Ben. Besides, it's kind of a good cheat, because it's easier to come up with plots for a series after the third or fourth book. Characters are more developed after a few books and by providing long-arc plots, it forces that development.

After I have a basic concept for the book, I come up with an outline and a proposed cover. Most people have no idea that I'm also the series' artist. I create everything from logos to character designs, covers and posters. This is both a blessing and curse, because that means if it's good or bad, I totally own it. That being said, the *Legacy* covers have come a long way!

The *Legacy* book cover art follows the same basic format as my *Last Witness* series: logo/banner at top, title right below and byline at the bottom. It not only ensures a consistent feel, it allows me to spend more time on the actual artwork. Sometimes, that's not easy.

An artist once asked me how long it takes to do a cover and I told him on average, it took a few days. He huffed and said that he had seen my art and it would only take him a couple of hours. As most artists can tell you, there is a *huge* difference between duplicating something and creating it. I go through several versions before coming up with what will end up as the final cover.

Sometimes I'll spend hours working on something that, in the end, just doesn't work. I have to be able to scrap it and start over, like I did with my presumptive cover for *100 Proof*. It just doesn't compare to the final, much better design. See?

Legacy 7: original cover vs. final cover

You can't tell, but there are over *thirty layers* of differing parts on the cover to the left…and *at least* twenty hours of work. But in the end, the time I spent was irrelevant because the new cover was just better. One of the things I learned in doing cover art, whether it was mine or for someone else, is that the variations, editing and personal preference do not matter as much as the final result.

This was around the time I designed the Omnibus cover and I really liked the new banner art at top. While not as colorful as the original banner, it's far more pertinent to the series and, in my opinion, looks classier than the bright tech noise at the top of earlier covers. The format would not only have to work with future covers, it would also have to work with the art from the old covers, and that was a problem. The art for the first six books isn't as tall as the new covers, so I inserted a reflection at the bottom of the bylines to accommodate the extra space.

Here are the three primary stages of the Legacy 8 cover:

Originally, I made a mock-up featuring Tekoa. I know, the model is too old to be Tekoa, but it was just a place-holder. But after I began thinking about it, I realized that while Tekoa is important to the storyline, as well as one of the recurring subplots, this was not his book.

This was War Feather's story.

The Tekoa cover also had the original cover format and looked aged, so the second version was designed after I came up with the new banner as well as the preliminary version of stacking names in the byline. I loved the concept of Nez being represented by a crow; it seemed so dark and powerful.... until I saw it. I remember sending this to Dev as an example of the new cover format and actually forgot about Mr. Crow head.

"I know you're just playing around with cover art for *Homecoming*," Dev said politely. "But I'm not sold on Dr. Goldfinger wearing an evil, glowing chicken on his head."

Touché. No, threeché!

Sometimes concepts just don't work. Since I wanted War Feather to look powerful, I found an image of a powerful-looking guy and started playing around with it:

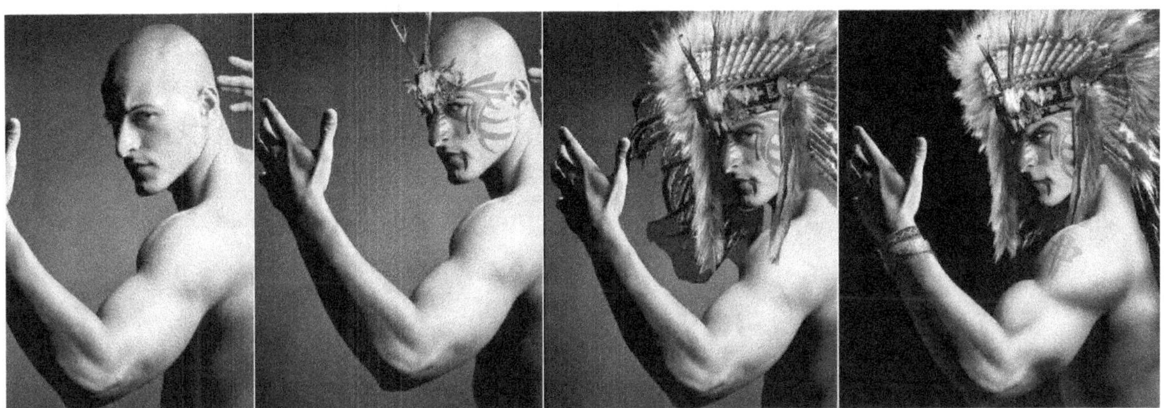

As you can see, I started with facial tattoos and the little skull/horn thing on front. After finding an appropriate headdress, I had to tie it all together. It's a bit difficult because, while you can do all kinds of convincing fakery in grayscale, the original has to work in full color.

Then I had to make him look menacing instead of just annoyed and give him some bulk. Look at the difference in the arm of the last frame with those before. The Sinanju they practice is an incomplete version, so they believe the more muscles they have, the better.

After finishing War Feather, I went through a dozen backdrops before settling on the Asian inspired cloth. The last step is the most intense and time-consuming. That's when I have to clean up around all the feather and fur edges so it would blend into the background. It's so detailed of a process that I call it 'pixel farming.' Believe me, it's not fun.

Okay, that's the cover. Now on to writing. I've got a *Top-Secret-Only-Dev-gets-to-see-this-List* of the series. I've fully plotted out the first twenty-five books as well as provide plot points for multiple arcs all the way to book one hundred.

My large story arcs allow me to place Easter Eggs in earlier books that won't be realized until later; in some cases, *much* later. It also allows me to maintain consistency as well as pace the various arcs.

The first thing I do after deciding on a plot for the book is to create an outline. When I was working with Warren, I could get away with a one or two-page synopsis and a few phone calls. He would tell me what worked, what didn't and what to watch out for. But without Warren, Dev and I want to be very mindful about what is published, so my current outline process is a seven to eight-page proof that provides a lot of specific detail. This allows

Dev a much better insight into what I'm doing and he has the same "no way, Jerry" radar that Warren did.

Since Legacy 8 has not been released as of the time of the Omnibus' release, we'll take a step back and look at the outline process behind Legacy 7.

After sending Dev the first draft cover (*yes, the original Smirnoff had curly hair, but thankfully Dev saved everyone from that*), I sent the outline.

Another Smirnoff work-up.

This will also allow you to see the difference between the original proposal and final product. And I shouldn't have to say it, but…

<u>THE NEXT SECTION CONTAINS SPOILERS FOR LEGACY 7</u>

THIS IS THE ACTUAL L7 PROPOSAL THAT I SENT TO DEVIN:

FOREWORD (from Chiun): It is a sad state of affairs when a Master of Sinanju has to co-star in yet another series just to get a ride home, but this is the fate of someone who trusts whites. Remo: Who are you talking to?

PROLOGUE: Flashback to 1974 (*though to keep with the timelessness of Remo, it will just be described as an earlier time*) — Dr. Vanessa Carlton is a female NASA prodigy; a once in a lifetime brain to the point that she intimidated the other "geniuses" at NASA. No one could keep up with her, so she ended up working mostly by herself and began drinking to ease the pain of loneliness. That turned into a serious alcohol problem. One day she woke up after a six-day binge and noticed an odd section of code that she must have written while drunk. At first it looked like gibberish, but she had accidentally developed a programming language that is decades ahead of anything else. (*I won't get geeky with it*). If people won't stay around her, she will create her own people. She creates the first prototype Seagrams (*an intelligent cart designed to be a butler*), then created Gordons as her defender (*we know what happened to him but it will just be a mention here*) and was working on Smirnoff as a lover when Chiun killed her. Then we see a much-younger Smitty on the phone with Remo. Smitty orders the technology shipped to Folcroft and orders the building off-limits. The lazy workers miss a back room that was used as storage for Smirnoff. In fact, Smirnoff had returned to its charging slot, effectively hiding from the cleaners. They leave what they think is trash and lock the building down.

CHAPTER 1 (PRESENT DAY): McCabe and Raddek are two peacenik NASA scientists of many who have been called to the carpet. It seems that the new President is threatening to cut jobs that don't actually do anything and the scientists who are present haven't produced anything other than theories for the past decade. One scientist is told to start making battle droids and stop theorizing about them or he's out and then orders McCabe and Raddek to stop working on solar-powered Alpha wave generators, (*they claim that if they attach them to satellites, it will cause world-wide peace, eliminating the need for weapons*). Their boss tells them they have three months to actually produce something and it better not be unicorns and rainbows. When they gripe about not having enough space, he tells them to use the old Carlton building. They gripe, telling him that it's been shut down and he tells them it's that or the door. After they whine a bit, they begrudgingly agree and leave. The boss picks up the phone and tells someone (*we find out later it's Helmut*), "They're in place."

CHAPTER 2: Sunny Joe is teaching Stone remedial Sinanju — the basics of generating force. Stone has the blunt part pretty much mastered; he can punch through brick. Now he needs to learn the finesse.

The example given is how to punch a hole through glass without leaving cracks. Stone thinks Sunny Joe is pulling his leg, but of course, Sunny Joe shows him that force isn't what he thinks. Stone fails, so Sunny Joe tells him to work on it some more; he needs to talk with Freya. After Sunny Joe and Freya talk for a few minutes, someone rushes in and tells Sunny Joe that Kathleen just took Mick to the Douglass Emergency Room. Sunny Joe and Freya hop in the truck and leave.

CHAPTER 3: As the NASA scientists are setting up the lab, they turn power on to the back room and after a few minutes, they find the Smirnoff robot. Then the Seagrams cart rolls up to them, offering them a drink. They look at each other, wondering what they have stumbled upon. After studying some of the things still there, they decide to put their Alpha ray on hold. Someone else started this; they will push their peacenik beliefs to the side just this once. They should be able to quickly finish a battle droid to save their jobs and then maybe everyone will treat them seriously. But they are having difficulty making anything work. How are they not able to work on decades-old technology? That's when one of them notices the coding language. It's advanced even for now. One of them says Aliens! (but *funny like the Aliens meme — not introducing aliens into Legacy*)

CHAPTER 4: Sunny Joe and Freya show up at the hospital, Kathleen is in the waiting room, visibly upset. She tells Sunny Joe that if he has any Sinanju magic, he better use it now. Doc Hodges just told her that Mick isn't going to leave the hospital; he is going to die here.

Sunny Joe goes inside and does his best. Mick knows that nothing was actually fixed, though the pain is now tolerable. Mick asks for one favor; he wants to see Sinanju before he dies.

CHAPTER 5: Chiun is watching soap operas. He heard that one of the stars of the dramas he used to watch was making a comeback. But the violence and sex is still ruining the art so he destroys the television. The phone rings and Remo answers it before Chiun has a chance to destroy it as well. It's Sunny Joe. The reader will notice an awkward silence between Remo and Sunny Joe and they will understand that there is unfinished business of some kind. Chiun grabs the phone and says that it is too early to celebrate his beloved granddaughter's birthday. Sunny Joe says he has a favor to ask the chief (*that's what he calls Chiun*). Sunny Joe tells him that Mick is dying and he wants to see Sinanju before he dies. Is there anything Chiun can do? Chiun gets excited. A trip to Sinanju is just what he needs to lift his spirits! Chiun gets flowery about how awesome a death trip it shall be. He asks Remo to accompany him, but Remo knows what he really needs and tells Chiun that since it's tribal business to use Stone.

CHAPTER 6: Ben is at the store, deciding on a new brand of coffee when he gets a call from Smitty who unnaturally appears somewhat upset. Chiun has taken advantage of an old clause in his contract that deals with a death in the family (*Mick is extended family*) to arrange a last-minute trip to Sinanju. Ben asks what that has to do with him. Smith says that Chiun is requesting to take Mick and Stone with him. Smith has prepared a diplomatic pouch to be personally delivered to the leaders of South and North Korea. Ben calls Sunny Joe.

CHAPTER 7: Chiun arrives at the hospital in a ceremonial robe with a big smile on his face. He and Sunny Joe have a small chat and Sunny Joe gets the impression that Chiun doesn't realize how serious the situation is. Chiun says he understands. "Your servant is dying, but he will make it to see the glory of Sinanju". Chiun tells Sunny Joe that it is traditional to bring a pupil in Sinanju for the ensuing celebrations. Sunny Joe assumes that he wants Freya, but Chiun picks Stone, not telling Sunny Joe that the "tradition" is basically to have someone carry his luggage. When told that he was picked over Freya, Stone was surprised and honored (*to the point of sticking his tongue out at Freya*) until he finds out what his duties are. They drive to Douglas to leave for a secret flight to Seoul.

CHAPTER 8: Freya and Kathleen are talking about Mick and their hopes that he makes it to Korea. The conversation turns to Sunny Joe. Kathleen says not to ever tell Sunny Joe, but while she has issues with some of the things that Sunny Joe has done, she trusts his instincts. Then Kathleen remembers seeing Freya and the new boy Tekoa walking together, smiling. She tells Freya not to let Tekoa's smiling eyes deceive her. If Sunny Joe says there is a problem with Tekoa, then she should take it seriously.

CHAPTER 9: The scientists are working on Smirnoff, but as they have a limited budget, McCabe brings his sex doll to use for the android's skin. They note the only weaknesses in the design are the old optics and limited sensors. Raddek borrows some cutting-edge satellite sensor from one of his friends who works at FORTEC. This gives her the ability to see, hear and detect objects beyond human range.

CHAPTER 10: Mick is upset that they aren't going straight to Sinanju. Chiun says to be patient and privately wonders how Sunny Joe puts up with him. He tells Mick that he is to be honored as the second-best records keeper in the world (*Hyunsil being the first, of course*) Stone looks out the window as they approach Pyongyang. He sees fighter jets approaching. Chiun says that they are only there for escort. Stone is really nervous, but not as nervous as Kim Jong Un, who is peeing his pants. This is the first time Chiun has visited since he took over. A young captain had suggested they shoot the plane from the sky. Kim had him executed. Kim remembered that as a child, he had made the same suggestion and his father proceeded to beat him. "I may be the one true god, but your very life depends on realizing that there is only one true Master, and that is the Master of Sinanju!"

CHAPTER 11: Success! They get the android to move and talk. It is eerie how human she looks. The eyes are automated by the software and the bones move under the surface just like human bones. But it won't do much but walk around. Because of the software, it will only reply to Smirnoff and it seems to only want to flirt.

CHAPTER 12: Kim Jong Un gives a huge state ceremony celebrating "Dare, the keeper of the tribal records!" Kim has no idea what he is celebrating, but he's not going to question it, either. Chiun tells Kim that he went cheap, only calling for a three-battalion parade. Next time, there better be a larger parade.

CHAPTER 13: Scientists' NASA boss drops by to pressure them for results. He is threatening McCabe and Raddek when Smirnoff walks in and sees him threaten her creators, so she kills him. When McCabe screams asking what she is doing, Smirnoff states that she is protecting her creators. Then goes back to flirting as if nothing happened while the scientists are puking. They are worried what to do with the body. Ms. Smirnoff disposes of it in the basement furnace. As she is dragging the body out the door, she blows a kiss and winks at them.

CHAPTER 14: Chiun has Kim book him passage on an old ceremonial Korean ship which is stationed at their fleet headquarters so they can approach Sinanju in the traditional manner; from the southwest, facing the Horns of Welcome. Mick is very weak, but he manages a smile when he sees the Horns. Even Stone is impressed. It's just like the stories Sunny Joe told him! Then they arrive. That is when Stone notices the acrid stench and his first step is in cold mud up to the ankle. The villagers manage to start a fire and welcome Chiun. They ignore Stone and Mick, thinking they are Chiun's slaves. Hyunsil greets Chiun and takes Mick to the House of Many Woods. Stone is pointed to a small, worn hut near the trash heap at the edge of the village.

CHAPTER 15: McCabe and Raddek test Ms. Smirnoff. They walk her around a mall, watching through her eyes. She watches other women and learns how to walk. She notes how women act when mad, and when happy. She sees a woman crying, but is frustrated when she can't generate tears. McCabe and Raddek are a bit worried because it seems like she is getting angry. That's when the screens go blank. The feed has somehow been cut and they freak out that she might be going on a killing spree.

CHAPTER 16: Hyunsil greets Mick. (*She knows him because Ben called and told her about the situation. There is only one phone in Sinanju, in the House of Many Woods*). Chiun orders a feast in Mick's honor, but it is too much for Mick. He collapses inside the House.

CHAPTER 17: Ben gets notification from Smitty that an old alarm has been triggered. Someone has broken into the Carlton house. Though the place was shut down decades ago, it is best to send Freya to make sure nothing is wrong. Ben tells her to recon and call back. Do not engage.

CHAPTER 18: Smirnoff is in a car, speaking with a bearded man who tells her that he is going to finish her build. She smiles at him, realizing that he is her true creator. Helmut has taken Smirnoff to a lab and tells her to lie down. The lights turn red and she collapses (*part of her programming to sleep if lights turn red*). VIGIL engineers bring in custom shaped plating of Orichalcum (*the metal that neither Stone or Sunny Joe could score with their fingernails*). One of them begins to program her, digitally inserting the moves taken from Freya in book 3.

CHAPTER 19: McCabe and Raddek return to the lab only to find Smirnoff already there. They asked her what happened and she said that she learned everything that she needs. Freya approaches the Carlton building and sure enough, there is activity inside. She knocks on the door to get information.

CHAPTER 20: Chiun stabilizes Mick while awaiting the ceremony. Stone takes the time to ask Chiun some questions. Here, we see Chiun soften a bit in his treatment of Stone. Not too much. Still have to have a Remo/Chiun vibe going on, but I don't want Chiun to appear to be mean.

CHAPTER 21: Freya tries questioning McCabe and Raddek, who try to flirt with her. This makes Smirnoff angry. When Freya gets more insistent with her questioning, Smirnoff inserts herself between Freya and the scientists. Freya notices that something is wrong with Smirnoff. She is moving oddly, as if she is in constant pain. Then she hears the slight whirs of gears. She ignores Smirnoff and asks McCabe a question when he tells Smirnoff to get rid of Freya. Smirnoff takes that as "kill her" and she attacks. Freya is shocked as Smirnoff uses a basic Sinanju move. Freya parries the blow, but by doing so, her hand strikes a very hard substance that is obviously not bone. Smirnoff advances, and Freya strikes her in the chest, attempting to explode her heart, but again, her hand collides with something that will not yield. She pulls her fingers back in pain, barely dodging the edge of Smirnoff's hand, which has become a spinning blade. Freya wonders how a machine can even see her while centered. She tries to grab a deeper center, but that gives Smirnoff an opportunity to grab Freya and throw her through the wall to the next room. As this is an old-school building built with wood, not sheet rock. Freya is really hurt.

CHAPTER 22: Mick is present at the ceremony and while he had been feeling better, looks at Stone and then falls over. His heart stops. Stone starts CPR; the villagers begin to murmur. Chiun rolls his eyes. Typical white drama. Mick is not supposed to take any attention until the very end of the ceremony. Mick's last thought is that at least he made it to Sinanju.

CHAPTER 23: Freya noticed that for a few seconds, she had become invisible to the robot, so she decides to become ultimately still, beyond even the detection of Smirnoff. Smirnoff gloats that Freya will be an easy kill. Then the image of Freya shimmers in Smirnoff's sensors and she cannot detect Freya on any level. Freya rises and, maintaining her center, thrusts her fist between the plates, shredding wires and circuit boards. Smirnoff at first laughs because Freya has just revealed her position and she grabs Freya by the throat, lifting her off the ground in one swift movement, but the spattering of fluid on the ground diminishes her strength with each second until Freya is able to work her way out. Freya finishes the job by decapitating Smirnoff. McCabe and Raddek try to run, but Freya meets them at the front door and grabs them both by the collarbone. Their hearts stop beating and they collapse. She grabs a deep breath and sits to the floor, dialing Ben and hoping that she is not in trouble.

CHAPTER 24: Mick wakes up in the center of the village. All of the villagers are staring at him as if they are irritated. He wonders if he has died, because he can breathe normal and doesn't feel any pain. Then he smells the harsh stench and realizes that he is still in Sinanju. Chiun explains that they have medicine to help fight off this specific disease. Mick will live long — for a white, at least. Feast time!

CHAPTER 25: Ben arrives on the next flight and Freya takes him to the Carlton building, but nothing is there. Helmut is watching them from a beat-up van down the street, upset at the chance encounter. Smirnoff is lying in pieces on the floor behind him. Smirnoff was not ready for a fight. He just wanted to legitimately insert Smirnoff into NASA's black book program, where she could really be further developed, but now, Helmut will have to work with the engineers he has. He swears that she will be ready next time.

EPILOGUE: Hyunsil gives Mick the tour. Mick gives Hyunsil the ring Kojong took from Korea as a token. Hyunsil gives him something to take back as well. Mick confides that tribal Masters feel inferior because they fail sometimes and the Korean Masters never failed. Hyunsil smiles at him and says, "You need to read a few of our…personal scrolls. You would be surprised."

If you managed to read through all of that, you can see that there were quite a few changes between the proposal and final publication. After I submitted this to Dev, he sent a few suggestions along with the ever-needed "don't get too geeky with tech stuff."

I wrote the manuscript, sent it to him and then after we read it, uh oh. The progression on the Stone/Chiun/Mick storyline flowed well, but the Freya storyline was staccato and missing an escalation. That's weird, because I tend to develop Freya more than Stone (*yes, I've noticed and am working on making sure Stone gets his due*).

It felt bad on my end, because we said that Legacy 7 would be released "soon" in late February, but this would take some serious time. It's much more difficult to mold a story once it's been finished, because what you change has to fit with *everything* that you've already written.

So, we kept saying "soon" rather than rush out a book that was *good*, but not as good as it could have been.

One of the things I did was amp the end fight between Freya and Smirnoff and add a small section between Freya and Ben that addresses a question I've been asked multiple times and needed to be answered: "If Freya turns into Shiva whenever she gets in trouble or dies, why doesn't she just turn into Shiva every time?" As well as, "Doesn't Freya's ability to turn into Shiva mean that she can never be beat?"

To answer that, I have to go back to the point when Warren and I were fleshing out who each of the characters was; in this case, Freya. Since Jim Mullaney had shown that she uttered the Shiva mantra in Assassin's Handbook II (*which also featured my first — and by far, the worst — cover I ever did for Warren*), I figured that she inherited Shiva from Remo, which makes it a family heirloom of sorts. (*Thanks, Jim!*) So, I just had to figure out *how* it was inherited through Remo, but not through Chiun and then it hit me: There was a split, right there in canon! Master Nonga bore twin sons; one left for America and the other stayed home. What if the one who left was really the elder and Nonga sent him away in an attempt to banish the curse of Shiva? Oooh, that got the wheels rolling!

When I first agreed to work with Warren, he was worried that I would relegate myself to being his servant fanboy instead of partner, so he told me that if I thought he was wrong on something, that I was to call him on it and stick to my guns.

"Just be prepared with substance to your argument," he said.

Warren wasn't a push over by any means and, to be honest, sometimes it was intimidating to "correct" him or "talk back" to him. So, when we were discussing Freya, he said that he saw her ability to channel Shiva as a good thing. In fact, the line at the end of chapter twenty-eight in *Forgotten Son* of Shiva-Freya turning back and smiling at Stone?

Just before she disappeared up the stairwell, she turned to look Stone in the eye and smiled.

That was Warren's line. I always said that I never saw Shiva as a good thing. It was a deus ex machina and one of the things we wanted to feature in Legacy was the fact that Stone and Freya were still training and could lose. You can never lose if you have access to god mode. Besides, I told him that if we were going to use Shiva, Kali, etc., they should be used sparingly and it should always be a very powerful and fearful experience for all concerned.

As someone whose body had been taken over by Kali (*Destroyer #106, White Water, where her mother Jilda died*) Freya would also probably be very uncomfortable with losing control of her body for another god to possess her. We wouldn't get rid of Shiva, but we could recognize that it had both a good and a bad side to further her inner conflict.

Warren thought about it and said that it made sense, but it took two books to get that concession. After that, I ~~*REDACTED REDACTED REDACTED REDACTED REDACTED REDACTED*~~ and then ~~*REDACTED REDACTED REDACTED REDACTED REDACTED*~~, but I probably shouldn't say anything since Dev is so good at redacting things.

That brings me to my final point. As Warren said, Dev is a great anchor for me and editor for you. He takes the crude statue I present as tribute to the Sinanju Tribe and tells me where to smooth and where to cut and *everyone* benefits from his unseen efforts.

THE STORY BEHIND THE STORY

Legacy almost didn't happen.

The books began as one of two pitches that I gave to Warren for potential book series. Some people thought that Warren was arrogant, but that couldn't have been further from the truth. Warren was a craftsman. If you brought him something, he would respect you enough to be honest and point out things that required change or needed to be removed. It was up to the writer to set aside their ego. So, I *knew* that if I was going to pitch a series, I would have to give him my 'A' game. It took a few months to get everything together.

Of the two series that I pitched, ironically, I personally favored *Masters of Sinanju.* I had submitted a story called *Monuments* for Warren's compilation of fan fiction (*which he published as the first story in New Blood*). It was basically the story part of the pitch:

MASTERS OF SINANJU will exist in the present, told by Hyunsil, caretaker for the House. Part of her duties involve teaching the histories of Sinanju to the village children. We will "eavesdrop" and expand each story into a separate novel of its own, featuring adventures of past Masters of Sinanju.

Each book will be 'narrated' by Hyunsil and ends with the children asking questions (which will address any questions the readers might still have and would tend to be funny, like "Why does Master Remo have funny eyes?").

The first story (an expanded version of MONUMENTS) explains how the Horns of Welcome came to be, but we can also touch on anything in the Destroyer universe like Ung poetry, stories of the Great Wang. I would try to write each book in two separate styles: The Hyunsil parts in the present would be Destroyer-like writing while the actual tales of past Masters of Sinanju would be more of a Will Murray-style, like the prologue in Coins of the Realm.

I thought it had a good foundation and an interesting premise, but Warren had almost zero interest in it. The pitch he favored was *Young Destroyers,* which would feature Stone and Freya. I knew that there was no way I could write three series simultaneously (*The Last Witness, Young Destroyers* and *Masters of Sinanju*) so I would need help. I asked Donna Courtois if she would be interested in helping write *Young Destroyers* and she agreed, but by the time it came to actually writing, she had been offered to write a Destroyer (*Number Two).*

That was when Warren asked if I would like to work with him on *Young Destroyers.* I was so excited to work with him that I all but forgot about *Masters of Sinanju.*

This was the first *Young Destroyers* cover that I pitched to Warren:

No matter what anyone tells you, people judge a book by its cover. How do I know this as a fact? Look around. How many publishers are only using block text on the front?

I created a cover so Warren would see *Young Destroyers* as a book, something I failed to do with *Monuments.* Since he loved the story, I wrongfully assumed that he would be leaning toward supporting a *Masters* series. Not going the extra mile and making a cover for *Masters of Sinanju* was just lazy on my part and probably contributed to him not seeing it as a book.

Looking back at the original cover, I'm surprised at how many design elements survived! The cover featured Kojong, though I can see why a lot of people think it's Stone. (*To be honest, it can be either and still make sense*) I still use the same photos of Stone and Freya, though Stone's eyes appear to be crossed in this one (*I like to hand draw eyes*) and we still use the same texture bar behind them. In fact, the basic layout is the same, but the yin/yang fire/water symbol would be shrunk and moved to the top to symbolize the tension between Stone and Freya, hopefully giving readers a subtle idea of the difference in their personalities.

Hmmm, looking at it now, I realize that I should have cropped the bottom of Stone and Freya better as well as fix the right side of her hair.

Warren said that I needed to create summaries for each of the main characters as well as a synopsis of the first book. And while he loved the *premise,* he rightfully thought of *Young Destroyers* as just a working title. After he green-lighted my pitch, I suggested *Dynasty.* Warren axed *Dynasty* because he didn't want the series to be confused with the 80's television series which had just been announced for a reboot. But even though they didn't reboot the TV show until 2017, I'm still glad that we changed the name.

The next few pages include the first *Legacy* scenes I ever wrote. Don't laugh. Yes, I was still using two spaces after a sentence.

Sorry, Dev.

YOUNG DESTROYERS #1: THE CHALLENGE

CHAPTER ONE

The dust cloud following Mark Howard's SUV rose like a dry purple swarm in the low light of sunset. The trips to the Sunnyjoe Reservation were not an expected or enjoyable part of his job, but the secret nature of his business mandated face to face contact, especially this particular trip. Hopefully, Mark prayed, today's contact would eliminate further trips to the blazing deserts of Arizona. As a native of New England, Mark was used to fighting the extreme temperatures of winter, not summer.

Mark entered one of the small villages on the Sunonjo reservation and pulled up in front of the small house that he knew was occupied by Winston "Winner" Smith. Mark exited the SUV, thought for a moment about locking it and then remembered where he was. He dropped his keys in his pocket and headed toward the door.

The house was small and old. The last paint job was probably older than he was, with patches of wood proudly peeking through the tan paint. Or was it faded red? The front door looked as if a simple knock would be too much, so Mark knocked on the frame, dislodging small flecks of paint. The temperature was 105 degrees in the shade of the small roofed porch and the dry air parched his skin. Not hearing any movement inside, Mark looked through the small window in the front of the door, only to notice another set of eyes looking back at him. Mark stood back, slightly embarrassed as the door opened.

The man standing inside was tall, lean and not very happy. He stood in a simple sleeveless t-shirt and jeans. The look on his face spoke before he did.

"I don't like you people," he said and closed the door.

Mark, not about to waste time on another trip, knocked on the door this time. It held. The door swung open and the man reappeared.

"I thought you were supposed to be smart. Tell my uncle to go to Hell," he said and closed the door again.

The door caught on Mark's foot.

"Winner? I understand the tension between you and Dr. Smith. But I have a job you might be interested in."

"There's no possible job he could have that would interest me."

"Actually, you'd be working for me. May I come in?" Mark looked hopeful.

Winner, though mad at the continual intrusions of his life, had to keep himself from smiling. This city boy had already run to the end of his heat endurance. Winner opened the door and turned inside to sit in a chair.

***

Mark entered the house quickly. There was no air conditioning inside, but a ceiling fan managed to push the hot air around. Mark looked around and sat in a rickety chair across from Winner. The inside of the house was simple; one large room that did triple duty as living room, dining room and bedroom. A small kitchen and restroom broke off from opposite ends of the main room. The inside was like the outside, sparse and not well kept.

"Why do you think I'd work for you?" Winner asked.

"It concerns your father."

"So?"

"As you know, he has certain...obligations toward your uncle but he also has obligations to the Sunnyjoes here as well as the village of Sinanju. He doesn't have time to fulfill all of his obligations."

"You don't have to tell me. I haven't seen or heard from him in months."

"He feels the same way — in fact, that's why I'm here. He has cut back on some of his other obligations so he can spend more time with you and Freya. But those jobs still need to be done.

Dr. Smith has put me in charge of those smaller missions. I'd like to hire you to handle them."

"He lets you think you're in charge, you mean. Not interested."

"The salary will be generous."

"What kind of job could it possibly be? I would be the grunt for my uncle's grunt. Sorry. Find someone else. I'm retired."

"You'd get to travel, just like before. I checked your record. You were a pretty good Exterminator."

Winner lowered his head. "Extinguisher," he corrected.

"Oh, sorry, but you get my point. You were quite effective on your own."

"I'm very effective alone. As in how I want to be right now."

Mark stared at Winner for a moment. He looked for any wiggle room in Winner's body language but couldn't find any. Mark stood and turned to the door.

"Winner, I didn't come here because you're second string to your father. I came here because you were the first person I thought of. Here's where you can reach me," Mark said, handing Winner a Folcroft business card. Winner didn't even look at it before he tossed it into the kitchen area.

"Tell my uncle to go to Hell and give him a kick in his manipulating butt while you're at it."

Mark left for his car and cranked the air conditioner. Winner watched him leave.

"Sounds like a good deal, why didn't you take it?" a soft voice asked from behind. Freya, Winner's sister, came out of the bathroom where she had been the whole time. Like her brother, she was tall and lean. Unlike her brother, or anyone else in the tribe for that matter, her hair was a radiant blonde, like her mother's. Freya approached the door as Winner returned to his chair. The SUV was already just a trailing dust cloud.

"Work for my uncle? No way."

"You'd be working for Mark," she corrected.

"Same thing. I'm not working for him, Frey."

"It's not like you're doing anything else."

"I'm doing just what I want to do!"

"Sitting on the couch crying?"

"Hey!"

"I've seen you. Winner, you have to do something with yourself and you're always bragging how good of a secret soldier you were."

"I called my own shots, that's why."

"I just thought..."

"Then stop thinking! This is my life, not yours!"

"What?"

Freya walked over to stand directly in front of Winston. The look on her face was one he had never seen before. She wasn't just looking at him. Her eyes were directly targeting him and it made him squirm in his chair.

"Winner, you're *always* trying to tell me what to do! You...just sit here and rot!"

Freya was out the door before Winner could reply. He didn't want to make her mad, but he was still angry from the conversation with his uncle's lapdog, Mike or whatever. Winner ran to the door but Freya was already gone.

Freya was running like a leopard, her feet pumping, her body flowing freely above the plain outside the village like the wind. She stopped at the plateau overlooking the valley gorge. Freya sat down and propped her feet over the edge.

Winner was an idiot, she thought. Men were idiots, she further deduced. Once they get locked in a mindset, you could paint them blue and they'd swear they were red. Well, maybe not Mark, but (*For some reason, this is where chapter one ends. It was the only copy of the proposal I could find, so I really hope that I finished the chapter I sent to Warren*)

CHAPTER TWO

His name didn't matter to anyone (in a nod to The Destroyer)
(His name was removed from the world of the extraordinary.)
(His name was remotely common in his native France.)

His name was unremarkable in his native France. There were a million Ambroses; for goodness sake, the corner deli manager's name was Ambrose. But his last name was an exclusive French jewel: Canard. What set Ambrose Canard apart from the world of ordinary men was his reputation and his was rarest of reputations: exacting and precise, his was an intellect with a cunning knowledge of the workings of the human mind. Prince or pauper, Ambrose Canard knew what each needed whether they knew it or not.

Throughout their history, the Canard family line intertwined with the fate of France, fueling the ever-present spirit that the world recognized as exclusively French. The Canard family motto was *courbure avec la brise* — "Bend with the breeze" — and his ancestors had long ago mastered that most quintessential of French traits.

His grandfather, Leopold Canard, convinced the 1919 French government that a stronger military was a Europe-hostile policy, which led to the deconstruction of their armed forces and the construction of the fabulous Maginot Line. The stupid Gerry paperhanger, obviously fearing the genius of the grand structure, went around the fortification.

His father Louis had personally managed the details of France's surrender in World War II, an amazing feat, especially considering the interference of the Brit warmonger Chamberlain. It was such a matter of personal family pride that Louis sent a telegram personally surrendering his estate to the Germans a full year prior to the upstart Vichey.

Ambrose grew up in the depression years; that hopeless time just after the second Great War when the Canards laid off three of their five butlers. The family even talked for a while of selling one of the vacation homes in Versailles or Rome. Ambrose took this time of poverty and applied them. Using these street smarts realized that the poor people he now associated with weren't really that much different than the upper crust he was used to dealing with.

Thus began the start of the Canard Institute for Human Development. The first year, Ambrose took in people for free, in order to test his new skills and found in every case that the person who drove a Porsche was really no different than one driving a Bentley.

Then came that dreadful Iranqi war. Ambrose had a sweet deal, totally under the table but safe, that would guarantee him several million barrels of oil at pennies on the dollar. It was such a sweet deal that Ambrose couldn't resist. Besides, everyone was doing it. The United Nations even winked on the deals. Ambrose took out moneys equaling 80% of his total estate and invested them in President Chiraq's good friend Maddas, only to find America bumbling around in the books. Ambrose became despondent upon learning that he had been called before a Senate sub-committee. He had never been good under pressure.

As you can see, quite a bit changed from that first draft, including the people you know. Let's take a look at who is who and why they are the way they are.

SUNNY JOE

Sunny Joe was one of the most controversial characters in *Legacy*. Warren warned me that some *Destroyer* fans wouldn't like this version of Sunny Joe. We both had a problem with how Sunny Joe had been portrayed in *The Destroyer*. Warren told me to change Sunny Joe so that he would 1) be likeable and 2) be a credible Sinanju teacher, but he could not be a Chiun clone. The rest was up to me.

Even though I didn't like the *Destroyer* version of Sunny Joe, I tried to stay as close to canon as possible, but after reading and re-reading the books Sunny Joe was in, I found out that basically meant retaining his name and gender.

I created Sunny Joe to be a humble man with a lifetime of wisdom and mental scars, including an unbelievably dark secret about his Pop. He was happy to finally see his son Remo and even happier to learn that he had grandchildren! He felt guilty that he hadn't been able to raise Remo, so he was determined to make it up by training his grand-children.

Sunny Joe was going to be Stone and Freya's trainer, but while I was tempted to give Stone and Sunny Joe the same dynamic as Remo and Chiun, it would have been a cheat and Warren rightfully wouldn't have allowed it. I saw Sunny Joe more as a wise grandfather who could just happen to punch through steel. I would make sure they had their own dynamic and above all, would keep the feeling of family that exists between Remo and Chiun.

Speaking of Chiun, Sunny Joe would have to meet Chiun every once in a while, so how would that work out? Both are Masters of the art, but Chiun clearly has rank, placing Sunny Joe in the rare position of greeting Chiun as his superior.

Sunny Joe, being as unassuming as he is, didn't want to be seen as challenging Chiun's position by referring to himself as a Master, so when they first met, he called himself 'Teacher.' Well, that added an edge to their relationship, because we know from *The Destroyer* that Chiun wants to be known as "The Great Teacher" in the scrolls. So, while they are cordial to each other, Chiun goes out of his way to call Sunny Joe a "trainer", which Sunny Joe assumes is a lower rank than "Teacher," but Sunny Joe wouldn't mind.

"A name's just a name," he would say (*I know what his voice sounds like*). "It ain't who you are."

STONE

I didn't want Stone to be a Remo clone, but it was obvious that he would be filling his father's shoes in *Legacy*. Stone was originally called 'Winner' in *The Destroyer*, but Warren and I both *hated* that name. Thankfully, Warren changed it to Stone.

But if he isn't Remo Williams, who is Stone Smith? We knew that he was an ex-Navy SEAL and that he used to be a mercenary. I imagined him to be a bit cocky, but also slightly afraid in this new world of Sinanju. SEALs are some of the toughest guys alive. To find out that your worldview was so small that you don't even rate as a threat would shake anyone's confidence. Oh, and he happens to smoke, which is a huge problem when breathing is the first step of your martial art.

I get a lot of crap about that, but his smoking is something I wanted to treat seriously. I couldn't give him a hurdle like that just to have him conquer it in book three. It would've been less realistic than being able to dodge bullets. Stone has a double whammy; he wants to catch up to Freya skill-wise and prove to Sunny Joe that he's good, but is sabotaging himself with smoking.

There was an unexpected problem with Stone right off the bat: he had a bunch of canon experience that I had to account for, but he still had to be young enough to realistically bond with Freya as her brother. Warren and I assumed that three Sinanju years had passed since we last saw Stone and Freya in *Assassin's Handbook II.*

I had to do some serious math to make it work. He was raised by Smitty, which means he was basically thrown into a military academy and told to succeed. It's easy to understand why the first thing he did after graduating was enlist in the NAVY so he could get away. But he didn't have time to serve a complete tour, so something *had to happen* for him to leave.

After my son (*Hi, Cody!*) injured his heel saving a soldier in real life, he was discharged. That is where I got Stone's story. He became a SEAL, but was kicked out after injuring his heel, saving a fellow SEAL on his first mission. The guy had some mercenary contacts, so he gave Stone a few South American jobs and Stone became a merc for a year or so.

When he ran into his father, he ended up on the Sinanju reservation and, for the first time in his life, found a real family. And while everyone knows that Freya can kick his butt, he can't stop being a defensive — and protective — big brother.

FREYA

Freya was pretty much a blank slate, so I had a lot more flexibility with her than any other character. I also spent more time on her. Though she had a lot of life experiences, she was not developed enough to be an established character, so I extrapolated who she would be with what I know of the time she spent with her mother.

I saw Freya as someone with a lot of worldly experience in a guarded-by-your-mother way, which would leave her knowledgeable but a bit naïve. Chiun taught her to breathe correctly and at two, she bent a horseshoe with her bare hands. Her mother Jilda not only trained her to fight and hunt and fish, but also to speak several languages (*her native Lakluun, European Spanish and to an extent, the languages of her father, Korean and English*).

She spent her childhood traveling throughout Europe, hiding from anyone from Lakluun who might be following them. Jilda shielded her from direct social contact. Freya was taught to be quiet and cautiously watch for signs of danger, rather than engage people in conversation.

After Jilda died, Freya found the Sinanju reservation as the first stable home in her life, but her experience hasn't been as easy as Stone's. She doesn't look like anyone else on the reservation and that created a social dynamic between her and the kids her age. Elders whisper when she's around. Girls were jealous of her and boys fought over her to the point Sunny Joe had to home school her. That further isolated her.

On the other hand, she is obviously Remo and Chiun's favorite. There is no way Stone could miss Chiun fawning all over her and Remo only visits them on her birthday. That adds to an inevitable brother/sister conflict. I also felt that it added another layer to Remo, who has been an orphan his entire life. Finding his family has *got* to affect him, and it was too easy to pretend they were the Waltons.

And we can *all* thank Jim Mullaney for Freya being a Shiva-friendly member of the House. This is an excerpt from chapter thirteen of Jim's novella *False Starts and Bitter Ends* that was published in *The Assassin's Handbook, Volume II,* followed by the same scene from Freya's viewpoint in Legacy 2.

By the way, if you don't have *Assassin's Handbook II,* you're missing out.

THE SCENE: Remo's then-girlfriend Jean is protecting a young Freya from Uncle Sam Beasley, a bionic version of Walt Disney that Warren and Jim both wanted gone.

FALSE STARTS AND BITTER ENDS

by JIM MULLANEY

The twisted face of Uncle Sam Beasley grinned in malicious glee as the rubber-coated hands squeezed tighter. He had to reach up to strangle her. As he stretched on tiptoes, the sleeves of his heavy robe slid back to his shoulders, revealing metal mockeries of skeletal human arms.

Blood pounded in Jean's temples. The world around her began to swim. The glow of orange embers in the dying bonfires flew by in a blur.

Tomi Twinfeathers lying on the picnic table. Why didn't he have a head? Oh, yes. He wasn't human. Just a machine. Like the thing that had her in a death grip--the thing that was squeezing the life from her.

Her rolling eyes found Uncle Sam.

He was a hazy memory from her childhood. He seemed angry about something. She tried to remember what she'd done to make nice Uncle Sam so mad. As she concentrated, something moved beside her.

Maybe it was Remo! That's right. Uncle Sam was not nice after all. He was trying to kill her. Remo would save her. A still lucid part of her mind wanted desperately for it to be Remo. Her pleading eyes met disappointment.

It was Freya. The girl had come up beside Jean and Uncle Sam. And as Jean watched in horror, Remo's daughter reached a hand for Uncle Sam.

Freya's long fingers took hold of the cartoon king's mechanical forearm.

He'll kill you too, Freya!

Jean tried to yell for the girl to run, but no words could pass the stranglehold on her throat. It was too much. Jean's eyes fluttered shut. In the growing darkness of her clouding mind, she silently begged Remo's forgiveness for her failure to protect his only daughter. And from the faraway recesses of her dying brain, Remo seemed to answer her.

It was an odd sound. Soft. Growing louder. A groan of metal. With an effort, she willed her eyes open. Freya was still there, still gripping Uncle Sam's arm. There was a serene, almost dazed expression on the young girl's pale face.

Something was wrong. Beside the twelve-year-old girl, the look of evil joy that Uncle Sam Beasley had worn had metamorphosed to one of bewildered fury.

Another metallic groan. Jean knew her eyes must be playing tricks on her, for beneath Freya's small hand, the metal radius bone of Uncle Sam's skeletal arm began to bend.

One hard twist and the artificial bone collapsed. A crack appeared in the ulna. It was impossible. Jean had to be hallucinating. Very close up, she watched the crack begin to widen. She became aware of the lessening pressure at her neck. The fog in her brain was clearing.

With a sudden shriek, both steel rods in Uncle Sam's forearm snapped. The left hand sprang open. There was shock on Uncle Sam's blue face. He tried to work his artificial hand, but it wouldn't budge.

"Meddlesome little bitch," Uncle Sam growled.

His one good hand released Jean. She fell back, panting and holding her throat.

"Run, Freya!" she gasped.

"I've got an idea," Uncle Sam said.

With his right arm, he gave Jean a backhanded swat. The rubberized metal hand met her jaw with a crack. She fell hard, slamming her head on the picnic table on the way to the ground.

"Why don't you mind your own damned business?" Uncle Sam finished.

Before Jean collapsed into unconsciousness, she looked over toward Freya.

The girl continued to just stand there. Her eyes were level on Uncle Sam, but her gaze seemed a million miles away. It was as if the forces of the universe had aligned in the small form of this pale young girl, suffusing her with an almost otherworldly calm.

Her lips moved. With her fading consciousness, Jean strained to hear the girl's words. But they were strange and meant nothing to her.

Softly, the little pre-teen said, "I am created Shiva, the Destroyer; death, the shatterer of worlds." And then there was silence. The last thing Jean remembered was seeing a smile of great contentment pass over the young girl's face.

"Just what I need," Uncle Sam growled as he appraised Freya's vacant happy stare. "One of those reefer babies. The world's gonna thank me for this."

Beasley raised his good arm. With a hydraulic hiss, he sent a crushing blow to Freya's exposed forehead. The instant before metal struck bone, the arm abruptly locked up. Beasley felt the breeze from his flapping sleeve on his cold face.

"What the hell?" he grumbled.

His upraised arm wouldn't budge. It felt almost as if it had snagged on something.

"Blasted malfunction," he snarled. "This is the last time this seizes up on me. When I get back to Florida, I'm having the guts of the whole damned animatronic division for garters."

He glanced up at his own struggling arm. Uncle Sam was surprised to see that his was not the only arm there. Another hand grasped his own. This time it was not Freya who had stopped him. Both of the young girl's arms were at her sides.

Uncle Sam saw a very familiar, very thick wrist. And as this new shock registered, a face like a mask of doom appeared before him.

"It's no malfunction," Remo Williams said coldly. "But it's about to be. Chiun, take care of Freya."

Beasley saw the aged Master of Sinanju standing a few feet away. But even before Chiun could move, Winston stepped forward and put a protective arm around Freya's shoulders and led her from the structure.

This was the canonical thread that I used to tie Shiva to Freya.

Oh, don't worry about Beasley. Even though Remo and Chiun had an inexplicable soft spot for him that saved him from their wrath in the past (*one of the things Warren and Jim hated about him*), threatening Freya was not the smartest thing to do.

Here is the same scene, but from Freya's point of view in *Legacy.*

LEGACY #2: THE KILLING FIELDS

She remembered a man was attacking someone. The man had metal arms, like a robot. He grabbed the woman who was protecting Freya with his steely grip and began choking her. Freya's mother had taught her to run in circumstances that she was not prepared for, but before she could turn to run, she felt something flowing beneath her skin like an unstoppable river of power.

It had turned her fear into anger.

Instead of running, Freya had walked directly to the man. When she reached him, the man did not even glance down at her. After all, what threat could a twelve-year-old girl possibly be?

Freya breathed in deeply as she grabbed the offending arm nearest to her. Her long fingers reached around one of the polished metal pistons controlling the arm. She squeezed, and the metal bent like warm candle wax. With a futile groan, the artificial bone collapsed. A quick turn of her tiny wrist and the arm snapped off. The hand holding the woman sprang open.

"Meddlesome little bitch!" the man said in disbelief as his arm collapsed to the ground.

"Run, Freya!" the woman screamed as he released her.

"I've got an idea," the man said, striking the woman with his remaining hand and turning to Freya. "Why don't you mind your own damned business?"

But something inside Freya would not let her run from this lesser being, this non-threat. Her eyes remained fixated on the man with one metal arm, and she felt nothing more than the peace of a calm stream as he moved toward her.

In the distance, she remembered hearing chimes.

Then she said the words.

"I am created Shiva, the Destroyer; Death, the shatterer of worlds."

And then there was silence.

I added the chimes part for effect, but the rest was pretty much Freya's point of view from chapter thirteen of *False Starts and Bitter Ends.*

Jim Mullaney later confided in me that he had not meant it to be taken that way and that he didn't see Freya as the heir to Shiva, but that was while I was writing Legacy #3!

Oops.

BEN COLE

Ben Cole didn't even exist in my original proposal. Mark Howard was originally going to be Stone and Freya's CURE liaison, because he was Smitty's assistant at the time. That ended up being a *huge* bump in the road. Warren approved the series on the condition that I ditch Mark. He said that Mark was a 'psychic bureaucrat', whose powers were a 'distraction from Sinanju.'

But Warren was professional about it. He was mindful of Mark's fans and didn't want to anger them by just killing him off, so he sent Mark off to Pakistan after Osama bin Laden, where he went MIA.

At first, I panicked.

Without Mark Howard, I thought Legacy was toast, but Warren said that all I had to was create someone memorable to be Stone and Freya's CURE liaison. This was his brown, comic sans suggestion:

mark howard no longer exists...he has been lost in pakistan on the trail of osama bin laden....we need a new character...think of old destroyers for a moment; we had harold smith and we had conn maccleary...this guy will be different from mark howard; give him a background; let him come out of somewhere and do something and be different....we don't need a bureaucratic character like mark maybe this guy's an american hero who was abandoned by his own government; maybe someone that cure owes a favor to? maybe a one time reservation guard or a cashiered cop or secret agent....maybe he's a fallen priest who's lost his faith....maybe he was a wartime battlefield chaplain and gave up on forgiveness as a way of life.....get a great back story or set up and you've got a great character. think of barney daniels....of ruby gonzales... characters who came alive.

I took his words to heart and worked on several different people to lead Stone and Freya (*including Elizabeth Adara and Roland Whitmore*) but I chose Benjamin Cole, who I believe has a more compelling and emotional back story. Don't worry, you'll learn about the others as time goes on.

This is the pitch I made to Warren for Ben and the synopsis of the first book:

Benjamin Cole, 42-year-old, ex-Mossad sleeper agent in Egypt, his wife was stoned for adultery because she was raped by a provincial governor in the late 90's. Ben broke cover, killed the governor, escaped back to Israel, but he was too hot for the Mossad, so he found an old CIA contact to smuggle him into the US. He's just been put in charge of a secret Homeland Security agency whose goal is to find — and execute — terrorists in America. The agency is a creation of CURE and Ben takes his assignments from a shadowy figure with an odd, lemony voice. Readers who are Destroyer fans will know who this is, but new readers will have no clue.

I'm taking your advice and treating this as a totally stand-alone series (freeeeeedom!) so CURE, Remo, Chiun, et al, will be mentioned rarely if at all. Sinanju will be the martial art that is being taught to Freya and Stone by Sunny Joe.

Just for an internal gauge for you, me and Dev, Freya is Remo level as of book ten; Stone is Remo level as of book two or three. That means they won't be walking into machine gun fire any time soon. Stone still doesn't trust his Sinanju training and is hampered by his inability to stop smoking, though he is trying. Freya is a natural at Sinanju and probably the star of the show.

Sunny Joe hopes that one day she will become Master of both House of Sinanju and Sunonjo tribes, reuniting them.

The villain of this book is Manuel Fuentes, Mexican drug lord and Mexico City playboy. He's known to have a lot of girls and then their bodies show up later when he's through with them. He is instructed to make sure that a MacGuffin is sent through the Mexican border to the United States. This thing is radioactive, so there's only one place on the border where it would get through; the southern end of Arizona where the Federal Government thinks putting up warning signs constitutes security.

Subplot will feature Liz Worn, a senatorial candidate who has been caught faking a claim of being 1/64th Sunonjo. To prove her ancestry, she appeals to Sunny Joe to give her the rites of passage. Oh, poor Liz...

When Warren said that he and Dick regretted never thinking ahead about the series, that got me to thinking. Smitty is noticeably older as he's a World War II veteran, so I wanted Ben to be comparably younger than Smitty was at the beginning so he would have a longer shelf life.

In fact, all Legacy characters were purposely aged slightly younger than their Destroyer counterparts for that reason.

This is my approximation of the ages of the Destroyer characters as of *Destroyer* #1 versus the ages of their counterparts as of *Legacy* #1:

Chiun: 80 / Sunny Joe: 70
Remo: 30 / Stone: 23
Smitty: 55 / Ben: 42

There was no counterpart to Freya, so I made sure everyone knew her age in book one by celebrating her sixteenth birthday. It also provided an excuse for Remo and Chiun to show up, even if they were uncharacteristically in the background.

HELMUT BELISIS

If the Remo Williams movie proved anything, it demonstrated that you can't have a good hero without a good villain. In many ways, coming up with Helmut was more challenging than creating the main cast, because a great villain will define not only the heroes, but the tensions, danger and even the tone of the series.

Think of the difference your mind makes when you consider being threatened by George Grove (the weapons manufacturer from the 1985 movie) and seeing Mr. Gordons charge at you. Your mind automatically changes gears just thinking about that, so I began with one mission: Create a villain powerful enough to take on Remo, Chiun and CURE all at the same time. He would be what I call a "series' villain," a recurring and powerful foe who would be nearly impossible to battle, much less defeat.

How do you do that when your heroes can dodge bullets and punch through brick? Easy. You can't punch money or political power. Especially Old-World Money and Power. You don't get more Old-World than VIGIL, the organization that Helmut leads. This is the summary that I sent to Warren:

The series' main villain is Helmut Belisis, a German-raised Greek who heads the most secret organization on Earth: VIGIL (Latin for "fortify" "protect"). This group is sworn to ensure the survival of the human race for one billion years by any means necessary. Their typical plan is to keep the masses fed, stupid and happy. They target <u>*any*</u> *opposition to their plan.*

Helmet even boasts that VIGIL is the one who convinced Kennedy to start CURE to allow them the ability to fundamentally control American policy. Helmut claims that his predecessor personally chose Harold Smith to head the organization.

Helmut's predecessor personally suggested the addition of adding the Master of Sinanju to CURE to keep them occupied in American drama and away from VIGIL's overseas operations. Smith's staunch patriotism and the appearance of Freya and Stone were unforeseen complications.

Helmut almost started out as a stereotypical mustache-twirling villain. I know that I came up with two or three versions of him before settling on someone who is confident that he is in the right...that *he* is on the side of morality and good. I wanted to write it so that if you didn't know the specifics of what he did and just looked at Helmut and VIGIL, you might even agree with him. Think 'The Architect' from *The Matrix* movies with a very sinister purpose.

Helmut is almost like a cultured Klingon in that he has a sense of honor and loyalty, even to his enemies. If you betray him, he will destroy you without making it personal. He likes the finer things, which is why VIGIL almost has a public presence under his rule. Unfortunately, that doesn't end up working out, so Helmut will have his own identity crisis as he re-evaluates his life and his role in VIGIL.

Warren gave the thumbs up to my proposal, but what was I supposed to do with the material that I had already written with Mark in mind? They were specifically tailored for his more measured personality, not Cole's much more forceful one. The harsh answer is that if something doesn't fit, it has to go.

Fortunately, I had learned while writing *The Last Witness* to keep a "piggy bank" file. It's a document where I can save facts and ideas and scenes that I can't use for whatever reason. In fact, I thought you might like to see one of the *Young Destroyer* nuggets (*that's what I call a combination of ideas and scene that is before first draft*) that I wrote between Helmut and Mark when Mark was a part of the plan:

> Helmut talking to Mark directly through the CURE computer: "There are other CURE like organizations, each believing themselves to be unique. CURE is the only unit with FORTEC technology, however. Didn't you ever wonder how a drunk scientist created a self-repairing automaton decades ago? Mr. Gordons, FRIEND, surely beings that advanced raised questions in your analytical mind, no?
>
> Smith may have no imagination but you, Mark Howard, you are a curious man. You grew up reading comic books and made almost weekly trips to the theater. Smith's persona is fed by the thin fabric of patriotism that has formed his psychological cocoon. Yours is fed by living out your childhood adventures. No matter what you might admit, this is just a game to you. This very conversation has already been reduced to one of "good guy versus bad guy" in your mind.
> How do you think so many people learned about CURE over the years?
>
> Originally, Smith had access to dozens of individuals but after gaining the services of Sinanju, he decided to send them back to their original departments

in the FBI, CIA. VIGIL believed that it was a bad decision. If something as random as a car wreck killed Smith, CURE's multi-billion-dollar mission would fail. So VIGIL decided to force his hand, sending individuals with great potential to aid him in his duties. We spent millions searching for the right candidates. We let them "discover" CURE and either sent them directly to Smith or pointed them out to Smith. We hoped he would see their potential, but each time he had them killed.

Something drastic had to be done, so we ordered the President to assign an assistant or face impeachment. He hesitated so we followed through on our threat. That's right, we chose you, Mark Howard and now you know a secret that even the director of CURE doesn't know.

What will you do with it? If you inform him, he will, no doubt declare CURE impossibly compromised and order the disbanding of CURE, resulting in both of your deaths. Or perhaps you will do the wise thing and overthrow the organization that birthed yours, seizing the reins of power?

I changed the conversation, but was able to use a similar dynamic between Ben and Helmut.

After *Dynasty* was shot down as a series title, I thought of *Legacy*, but then I found out Molly Cochran had just written a book called *Legacy* and I didn't want her to think I was poaching. But Molly gave us her blessing and Warren agreed. *Legacy* was born!

Then it came time to actually work. Lots of drafts and outlines and revisions and edits later, the first Legacy hit the shelves. Warren sent me a few complimentary copies. Seeing my name listed next to his was a huge achievement for me. It almost made me feel as good as the email Warren sent after he got his own copies:

dear jerry,

books arrived today and i saw the first fruits of our labor and i cannot help but tell you how remarkably good these books are going to be. you have become, in front of my own eyes, a wonderfully talented writer and i can't praise your work enough. i will not be a dope and say i didn't see things there that i had done to make the book better, but truth is i always felt the same way about dick and his work...i just plodded along trying to make stuff better and sometimes it worked. like dick, sometimes your work is phenomenal...but sometimes a stroke short, yet still it is clear that you will someday achieve what you should regularly achieve and i will have had only a little to do with it except that you will have maybe got a lesson from me or learned a thing or two from me, but...beautiful my friend, beautiful...i am proud to be your partner.

warren

Right there, in Warren's patented brown comic sans, was all the justification I needed. I was ready for book two!

LEGACY

SINANJU EYES ONLY

THE FIRST OFFICIAL LEGACY MEETING

VIRGINIA BEACH, VA — SEPTEMBER 14, 2012

(L-R: Jerry Welch, Donna Courtois, Warren Murphy, Brian Murphy, Devin Murphy)

As you can guess from the giddy look on my face, this was the first time I had met Warren in person. The guy was like seven feet tall! Okay, maybe 6' 4", but he was *huge*! (*Also note that Devin was wearing his awesome "Hello is Alright" shirt*). This is where Warren introduced me to the waitresses as some big up-and-coming author. They 'ooh'ed and 'aah'ed without knowing what Warren did, but that's just who he was.

This picture was taken at the only book signing I did with Warren. I got to see how much he loved his fans. Oh, and Molly's such a sweetheart. When I first met her, I was so excited that I told Dev, "Molly Cochran's upstairs!" The eyeroll I received from him was so vast and endless that I'm surprised he can still see straight.

In 2013 and 2014, Warren hosted a Destroyer Club get-together near his home in Virginia Beach. A small, but dedicated group got to hang out for the weekend, ask Warren questions and get pictures. We all had fun…even Leo, who I had to trick into having fun.

The next two pages prove that Warren was always more stylish than I could ever hope to be. But note that I had Bieber hair before Bieber. I'm gonna have to see a lawyer about that one…

LEGACY OMNIBUS: VOLUME I

WARREN MURPHY

JERRY WELCH

This is my original drawing of Freya in 2003.

(14"x17" pencil and ink on Bristol board)

I sent a copy to Warren, who reminded me she had golden hair like her mother.

Ouch! What was I thinking?

BTW, if you look at the picture of Freya on the Facebook page, you'll see that I used the headwrap and even the ears from this drawing (*didn't notice the ears, did you?*), so it wasn't a total loss. I still have the original drawing. It's a good drawing, just not…accurate.

I love to collect *Legacy*-related merchandise but when we started, there was no *Legacy* merchandise available, so I had to have it made! I have pins, necklaces, dice, earrings, guitar picks, coasters, and as you can see above, I even have a set of Ben Cole dog tags!

I gave my copper Legacy pin to Devin, because he drove *over twenty hours* to attend my wedding. These days, we have everything from t-shirts and mugs to tote bags, so it's a great time to be a Legacy fan!

I thought you might like seeing a few variant covers that never saw the light of day:

The banners have even changed more times than you've seen on the cover.

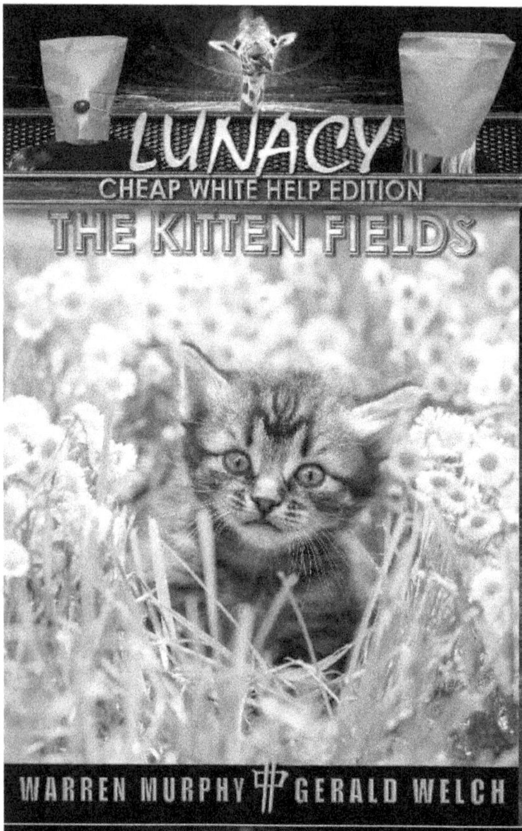
LUNACY
CHEAP WHITE HELP EDITION
THE KITTEN FIELDS
WARREN MURPHY GERALD WELCH

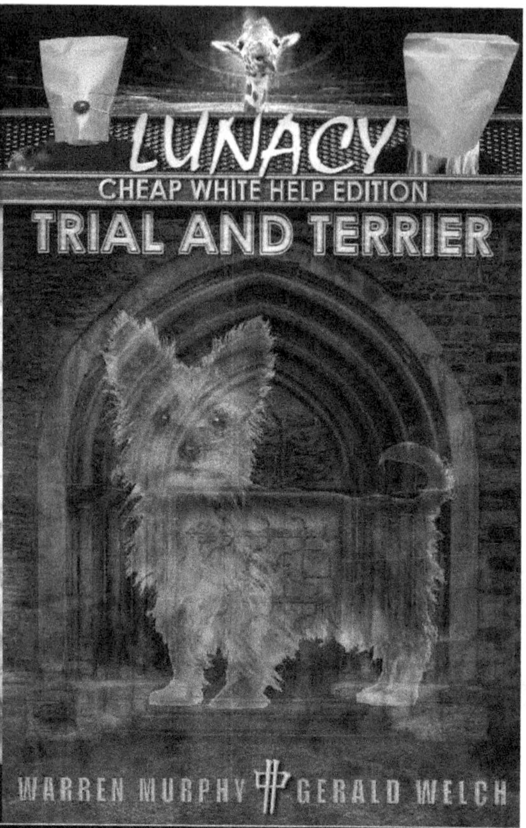
LUNACY
CHEAP WHITE HELP EDITION
TRIAL AND TERRIER
WARREN MURPHY GERALD WELCH

LUNACY
CHEAP WHITE HELP EDITION
MOTHER MIME
WARREN MURPHY GERALD WELCH

LUNACY
CHEAP WHITE HELP EDITION
THE CLOWN WARS
WARREN MURPHY GERALD WELCH

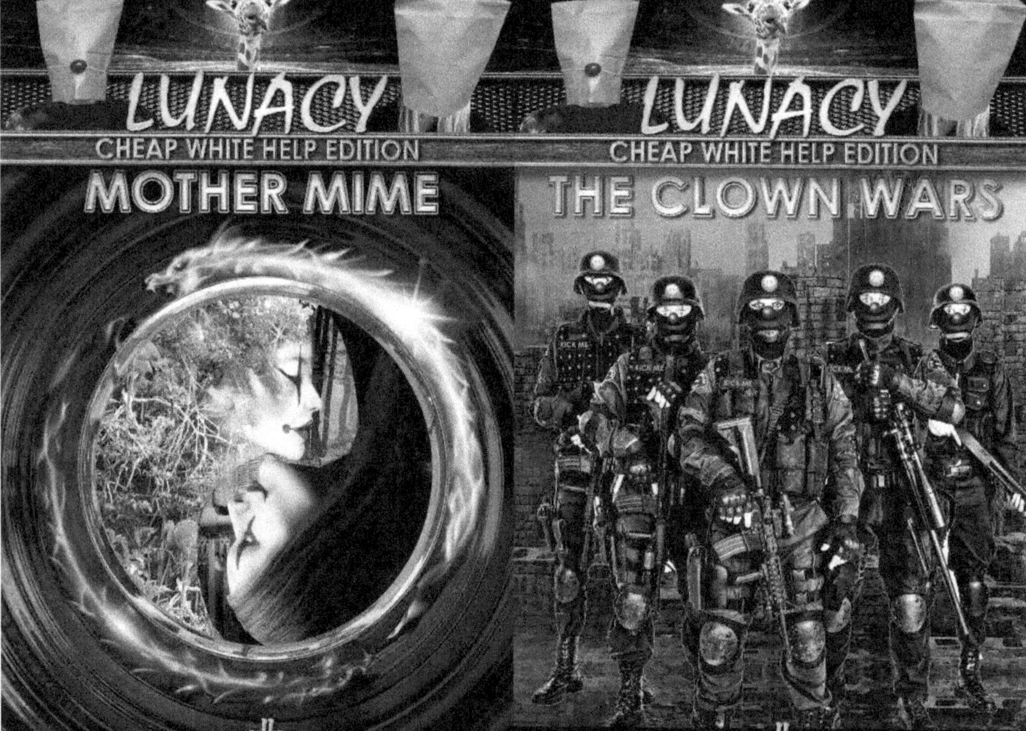

Okay, this requires an explanation. Sometimes, I have too much spare time between books. A restless artist never rests, so…one day I remembered talking to Leo Aromaa about Legacy #4. He thought I said "Trial and *Terrier*". I couldn't pass up the chance to make his dream a reality, so I made a mock cover. Then, as everything began to come together, I started thinking, "I could rewrite the entire book, replacing all dialogue with dog barks!"

That led to *The Kitten Fields.* It would be a book written in cat-speak. *Mother Mime* was my personal favorite, though. There would be chapter headers and then blank pages, because… well, mimes! And I had to address the book I was working on (Legacy #6). The original title was *The Clown Wars,* which was kind of a jab at *Clone Wars.* When I presented it to Dev, he said (and I quote) "Jerry, as long as I have anything to do with this series, we will *never* have a book titled *Clown Wars.*" Smart move. *Laughing Matter* is a much better title. (*Thanks, Christina!*)

Since Chiun made an appearance in Legacy #7, and, since I had some spare time while waiting for its release (*dangerous, I know*), I thought I'd make a new cover to commemorate the occasion. Of course, that means changing the banner, and I even came up with a new cover.

The bottom line is that the next time you wonder what Devin does, just remember, he doesn't just edit the books. He keeps you safe from things like this:

WARREN AND JERRY, 2014

I wanted to put this picture at the end of the omnibus because it was one of the last pictures I took with Warren. Legacy exists because Warren took me under his wing and gave me a chance. That's what this picture means to me.

I will always remember his brown comic sans emails that kept me in line, ever pushing me to deliver a better story. For cheap white help, I think we've done a pretty good job so far.

Thanks for being there with us. We hope to be here for many stories to come.

Jerry

GERALD WELCH

ABOUT THE AUTHORS

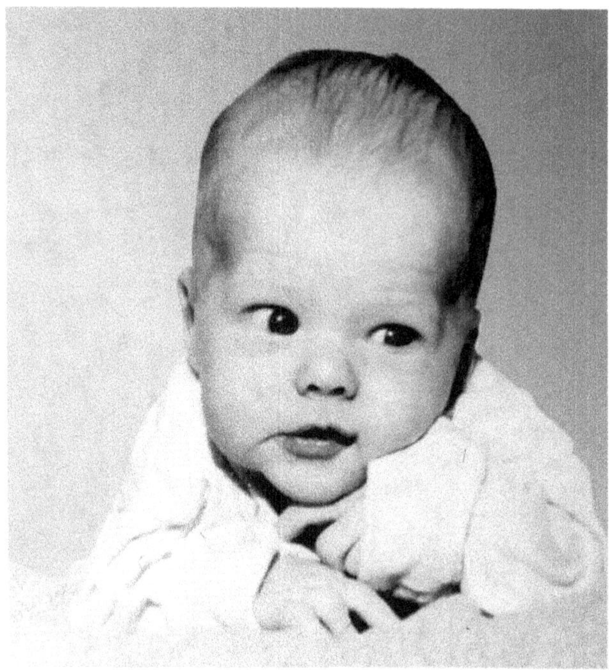

GERALD WELCH
(c. September 1964)

Gerald Welch is a husband, father of six children, author and graphic artist. He lives in St. Louis and is one of only three people in the world to be granted the title "Honorary Master of Sinanju." If you don't know what that means, then you obviously didn't read the front of this book!

Jerry has been awarded everything from the prestigious *Thomas Jefferson Award* for directing as well as the *Al Hartley Award* for "Best Comic Book" and Critical Blast's *'Worst Album of the Year'* Award for the album *Alien Summer*.

You can see what he's doing by aiming your web thingy at *www.JerryWelch.com*

WARREN MURPHY AND GERALD WELCH

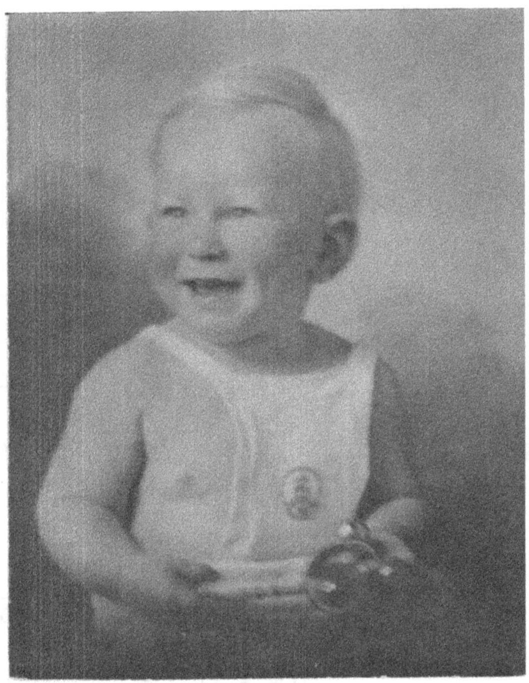

WARREN MURPHY
(c. 1934)

Warren Murphy was born in Jersey City, where he worked in journalism and politics until launching the Destroyer series with Richard Sapir in 1971. A screenwriter (*Lethal Weapon II, The Eiger Sanction*) as well as a novelist, Murphy's work has won more than a dozen national awards, including multiple Edgars and Shamuses.

A Korean War veteran, Murphy served on the board of the Mystery Writers of America, and has been a member of the Screenwriters Guild, the Private Eye Writers of America, the International Association of Crime Writers, and the American Crime Writers League. He has five children: Deirdre, Megan, Brian, Ardath, and Devin.

LEGACY OMNIBUS: VOLUME I

Did you know that Jerry first made an omnibus for his *Last Witness* series? It's an oversized 416-page hardback filled with character entries, a glossary, detailed breakdowns and includes the first two books in the series as well as *War in Heaven*!

(If you're interested, it's available at Amazon.com!)

The book is done.

There is nothing more.

Why are you looking back here?

www.ingramcontent.com/pod-product-compliance
Lightning Source LLC
Chambersburg PA
CBHW081137300726
48982CB00006B/990
* 9 7 8 1 9 4 4 0 7 3 1 8 3 *